W9-BML-960

F. Donald Logan 5·28·59

THE CAVE

Books by Robert Penn Warren

John Brown: The Making of a Martyr
Thirty-six Poems
Eleven Poems on the Same Theme
Night Rider
Selected Poems, 1923-1943
At Heaven's Gate
All the King's Men
The Circus in the Attic
World Enough and Time
Brother to Dragons
Band of Angels
Segregation: The Inner Conflict in the South
Promises: Poems 1954-1956
Selected Essays
The Cave

THE CAVE

Robert Penn Warren

Random House • *New York*

FIRST PRINTING

© Copyright, 1959, by Robert Penn Warren
All rights reserved under International and Pan-American Copyright
Conventions. Published in New York by Random House, Inc., and
simultaneously in Toronto, Canada, by Random House of Canada, Limited.
Library of Congress Catalog Card Number: 59–5719
Manufactured in the United States of America
by H. Wolff, New York
Design: Marshall Lee

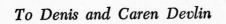

To Denis and Caren Devlin

You have shown me a strange image, and they are strange prisoners.

Like ourselves, I replied; and they see only their own shadows, or the shadows of one another, which the fire throws on the opposite wall of the cave?

True, he said; how could they see anything but the shadows if they were never allowed to move their heads?

Plato, *The Republic*, Book VII

THE CAVE

I

They were number X-362 in the Monkey-Ward catalogue, genuine cowhide, prime leather, expertly tanned, made to our specifications, on our special last, ten inches high, brass eyelets, top strap with brass buckle, worn and admired by sportsmen everywhere, size 9½B—which is not a big foot or a little one, for a man. But the man was not there.

The man had not, however, thoughtlessly abandoned the boots. He had, it was clear, loved them. He had loved them a long time, putting on new soles before shapelessness had set in, wiping the mud off before it could cake, working in saddle soap with his finger tips, while he sat under the sugar maple, in a split-bottom chair, in the grape-purple shade over near the unpainted lattice well house, if it was summer, or if winter, while he sat before the hearth, in sock feet, the wool of the socks faintly steaming, and

[3]

hot ash, pink fading to dove-gray, flaking infinitesimally off the hickory chunk.

Now the boots were set side by side, placed thus with prideful care. Be good, don't move till I get back. Children behaving very well, waiting. No, just boots, bearing the mark of their master's weight, strength, and strain, like a body when the soul is withdrawn in sleep, or death. Just boots, and one sags a little from the weight of the guitar propped over it.

The boots are set in the middle of a little glade benched into the ridge, and one strong ray of the June sun, past meridian but not yet well caught in the weight of westering, strikes through the upper frills of beech leaf and finds the guitar. The ray strikes the strings to a glitter, and you think that that glitter might almost be sound, so startling it is, a single chord stabbing the afternoon silence.

Then the silence is over. The locusts begin again, for this is the year of the locust. In fact, there has not been silence at all, for the air has been full of a dry, grinding metallic sound, so penetrating that it has seemed, paradoxically, to come from within the blood, or from some little buzz saw working fiendishly away at the medulla oblongata. It is easy to forget that it is not from inside you, that glittering, jittering, remorseless whir so much part of you that you scarcely notice it, and perhaps love it, until the time when you will really notice it, and scream.

The locust sound is like that, rising from the long, wooded ridges and the coves, hollows, gaps, water gaps, and valleys, westward where the land breaks toward the river, eastward toward the higher ridges that heave up, rock snagging above woods-growth. The locust sound unremittingly rises, and you live so fully in it that it is no longer sound. It is more like the dizzying heat-dazzle that, too, shimmers up from the woods and ridges, to make your vision shake. That distant, pervasive, persuasive sound never stops, and that is why, when the sound in your immediate vicinity does suddenly, and inexplicably, stop, you think you are caught in a breathless hush. You can't bear the silence.

[4]

Something has got to happen. So when the ray of sunlight strikes the glitter off the guitar strings, you hear it like a big *whang*.

But it isn't, and now the locusts in the vicinity are back at work. The ray of sunlight has moved beyond the strings anyway, to pick up the lesser brightness of mother-of-pearl on the instrument. The mother-of-pearl is in letters set in the pale-polished wood.

JACK HARRICK

HIS BOX

1901

Jack Harrick, whoever he is, is not here in the beautiful glade. Nor is it he who has taken off the boots, lovingly set them side by side, and propped the box across one. For Jack Harrick, a big, grizzled, heavy-headed old man, ruined and beautiful, is two and one-half miles away, sitting in a wheel chair, dying of cancer.

At this moment he is wondering if he smells. There is no reason to think that he does, but he is wondering. He is wondering this because his wife has just been in to speak to him, to bring him iced tea, to lay her hand on his great grizzled head, and her cheek against his, and say "John T.—dear John T.," and perhaps he would be happy, he thinks, if he did smell, but he does not know why he might be happy if she had to get his stink. Perhaps, after all, he would not want her to, and prays God that he does not smell—or prays that he does not want her to get his stink.

He then thinks about dying and how the body is nothing. It is a hunk of filth and they fling it into a hole before the smell gets too bad. Well, if he could get to smelling now, that would fix them. It would fix them all. He would like to rub their noses in it.

Then his eyes fill with tears, the terrible tears of an old man, not too old, and yet strong. He looks out the window. There is the white oak in the yard, the remnants of rope yet hanging from it where he had once put up a swing for his boys. No, for his older boy, years ago. How long did it take a piece of rope—good rope, too—to rot? There is the flower bed where his wife's nastur-

[5]

tiums shine yellow and red beyond the uncut lawn this side of the paling fence. He wishes he had fixed the fence like she asked.

He begins to pray again. What he sees out the window—tree, rope, fence, flowers—swims in bright tears. He does not want to smell. He wishes he had fixed the fence. He prays, but words mean nothing. He is simply saying over and over the grace his wife had long back taught their children: *God is great, God is good, make us thankful for this food.* His tears stop. He reaches down and lays his right hand on his genitals.

No, Jack Harrick is not in the glade. Nor is whoever it is who has left boots and box, and withdrawn. A jay bird streaks out of the dark of beech-shade, whips sharply up, and perches on the tip of a high bough. He looks black against the brilliant light. He drops off the bough, the bough quivers at his departure, and he drops straight down to find perch on the neck of the guitar. He peers beadily into the underbrush surrounding the glade, now here, now there. He makes you think of a little boy playing Indians, that histrionic alertness, that pathetic, bright air of savagery. You could put thumb and forefinger to the back of the bright neck, behind the wicked crest, and pinch out the light. With no trouble at all.

It is cool here in the glade. A man could lie here on the patch of blue grass, stare up at the sky and forget the locust-grind and the heat-dazzle. It is not merely the coolness of shade. Toward the upper side of the glade, where the outcrop of limestone marks the heave of the ridge, the biggest beech of all stands, trunk enormous and elephant-gray, boughs swooping down, great gray roots convolving and grappling the limestone. If you look close under the shadow of the down-swooped boughs with the small, dark-green, enamel leaves, you will see a longitudinal opening in the rocks, a vestibule, a jutting overhang of mossy limestone, and farther in, another opening, not nearly as big, a couple of feet high, three feet across. The opening of the vestibule, dark green with moss, fern hanging lacily over it, trefoil to one side, is very pretty. Coolness drifts from the opening in the

[6]

faulted stone. If you lie on the ground, on the grass, your cheek, the one toward the hole—ten feet away, fifteen feet, twenty—will be cold and calm, like marble, while the sweat on the other cheek dries stickily, making flesh prickle.

The jay bird flings up from the neck of the guitar, banks into a long dive into beech-gloom, and is gone. A thin sweet note vibrates spookily from the one string that the jay bird's heel has plucked. In the trees nearby, the locusts hush, as though to give the note a silence in which to die. It dies fastidiously into the sky, into the dazzled space over all the land. The locusts resume. The boy and the girl come out of the woods, into the glade.

The boy comes first. He is a young boy, seventeen, or eighteen, a likely boy, in blue jeans tight enough to show his good leg and narrow hips, with a plaid gingham shirt, red and white check, over shoulders wide but still kid-scrawny. His straw hat is a farmer's kind of hat, the kind that bends over tobacco plants at suckering time, over the hoe in the corn patch, but it is not worn like a farmer's. It is gallantly canted to one side, side brim pressed up like an Australian bushranger's. A couple of drake feathers, purple, black, blue, are stuck through the straw on that side. The face beneath the hat is not clearly visible as he enters the glade, just the tousle of yellow hair on his neck, for he is looking back, laughing, laughing at something, beckoning as he swivels on the clean hips, holding a hand back toward the girl as though luring a little filly with sugar or a fawn with the prospect of laying a silken tongue to the delicious salty, tingly sweat on the back of the hand, tolling the girl out of the woods and brush toward the spot where grass is soft as silk at the edge of beech-shade. As she comes toward him, out of the dark into the more dappled shade of the woods-edge, she is laughing, too.

She pauses at the very edge of the woods, sunlight striking across her pale yellow dress at the belly and downward, but her bosom and face yet in shade. The laughter still on her face, she

[7]

is poised there, looking up into his face as she puts out her hand toward his waiting one. Then the laughter is not there, and has left a sadness that is not yet at home on that face.

Her face, as he stares down into it, is in one of its moments of beauty. Her hair, very fine and dark, is worn loose, with a ribbon, yellow, at the back of the neck, and now with the sweat of the climb the hair is curling and tangling over one shoulder, and wreathes festively in a multitude of little damp-shiny tendrils about her face. Green leaves, dappled with sun and shade, are behind the head and the curling hair, framing it, as the hair frames that face from which the brook-brown eyes are lifting up at him with their new, unhabituated sadness.

It is a face that will not be beautiful forever. As the years come on, there will be no distinct architecture of bone to sustain its beauty. It will have only what the years give, the sweetness of the life process and the warmth of sympathy; or, with ill fortune, the dulled, unfocusing glance and the sag of lip or twitch at the corner of the mouth to indicate an old unformulated grievance. But it is beautiful now, and as the boy looks down at it his breath literally stops. He thinks that he cannot move. Her glittering glance, coming to him through the new veil of sadness which he has not yet identified as sadness, seems to offer him everything but at the same time to cut some nerve at the top of his spine so that he can never again move a muscle.

He has a plan, or a compulsion, in bringing her here today. But the first time he had brought her here that had not been so. In that period, which now seems so incredibly long ago, but was not, he had had no design upon her, beyond the necessity of being with her at every minute possible. In that period he had never even permitted her to enter the darkened room of his fantasy, or if she entered she would suddenly become faceless, and the world was ashes.

He had scarcely ever tried to force himself upon her, ever so little, as he used to try, in his clumsy, boyish way, to get at other girls last year, a thousand years before that afternoon when Jebb

[8]

Holloway, a lanky good old country boy, the captain of the basketball team, had nodded yonder toward two girls walking across the schoolyard and said: "Look at them Christmas bubbies that-air little Jo-Lea is stringing on herself. Mammy, rock me to sleep."

Actually, it had not been Jebb Holloway's remark that did it. He had flinched at the remark, had turned away, knowing he was flushing, afraid that the others might see it. Jebb Holloway's remark had simply made him notice, next day when he saw Jo-Lea go down the school hall, how she held her left forearm across her breasts as though, in shame, to press them back, conceal them, protect them. That gesture of guilt, or shamefastness, had evoked in him his own feeling of the day before, the flinch and the flush. With that evocation, his doom had been sealed.

It was sealed because he knew, not in his head but in his belly, how Jo-Lea felt—whatever nameless feeling it was—and knowing how she felt, he loved her. It was as simple as that. But he had not used the word *love*. He hadn't even felt the word, whatever it was he did feel. He had simply felt that he had to protect Jo-Lea —no, not Jo-Lea exactly, but Jo-Lea the bearer of that precious and shamefast, orbed softness.

For there were, in fact, two Jo-Lea's. There was the Jo-Lea whose left arm was folded across her bosom in that sad, unconscious, conquering gesture. And there was the other Jo-Lea, who didn't know or care how slick a guy handled a basketball, how sharp a forward a guy played even if he wasn't tall as some, how clean a guy could take a squirrel out of a hickory top with a .22 pellet in the eye, just like they said the old fellows who first opened up this country used to with a long rifle, how a guy could trail bear, and got one, too, by God, just last winter, or how a guy could set a broadax in white oak nigh to the eye. This Jo-Lea didn't know much of anything, anything important anyway. What could you talk about with somebody like that?

This Jo-Lea not only bored him, she somehow robbed him, casually and indifferently, of the prides by which he lived,

[9]

robbed him even of his identity as Monty Harrick, and left him feeling that everything he had ever tried to do was silly and vain. Sometimes he felt he just couldn't stand to be with this Jo-Lea. He had to get away and go do the things he was meant to do. Right this minute, the fellows were down in the pasture back of the shed which had once been his father's blacksmith shop, choosing up sides for baseball. Now who the hell would be pitching against Sam Butts?

As for the other Jo-Lea, even as she compelled him and he looked down into the shining brook-brown eyes veiled with sadness, and thought his breath would stop, he was aware, fleetingly, of an anger at what, leaping ahead, he knew would come later: the dusty staleness, like opening an old closet, that he would feel toward supper time when she left him at the corner of the road, just where the road turned into a sort of street, and walked up the patch of concrete toward her gate.

It was a brownish concrete, full of cracks and crumbles, running along the iron fence of her father's place, the only iron fence in Johntown, that enclosed the brick house with stained-glass parlor window and little fish-scale pointed tower, set back beyond two umbrella trees, accurately placed, two catalpas in purple bloom now, and the maples random along the fence.

Sometimes he could think of that patch of concrete, one of the few patches in the settlement—in town, as Jo-Lea and the kind of people who had the stores and the bank and such would say—and he felt miserable enough to die. He would see her walking away from him—the narrowness of the heel tendons moving, one-two, one-two, the skirt slipping and swaying over her narrow hips, the opulence of her breasts, punished and defended by her gesture, being borne away, away from him—to what?

He could not bear to think what she would do upon entering, the ordinary casual things somebody might do on coming home, saying hello, kissing her mother, washing her hands, putting food between her damp, warm lips, sitting on a toilet seat, a real toilet you could flush by pushing something or pulling a chain.

[10]

Going to the toilet was a defilement, and the thought of her doing it made his skin run prickly up the back of his neck. He hated the thought, and was, in fact, afraid of it, it made him feel so different, his face feeling thick, eyelids thickening, lips thickening, breath heavy, his arms heavy and dangerous, and an anger growing and swelling upward in his being, like a big bubble deep in a mud swamp, released from some decaying vegetable matter to rise up, viscously up, to burst with a *plop* at the surface.

He thought of her going into the house, moving into the gloom of the front hall, with the pale golden oak curlycues everywhere on cornices and mantel, moving through the bead portieres, which would make a faint clicking sound, into the deeper gloom of the back hall and body of the house, or going up the stairs with their golden curlycues into an even more mysterious and shadowy region, and he simply could not bear to think of the things she might do. Any of those things she might do was, in fact, a defilement—and a betrayal—like going to the toilet. He could bear to think of her only after she had overpassed the common life of evening and lay in her bed, on her back, her narrow heels close together in a painful precision, her face calm, eyes closed, preferably with moonlight falling across her face, her right arm flung back on the pillow, crooked over her head, her left arm laid across the mounds of her breasts.

Even that calm image, however, might suddenly be a betrayal. Not by defilement, by something else. He might suddenly think of her as lying under the soft, suffocating weight of her own breasts, as though a big purry cat, soft as cloud and heavy as lead, were crouched on her chest to do what cats do when you are sleeping, suck your breath. He would feel, then, like crying out, to warn her.

But she wouldn't want to wake up. She wanted to lie under that suffocation, the pressure more and more imperative and conniving on her chest, breath shorter and sweeter, drowning deliciously under the weight of softness of self into the deeper and softer recesses of herself, like a body relaxed and glimmering

[11]

whitely into the darker depth of water, swaying and shelving downward, surrendering itself in voluptuous fluidity to the element. She would be, somehow, both the body glimmering whitely down and the dark envelopement, the self drowning into self, self-glutting in its own fulfillment of softness.

He could not bear the thought. It was as though he were being betrayed. No, it was as though he himself were drowning. He wanted to run out, into the night, and gulp the air. He wanted to run away, over the moon-bathed ridges and cove shadows, where whippoorwills called from cedar-dark. He wanted to feel his own bare feet bleed on the rock as he ran. He hated her, for she involved him in something. In what? In her own being and destiny.

No, it was not that. He hated her because she was so completely herself and did not involve him. As night after night, under the cloudy-white weight of self, she drowned darkly inward into herself, he felt that she had no need of him. Even after what had happened between them. Even after that, there was no place for him. No place with her, and she had robbed him of whatever place he had had in the world before.

Sometimes he wished he had never seen her. In her softness and indifferent compellingness, she had robbed him of something—and even this minute down in the pasture, the fellows, God darn, were choosing up sides for a ball game. He bet if he dropped her he could get another girl that wouldn't make him feel so much like he didn't amount to a thing. Durn it, here he just graduated from high school, and she made him feel like he was nothing. But some of those girls at school, they had looked at him like they thought he wasn't a bad-looking fellow. Sometimes in his room he would stand in front of the mirror, suck his guts in till they clamped round his backbone like new bean vines on a beanpole, pull his broad leather belt to the cruelest notch, cant his hat, with the drake feathers, to one side of his head, set his lips in a ruthless line, narrow his eyes, ever so little, then turn his head, very slowly, to one side, as far as he could turn it toward

[12]

profile and still see himself in the mirror. He wished his nose were bigger and not turned up. Not that it was turned up much, just a little.

Monty Harrick wished his nose were like his father's, a big jutty nose like the nose of the Indian on a nickel—and folks said the Harricks had Indian blood, Cherokee blood, blood of a chief's daughter back from the early times when, as folks said, the Harricks had fought and fucked over the mountains into Tennessee. Well, even if Monty Harrick didn't have that nose, folks knew, the girls knew, that he was Old Jack Harrick's boy, a chip off the old block, the son of that Jack Harrick who had known every laurel-slick where a he-bear might lie easy and reach for his wild grapes, and every ivy-slick where a wild boar would wallow, and every likker trail and still track in East Tennessee, and had helled over half the ridges and up half the hoot-owl hollows from Chattanooga to Nashville and as far over as Abingdon, Virginia.

For thirty years Old Jack had dragged jugs dry, whipped his box till folks fell down from dancing, cracked jaws with his fist like hickory nuts under a claw hammer, and torn off drawers like a high wind in October stripping a sycamore to bare-ass white, all over Kobeck County, counties adjacent and contiguous, and other points of the compass wherever a farm wasn't too perpendicular or a crossroads store set too slantwise to allow a fellow foothold for one punch to the head, or wherever there was enough shade-privacy for a maiden's shame-fun, enough grass so gravel wouldn't put a crick in a lady's backbone, and ground wasn't so tilted you'd have to use one hand to hold on to a sapling to keep from rolling downhill to the settlement to advertise fame, envy, and consternation before you could get unclamped. Not that a little tilt, as old folks reported Old Jack to have said when young, didn't spice sport, heads downward, and reported that after a certain set-to the boys found what had been good pasture grass and clover now looking for fifteen feet like where oxen had passed dragging a log from logging operations.

That was what the old ones, dreaming back, said about him,

the ones left, especially Old Jim Duckett, butt-sprung and smelling of corn likker, tobacco juice beading yellow down his whiskers, no good and never had been, sitting in front of the harness shop, in the shade, reaching out to snag Monty by the sleeve, saying: "Durn if it ain't Ole Jack Harrick's boy— Boy, you made like him?"

Then tee-heeing in an awful old-man snicker, before launching into the praise that somehow was intended to make the praiser the peer of the praised: "Yeah, Ole Jack, he was a heller. He was ring-tail. Hard-working between times and made that anvil sing, but when he tuk over the ridge, he was shore Hell's own unquenchable boy-chap. Yeah, a pearl-handle in his hip pocket—.38 on a .44 frame—and one button of his fly unbuttoned to save time and didn't give a durn which he might git aggervated to use fust, pistol or pecker. I'm a-telling you, strong men, when they met him they give him the high side of a hill track and fust on the creek log, and wasn't no woman under age fer putting on the calico cap didn't swaller sweet spit and look back over her shoulder when she passed him on the big road, her married or not and hit Sunday.—Yeah, you Ole Jack's boy?"

And at Monty's sick-faced nod, Old Jim Duckett had gone on: "Yeah, and that Jasper Harrick, yore Big Bubba? Yeah, and him a Big Bubba to have now. Yeah, he's the spit and image of Ole Jack. A chip off the old block."

And the old-man fingers would, with their insinuating feebleness, reach out to pinch his thigh through the jeans, and the whiskered baby-pink lips would peel back from the yellow teeth: "Yeah, and you—air you a chip off the old block—hee-hee?"

But he knew he wasn't. Maybe his Big Brother was a chip off the old block, but he wasn't. He didn't know what he was. He was nothing—that was what some deep part of him felt as he smiled down at the girl-face in the dappled shade, reaching out his hand now to toll her out of the brush to try to make her do again what they had done five times near a month ago, but she now kept putting him off from. Durn it, it looked like five times

[14]

would give a fellow a sort of right, or at least the right to know why she kept putting him off. But she wouldn't even say why, and when he insisted the tears brimmed up in her eyes till he himself felt all torn up or, durn it, ready to run off and never see her again.

If it weren't for this girl, drat her, maybe he would be a real chip off the old block. Other girls looked at him, at Monty Harrick, and he knew durn well what they might be thinking. Being with some girls, a guy felt sort of free and easy. But with Jo-Lea a guy felt trapped. She made you feel like the pith had been drawn. It was as though her being so pretty did it to you. Those other girls—Jo-Lea plain cheated him out of what he might be getting off them, or they might be crowding on him to take: and he saw the face of Sallie Mapes, the way it was that time in the lumber room.

The lumber room, as they called it at school, was a sort of big dark closet for storage, one little window up high, off what they called the gym—which wasn't much better than a tobacco barn with boxed walls and tongue-and-groove floor, with a few chest weights stuck on one wall and basketball hoops at each end. The lumber room was full of junk, broken desks, folding chairs they put around the edge of the shed for the audience when there was a game or a shindig, and the vaulting horse.

Long back there had been a principal from Nashville with fancy ideas and he had put up the chest weights and bought the vaulting horse. The cords on the weights lasted about one year, and who cared, and in two years they busted the vaulting horse down, and who cared. The weight frames stayed screwed to the wall and the horse was shoved back into the lumber room till someday another principal with fancy ideas might come along and get it all fixed. So there it was that afternoon, after basketball practice, when Monty came back to hunt his lunch bucket and, thinking somebody might have set it out of the way, opened the lumber-room door.

There was the vaulting horse and there was Sallie Mapes, but she was not vaulting it. Whatever vaulting was being done was not being done to the busted vaulting horse. In the first surprise, and dim light, he just stood there and gawked and didn't catch on to what she was doing, or was getting done to her, cocked there, belly down and bubbies banging across the low end of the horse, the busted end, like a plump-tight bolster over a chair back, her hands hooked back to the underpinning of the vaulting horse for purchase, her head sort of lifted up, straining up so he could see the veins in her neck, her mouth a little open, the bottom lip slack-down and damp-looking, and her eyes blue-wide and starey, but not seeing anything, not seeing him at first even if she was looking right at him, her gaze fixed like she was studying on something and had to have the answer, and by God she almost had it, she almost did.

Then, in two seconds, or two years, he couldn't tell which, after he had stood there in the dim light, gawking and not realizing, he realized. Beyond, he saw somebody—Jebb Holloway—sort of leaning over. He saw one lanky arm was reached out to latch on to the near hand-hold on the vaulting horse. He saw the other arm reached out and the hand clamped on the scruff of Sallie Mapes' neck. That was why, he suddenly realized as his guts turned over, Sallie Mapes was rearing her head up so hard, nearly to bust the veins in her neck, to get the most out of that handgrip on her scruff. No, it was not quite accurate to say he realized it. His own hand realized it, with a prickle and tingle in the palm, and the fingers tensing out like ice hooks, but nothing to hook to.

That was the way, lanky arms out and ham-big hands clamped, that Jebb Holloway was keeping things in order before the door flung open and everything froze. Then it unfroze. "God durn," Jebb Holloway said in a voice tight as murder, "shut that door!"

So Monty managed to get out, and shut the door.

Shutting the door didn't end anything, though. It began it. At school, in study time, or class time, citizenship or plane geometry, he would watch her, a plumpish girl, not too well shaped, but

[16]

plentiful, bulging a baby-blue sweater, with light-brown hair done in curls, skin white as buttermilk and maybe smelling a little like it, and big blue starey eyes, starey to some extent even when she was not distributed over a vaulting horse. Then he discovered that she was watching him, and when she watched him her eyes weren't so starey. They narrowed some, as though she were peering at him from the brush.

Then one day, when he happened to look up and catch her eyes on him, he didn't jerk his gaze away as quick as usual, and he saw her suck her lower lip in, staring right at him, and bite it. He could see how white the teeth were that pressed down on the soft pink-wet lip. Then she let the lip go, suddenly, so it popped out and down. You could almost hear the little soft, wet *plop* it would make, snapping free. Then, looking right at him, in the middle of class, she did it again.

That was what that Jo-Lea was cheating him out of. Sallie Mapes was his. She was his as sure as God-a-mighty made little green apples. Hearing in his mind that soft, wet, soundless *plop* of her lower lip suddenly released by the white teeth, he knew what he ought to have known all along, that the second he had opened that lumber-room door and seen her face straining up and she had seen him seeing her, he was the thing she had to have, and she was his more than she ever was Jebb Holloway's, she was absolutely his and nobody else's. If it weren't for that Jo-Lea. Drat Jo-Lea.

Then one evening, when he had sneaked off down to the pool-room with his Big Brother to shoot a game, the fellows down there, Jasper's age, five or six years out of high school, if they had ever been in, got to kidding Jasper. It was not horsing around for fun. It was to work up trouble between Jasper Harrick and Jebb Holloway, for Jebb was there, too, and getting redder in the face. Jebb, being younger, would have had to prove something even if Jasper wasn't a man you'd want to fool with. Jebb might have had to call Jasper out in the alley, bare knucks, or knives, or broken bottles, or cue sticks right there—who knows what?—if

[17]

Jasper, in that easygoing way of his, hadn't stepped over and slapped Jebb on the shoulder, and grinned, and said: "Hell, boys, Jebb's my buddy. We buddy up on nigh everything, don't we, Jebb? And Sallie—hell, there's plenty of Sallie to go round. Ain't it, Jebb?"

Jebb, being younger, was flattered—especially since he wasn't, and never had been, a buddy of Jasper Harrick's. Grinning back, even if a little sickly, and saying yeah, yeah, made him more of a man now. A man like Jasper Harrick, a hero not long back from Chink-killing in Korea, who everybody knew was a man if there ever was one: a chip off the old block.

It was awful, walking home in the frosty dark, with Jasper, and knowing about Sallie. Then, suddenly, it wasn't awful, for it was his brother, his Big Brother, she had gone to, to do what she'd done. She'd gone to Jasper because she couldn't get him—him, Monty—and Jasper was the closest thing. Yeah, he, Monty, he'd shown her. She couldn't crook her finger and pop that underlip and expect him to come running. Striding along now, he hitched up his belt, squared his shoulders, and got his ruthless feeling. He could feel the ruthlessness on his face, as he strode along beside Jasper under the winter stars. He felt a little superior to Jasper, and more knowing—that for the first time, and it was a heady, windy feeling.

Then Jasper, musing out of his long silence, said: "That Sallie."

Monty waited, striding along, feeling superior.

Then Jasper laughed. "A fellow getting in a fight over Sallie Mapes," he said. "Imagine that. Why, she flings it round like a drunk man with a scatter gun. She would do it bare-ass on cockleburs. No other place handy, she would tell the bacon to move over in a hot skillet for butt space, and not care if you took the turkey wing to fan the fire up." Jasper laughed again, fell silent, then said again, with a contemptuous indulgent tone, shaking his head: "That Sallie, now."

It was as though somebody had kicked him in the pit of the stomach. His fine feeling was stripped off in one flick, like skin.

[18]

He felt naked as a skinned squirrel, and the gut-knife ready. Oh, he wasn't off the old block, not him, not Monty. It was Jasper who was, Jasper striding along musing and laughing to himself in that contemptuous, good-humored way at a Sallie Mapes, just because he was Jasper, a chip off the old block, and girls—not just those drawers-happy ones like Sallie—would do anything for him, roll over like puppies and lick his hand, and he would toss 'em what they craved and just laugh his easygoing way and off to the woods again, or drift down the river in his skiff, miles and miles, nobody knew where, flat on his back in the skiff, his hat over his face against the sunlight, dreaming in the darkness of his head, drifting on past afternoon into bullbat time, into night-time, all night long, and alone, or go wandering off, not merely to deep woods or down river, but crawl down in the ground, in the caves, deeper and darker, lying in the ground with his dreaming, as though he had cave-crawled into the earth like it was some sort of joyous dark-dreaming he was crawling into, to lie snug and complete with the whole earth tucked in around him.

No, nothing ever held Jasper back. "Be seeing you," he'd say, and be gone.

"Where you going?" somebody would ask.

"Can't ever tell," Jasper would answer, and laugh, and be long gone, whistling off yonder into dark or distance.

He had that trick of being himself so completely, it looked like he wore the whole world over his shoulders like a coat and it fit. That was why everybody reached out and tried to lay a hand on him, get a word off him, have something rub off him, hold him back a minute, before he moved on toward wherever he was going.

So that night Monty strung along beside Jasper as Jasper strode through the winter-bright night, so tall it looked like he had to duck for stars, that is, for the specially low-hung ones, laughing to himself, being Jasper Harrick, but Monty knew that he, Monty, wasn't like Jasper, his Big Brother. He couldn't even be himself, whatever that was.

[19]

It was that Jo-Lea that had prevented him. She had prevented him from being himself. And right now, with that sad, glimmering beauty of her brook-brown gaze, she prevented him from being down in the pasture back of the old blacksmith shop ready right this minute to pitch against Sam Butts, his fingers closing on the ball, his eyes narrowing as he studied the batter, and *strike!*—strike it would be. She prevented him from striding along in starlight and laughing indulgently because some Sallie Mapes had cocked herself up to him. She had prevented him— drat her, drat her, oh, durn her soul—from going into some world where, in winter, you got messed up together under an old lap robe in the back of a Chevrolet, or where, at night, in summer, in a place smelling of clover, white thighs moved slow and glimmered white like a moon flower in the leaf-patchy moonlight, and you-know-what winked like glory. Yeah, she prevented him from being himself. That Jo-Lea.

And now poised at the edge of the glade, as she reached out her hand to his, he looked down at her face and saw the damp-dark curling tendrils of hair framing her face into more than usual pinkness and pallor, saw the glistening of tiny drops of sweat just at the hairline and gathered on the temples, saw how bright the brook-brown eyes were. So something just tore the words out of him. It was as though a cold hand had gripped his middle, right through his hide, and jerked the words and his guts out together. It was as though the words had been hidden right in there in his hollow, deep and dark as his innards—or were the same thing, his very innards themselves—and now got jerked out into light. "Jo-Lea, Jo-Lea," he heard his voice in a painful grating sound, as the words were ripped out, "durn it, Jo-Lea, I just love you!"

He had never said those words before. That was the first, shocking thought he had: *I never said that before.* He shook like a leaf. He had done something that made everything in the world different. It was like jumping off a cliff.

Then he knew that he had, as a matter of fact, said the words before. No, he had merely uttered the same sequence of sounds. For he knew that it had, before this time, been only a sequence of sounds, as without meaning as wind making the rusty hinges of an old shed door scrape, sounds he had uttered mechanically as a duty, a reflex, or as an apology and justification for the act he had performed upon Jo-Lea Bingham.

But now the words had burst right out of him, like his own very innards, and therefore were truly words, and he felt as empty and pale-thin as though his insides really had been jerked out. He looked down at her face, and saw growing on it a smile that was both bright and sad, for the brightness was partly the brightness of tears swimming in her eyes, just under the point of breaking. It seemed to him that right that instant when he had said he loved her and meant he had to be close to her or die, the smile was coming from a great distance. But suddenly it was withdrawing into a greater distance, and he would be left alone, forever.

She could not see the awfulness of what had happened to him, the awfulness of hearing the words *I love you* come ripping and painful out of a fellow's very innards. The pity that was in the smile as it withdrew into distance—that pity made things worse. Pity, it wasn't pity he wanted. All he wanted was for her to know the gut-chilling God-awfulness of what could happen to a fellow. All of a sudden he hated her for that brightness of tears and sweetness of pity. "Listen!" he said. "Listen—"

And he drew her out of the brush, and seized her.

For a moment, with her head dropped back, and the smile on her face still withdrawn into its distance as into a wisdom to which he might not attain, she seemed unaware—or worse, contemptuous—of what might happen to her body. It was as though her body were nothing, and because that body was what he had

[21]

seized, and was all he could seize with his hands, it seemed that her contempt for it was a final contempt for him.

"God durn it!" he burst out, and held her tighter, and began to kiss her on the throat and face, with an angry randomness.

For a moment, she accepted that, with the same unawareness, or contempt. Then she said, very gently: "Don't. Don't, Monty."

The gentleness was the worst part.

"God durn," he said, and held her tighter.

"Don't, Monty," she repeated.

The gentleness was what did it. If she had just tried to push him off, or something. But she didn't, and that gentleness was part of whatever it was in her that made a fellow feel trapped like that bear that got his paw caught in the honey tree.

He knew it was over, the chance of doing what he had felt compelled to do, but a new kind of compulsion was on him, a compulsion to drive on to some other kind of crisis in which she would struggle or strike him or do something to make him angry, to make him fling her aside and run away and never see her and be free and shed of her.

"God durn!" he gritted out. "You been doing it and now—now—"

But she wasn't even hearing him. She wasn't even feeling him as he gripped her. She was staring across him, and beyond him. He had to loosen his grip, and look, too.

"Oh," she said, "oh," and had jerked from him and was running over there by the mouth of the cave. She was leaning over something in that bright space over yonder.

Numbly, he moved in that direction.

"Look!" she cried. "Look—he's been here—he's here!"

Monty Harrick saw the boots. He saw the guitar propped across one boot, bending the top a little. He stopped for a second, while the girl lifted her head, looking here, looking there, searching. Then he came over, and stood facing her across the abandoned objects. No, not facing her, looking down at the objects, while in him grew a numbness that might be pain.

[22]

"Yeah," he said, not looking up, "he's been here."

"But he's here," she said, a little glint in her tone.

He looked up at her.

"He left yesterday afternoon," he said indifferently. "The way he does. I saw him getting some grub out of the safe in the kitchen, fixing something to take. Some corn pone and cold shoulder meat and something. I didn't ask him where, and anyway he might not of named it to me. Anyway, I didn't ask him because he had just come out of Pappy's room. I told you how it is. When he goes in to sit with Pappy. He comes out not looking like himself, sort of streaked and white in the face. Then Pappy, after Jasper's been with him a spell, he—"

He stopped abruptly, looking at her averted face.

"You aren't listening," he said.

"I'm sorry," she said, and humbly laid her hand on his forearm.

"I figured he was going down river," he said. "Fishing. Or just going. The way he goes."

"No," she said, "no."

"What?"

"No," she said, "he's here." She turned and pointed to the dark cavity among beech roots.

"Huh," he snorted contemptuously, "what would he be doing in a mole hole like that? Heck, he wants something to really go down. Really explore. Like Moon Cave. Heck, this little old rat hole, you can't go back thirty feet before it gets too low. To crawl, even."

"He's here," she said, even more quietly.

He studied her face. "How you know so gosh-durn much about it?" he demanded.

"He broke through," she said. "He figured that that cold air was coming from somewhere, and broke through."

"How do you know so much?"

"He broke through to something big," she said. "And beautiful and grand and stupendously inspiring. Like they say Mammoth Cave is."

[23]

He reached out and seized her wrist. "Durn it," he said, "how do you know?"

She looked up at him, very calm and sweet. "I thought you knew."

"Well, I don't," he said.

"Daddy told us at supper, last night," she said. "Jasper and that Isaac Sumpter came to the bank to get the paper drawn."

"What paper?"

"To go shares," she said. "This is Sumpter land, what's left of the old Sumpter farm, Daddy says. Left, Daddy says, because you couldn't even grow a mortgage on it and nobody would buy it. That's the way Daddy talks."

"What paper?" he demanded.

"I was just telling you, silly," she said crossly, drawing away from him. "If you weren't so silly you could guess. To go halfers. It is Isaac Sumpter's land, for his Uncle Bob left it to him, and Jasper gets halfers for exploring it for him, and all. It would be an attraction. A tourist attraction. Like Mammoth Cave. Everybody would be rich. Jasper would be rich."

"Rich?"

"Yes, rich," and she nodded gravely.

"What would Jasper do with money?" he demanded. "Him, he'd just whistle and walk away from it. Like he does. Away from everything." And all at once, saying that, Monty felt free and proud and high up, happy as though wind were ruffling his hair.

"That's what Daddy said," she said, nodding. "Yes, Daddy said, give him ten thousand and what would he do? Just buy a new shotgun. Yes, Daddy said, what's money to a hill—"

Abruptly, she stopped.

"Go on and say it," he said calmly.

She was staring up at him, her lips quivering a little, her head seeming about to shake in a denial, her eyes beginning to brim.

"Say it!" he commanded ruthlessly, some sort of elation growing with the ruthlessness.

[24]

She was staring up at him, with her brimming eyes. "I'm not my daddy," she said, in a small, painful voice. "I'm me."

"Say it!"

She continued to look up at him with the deep, sad appeal.

"If you don't say it," he asserted calmly, feeling himself high and absolute in a dizzy, heat-dazzled light, "I'll never speak to you again."

She gathered herself, blinked back the brightening wetness of her eyes, touched her lips with her tongue as though to relieve the parchedness, and said: "Hillbilly."

"Yeah," he said, "yeah," with a slow, husky, glutted tone. "My pappy was a hillbilly. He was a hillbilly blacksmith. And he was a hillbilly heller. He got put in jail. Yeah, don't forget that."

She reached out to touch his arm, and he jerked back.

"Yeah," he said, "and sitting up there now, dying of cancer. Yeah, don't forget that—cancer. He's an old hillbilly heller dying of cancer. Yeah, don't forget it."

The elation had gone. It had gone before she reached out to touch him. It was gone, and there was just some kind of grinding dryness in his chest, but the words kept coming up out of that as though something had stirred up that dust in his chest and it rose up in his mouth and he tried to spit it out.

"Yeah—and my brother, he's a pore cave-crawling hillbilly, he's a—"

He stopped. His pecker was hurting, and he was looking right at the hole in the ground, over yonder under the beech roots. All at once he was over there. He hadn't run exactly, but he was there of a sudden. He was leaning down, sticking his head into the cool dark of the hole, beyond the drooping fern fringe, yelling: "Jasper! Jasper!—You there, Jasper!"

There was the echo of his voice from the dark, then nothing. He rose slowly, turned around, and moved forward, his eyes now sun-dazzled after the dark of the hole. He felt dizzy with the light, and letdown. Jo-Lea was looking at him across the little distance of green grass.

"You can see it," he said, in a dull, apologetic way. "You can see where he scraped the moss going in. Scraped it back off the dirt and rock."

She didn't answer, watching him in her humbleness and unhappiness.

"He must of been sort of dragging his short pick," he said. "Or something."

He came toward the boots and box, and looked down at them. All at once he leaned over and picked up the instrument, and gave it a few idle whacks. He let the sound die away, then looked up at Jo-Lea.

"He plays pretty," she said.

"He plays good," he said, "but never as good as Pappy, folks say."

He gave the box another couple of aimless whacks.

"One time I heard him—" Jo-Lea began, then stopped.

"Pappy?"

"No, Jasper. It was a time back."

He whacked the box, not looking at her.

"I was with Lolly Hanks, down by the river. We were hunting four-leaf clovers. For luck." She stopped, smiled a little wispy self-deprecatory smile, then added: "That's how I know it was a time back. Looks like I stopped hunting four-leaf clovers. I gave it up a time back."

She smiled the wispy smile again, and he suddenly saw her, in his head, the way she used to be, when she was young enough to walk down the river bank with Lolly Hanks, their arms twined around each other's waist, peering studiously down into the grass until one would cry out with excitement, then break apart from the idle embrace and lean to pluck the treasure. Then he realized that, in his mind, he wasn't now seeing that slender little-girl Jo-Lea of a time back, crying out and leaning for a clover, but this Jo-Lea leaning, in his mind, her right arm stretched down for the prize, and her left arm pressing up tight against the weight and sag of the breasts as she leaned over, the breasts that had not

[26]

been there whatever time that was, down by the river, she was talking about.

And now saying: ". . . and on a big rock, a gray rock, there where the water came down riffling, he was just sitting there—"

"Who?" he demanded.

"Silly," she said. "You know who. Jasper—we were talking about Jasper and him playing. He was wearing a red shirt."

"Yeah," he said. "Yeah." And thought of her leaning for lucky clover, the little girl now, leaning.

"He didn't see us," she was saying, "and we just stopped still, Lolly and me, it was so pretty. It was a song I never heard, he was playing, and singing it too."

She stopped. The musing note in her voice trailed off into silence. He looked at her face, somewhat averted now toward the hole in the ground. The locusts had stopped. Now, all of a sudden, they took up again, chewing up the sunlight like a million-size buzz saw hitting pitch pine.

"I never heard it since," she said.

"One of them he made up, I bet," he said. "He must of made up a thousand," he said. Then as though to be sure that some contempt came into his tone, he added: "Just sitting around. On a rock or something."

"I wish I could hear it again," she said, looking now slowly and fully at him, appealing and deep-eyed, as when brook water runs from sun-sparkle into shade, and he felt ashamed of himself. Of what? Of having put that edge of contempt in what he had just said.

He found himself leaning over the guitar. "Maybe it was this," he said humbly, and, picking out the tune, began to sing.

"Mist on the mountain
Fog round the hill,
I'll still be loving,
Do what you will:
Do what you will."

[27]

He stood, backed by the beech tree, his weight firmly on the left leg, the right leg crooked, right heel lifted, only the toe touching ground, left shoulder low, right shoulder skewed up higher than necessary, the unnecessarily loose red-check gingham of the right sleeve flopping a little with the movement of the right hand, his head canted back with the gallant straw hat and drake feathers stuck on it, the eyes slightly squinting against the full light, and sang with the nasal quaver of the back country, through the verse, then repeating the last line, in a fading minor. Then hesitated, and resumed:

> "Ice on the bucket,
> Frost on the ground,
> I will keep loving,
> Spite my heart's wound:
> Spite my heart's wound."

And went on:

> "Pone in the ashes,
> Meat in the pan,
> I will keep loving,
> Well as I can:
> Well as—"

He stopped abruptly. The locusts were still busy. He let the guitar slip down across his body, and hang straight down from his left hand, holding it out to one side as though he were holding a goose out there and throttling it. "Is that the one?" he demanded.

She shook her head. "No," she said, "but it's pretty." Then: "I didn't know you could play."

He didn't say anything.

"You never played for me."

"Every fool that can pick a box don't have to go round showing off," he said.

[28]

"You play pretty," she said. "Did Jasper teach you?"

"Any fool can pick something out of a box," he said. He leaned over and laid the instrument where he had found it, propped against the left boot, laying it down with some scrupulosity, an expiatory care, a need to place it exactly as it had been.

When he raised up, she was looking down at his feet, staring at them with such intentness that he himself looked down, too.

"Your boots," she said, then looked at the pair under the guitar, "they're just like those—like his."

He looked at his own boots. Yes, they were the same. Oh, yes, the same; and a shock of guilt, and exposure, ran through him. The same, but to make matters worse, make exposure more certain, his own were bright and new, not with the casual confidence of long use, not a scar on them, only a little dust on the yellow newness. He scuffed a foot as though to kick up some more dirt on them. But there was only the thick grass. No dirt.

"Boots are boots," he said bitterly. Then, turning away, added: "Even Monkey-Ward boots."

He was moving away, over yonder, around the beech tree. It was as though he were being pulled by a string, and he wasn't even himself while the string pulled him away from those boots and that box, and durn it, why had they had to be here anyway!

He felt Jo-Lea's hand on his arm, but did not turn.

"Monty," she said, so he turned to her.

"Monty," she said, "your playing—I thought it was real pretty."

He looked down at her.

"It was real pretty," she said. "It was as good as radio. Or even TV."

"Yeah," he said. Then: "Any hillbilly can pick a box." He drew from her, and added: "Didn't you know that?"

"Oh, Monty," she cried, "you don't have to be that way!"

But he had turned from her.

He moved on around the beech, steadily as though he had a long, stubborn way to go. But all at once, at the verge where the grass gave out and the brush began, he stopped. "Durn it," he

[29]

said, not knowing exactly what he was durning, and dropped down on the grass, belly down, on his elbows, staring into the green brush and woods-dark.

Her feet on the grass made no sound, but he knew she was coming. He knew it, because he wanted it so much—or didn't want it. He thought, in a crazy flash, of how at school they used to put some iron filings on a piece of tablet paper, and then bring a little red-painted, horseshoe-shaped, dime-store magnet closer and closer on the bottom side of the paper, and how the filings would quiver, then stir, then all begin to shift and point. That was what he felt like, one of those filings. No, he felt like a whole mess of them, like he was nothing but a paper sack full of them, and they were quivering, and quivering, ready to shift.

She was closer. He knew she was. He heard a slight rustle, a movement, perhaps her breath. Then everything was quiet again. Except, of course, for those locusts. But he wasn't going to turn around. Durned if he would. A fellow had to hang on to something. Durned if he would turn around.

Then he did. He rolled over and propped himself up on one arm.

She was sitting there very quietly, her legs bent back under her, her yellow skirt evenly spread to make a circle on the green grass, her hands lying supine, slightly curled, and empty on her lap, in a sweet humility, her waist rising very straight and small from the spread circle of the skirt, her back very straight but her neck gently inclining to one side, as she fixed her deep, patient, unexpectant gaze on him. The deep green of the beech leaves was behind her head. He did not want to look into her eyes. Then, truculently, he did.

All right, he might look at her. But he wasn't going to show anything. He adjusted his ruthless expression. He tied it on tight.

Then, in that small voice, very small under the sky and against the beech tree, she said: "I'm me."

He wasn't going to say a thing. Be durned if he was.

"I'm not my daddy," she said. "I love him, and he's sweet, but I'm not him."

He waited.

"I'm not anything he says or thinks," she said.

He kept on waiting. Let her wait.

"Don't you see?" she said.

Let her wait.

But she was rising a little to her knees, leaning, reaching out timidly—and demandingly—with her right hand, saying: "Don't you understand?—don't you understand?—I'm just me."

He was caught in the demand of her gaze, then dropped his eyes, not ready to answer. What he now saw, and was caught in, was the way, when she leaned in that posture, the loose neck of the yellow dress hung down, and her breasts, unself-conscious, not defended now by the left arm pressing, hung there, in her shadowy underness of body, with natural weight and fullness, as though about to escape from their bindings.

He couldn't lift his eyes to meet her. For shame? For shame at her shame? For shame in his uninnocence before her innocence— her innocence as she proclaimed her identity? For shame in some guilty anger that had been piling up in him? For shame of Old Jack and his cancer? For shame of Jasper, who was a pore cave-crawler, and wouldn't know what to do with ten thousand dollars? For shame of his own hillbillyness? No—for shame of something else, something more deeply himself?

Anyway, unable to lift his eyes for shame, staring at those shadowy breasts pressing to be free of their binding, he suddenly felt some awful, throttled, guilty stricture in his own chest give way. It was as though that sight had broken something inside him. He thought he was going to cry. He wasn't sure he wasn't already, in fact.

Abruptly he shoved himself up to a crouch, groped out for her outstretched hand, and as she came up to her knees, he put his arms about her body and, crouching, closed his eyes and pressed

[31]

his head against her bosom. He hung on to her, with his eyes shut, and thought he was really going to cry now. He even thought, for a second, with a flash of fear, that something inside him really had busted.

But that wasn't true, he knew. It was just the crazy awfulness of feeling forgiven, completely forgiven, for something, and you didn't even know what the thing was. After a minute, when things had sort of settled down inside him, he could hear her heart beating. It was making a strange, dark-sounding, juicy-sounding *bumpity-bumpity*. Like a sound down a well. Or in a cave.

The position was awkward. He slipped out of the strain of the position, getting his legs straightened out so that he was sitting. She slipped down across his lap, in a movement somehow will-less, and weightless too, though she wasn't exactly a small-built girl. She lay there across his lap, her body out straight and simple, feet together, knees together and crooked ever so slightly, hands set supine, lax, and empty, as though they had been dropped and abandoned in her lap, which wasn't a lap any more, now that she had slipped back, her neck over the crook of his left arm, her face upward, very calm, in the watery-waviness of beech-shade over it, and eyes closed. For an instant he was afraid that something had happened to her, something awful, you didn't know what, and he was stuck with it. He leaned over to peer into her face. He was aware, then, of her breathing. He thought his heart would break, she was so beautiful.

When, at last, he lifted his eyes, he was looking, he found, across that wide, grass-deep circular area under the big, down-swooping gloom of beech boughs, toward the sunlight over yonder in front of the cave. He found he was looking at the objects over there in the bright patch of sun: the box, the boots.

He was staring at them, it seemed, without really defining them. It was as though they were objects he had never seen, nor any like them. They were, it seemed, nothing but a set of shapes,

[32]

a smudge of color, the metallic glint of sun on string, and he didn't know what the hell they were.

Then it was as though his own hand, his right hand, wasn't his. It was as though that hand was doing what it was doing on its own responsibility. He wouldn't even have wanted to. Not with her so beautiful. As beautiful as that. But that hand didn't care, not a bit. Why did she just lie there so soft? Drat her, drat her, it wasn't his fault. He wasn't even looking at what that hand was doing.

Just as the hand wasn't his, so the words in his head weren't his either. They came flying there, hard, bright, dark-glistening words, and settled there in the dark of his head, like a flock of grackles swooping into the inside shade of a tree to set up that gosh-durn bright, creaky racket, and wouldn't stop:

Not buttons. No, it wasn't buttons. It was elastic. It was like the kind you saw in advertisements, and kicking high-jinks. Yeah, it would be the kind cost good money, but what the hell, she was Old Man Bingham's girl, and he had that bank. It would give. It was giving easy, and durn if he wasn't surprised that that old to-bacco-stick, squint-eyed witch of a mother hadn't wrapped her gal's tail up in croker sack and barbed wire for safekeeping, but he'd fix her. Boy, he would sure fix her. Yeah, he just wished old Mrs. Bingham would come busting through the brush. Yeah, if Jasper came crawling out of that hole, boy, would his eyes bug out? Yeah, and Old Jack Harrick, that old hillbilly heller and his cancer—just let him turn up, wheel chair and all—it would fix him. It would fix them all—bare-bottom in beech-shade, hurrah for the month of June, and pumping that bicycle. Yeah, Old Jack and his cancer—

And all of a sudden the birds gave a crazy squawk and a big gusty flurry and were gone out of the dark tree of his head, gone for good, and he was going to love Jo-Lea. He was going to love her forever, and ever.

"Jo-Lea—oh, Jo-Lea," he cried out of the fullness of joy, and

[33]

tried to lean over her, to see her face. He wanted to see her face, and know for true who she was.

Her face, he saw, was averted. Her face was turned toward that shadowy space under the beech boughs. Her eyes were open, and she was staring across over there, to the sunlit space, beyond. She was staring over there at the boots and the box.

In a flash, he saw this fact. Then, before he could realize the full fact, even as her name burst from his lips, she had jerked free, was pushing herself up, jerking completely free, had got to her feet, had tried to run away, had stumbled and almost fallen flat, her knees hobbled in those panties that had cost good money and come down so gentle.

She leaned over. She tried, or seemed to try for an instant, to pull the panties up. But they were caught, or twisted, or tangled. So she jerked them off, stepping out of them in a complicated quick, tricky way, like a trick you learned to show off. She was running around the beech tree, leaving the panties, running toward the bright spot, toward the box, toward the boots, toward that hole in the ground. "Jasper!" she was calling, "Jasper!"

The boy managed to get up and run after her. She was bent over, at the hole in the ground, calling into the hole. She turned around as he came up, and pointed to the box.

"Look," she said, "look!"

"What?" he said, staring stupidly.

"Don't you see, don't you see?" she cried out.

"See? See what?"

"We're fools, we're fools!" she cried out in anguish. As he stared at her, she reached down and seized the box and held it cradled in her arms. "He never would have left it out," she said. "Oh, don't you see—he wouldn't ever have left it out all night for the dew to ruin!"

He was staring into her face, while the whole glittering askew world swam and tried to come back into shape to make sense.

Then she had dropped the box and was tearing across the glade, not looking back, whipping into the green brush like a stung filly in sweat-fly time. She was grading down the mountain so fast that when she broke out of the trees downhill she would be fifty yards ahead of her shadow and it would not catch up till she stopped to draw breath.

II

Mr. Timothy Bingham, chief stockholder, president, and cashier of the People's Security Bank of Johntown, Tennessee, wore pince-nez glasses rather than plain steel rims, which he would have preferred, because his wife, between whose legs he had not managed to get in five years, thought pince-nez more refined and suited to his position, and hers.

Mr. Bingham dressed neatly in dark wool, summer and winter, suits cut well enough to show his good, not yet quite stooped, shoulders, parted his not yet too thin brown hair in the center, kept his black shoes, box toes, well polished with a handy home kit stored in the back hall by the broom closet, taught Sunday School, out of civic duty, not conviction, at the Baptist Church, there being no Presbyterian communion in Johntown, sang in a pretty good baritone, read the *Saturday Evening Post,* the Kobeck County *Weekly Herald,* the *Reader's Digest,* and the *Wall*

Street Journal—the last being left exposed like a ritual wafer on the desk at the bank, the desk where he rarely had time to sit in his role as president—thought of the future only when forced to do so to calculate interest, and thought of the past, resolutely, not at all.

He was forty-six years and eight months old, having been born October 3, 1908. He had gone two years to Teacher's College at Nashville, had got married young, to Miss Matilda Bollin, a sickly, pertinacious, culture-hot and cold-bellied girl several years older than he, who had delivered him first a stillborn son and then a beautiful daughter; and now he was leaning over the counter at the bank, sorting checks according to the foreign banks on which they were drawn—that is, banks not of John-town, Tennessee, but of Nashville, Chattanooga, Louisville, Russellville, Murfreesboro, Guthrie, Clarksville, McMinnville, Atlanta, Bowling Green, etc., and even New York.

To say that Timothy Bingham was sorting the checks is not precisely true. His fingers were sorting the checks, with only a disturbed and fitful supervision from the inner reality which was Timothy Bingham, a supervision so fitful that several times already the fingers had made grievous errors, perhaps even malicious errors, errors which the inner, the essential self of Timothy Bingham, caught in its anguish, had detected only in the appalled nick of time. While the strong, clean white fingers distributed the checks to appropriate, or inappropriate, piles, like cards in a game of solitaire that those fingers had played almost daily for twenty years, the self of Timothy Bingham endured its awareness.

It was aware of two things: the *click-clack* of the ledger-posting machine behind him, and the fact that the bank examiner was in the little conference room behind the fake mahogany door to the left of the vault.

There was a third thing, but the self of Mr. Bingham could not bear that awareness. He could avoid it, until the Greek came.

[37]

That insinuating *click-clack* that he heard behind him was the sound of the ledger-posting machine, which Miss Dorothy Cutlick, the bookkeeper now for some three years, expertly operated. She was a good bookkeeper, for he had taught her himself, all that hot summer, three years ago, when she had come out of high school, a towheaded girl, the mark of the hill farm yet on her even after four years in the settlement. She had been overage for her graduating class. She had had to nurse a dying mother before she could break out of the shack and come down to high school, and then had managed only after a blazing row with her old man, who had, as a matter of fact, laid her scalp open with a glancing blow from a handy length of firewood. Happily, the force of her father's assertion of her attachment to his hearth side had been somewhat modified by the fact that he was, at the moment, on the downgrade side of a high toot and sliding rapidly. Her skull was not fractured, only well bloodied, and he had had no second try. The miscarriage of his first try started him in a long staggering dive, and his head nearly knocked a chunk of limestone out of the chimney, the chimney being the only reliable and firm-set thing about the shack. He lay on the hearth, and she let him lie.

She ran out, blood and all, into a night of black frost and brilliant stars, down the rutted track, under the black, leafless oaks and whirling black void of sky. At a neighbor's cabin, they took her in, and somebody got up the ridge in time to pull her father off the hearth, where he lay with hair singed off one side of his head, and the brains under the hair seething and bubbling from the inner heat of his own homemade ninety-proof panther-piss and the outer heat of a hickory fire.

Dorothy Cutlick was not to see him again for six years or so—after she had been working in the bank for two years, that is, and Old Man Cutlick, brooding in the shack sliding down the gully-wash and scrub-oak north haunch of his ridge, with cash absent

[38]

and whisky short, had had time to figure out that his gal must own the bank by now and owed him a half interest. The occasion of his visit had been definitely messy.

It was so messy that Dorothy Cutlick couldn't bear to remember it. It wasn't just the messiness of things that had happened there in the bank, with town eyes staring at her in such respectable consternation and vindictive curiosity that she felt all her striving and struggle had been in vain. That was bad enough to make any girl wake up in the middle of the night and feel her flesh prickle down her spine and despair gather deep in her throat like the back-flush from a sour stomach, and say: *My God, my God, oh, Lord, Lord,* while moonlight fell serenely through the lace curtains she herself had put up because Mrs. Putney was too chinchy to have more than some lengths of flour sacking and a cracked green shade in a rented room.

No, it wasn't just the mess that had happened outside her that made it so she couldn't bear to remember it. It was something that had happened inside her. She didn't know what it was, but she did know that it was something even worse than the memory of the first years in Johntown when she had worked in Mrs. Torvey's house, while Mrs. Torvey was taking her time about dying, and she had scrubbed floors and washed sheets and emptied bedpans and sat up all night reading the Bible out loud because the old fool was afraid to die.

Whatever it was she couldn't bear to know was worse, even, than the time after the old fool was dead and she had been the supper-time waitress in Ye Olde Southern Mansion Café, the only eating place in Johntown, where the truckers parked their rigs to take on extra coffee and Don't-Doze if they were heading up the mountain, and to buy a pint under the counter if they had just made it over, heading west. She had learned to keep her mouth shut and her knees tight, though sometimes things were so awful she'd go back to the washroom to cry.

Sometimes they'd say things to her so embarrassing she'd blush, even if she knew that when she blushed the scar coming out on

[39]

her forehead from under her tow hair turned so red you'd think Old Man Cutlick had just that second done his logical and fore-ordained work with the length of firewood, and blood was only now about to pop. Sometimes they would talk that way just to make her blush, and then kid her about the scar. Then she would go to the washroom to cry. If there was time.

What the truckers said to make her scar flare up was worse, it seemed, than what actually happened to her in the end, there in Ye Olde Southern Mansion Café. The money she got just wasn't enough to make it on, even if the Greek let her cram her belly full every night. She would sit by the kitchen table, humped over so her face was nigh the table level and she wouldn't have to tote the ammunition so far, and grimly load up for the twenty-four hours to come. She would pack the greasy grub into her gullet like packing a sausage sack, now and then sluicing down some recalcitrant gobbet with a douse of lukewarm coffee. If she ate enough, she thought, she wouldn't have to eat much tomorrow during the day and could save a nickel, or maybe a dime.

No, it wasn't as simple as that, the remorseless grub-stuffing. It shared something with whatever it was that made her study her lessons, grimly on till dawn if necessary, until she was letter-perfect. It looked like she just had to get all there was of whatever it was she was suffering so much to get, even if the real thing wasn't grub or lessons. Grub and lessons, they were simply elements in the process. Stuffing them in was simply a sort of paradigm of the more fundamental and unnamable process she was trapped in. She was aware, in some dim way, that you could fling T-bone steak (often just the tail part somebody had left, cold, on a plate) and apple pie and the pons asinorum and the Declaration of Independence and 1776 and all the Latin declensions to boot, the kit and caboodle, fling them all into her and tamp it down, and it wouldn't fill up the empty ache which was the realest thing about Dorothy Cutlick, and which Dorothy Cutlick had no name for, for a person's name is not a good enough name for the ache a person is.

[40]

Anyway, the three dollars a week and what grub she could stuff, or slip into an apron pocket, wasn't seeing her through. There was rent, not to mention books and clothes, though God knew the clothes weren't much to brag on, even if she had been observed standing for more time than seemed appropriate before the show window of the Johntown Ladies' Wear and Department Store. So she told the Greek, with hemming and hawing, and the scar going on and off like a red blinker at an intersection in a place bigger than Johntown, that she wasn't making out. She asked for six dollars.

The Greek was not a bad fellow for a Greek in business in Johntown, which was a place not designed to bring out the best qualities in a Greek in business there. Nick Pappy—which was what Johntown had decided was a good enough name for Nicholas Papadoupalous—was not a bad fellow, but he had his troubles.

For one thing, he had failed three times in the restaurant business, Cincinnati, Louisville, and Nashville, in that descending order. And he was convinced, in the deep, dark, angry, tear-sodden secret center of his being, that he was going to fail in Johntown, and fail past Johntown, and fail, and fail.

The Greek was broad-built and burly, with a blue chin, narrow eyes, and a head gone shiny-bald. The head, however, gave the general impression that it wasn't natural baldness but the baldness of a wrestler whose hair had got prematurely worn off from slipping out of headlocks before he got ready to break the bastard's back. He was so burly he always seemed on the verge of popping a seam. His thighs were so tight-packed with muscle that he wore slick places on his trousers, halfway between knee and crotch, where the bulge of muscle on one leg wouldn't clear the bulge on the other when he walked. You knew he would have a black pelt on his belly like a buffalo robe, and have a scrotum like two doorknobs stuck in a chamois bag. His hands were ex-

[41]

cessively white—as though the dishwater of the years of his apprenticeship in his chosen vocation had had permanent efficacy—and were sprigged with coarse black hairs, with square-cut nails, strong and sharp-edged like the business end of a three-quarter-inch chilled-steel wood chisel. And in that deep, dark, angry secret center of his being tears fell without ceasing.

Nick Pappy, much to the astonishment of Johntown, wore a diamond ring on his right hand, but the hand looked so awe-inspiringly competent that no citizen of Johntown ever expressed the astonishment. Nick had the best car in Kobeck County, a Cadillac, new at that, or at least new by the standards of Johntown, Tennessee, and his idea of the Good Life was to take Sunday afternoon off, drape his bulk in his expensive hound-tooth tweed jacket, which he had bought in Nashville, clamp a cigar in his left jaw, establish his wife beside him, with her drugstore blond hair advertising itself, and him, to the hicks, and cruise contemptuously up hill and down dale over half the natural beauty and historicity of the Volunteer State. Then to round out Sunday, his idea would be to come home, to the shotgun bungalow he rented and called home, take off his shoes and hound-tooth tweed, drink a half pint of Jack Daniels on the rocks, and lay his wife.

But Nick Pappy was not now living the Good Life, even on Sunday afternoons. He had the yellow Cad, yes, with only a few payments yet due, and the hound-tooth tweed jacket, and the Jack Daniels, but Mrs. Pappy lay up in bed all the time now, sick and fat, and the blond was fading out of the hair. Nick Pappy, though hefty himself, could not abide heft in intimate relations, and if hair was not blond you could scalp it for all of him and give it to the Indians. As a matter of fact, it had better be platinum blond, and in the good days he had best enjoyed his Sunday afternoons when he had shut his eyes tight and pretended that Mrs. Pappy was Jean Harlow, a platinum-blond, swivel-built movie queen, even then long since deceased, who had made a deep impression on him in his formative years.

Mrs. Pappy, like Jean Harlow, had been in the show business,

[42]

and what she had offered to show was every square centimeter
of herself, veiled only by the shifting blue haze of the cigarette
smoke of various honky-tonks in Chicago, Cicero, Minneapolis,
Pittsburgh, Denver, St. Louis, etc. A few years back, in Indianapolis, standing in a pocket-handkerchief-size patch of open floor,
swathed in cigarette smoke as romantically blue as duskfall in a
Maxfield Parrish painting, the artiste Giselle Fontaine—whose
real name was Sarah Pumfret, and who was descended, though
she did not know it, from a long line of learned New England
divines and talented Pequot-killers—had thrown her head back,
shut her eyes, twitched her neck with metronomic precision in a
way to make the pale hair jerk and jerk, supported her breasts
lovingly and delicately with the tips of her fingers, and executed,
with other parts of her body, certain motions which convinced
Nicholas Papadoupalous that he could not live without her.

He felt that he could not live without her, because he suddenly
loved her. Or rather, he thought he loved her, which is sometimes
the same thing, and sometimes even better. He loved her, because something in the scene before him was different from the
hundred or so such scenes he had witnessed in the fifteen years
before. Something was different, too, from the number of similar
scenes which he had witnessed at closer quarters. Something,
perhaps the way the blue smoke coiled and curled like a dream,
perhaps the way the yellow hair twitched and twitched with the
neck-jerk, made him feel that time had stopped and this was
Truth.

Time, as a matter of fact, had stopped, because some mysterious element in the scene—the smoke-veil, or neck-jerk—made an
old forgotten fantasy come alive. It came alive out there on the
handkerchief-size patch of floor, in the stunning, shattering,
noiseless collision of the dimension of Time and non-Time,
Dream and non-Dream, which is what we call Truth with a capital T.

Nicholas Papadoupalous, sitting there in the honky-tonk, while
the tom-tom rhythm picked up, had wept, unashamed. He wept

[43]

out of some deep inwardness of vision. For the first time in his life, he knew what joy is.

Two days later, voice quivering, shy as a boy on his first trip to a whorehouse, he asked Giselle Fontaine to marry him. She had been sitting at a honky-tonk table, with a half-empty bottle of Asti spumante in a tin bucket of melting ice and a saucer of dead cigarette butts before her, shivering inside her rabbit-fur wrap, even though the room was hot as a Turkish bath. She stared into the brown eyes, where tears gathered. This crud, sitting across from her, said he loved her. Then this crud started to get tears running down his face.

With surprise and contempt she watched the tears run down the crud's face. With further surprise, of a different order, she realized that the tears were running all the way down to a chin which a 6 P.M. shave had left the color of the steel of a Luger automatic. The crud's tears and the color of the crud's chin, they just didn't seem to go together. That was what surprised her.

This new surprise gave way to a new contempt when the crud asked her to marry him. But within the orbit of that contempt, while she stared into the tear-wet brown eyes, Giselle Fontaine assembled certain data. She knew she was tired. She knew she was very tired. She knew he owned a restaurant, or said he did. It was down in Nashville, hip-deep in hick country, but he said he owned it. She knew he had a yellow Chrysler Imperial parked outside, this being shortly before the Cadillacs had the first fishtails and before Nick Pappy discovered he couldn't live without a yellow Cadillac convertible, with fishtails. She knew that that chin was gun-metal blue, even if the crud was crying. She knew that gun-metal chins were, on her private statistical curve, to be correlated with a fairly high percentage of agreeable experiences. She knew, also, that for three weeks now she had been spitting up blood in her handkerchief.

She had scarcely assembled her data, and riffled through them, when the crud scraped his chair on the floor, reached over to take her right hand, and drew it, palm up, toward him, and as

[44]

abruptly as though a blackjack had been laid at the back of his skull, dropped his head forward to let his forehead lie in the palm of her hand. From a great distance, in a thin, innocent voice that could not possibly be his, but was his, she heard him say: "I cannot live without you."

She couldn't believe it, but that was what he said.

She was looking down at the top of his big bald head, that looked as hard and slick as polished marble, when she heard those words. Incredulously, she repeated the words, inside herself, without sound but with her lips working. It was as though she had to make her lips make the motions of the sounds, though without sound, in order to conquer the incredulity that such words had ever been uttered by anybody, any where, any time. Then, that general incredulity being conquered, she had to repeat them again to overcome the particular incredulity that that crud with the gun-metal chin had uttered them to her. Then, this second incredulity being conquered, she had to utter the words again to conquer the incredulity that, as she stared down at the marble-hard bald head and felt tears wet her fingers in which the head lay, the same words were rising in her, not now as the echo of his words, but as the release of a feeling, profound, agonized, and joyous, that ripped upward from her vitals.

In that moment, all the data she had just assembled for review were whirled away in a gust of feeling, and she said, out loud now: "I cannot live without you."

He lifted his head from her hand, very slowly and painfully, like a man roused to face reality and afraid to do so, and stared dumbly at her. She withdrew her hand, and rose from the table. He rose, too, in massive somnambulistic retardation, never taking his eyes from her face. They stood there under the communal gaze of the awe-struck honky-tonk. She moved toward the door leading back toward the secret regions of the place, and he followed in that same massive retardation. Just as they passed the last table, a client seated there whistled.

Nick Pappy stopped, and with a tired, sad, numb heaviness

turned toward the client. His gaze on the client was reproachful and appealing, but inside him a sense of outrage was growing. It was outrage that some new-discovered sweetness and purity should be so soon defiled. He was not yet, however, aware of the outrage when, staring at the client in reproach and appeal, he said: "You hadn't oughta done that."

The client was a big man, and burly, bulging inside expensive fabric. He was flanked by a brace of appreciative sycophants of equal heft, though less expensive tailoring. He rose to his feet, and said: "Yeah?"

Nick Pappy had still not become aware of the outrage growing in him when he felt that client's jaw give and lips squush under his fist. He was, in fact, greatly surprised at the event, as surprised as though it were an accident and he had had no part in it. He looked down at the body lying calmly on the floor and took a step, leaning a little, as though to apologize. It was a misinterpretation of this gentle movement that caused the nearer sycophant to sink back into the chair from which loyalty had prompted him to rise. It also caused the second sycophant to bow his head in a sudden and decided interest in the condition of his well-manicured nails.

Nick Pappy did not actually apologize to the client on the floor. He looked at him curiously, and then looked down at his right hand. He lifted the hand into the light and inspected it, almost as though preparing to rebuke it for error. He seemed to be deterred from this only by the fact that the hand had already suffered enough. It was bleeding across the knuckles, where, presumably, the client's teeth had made themselves felt before they crumpled under the impact.

As he stared at the injured hand, Giselle Fontaine took it, leaned to it, and kissed the blood. It was a gesture as unmeditated, as natural, as that of a mother leaning to kiss a child's hurt to make the hurt go away. It was a gesture instinctively performed in humble joyousness, but the instant the faint, salty taste of Nick Pappy's blood had reached her tongue, something else fused with the joyousness. The taste of the blood reminded her of the blood in her handkerchief, her own blood, the reminder now bringing, first, terror, then desperate avidity as she parted her lips and licked in, sucked in, swallowed in, what blood of Nick Pappy, the crud, was available. She felt, as it were, that his blood might mystically replace whatever blood she had lost, or might lose; that blood-taken-in might, by a mystic homeopathy, cure the disease of blood-going-out.

Then, when there was no more of the mystic medicine on Nick Pappy's knuckles, she raised her head, and while her throat made a couple of last automatic swallows, getting only saliva now with blood-flavor gone, she stood with queenly calm and lifted head under the fascinated eyes of the honky-tonk. Her heart was full of peace. All would now be well.

All seemed well, at first.

When they got back into the rear regions of the honky-tonk, he gave her a chaste kiss, then waited outside her door while she got ready to go. She rejoined him, carrying a little suitcase, but in it were not the gewgaws and Oriental rig of her trade, the stuff to be cast off before the tom-tom began to get compulsive. She left that stuff lying on the chair in her dressing room, where an attendant, whose job was to collect it off the floor after the performance, had left it.

Nick Pappy put her into his yellow Chrysler Imperial, and drove her to her rooming house. He saw her to the door; kissed her once; held her hands tight; with a cold, spiritual elation, stared into her eyes; then wheeled and strode powerfully down the steps and drove away. He was back the next morning, shortly after the milkman, waiting in the yellow convertible. They got married the day after, and all that time, while waiting to get married, he never laid a finger on Giselle Fontaine. He would have died first. He did not know that the whistle of the well-tailored client at the honky-tonk was what prevented him. He

[47]

would have died before degrading the beauty and terror of his vision to the level predicted by the whistle.

Things still seemed well when they got to Nashville, down there hip-deep in hick country. There was the restaurant, a pretty good restaurant, though she did not know about the condition of the bookkeeping. There was a hotel apartment, which she populated with cute stuffed dogs, *moderne* versions of the kewpie doll, and a live Siamese cat. She had not been too wrong, either, about the gun-metal blue chin. But she was somewhat puzzled by the times and places he seemed to prefer for the exercise of his not inconsiderable talents.

After the first few occasions, his interest in the ordinary operations, conducted in the ordinary way, in ordinary comfort, seemed to flag. But things were quite different on the bathroom mat, where she might suddenly find herself in business when she stepped from the shower with nothing more serious on her mind than paring her toenails or writing a belated announcement of her marriage to her aged mother, who was a public ward in an old folks home in Iowa. Things were also quite different in the middle of the apartment floor, or in the dark closet where, almost finished getting herself ready to go out, she might be reaching for a dress when he would seize her and thrust her, upright, among the hanging garments. Things were different, even as far as the bed itself was concerned, if he happened to fling her crosswise, down toward the bottom, best with her head hanging off the side a little.

Things were different around him, she had to say that. They were real different, a girl simply had to admit that much. And admit, too, a certain value in surprise for its own sake, even if waiting for surprises can sometimes be as boring as not ever being surprised, and even if some locations were distinctly harder on a girl's spine than others, and even if a girl's lingerie took a certain amount of wear and tear, particularly the latter. Well, she should worry about that, for he was the guy paid for it, and she didn't yet know about the condition of the bookkeeping at the

[48]

Marathon Marvel Restaurant and Steak House, Banquets and Supper Parties a Speciality.

Things were different, but, on the whole, quite satisfactory. It was just that she was sometimes puzzled, as she was that time when she already had her coat on, and even her galoshes, and then found herself across the foot of the bed and in business, nearly as quick as you could bust off a button and say Buster Brown. It wasn't the surprise itself that was so surprising. She had got rather used to surprises. What she found so surprising, and puzzling, was the fact that, after the surprise party was over, he was kneeling on the floor beside the bed, holding her right foot in both hands and kissing her ankle, as low down as he could with the galosh still flopping on her foot.

When she pulled herself to a sitting position on the bed, and looked down at the goings on, her first thought was that those awful, floppy galoshes made her look bird-legged, she was getting so thin. Then he lifted his face toward her, and she saw that it was working with an agony of despair, remorse, or something. He stared up at her with an expression of wild appeal, as though he were a man drowning and the bed were the shore and she sat there not lifting a finger to save him.

It was all so sudden she didn't have a chance to make head or tail of it. Then he dropped his face and again was kissing her ankle, or missing the ankle and kissing the dirty galosh. As a matter of fact, it seemed to her on subsequent reflection, he wasn't missing the ankle; it looked like he was kissing that dirty galosh on purpose. On purpose or not, between kisses he was saying: "I'm sorry, I'm sorry," over and over, now and then looking up at her to say it again, with tears brimming in his eyes, before his head again dropped to the work.

She didn't know exactly what to make of it, or even what he was sorry about, except that he had sure rumpled her past superficial repair, and they'd surer than cow patties aren't codfish cakes be late now to the main feature.

But the immediate disturbance, or puzzlement, was lost in

[49]

something else. For one thing, she felt—as what girl wouldn't with a competent-looking gun-metal chin kissing her foot with such tenderness?—rather queenly. For another thing, this queenly feeling, and the sight of the marble-slick bald head bowed before her, carried her back to that night at the honky-tonk and the joy that then had risen in her. So now, as unawares as when in the honky-tonk she had said to him that she couldn't live without him, she was saying: "It's all right—it's all right—it's all right, baby—" and reaching out to touch that marble-hard bald skull.

It was all right, for the moment. It was bound, however, to occur to her that his having rumpled her or made her late to the main feature would scarcely account for all the griefful goings on. This puzzlement increased with time, fed by his practice of leaping from ambush, his bursts of unspecified contrition, or whatever they were, and his habit, which she remarked more and more with the passing months, of keeping his eyes squinched tight while she was in business. Even when she couldn't see his face, and when, in fact, his face wasn't what she should have been concerned with, she was darned sure he had his eyes squinched tight, the crud. She couldn't get her mind off the fact, and it sort of got in the way of whole-hearted effort.

Besides, there was more blood in her handkerchief now. Her eyes could see it. Even if her mind denied the fact, crammed the fact down to the bottom of things in her head, like the dirty handkerchief crammed down in the bottom of the laundry basket, her eyes had seen it. It was blood.

Then, when the Marathon Marvel folded and they moved to a crummy room in an area back of the railroad yards in Nashville, waiting to salvage what they could, and then on to Johntown to the shotgun bungalow and Ye Olde Southern Mansion, Nick Pappy didn't pay her much attention for a while. But once settled in Johntown, with business promising and the yellow Chrysler swapped in for a yellow Cad, he got a second wind. It was like a new honeymoon, only with more ingenious dramas and surprises. The surprises didn't surprise as much, however, and she found the regularly squinched eyes and the occasional burst of contrition more puzzling and distracting than ever. And more and more, on those occasions when they were in business and she knew his damned eyes were squinched shut, she felt like she wasn't there. She felt like a spook. She felt like something he just grabbed, like a bolster. She couldn't figure out what the crud was up to.

The crud couldn't either. But down beneath the inner confusions and the shifting shadows shelving always deeper, he felt himself trapped in an agony of infidelity. If each of two women had a claim on a man's fidelity, he sure couldn't be faithful to one without being unfaithful to the other. He had to be faithful to Giselle Fontaine and his moment of vision in the honky-tonk. But he also had to be faithful to poor Jean Harlow, who, for all her platinum hair and swivel-build, was now nothing but a handful of burned ashes over which a big to-do had been made long ago, in Hollywood, California.

Back yonder, that night in the honky-tonk, it had seemed for a moment to Nick Pappy that there was no conflict in loyalties. What was going on to the throb of tom-tom, swathed in blue cigarette smoke out there on the patch of floor, had seemed like the projection of the fantasy which had underlain, underpropped, all life. The two things were one thing, and its name was joy.

But the two things—the fantasy and the real woman named Giselle Fontaine—started to fall apart. They got ungummed.

In the early days Nick Pappy had been so sure they were one thing that he had been in business with his eyes wide open to add to the relish. But something was wrong. Immediate satisfaction gave place to a grinding misery in the vitals, an insufferable pang of conscience at the soundless cry of the poor platinum-blond, swivel-built darling sunk in the suffocating depth of her nothingness. All the impromptu dramas and surprise parties were only a way to make actuality take on the ideal intenseness of fantasy, a ritual to call down, to the sprawl of the bath mat or

[51]

the tangle of the clothes closet, the romance, the mystery, the *mana*, the glory, of the dream that had glimmered in the dark of his head.

The impromptu drama, the ritual, the squinched eyes, never quite accomplished, however, what they were supposed to—that is, the fusion, the identification, of the dream and the actuality. Either the thing didn't work at all, and all he had a grip on was the actuality which some nagging something deep in him said wasn't so damned different from other actualities that he had to be in such a mess about it. Or the thing worked too well, and with his eyes squinched tight, he clasped the expensive, swivel-built dream with the breath of honey and his name on her tongue, and he was unfaithful to Giselle and his moment of vision in the honky-tonk.

Anyway, whichever way it went, he was bound to feel bad afterwards. There was bound to be an infidelity and the anguish of remorse, and worse, much worse in the end, the anguish of not knowing what it was all about. Then that remorse, and that anguish, shaded over into a different kind, and even worse.

The time came when Giselle Fontaine's fear at what she saw in her handkerchief overcame the fear-prompted denial of the thing seen, and she went to a doctor. It was high time, for she was thin now as a broom handle, and looked bird-legged as a flamingo, even without galoshes. That doctor stuck her under the X-ray and it could see right through you, right to the spot where she was going to pieces.

So she went to bed, and stayed in bed. She ate raw eggs and filet mignon and mashed potatoes and drank gallons of Grade-A milk and pints of cod-liver oil, and it was darned lucky for the crud that the crud could get it wholesale, all except the cod-liver oil, and she read *True Confessions* and *Real Romances*, or lay on her back and stared at the ceiling and didn't care what she had read in the *True Confessions* and didn't care what she herself had to confess or what she wished she had to confess, but had about given up hope she would ever again have anything to confess, for everything seemed so small and far away, and Nick Pappy sat by the bed and held her hand.

As for Nick Pappy, he felt, week by week, the hand he held getting puffier and puffier. He saw the shape on the bed getting more shapeless. He saw the face puffing out moonwise, vaguer and vaguer, till it looked like the moon rising deliquescently beyond gray mist over marshland. He saw the platinum blondness of the hair retreat, day by day, week by week, toward the end of each strand, strand by strand, and the muddy brown crowding up from the scalp.

Everything was the violation of everything, and it was bye-bye, my billion-dollar baby, and far away in Glendale, California, her mausoleum surrounded by the artificial, arsenical greensward of the famous Forest Lawn Cemetery, the platinum, swivel-built darling fell more vindictively into nothingness, and Giselle Fontaine swelled more and more into her somethingness, which was worse than nothingness, and Nick Pappy blamed his luck sometimes, but more often blamed himself, for it was as though what was happening to Jean and Giselle was all his fault, and all had come by a defect in fidelity.

So Nick Pappy, late at night, might go into the kitchen of the shotgun bungalow and fetch down the Jack Daniels, Black Label —for he always liked the best—and get a glass and a tray of ice, and go into the living room and sit on the couch among the tapes-try-covered cushions, which exhibited scenes from a harem, and take it on the rocks, and try to forget the note for $2,000 which Mr. Timothy Bingham held over at the People's Security.

Or he might simply get into his yellow Cad convertible, and go gliding or throbbing, swooping or shelving, up, down, and around the dark hills of Tennessee under the Tennessee night. But he would have to hurry back, before too long. Sarah Pumfret, who had been Giselle Fontaine, might need something.

Things stood this way, when, one night at closing time at Ye Olde Southern Mansion Café, Dorothy Cutlick, twisting her wait-ress' white smock, somewhat soiled now, stood before him and said she wasn't making out on three dollars a week. She had to have six.

Nick Pappy had never really noticed Dorothy Cutlick. She had been, simply, a not too satisfactory mechanism for heaving out the hash. In fact, for some time now, sunk in his numbness, he had not noticed anything. But now he noticed her. It was the scar that made him notice. The scar ran out from under the hair on the left side of the forehead, and under ordinary circumstances it wasn't too obvious. But now, in anxiety and embarrassment, she was blushing furiously, blushing and going pale, and the scar got the blood-red benefit.

At first, as Nick Pappy's gaze fixed on the scar, he felt revulsion. His first thought was to fire the girl. He hadn't ever really noticed the scar before, but now he thought he would fire her, for that scar seemed to absorb and compound all the anguish time was dishing out to him. Then he noticed that the scar ran back into her hair, and Lower Appalachian towhead is the nearest thing in nature you will get to platinum blond, barring albinos. Dorothy Cutlick was real Lower Appalachian towhead, prime specimen, every hair platinum down to the precious follicle whence it sprung, and no muddy brown crawling up from the scalp, strand by strand. Nick Pappy was staring at the hair.

Detaching his gaze from her hair, he began to notice the rest of her. She was talking—stammering, stopping, then talking again—but he wasn't hearing a word. He noticed that she wasn't built bad, as far as you could tell under that smock that was shapeless as a laundry bag. He noticed that she didn't have a bad face—nothing to brag on, but not bad. He noticed, as his silence seemed to deny the request being made him, that the blue eyes that were staring up at him had taken on, with the desperation, a deepening violet hue. The face was asking him for something.

[54]

"I got expenses," he heard his voice saying. "You know my wife is sick and I got special expenses."

She said she was sorry. She was sorry about his wife, and the desperation in her voice sloshed over into his desperation, and mixed with it, and that mixing seemed to give a deep, troubling sincerity to the sympathy the words abstractly defined. She was sorry, and something was stirring inside Nick Pappy, the need to hear somebody say they were sorry, sorry, sorry for Nicholas Papadoupalous. Nicholas Papadoupalous was so tired, and the tears fell unceasing in the dark, secret place of his soul.

She said she was sorry, but she had to have the six dollars. Please, she had to have it.

"How much rent do you pay?" Nick Pappy heard his voice asking. He was surprised to hear the question asked. It was as though he were eavesdropping on a total stranger and was awestruck by the stranger's astuteness at negotiation.

She paid two dollars. Two dollars a week.

Nick Pappy waited to hear what the astute stranger was going to say. The stranger waited, to let the girl's suffering pile up a little more.

"I got expenses," the astute stranger said on behalf of Nicholas Papadoupalous, and waited. Then he said: "But I'll tell you what. I'll give you four dollars."

The girl managed to gasp out that she couldn't make it. Not on four dollars.

"Well," Nick Pappy heard the astute stranger say, "I'll tell you. It will be four dollars. But you can move out of where you are staying. You can have that little room back of the storeroom here. It's got running water, just cold now, but I'll get the hot hitched on. You can use the ladies' john in here. I'll get the nigger to clean the room up tomorrow and maybe kalsomine the walls. There's a bedstead and such up at the house in the basement. Nothing fancy, but it will do. I will give you four dollars. You will save two on rent. That makes six. What do you say?"

[55]

She said nothing.

Then the stranger, after waiting, added in an offhand voice, which provoked Nick Pappy's admiration: "Well, take it or leave it." And he turned away, adding however, like an after-thought: "If you take it, you can have breakfast free. You can have the forty-five-cent special, with waffles, if you want."

The offer of the forty-five-cent special—that proved that the astute stranger was real astute. It wasn't just the forty-five cents, which was money, all right; it was the idea of sitting down at the counter and eating something hot for breakfast, not standing in the middle of her room in the Putney house to cram down some dry bread and maybe a piece of grease-congealed meat smuggled out of Ye Olde Southern Mansion the night before.

But the mention of waffles—that was the touch of the master. It wasn't that Dorothy Cutlick liked waffles particularly. It was, simply, that waffles stood for something in her mind, something never tasted, or even seen, in any cabin back in the bobcat coves or shacks clawing for hand-holt on the bare rump of a ridge, something belonging special to town, something exotic, re-fined, genteel.

"Waffles," Dorothy Cutlick said in a weak voice, musing.

"Yeah," the astute stranger said, clearly knowing that all he had to do now was pick up the marbles, move in for the kill. But artistry, it was clear, prompted him to wait, to let the Lower Appalachian towhead stand there, brooding on a waffle floating in her inner darkness, oleomargarine melting on it, and the syrup ready to pour, before he indulged himself in a last flourish of virtuosity. "Yeah," he said, "and you can let the nigger cook 'em for you. Cook 'em and set 'em on the counter in front of you, like a customer and a lady."

Dorothy Cutlick didn't say anything to that. She stood for a moment, benumbed. In that moment, the astute stranger was gone, and Nick Pappy stood there, also benumbed and uncer-tain, a little baffled now that the stranger had gone and left him with all the responsibility. Heavily, he drew out of his benumbment, mumbled something about having to get on home, on home to his wife, she was sick and he had expenses, and went to the door, and switched off the main light, and waited for the girl to swap the smock for her coat, and head off down the street toward the Putney house. He left the night light on, locked the door, crossed the street to the yellow Cadillac, got in, and with hands on the wheel, the motor yet dead, stared through the windshield, and watched Dorothy Cutlick pass under a street light at the end of the block, the towhead looking paler than ever. It looked damned near albino, under the light.

She turned the corner. He touched his starter, first a whir, then a hollow cough that wrenched the night, then the authoritative pulse. But he did not engage the gears. He let his head sink forward on the wheel, feeling the pulse of the motor transmitted up the steering shaft to his forehead, and said: "Jesus. Jesus Christ."

But Jesus, Jesus-Christ-what, he didn't know. It was just that things changed. Something that was coming never came, and what did come changed on you. Before you got a good grip and knew where you stood. It changed before you knew the score.

It wasn't any real surprise when it happened. Nor was it a non-surprise. It was an event outside of the dimension in which you expected, or didn't expect, something to happen, either above or below or slantwise off yonder where you didn't have to look at it. But it came later than anybody who might have been able to think about it in the dimension of expecting would have expected.

Dorothy Cutlick had been installed in the room back of the storeroom for three weeks, and had had waffles every morning for breakfast, when, one night, late, after she had done her geometry and her Latin, after she had undressed and put on her wrapper, she came back to her room from the ladies' john to find the light out. At first she thought a fuse had blown, remembering that that was what folks said was the trouble when the lights went out. But she didn't really know what a fuse was. So she stood there in the narrow passageway, which had some light from the night light up front. Then, wondering if she had absent-mindedly turned the light off when she left, she entered and laid her hand to the switch by the door. Nothing happened.

Then the voice said, husky rather than whispering: "I cut it off over here."

Her heart, naturally, jumped into her throat, and that was all that prevented her from yelling. But before she could make a second try at the yell, the voice again spoke: "It's all right. It's just I cut it off over here."

The yell wasn't going to come now. It had gone away.

She saw the shadowy bulk sitting over beyond the little table where her books and papers were, she remembered, spread out under the unlit lamp. She wondered if he had messed up her papers.

"Shut the door," the sad, husky voice said, from over yonder.

She shut the door. A little light from off in the alley came through the high-up back window. It came through the sweat and frost that was forming on the glass.

"It's all right," the sad voice said. "You can get on to bed. I'm going to sit here awhile. It's all right."

She did what the voice said, already having crossed, at the moment when the scream went away, the line between the dimension of expecting and non-expecting into the dimension where the event would be. She lay there in bed quite a while, trying to hold her breath, hearing his breath go in and out, in and out, sad and slow. It was almost as though she might just die from trying to hold her breath—or go off to sleep, she was so tired, and wake up to her alarm clock at six thirty, and he would be sitting there, sad and heavy.

When he finally got up, it wasn't all right. But it wasn't not all right, either. It was just something that was happening and yet not happening.

No, it was like something that had been happening so long it

[58]

could not be called a happening, but the unbroken continuum in which other things could be said to happen. This was simply the extension of what had begun to happen years ago, when her mother first got sick, off yonder in the hill shack, so sick she couldn't move, and she—she, Dorothy Cutlick, thirteen years old, lying on the shuck pallet in the lean-to room, in the dark—had heard the furtive clawing at the door, the creaking of the door, had heard the shambling stealth, had heard the breathing and the whisky-belch, had smelled the whisky.

Her mother had been so sick she couldn't move, but all at once from the dark beyond the plank door, there had been her voice, saying: "Sim! Sim!"

It was so weak it seemed a thousand miles off, or not there at all—perhaps just something that Dorothy Cutlick wanted to hear and that Sim Cutlick didn't seem to hear at all. But, then, it came again, not louder, weaker in fact, but with something in the weakness more terrible than any loudness could be, saying: "I know you—I know you, Sim Cutlick—"

Then a faint movement, for even if Sim Cutlick's woman was so sick she couldn't move, she was Dorothy Cutlick's mother, too; and then there was the voice, even weaker, saying: "—come in here—I'm up—you don't come in here right now, Sim, I'll blow yore brains out—"

And there was the sound of an object being dragged on the plank floor. It sounded like a shotgun being weakly dragged.

From that moment to the time Sim Cutlick had tried to bend the length of firewood around her scalp, and from that moment when he had dived his own head against the limestone chimney to now, in the back room of Ye Olde Southern Mansion, it had been like the same happening. But that happening had been going on in its own way so steady it wasn't a happening at all, for it lay outside of and, as it were, included other happenings, the kind that fill up, and are, life.

What was transacted now in the back room of the restaurant had, therefore, no relation to life. When it happened, the surface of life could close over it, like pond water over a stone—or better, like flesh healing over a wound, but healing at an incredible speed as when you see some such slow natural process photographed on film and the film then run off at a speed to compress all time.

So ordinary life went on. Nobody in Johntown knew what was transacted in the back room—and not to know was very peculiar for a town the size and kind of Johntown, where everybody knows everything. It was even more peculiar for Johntown not to know than for Dorothy Cutlick not to know. For it could be said, quite literally, in one sense, that Dorothy Cutlick didn't know what went on in that room. At least, one Dorothy Cutlick didn't know—the towheaded girl that heaved out the hash, that wolfed down the genteel waffles, that slipped as quiet as smoke, in shabby gray coat, up the street of Johntown, that would steel herself, when question time came at school, to put up her hand, and then would answer in a thin, shaky voice. But the answer would be, almost always, right.

Except, that is, in the Latin class, there still being such a thing as a Latin class even if only two years, elective, and populated only by five queer ones. There could be a Latin class in a hill county like Kobeck where the benefits of advanced theory came late, and a hatchet-headed old maid, a she-pillar of the Baptist Church and last prop of good learning, terrorized the principal and grimly held at bay the forces of the teacher's college down in Nashville. Old Miss Jessamine Abernathy didn't have any theories; she simply liked to teach Latin. Dorothy Cutlick didn't like Latin, and it was the only thing she wasn't good at, or couldn't make the midnight hours of work pay off in. But she took it because it was there, cramming it in the way she had crammed in the free grub at night in the restaurant, forcing it down, to the retching point.

Now, suddenly, her Latin began to improve.

It was this way. During those transactions in the back room, with her eyes squinched shut—as, unknown to her, were the eyes

[60]

of Nick Pappy—she would find herself going over in her head all the declensions. A voice in her head just went on with them. Suddenly, even the ones she didn't know would be there in her head, spoken by that voice, beginning with *agricola, agricolae, agricolae*—and going on and on to *rebus, res, rebus.*

Sometimes, fairly often, she even got into verbs, not the easy ones, the hard ones, and once or twice she got fairly dizzy with subjunctives, but ordinarily she didn't get that far.

In any case, Dorothy Cutlick greatly improved her standing in the Latin class. When she graduated, age nineteen, in the summer just before she turned twenty, she had made an *A* the second term.

That was the summer Mr. Bingham's bookkeeper in the People's Security Bank got married to a merchant in Athens, a widower, and moved away. Mr. Bingham asked the principal of the high school if he had a girl graduating who was good with figures, was honest, and wouldn't fool around with some boy and get married. The principal said he was happy to say he thought he had a jim-dandy article to fit those specifications. So, on half-salary, Dorothy Cutlick came to the bank to get, as Mr. Bingham put it, broken in.

She had got broken in fast. For all her shaking hands, faltering voice, and downcast eyes, and for all the fact that she was terrified of Mr. Bingham's icy precision and glittering pince-nez, she had a mind that, like a patented mouse trap, clicked with murderous deftness onto whatever gave it the slightest nudge. Or it was, in fact, like the very machine she was supposed to operate: if the buttons got punched right, the right answer came out. By the end of July she was expert. There wasn't anything about the day's work she couldn't do.

Long since, she had left the room in back of the restaurant. It had been a Wednesday when Mr. Bingham hired her, telling her to come to work the following Monday morning. On that very

Wednesday afternoon she went to Mrs. Putney's house, and asked if she could have her old room back, the room she had left nearly two years before. It had been occupied by one of the teachers, who wasn't coming back to Johntown, and anyway Mrs. Putney was glad to get twelve months a year instead of only nine, and glad, incidentally, of the chance to ease in, without discussion, a rent raise of fifty cents a week. She promised the room for the following Sunday night.

Dorothy Cutlick didn't say anything to the Greek. She was back on that Wednesday night, heaving out the hash and then going on back to her room afterwards. She didn't know what to say to the Greek. Besides she had to think of her meals for the next four days.

On Sunday afternoon, when the Greek went home during the three o'clock lull, she collected her skimpy belongings into a couple of suit boxes tied with twine, and carried them to Mrs. Putney's. She got back before the Greek did, and was ready with her white smock on, wiping the Formica counter to a high polish in preparation for trade. It was a brisk evening, and when it was over, Dorothy Cutlick slipped off the smock, which was paid for by Ye Olde Southern Mansion and had that name embroidered in green across the breast, and walked out the back, and was gone down the alley, moving through a darkness lighted, as it were, by the severe glitter of Mr. Bingham's pince-nez.

The Greek, having closed up shop, and given a cautious look around, moved down the back passageway to the room. There was nobody there. He thought, at first, that maybe she had gone to the ladies' john. He waited a reasonable time, then went to the john. When there was no response to his decorous tap, he entered. There was nobody there. He rushed back to the room. As before, there was nobody there. Further, he noticed what he might well have noticed before, that there was no mark of anybody there. The books, the papers, the comb and brush, he realized with sudden terror, were gone. He opened the closet. It was empty. The drawers of the dresser were empty. Then he noticed the piece of paper on the dresser, a piece torn off the pad the restaurant used to put the customer's bill on. He read what was written there:

I will not be back. I have got a better job. Monday I go to work in the bank.

The Greek's mind focused on the word *bank*. The terror which he had experienced on discovering that the room was stripped now became the terror of that word. He was making good money, and even with Giselle going on like she did he managed to keep some of it. He had money in the bank, and he aimed to pay some on the note. But that word *bank* said there would be a day when he would have no money there, when the overdraft notice would come, when bum checks would come whirling after him like dead leaves sucked behind the gust of the yellow Cad, and him doing sixty down the mountain, when the sheriff would tack up the sign. He was sick at his stomach. His breath came hard. It wasn't fair, not when he worked so hard. It wasn't.

Then the anger shook him.

Out of that anger he hated *them*. He hated *them* as much as he had always admired *them* and even yearned to have a word of human recognition from *them*. *Them* was the kind of people in banks, people like the bank man in Cincinnati, in Louisville, in Nashville. Like that snot Mr. Bingham, with his buttoned-up black suit and those snot glasses on a gold chain. Even like him, the snot—even in an ass hole like Johntown, Tennessee.

Those people—they always thought they were better than you, and nothing, nothing in the world, no matter what you sweated and slaved to do, could make them change. No matter if you had a yellow Cad, no matter if you had a hound-tooth check coat, no matter if a platinum-blond, swivel-built darling whom all men yearned for lay down by your side every night all the nights of

[63]

your years—oh, nothing could help, for their eyes fixed on you and stripped you.

And he felt, all at once the unmanning pain he had felt more than thirty years ago, in a schoolyard in the Bronx, when the mick, a dirty little mackerel-snapping mick, and only half his size, too—oh, that wasn't fair either, to be half his size and then do it!—had kneed him for no excuse, just when they were in the middle of nothing more than a half-hearted scrap, just scrapping because the guys worked it up. He had fallen, grabbing his crotch while everybody laughed. Then the mick had neatly kicked him in the side of the head, and let him lie, precisely disposed north and south between an old banana skin and a gob of glimmering gray mucus on the black asphalt.

It was that pain that now drew his gaze to the bed. The sight of the bed gave, then, a new stab of pain. And it was the aggravation of the pain that, paradoxically, drew him toward the bed, as if he had to test something, know something at last. He lay down on the bed, on his back, staring up at the ceiling, suffering, relishing the throb of pain.

If she hadn't just walked out. If she had only had a row, or something, some reason. Or if she had just walked out and hadn't left that note: *Monday I go to work in the bank.* He moved slightly on the bed, to test the pain.

The fact, the awful fact dawning in his guts, was that what had been transacted on this bed—all his sweating and trying, and it wasn't fair!—had never meant a thing to Dorothy Cutlick. He was not prepared to face the awfuller fact that it had never meant a thing to him, either.

So Dorothy Cutlick was working in the bank, and had been for three years now, and two ten-dollar-a-month raises. She had learned everything about her job, and a good lot besides. She had learned to go to Nashville every fall and spring and get herself some clothes, nothing fancy, rather severe in fact, even middle-

[64]

aged, but nice, real nice. She had learned to keep on her nose a
pair of pince-nez, which she didn't really need but which she had
had a deep compulsion to buy—only she had not had the temer-
ity, or even the desire, to get a gold chain like Mr. Bingham's, settling for a silver one. She had learned to go into a big hotel in
Nashville and order a big dinner. She had even lived through,
and past, the time old Sim Cutlick descended on the bank,
drunk, demanding money, coming round inside the cage, threatening her, threatening Mr. Bingham.

Mr. Bingham, not knowing what else to do, had, for the first
time ever, pulled the pearl-handled Smith & Wesson .38 out of
the drawer and had held it gingerly pointed at the floor. He
didn't even know whether or not it was loaded. As Sim Cutlick
edged at him, blaspheming and unsteady, he retreated, saying
over and over: "Get out of here! I tell you to get out! You have
no right in here!" Then when Sim Cutlick, in the midst of blaspheming, reached for his hip pocket, Mr. Bingham, who knew
about the terrible things hillbillies might do, retreated one more
step and bumped the desk behind him. At that moment his forefinger closed on the trigger of the .38, which was, after all,
loaded.

At the explosion, Mr. Bingham nigh fainted back over the desk,
and Sim Cutlick sat heavily on the floor and began to scream. He
screamed that he was dying.

That was not true. But he was wounded. When people came
rushing in and lifted him up they found that his backsides were
soaked in blood from having sat down too hard on a pint bottle
of moonshine for which he had been reaching to strengthen him
in his fight for his rights as a true-born American citizen. The
bullet had been deftly planted between his feet, as the hole in
the floor testified.

Dorothy Cutlick, in shame and horror, had thought she was going to die. She sat in a chair, racked by dry sobs, and Mr. Bingham, with his eyes fixed on the mess on the floor which was Sim
Cutlick, abstractedly patted her shoulder and said for her to pull

herself together, everything was all right now. She hung on to the edge of his buttoned-up black coat and continued to shake with dry sobs. If she looked up, she would find, she had thought, all the eyes of town staring at her.

Mr. Bingham had gone to the sheriff and got him to let Sim Cutlick out of jail and warn him never to come back. "Just tell him not to come back," Mr. Bingham said, with a tone of authority befitting a new standing which, somehow, he felt he had in the community. "Tell him if he comes back I won't be responsible," Mr. Bingham said, for the wine was heady, and he felt his finger closing on the trigger, and his eyes narrowing dangerously.

"Yes, sir," the sheriff had said, and had said it with respect.

So Dorothy Cutlick hadn't had to live through a trial, or in the knowledge that her father was in the same town, in jail. And now, on a June afternoon, while Mr. Bingham was sorting the foreign checks and she was working the posting machine, he could hear the *click-clack* of the machine. But he did not look around. He knew, without looking around, that when Dorothy Cutlick swung her body, as she did, ever so little, when she pushed a button of the machine, her right buttock rose—ever so little—inside the real nice blue real-linen dress she wore, cut plain, with some white rickrack, and half-sleeves.

He had never before been aware of what happened when Dorothy Cutlick pushed a button. Yet he must have been aware, he allowed himself to think with a shocking flash of candor, quickly extinguished. He must have been aware, for if he was aware now he was aware without looking, and the looking must have occurred some other time, and the awareness that came with the looking must have been there, somewhere, all the time. In any case, the awareness was here now, with a strong mixture of elation and guilt.

The elation fed the guilt, like oil to flame. How could a man feel what he felt about that *click-clack* in his head after the awfulness of what had happened last night? The worst part of the guiltiness was that the awfulness of what had happened last night had, in some way, brought this awareness into his head, with the elation that, inexhaustibly, fed the guilt. How could the most awful thing that had ever happened to him stir up all these things in a man?

He tried, once or twice, as a flight from the present moment, to think of last night and the things his wife, Matilda Bollin Bingham, had said, but it was too awful. His mind couldn't dwell on it. As soon as he tried to dwell on it, his mind slipped to the awareness of the bank examiner back yonder in the little conference room behind the false mahogany door to the left of the vault, the room where Mr. Bingham would sit, armored with the glint of his pince-nez, while some reckless, or unfortunate, citizen of Johntown whined or blustered that he needed extension on a loan. Aware of the bank examiner in that same precinct where he himself had so often had to harden his heart, Mr. Bingham felt a growing fear of retribution, the despair of a man who has sinned and knows that all will be brought to light.

He wondered if it was time for the Greek to come.

But he couldn't bear to look at his watch. Or at the clock, which he would have been able to see by the slightest movement of his head.

He heard the *click-clack*. He saw, in his mind, the finger of the examiner running down a column of figures. He felt despair. But the funny thing was, he knew that his books were in apple-pie order. He knew that they were in perfect order.

He wondered if it was time for the Greek.

Nick Pappy was glad that the weather was warm enough to have the big plate-glass double doors of the bank open. Now he wouldn't have to put his hand on the brass handle and push it open and hear the little screak or grind it might make. These days, even when he went to make his deposits, even when the deposit was good, he dreaded what seemed the awful weight of the door, and the sound that would draw the glittering gaze of Mr. Bingham upon him. That was what happened to you when you owed money. The $2,000 he had owed three years back had, for a time, grown to $5,000. Then he had cut it back to just a little under $4,000. He might have got it all paid if it hadn't been for Giselle having to have that nurse. And all those French nightgowns. And a new TV. She said she had to have something, and when he said he owed money she said the shape she was in was all his fault, ruining her health, the way he had done things to her.

He might have paid off more, too, he was compelled to confess, if he hadn't turned in the old Cad. Not that he had turned it in on a new one, but on a year-old one. When that model came out he felt he couldn't live without it. For a year he had endured the pang of desire. He would wake in the night, thinking of the Cad, thinking of himself sitting in it. When finally he had gone in the agency door, down in Nashville, he had told himself he was just looking around. He had told the salesman that, too. The next thing he knew he was driving the car into Johntown, thanking God it was night so that nobody would see it. He never drove it past the bank. Not even at night, past midnight, with the town empty as a sardine can in moonlight, in the alley, after the tongue of the stray cat had finished work.

He wondered why Mr. Bingham had left that message this morning.

He wondered if Mr. Bingham knew about the car.

But a man had to have something. A man had a right to be something.

And there was Mr. Bingham sitting in there in the middle of all that money, and in there with him was Dorothy Cutlick who, without a word, took his deposits when he brought them into the bank and who three years back had just walked out of that room back of Ye Olde Southern Mansion Café without so much as a good-bye, as though what had happened on that bed back there

[68]

had never meant a thing to her. She probably knew that he owed $4,000, and that thought, when it lunged at him out of the dark, was like getting kicked where a man ought never get kicked.

He managed to get in the bank door, quiet as melted margarine soaking into a sliced bun. He didn't look, because he did not want to see Dorothy Cutlick. If he did not see her, he might not think of how she might know about that note. The note itself was worry enough at one time. He did not want to think of what she made him remember, and one of the things she made him remember was how, after she had walked out, he had gone to Knoxville to a hotel and got a girl sent up and he might as well have stayed home for all the fun he got. It was funny how you could do something and it was not fun.

He was around the end of the cage, with a side glance on Mr. Bingham, and Mr. Bingham still hadn't looked up, he was sliding past so quiet. He suddenly wished to Christ Mr. Bingham would look up and get it over. So he could breathe. He had been holding his breath.

Mr. Bingham looked up.

Mr. Bingham came around to the side and beckoned to him, on the sly it seemed. "Good afternoon," Mr. Bingham said, almost in a whisper. All of a sudden Nick Pappy thought how Mr. Bingham looked like an undertaker, with that black wool suit buttoned up, and his face so pale. He wondered what it would be like to be dead and have somebody like Mr. Bingham draw the blood out of you.

"We'll go through here," Mr. Bingham said, and moved spectrally toward the fake mahogany door. With his hand on the knob he turned and said, in his hushed tone: "The bank examiner is in here. We'll just go through."

He opened the door, let Nick Pappy precede him, then soundlessly closed it and led the way across the room, and *Jesus Christ* thought Nick Pappy, if he wasn't tiptoeing. Nick Pappy stole a look at the examiner, with a lot of books over at a desk. The examiner hadn't even glanced up. Mr. Bingham opened a door beyond, again stealthily. It was a larger room, with a long green-baize-covered table down the middle, a lot of chairs around the table, in mathematical order, a horsehair couch against the wall near a metal cabinet, a picture on the wall, with a big walnut and gilt frame—Rosa Bonheur's *Horse Fair*—and two windows rather high up, giving on the alley. Nick Pappy had never been in this room. He had always done business in the smaller room where the examiner now was. Business in this room must be that much awfuller than business in the smaller room. Nick Pappy wet his dry lips and thought how he didn't have $4,000. Maybe he could offer to sell the Cad. But that wouldn't bring $4,000. Maybe he could offer to fire the nurse. Maybe he could run up to the house often enough to take care of his wife. If she would do what you called co-operate. Maybe, he thought, he could die.

Mr. Bingham had said something.

"Excuse me," Nick Pappy said, "what did you say?"

"I said, won't you be seated," Mr. Bingham said.

The way he said that—not just "Have a chair," but this way—almost scared Nick Pappy to death. It was going to be bad, he knew, if they started talking like that. But he managed to murmur thanks and slid into the nearest chair, which creaked ominously.

Mr. Bingham had turned to the metal cabinet, and now held a box in his hand, approaching Nick Pappy. But Nick Pappy didn't look at the box, his eyes were so firmly fixed on the face above it, which he was trying to read. The face looked pale and sick. It was going to be awful, if it made even Mr. Bingham feel that bad.

"Have a cigar," Mr. Bingham said, and still not able to take his eyes from that pale face, Nick Pappy groped out, and found a cigar.

Mr. Bingham leaned at him and lighted the cigar. Nick Pappy had forgotten to bite the end. He had to do that now, while the match burned down and down to Mr. Bingham's wax-white finger

[70]

tips. You expected them to start melting, like tallow. But somehow Mr. Bingham held on till the cigar was lighted. Nick Pappy was watching the finger tips all the time. He didn't know how a man could stand it. *He ain't human,* Nick Pappy thought. *He don't feel fire.*

It was going to be bad. Sometimes they got cold as ice and told you about the note. Sometimes they got red in the face, and yelled at you, and that was worse. Sometimes they explained how it was all your own fault, and that was even worse. Sometimes, they said they understood your troubles and hoped you understood their position, and that was worse yet. But this was the worst ever, giving you a cigar, and then lighting it and not feeling fire burn down on the fingers.

"I don't smoke, if you will excuse me," Mr. Bingham said.

He sat down in the head chair, which had black leather arms, at the head of the table. It was three chairs away from Nick Pappy, but it was clearly the chair where Mr. Bingham belonged, who was here in the middle of all this money.

"Mr.—Mr.—" Mr. Bingham began, and stopped.

"Papadoupalous," Nick Pappy said, and for a split second seemed to wonder who the hell that name could belong to, here in Johntown, Tennessee. It was like remembering a name of somebody you used to know, but you couldn't remember where, or even the face.

"Thank you," Mr. Bingham said, "I hope you have always found our relations satisfactory."

"Yes," Nick Pappy said, past the chunk in his throat, the dryness of his tongue, and the cigar, which suddenly tasted like smoke off a town garbage dump.

"We want to give service," Mr. Bingham said. "We want to give service to the community."

"Yes, sir," Nick Pappy said.

For what seemed a long time Mr. Bingham didn't say anything. He was looking down at his clean white nails. He seemed to be drawing away from you, and you felt lonelier and lonelier.

[71]

It was bad enough to get called here to Mr. Bingham, but it was worse when Mr. Bingham just went off in the distance and left you.

Then, not looking up from his clean nails, Mr. Bingham said: "You lived in a lot of places, didn't you, before you came to John-town?"

So that was it. Not just the $4,000, but everything. All the places he had ever lived, the tenement hole with the drunk aunt, the asphalt schoolyards with the sputum and banana peel, the stinking dishwater of all the years, the face of Jean Harlow smiling perennially through the dirty-gray steam, the hotel rooms, the flickering spots on dice, his name written at the bottom of promissory notes, the sweat of flesh going cold against him, the yellow Chrysler Imperial, Giselle's voice saying: "I cannot live without you," when his head was bowed over the honky-tonk table to lie in the palm of her hand.

It seemed that Mr. Bingham knew everything, and a man couldn't live with everything his life had been. If somebody else knew it, then it was real, and a man couldn't live with it if it was real.

"You lived in New York, and Chicago, and big places like that," Mr. Bingham said. "Didn't you?"

Nick Pappy nodded.

"I used to live in Nashville," Mr. Bingham said. "I have been to New York and Chicago, but I never lived there."

He paused a time, then said: "I know the way they live is different there."

Nick Pappy nodded.

"You are the only person in Kobeck County," Mr. Bingham said, "who has lived the way they live in places like that. Now in Nashville, I know some people there, but not many any more. Just some bankers, I reckon, even some of the big bugs in the Association. But I'm a banker, and look here, Mr. Pap-a-doup—What I mean is"—and he leaned forward, probing and appealing, staring into the Greek's face—"I can't just go in the office of

[72]

one of those big bugs and say, 'Look here, can you tell me where I—' "

He stopped suddenly, appalled, like a man shaking at the brink of an abyss. "I couldn't do that," he whispered. "Now could I?"

He stared nakedly into Nick Pappy's face. "Now could I?" he repeated, in less than a whisper now.

"No," Nick Pappy said, "I guess not."

Mr. Bingham looked down at his nails.

Nick Pappy looked down at his own hand, which was shaking. A bit of ash fell off his cigar, and hit the green baize of the table. He looked at it there on the green baize, then up at Mr. Bingham. He didn't know what to do about it.

Mr. Bingham was looking at him again. As Nick Pappy lifted his eyes to meet him, Mr. Bingham, from behind the glint of the pince-nez, was saying: "I have no one else to turn to. I hope you will help me. I hope you will be my friend."

Out of the first incredulity, like light with infinite pearly calm dawning from mist, a joy suffused Nick Pappy's soul. He knew he was sitting here, in this secret room with Mr. Bingham, the president of the People's Security Bank, but he had to shut his eyes to believe it. He shut his eyes and it was like being in a deep, sunlit, grassy glade, with cool water running, where you could rest, in joy, forever.

Jesus, he thought, *Jesus Christ,* and was afraid to open his eyes.

Then he had the crazy thought that now he could drive the yellow Cad up to the bank door. Then the crazier thought that he might take Mr. Bingham for a ride, and into his head came the image of riding along with Mr. Bingham, at night, with the top down, moving fraternally, with enormous power, under a starlit sky, while the dark ridges reeled. *Jesus,* he thought, and opened his eyes.

Mr. Bingham was looking at him. "I have no one else to turn to," Mr. Bingham said.

"Jeez, Mr. Bingham," Nick Pappy began.

Then: "Jesus, Mr. Bingham."

Then: "You can cut me in, Mr. Bingham."

Mr. Bingham was looking again at his nails. Nick Pappy wanted to shut his eyes again, but he didn't dare.

"I don't know what to do," Mr. Bingham said, not looking up.

"What did you say, excuse me?"

"I don't know what to do," Mr. Bingham repeated, "when a woman—a girl—is going to have a baby and you—"

He stopped.

"—and you have to—"

He stopped again.

"—and you have to—to—" he said.

He stopped.

"—prevent it," he said.

Prevent—he had found a word he could manage to say.

Nick Pappy's first feeling was like having a rug pulled out from under you. Then he had to make sense of that feeling. Then he realized that the joy he had just had had been jerked away. The anger overwhelmed him, and his mind was saying: *The dirty bastard.* Then he knew. He knew, with the sense of betrayal, that all those people, those people with their dark coats buttoned up, were no better than you were, and all your secret yearning was wasted. It was a dirty joke.

"I have to prevent it," Mr. Bingham was saying.

Then Nick Pappy thought: *It is Dorothy Cutlick.* And the first sense of betrayal was compounded with this other betrayal.

"I don't blame you for being shocked," Mr. Bingham said, humbly. "It's an awful thing. It's just I have to do it."

Nick Pappy looked into his face and thought: *I owe the dirty bastard four thousand dollars.*

"I had rather die," Mr. Bingham was saying.

Nick Pappy stared into Mr. Bingham's face.

"I want to—to make it worth your while," he was saying.

Nick Pappy took the cigar out of his mouth, held in between

[74]

the index finger and the next of his right hand, and twitched it ever so little, not caring if the ash did fall on the baize. He hooked his legs back, one on each side of the chair, and the chair creaked with his heft as he leaned forward, staring into Mr. Bingham's face. "Listen," he said, "you are a big man. You got a reputation. People look up to you. You can't get mixed up in nothing. You got dough. You stick your neck out and somebody will chop it off."

"I would give all I own to have things different," Mr. Bingham said.

"I got to think," the Greek said. He rose abruptly from the chair, shoving it back with a scraping sound. "I got to work it out so they won't strip you bare-ass."

"I'll pay whatever it costs," Mr. Bingham said.

"It's not what it costs. You can get it for three hundred dollars."

"Your trouble—I'll make it worth—" Mr. Bingham began.

But the Greek looked down on him, moving his thick lips back in a sad, sweet smile. "Listen," he said, "you said I was your friend."

"Oh, you are—you are. I haven't got many friends. It looks like I am not that kind of man. But if you will be my friend—" Mr. Bingham said, leaning forward, lifting his gaze beseechingly toward Nick Pappy's hulk that had heaved up there like a boulder in a seersucker coat, with sweat stains under the armpits.

"I got to go," Nick Pappy said. "I got to think." He got to the door, and turned back, hand on the knob. "Thanks for the cigar," he said, and was gone.

Nick Pappy crossed the little room, making no pretense of not disturbing the bank examiner. That was the guy Bingham was afraid of, but he, Nick Pappy, was not. Maybe now Nick Pappy was not afraid of anybody.

He went out the other door, and damned near slammed it, and

[75]

stood there a second to enjoy the sensation. He took a couple of steps up even with the cage and looked in at Dorothy Cutlick, who was working that machine. He stood there staring at her inside that blue linen dress and he had one on like a tent peg. He could sure teach her now. It would all be different. Half a chance and he would break her back.

Jesus, he thought, and eased himself out of the bank, almost on tiptoe. It was not because he was afraid of anybody. It was just that he sort of felt afraid of something in himself.

He stood in the early afternoon sun, balanced on the curb in front of the bank. He reached up and took the cigar out of his mouth and stared at it as though it were something he had, surprisingly enough, just discovered. Then he flung it down on the sidewalk.

He set the ball of his right foot on the cigar and let all his weight come on it, with a slow, grinding motion. But suddenly, standing there in the bright sun, his heart filled with unutterable yearning. He thought of laying his head on a woman's breast and she would murmur that everything, everything, would be all right. He stood there and had to blink back the tears that washed all the sunlit street askew.

Then he pulled himself together. He strode off toward the restaurant, got the yellow Cad from behind it, and eased slow right down the middle of Main Street, right past the bank, not even looking.

But driving the yellow Cad down Main Street couldn't have mattered less, for Mr. Bingham still sat in the head chair at the end of the green baize table, and stared down at his clean nails. For a moment after Nick Pappy's departure, he had sat there drained and at peace, as though Nick Pappy, his friend, had carried his burden away. *He is my friend,* he thought.

That thought released, as it were, what he had been all morning able to keep from thinking of. He sat there, staring at his

[76]

nails, and what had happened the night before between him and
Matilda Bingham was happening all over again in his head.

"It is not possible, it is not possible," he whispered, sitting there
at the end of the green-baize-covered table.

But it was possible

After a while Mr. Bingham managed to rise from his chair and
go into the room where the examiner leaned over the books. He
tiptoed across, and felt the guilt again, worse than before, recognized as worse, but somehow detached from his self and the
thing that that self was enduring.

He went out into the hall of the bank, laid his hand on the
little wicket of the cage to steady himself, then entered. He wondered why he felt that way about the examiner. His books, he
was telling himself, were in apple-pie order. At least they were
all right.

He was telling himself this when he heard, from Dorothy Cutlick, a ladylike squeak of surprise. He turned to find her staring
through her pince-nez, through the bars of the cage, through the
plate glass of the bank out into the street.

"Oh," Dorothy Cutlick exclaimed, "she fell down!"

Jo-Lea Bingham had, for a fact, fallen down, right there on
Main Street, in Johntown, and right now was there on hands and
knees, her head hanging forward and her hair, jerked loose from
ordinary moorings, flung forward over her head. She was, for the
split second that Mr. Bingham stared incredulously at her, perfectly immobile. It seemed, preposterously enough, that the girl
had chosen that spot of all spots to sun her hair, the way girls do
after washing it, flinging it forward and letting it hang so that the
back underhair gets some sun, too. Jo-Lea was in precisely the
same position Mr. Bingham had so often seen her take, on a blanket out on the lawn, in summer, to dry her hair, and sometimes,
seeing her thus, he had felt a deep surge of joy, like pain, like
ice cracking over dark water, like trees cracking after an ice
storm, with the sound like ripping, like gunshot, like a thousand
windowpanes knocked out for hallelujah, while all the woods glit-

[77]

tered unbelievably in morning sun over the miracle. It was a feeling like falling and flying in a dream, with fear and glory mixed up, and you had better wake up quick.

On such occasions, Mr. Bingham, standing rapt on his concrete walk, inside his iron fence, between his two clipped umbrella trees, staring at the girl, his daughter, on hands and knees on the blanket, with hair loose in the sun—he had always managed to wake up quick. He knew enough to know that a man had better not mess with joy. A man better have no truck with joy, for there was no telling where it might end. He would stand there and feel himself being tucked back into his body, the body he had lived in for more than forty years, tucked in like old keepsakes, gone dim and moldy, being put back into the trunk you had accidentally opened in the attic.

Now, staring out at Jo-Lea fallen there on Main Street, in Johntown, Mr. Bingham felt that surge of joy. Idiotically, he said: "She's washed her hair!"

Dorothy Cutlick, in God's mercy, hadn't heard that idiocy, for she had taken a step forward, staring, saying: "She was running —she was running and fell!"

At that instant, Jo-Lea collected herself, jerked to her feet, and, before some gaping citizens had managed to get at her, ran, gasping visibly, down the street, out of range of vision of the plate-glass window.

Mr. Bingham ran out of the cage, out of the bank, into the street. In a dreamlike way, he was aware of the eyes of the citizens on him, a man here, a woman there, set like posts along the sidewalk, in sun or in the shadow of the occasional corrugated iron awnings, posts with, as it were, the awfulness of eyes. He was running down the street under those eyes. Yonder, ahead, was the yellow of the girl's dress, like a flickering focus of the blazing June sunlight. She fell down again, then rose, and ran.

Mr. Bingham tried to call out, to stop her. It was then, suddenly, that he simply couldn't run any more. His throat seemed to swell, worse than tonsillitis. His knees shook, then gave down.

[78]

He was sitting flat on the ground. He felt like floating, but he was actually sitting there in the dust, when the people came up.

Somebody was trying to help him up, but he waved them back, and collapsed again, now on the curb of the brick walk. A boy about twenty—a hard-faced, slick-faced boy, with his face held straight as a hickory shingle but some joke behind that straightness, his voice too unctuous, too solicitous, the kind of boy Mr. Bingham hated—was saying: "You want me to run her down for you? You say fer me to, and I'll run her down."

"My car," Mr. Bingham managed to say. "Get my car. My car, please."

The slick-faced boy stood there.

"Please," Mr. Bingham said.

"I ain't got the keys," the boy said.

Mr. Bingham fumbled in his pocket. "I can't find them," he said. "I just can't find them."

"I can't get no car without the keys."

"They're at the bank," Mr. Bingham said. "They must be at the bank."

The boy, taking his time, moved off toward the bank. Mr. Bingham leaned forward over his knees, and some white cottony saliva, mixed with bile, rose in his throat and threaded out of his lips. He wanted to retch, to spit, but he couldn't. His lungs were burning like fire. He thought he was going to die.

He didn't know what he felt about the fact that he was going to die. Somewhere in his being, he was troubled because he didn't know what he felt about it. A man ought to know. It wasn't tidy not to know. It wasn't businesslike. What would the bank examiner say if he found out that Mr. Bingham—the Mr. Bingham who was president, who had never had a breath against him, whose books were in order, yes they were, they were!—didn't know how he felt about the fact he was going to die?

He leaned forward to let the saliva run out, and it was as though his head had suddenly gone enormous as the sky and he was under that sky, a dawn sky, cold and autumnal, blue coming

[79]

out of darkness, buttermilk white streaking pale blue, cold saffron coming on the horizon. It was a scene from his boyhood, him duck hunting with Joe Buttons, old Joe Buttons, old hairy, no-good Joe Buttons, no good except in the woods, and now long dead and not good for that, and Joe Buttons saying: "Boy, them ducks. You ever see such ducks, boy? God-a-mighty, boy, and that sky jist workin with ducks. Workin with ducks, thicker'n maggots in the side of a dead gray mule and him gone blue. Boy, look—them ducks. Boy, ready—boy, ready—"

And they came streaking over the cold, buttermilk-blue and saffron sky, which was the inside of his enormous head, moiling in the sky, streaking down with the nervous twitch of wing, necks out, necks out in longing—yearning like lost hearts—streaking in, plunging toward the unwavered water, which was the color of sky, waiting for the boom of the .12 gauge.

Mr. Bingham, sitting on the brick curb, the bile in his throat, thought he was going to cry, something was so beautiful. It was so beautiful, and it was gone, and it was not gone, both things being true in his enormous head. He wondered why he had not stayed there forever, in the cold saffron dawn.

He wondered why Jo-Lea was running down the street. He wondered why his Little Honey-Baby, Daddy's-Sugar-Girl, his child, was running.

The room was like a big box, wooden. The floor was pine, tongue-and-groove, but unvarnished, unstained, unpainted. The walls and ceiling were pine beading, nailed up with moderate skill. The door was wood, with a black iron latch, the sill under it long since worn down paper-thin so that the nailheads stood up to trip you. There was a big roll-top desk, untidy; a wicker couch, such as is made for porches, with two faded sofa cushions on it, along the wall opposite the door; a broken-down Morris chair, with a stack of books and papers in the seat; a bookcase of books; two pictures, one a tinted photograph in gilt frame, ten by fourteen inches, on top of the bookcase, the subject a woman, the other a very large sepia photograph of the Valley of Jehosaphat, ruined tombs in the foreground, the Mount of Olives in the distance. There was a small rag rug in front of the couch. Morning-glory vines, blue blossoms shriveling sadly inward with the afternoon heat, grew on a trellis outside the window, and the leaves gave the light of the room a greenish flickering, like the light you see when you open your eyes after a dive into a woodland creek, in summer.

This was the study of Brother Sumpter, of the Baptist Church of Johntown.

Brother Sumpter now knelt on the little rag rug before the couch. His big hands, sinewy, corded with blue veins, were clasped before him, on one of the faded cushions. The water-green light of the vine leaves flickered over his gray head, inside which the pain now seemed localized as though a nail were driven directly down through the skull. It was better when the pain seemed to be in one place. It was better when it seemed to be only from a nail driven in.

He lifted up his hands in the green light and said: "My son, my son!"

He clasped his hands till the veins stood out, blue to bursting.

"My son, my son!" he said, with eyes tight shut. "Would God I had died for thee."

He heard the movement in the room above him.

He opened his eyes, and looked at the ceiling above him. Then he turned his eyes to the tinted photograph of the woman. From the photograph you could tell little of what that woman had been like, not pretty, not unpretty, not old, not young, with dark hair and dark eyes—yes, you could tell that much, the eyes were large—wearing a dark-blue dress, with a round white collar, held by a brooch. The coloring of the photograph was abominable, like a mortician's fancy work.

Brother Sumpter rose from his knees to his rickety height of black trousers, white shirt, and cheap white elastic suspenders, and stared across at the photograph. "My son, my son," he whispered, "I did not die for thee."

He approached the photograph, and added, whispering: "She did."

[82]

Yes, Mary Tillyard, whom everybody had called Tillie, but who, to MacCarland Sumpter, had always been Mary, had lain in a big walnut bed upstairs and ejected from her body the burden that was to be known as Isaac Sumpter, and then nobody could stop the blood.

"She died," MacCarland Sumpter whispered, and the old deprivation overcame him, as though a level of black water rose from the floor to overwhelm him, as though he himself were only an agony of emptiness, into which the blackness flowed. But at the same time his arms hurt with emptiness to reach out and embrace something, draw something—even the agony—against his body that he might not be empty.

Something—but what could that something be? For the body of Mary Tillyard was nothing, twenty-two years now under the earth on the high side of town, and even the name on the stone was dimming a little with time, as he noticed when he went there every Sunday, flowers in hand if flowers were in season, to kneel and pray, in rain, in snow, in sleet, in sun, and to try to summon up the joy to be his when, on the single stone, the space for the second date under the name of MacCarland Sumpter should be filled out, and MacCarland Sumpter should greet his beloved on the Farther Shore under the Throne of Grace.

But now, in this moment, he felt that there would never be joy. There was only the rage that time had drawn from him forever that parcel of flesh which his arms had once clasped and wrenched against the need of his body. And in this moment now he knew that flesh is all, and all else is delusion.

"God help me," he was saying.

But God did not help him, for in that moment there was again a sound from above, where Isaac Sumpter moved, and MacCarland Sumpter stared at the ceiling and thought the thought which he had never before allowed himself to think: the life of the young man in that room above was one term of an agonized equation of which the other term was Mary Tillyard's death.

[83]

MacCarland Sumpter was shaking with the horror of the thought.

"God help me," he said. Then: "This is not me."

But it was, and God did not help him.

He said: "I love my son whom God hath given me."

But knew that he stood there sweating.

He wondered if it was possible for a man to hate his own son. He stood there and shook with the thought that it was possible, and with the certainty that it was damnation. Then he thought that his damnation would be punishment for an older crime.

In 1916, MacCarland Sumpter was ordained and preached his first sermon in the Baptist Church of Johntown, on the text *Be still and know that I am God*, from the Forty-sixth Psalm. In the church sat Jack Harrick, Hell's own high-stepper, perdition's beauty-boy, bursting blue serge with muscle, holding high his head of crisp curly black hair, letting his blaze-blue glance flicker over the congregation and come to rest on his old friend and coat holder, Ole Mac, up there horsing away in the pulpit.

MacCarland Sumpter saw the pose of indolence and power, saw the grin not bothering to conceal itself on that face, the grin that could infect men and women like corruption, and knew that he and Jack Harrick had sat on the same log and lipped likker from the same jug and not even bothered to wipe off spit as they passed it back and forth. He knew that he and Jack Harrick, in the bushes, up back of the cemetery on the high side of town, had taken turns with Sadie Sparks, who would do it with anything from a brown bear to Beelzebub for fun and four bits, and give credit for the four bits if the bear didn't happen to have it handy.

MacCarland Sumpter looked at that grin and felt fear.

It was fear for his own soul, for the grin seemed to know, not what iniquity and filth had passed, but what was to come. He had to preach at that grin, to conquer that grin, or the grin would damn him into the fire of the pit. He looked into the blue eyes and the amiable contempt of the grin, and proclaimed the awfulness of God.

Then he realized that Jack Harrick was secretly fingering the arm of a dark-haired, dark-eyed young girl beside him. He saw the flush slowly mantling the girl's cheek. He felt sick, as though a jagged blade that instant, the instant before pain could become pain, had ripped out the bottom of his vitals. He knew that his voice had weakened to a whisper and that sweat was in the palms of his hands.

Overcome, he managed to utter a hoarse whisper: "Let us pray," and sank to his knees beside the pulpit, and called out in his pit of private darkness toward God. "I am called unto this people," he prayed, "to declare unto them the word and the ways of God. Oh, God, help me in my unworthiness, for what I have said is foolishness and what I have done is folly. I am a man," he cried out, "and I cry unto Thee, oh, God, for I have sinned in man-foulness, and health is not in my soul. Speak to me, oh, God, and let Thy breath stir the hair of my head and cool this forehead wherein foulness hath held habitation."

Some in the church wept without shame. They knew they had a preacher. Young Mac Sumpter, he could sure deliver. He could lay out the language faster than grease would spatter on a hot stove.

The girl with whom Jack Harrick had sat that day was Mary Tillyard, daughter of a man who had just moved to town to open a harness shop. The man and daughter, the mother being dead, brought their letter from a church in West Tennessee and were accepted forthwith into fellowship. Mary Tillyard—Tillie—was a good Christian girl. She came to church every Sunday, morning and evening. She conferred with the minister about church work. She also had dates with Jack Harrick.

No one told Mr. Tillyard what Jack Harrick was like. Perhaps

[85]

they thought he was settling down. It was time. He was over thirty. He would marry a good, clean, churchgoing, God-fearing, tight-tailed girl and settle down.

Then Mary Tillyard called on her minister. She had to tell somebody. She had no mother to tell. She could not tell her father. She told her minister. She was pregnant. Yes, she was certain. The man—the man's name did not even get mentioned —would not marry her. Yes, she was certain. He would give her money to go to Nashville and get fixed up. But he would not marry her. He was not the marrying kind.

That evening Mac Sumpter called on Jack Harrick. "Look here, Mac," Jack Harrick said, "I'm not denying but one thing. I'm not even denying she hadn't ever been pricked. I'm not denying she was a virgin. But I never made her a virgin and it's not my fault. But virgin or not, I tell you she has natural talents. I tell you she has talents that would make a circus pony look like a plow-broke mule and the band playing 'Dixie.' What I mean is, when a girl's got talent like that, somebody's bound to be in the line of fire when she finds out she has got something to live for. I'm not denying I was standing there when the tree cracked and nobody yelled 'Timber.' I'm just denying that I throwed her down, like you seem to imply. Hell, I had to hold her up. What I mean is, when her knees buckled under her that first time, I plain had to hold her up. Hell, I'll tell you—you know that track up by the old Folsom farm? We was walking along on a spring night, 'bout the middle of April, you know, strolling, looking at the moon and noticing how the dogwood was spook-white and listening to the peepers down the valley. You know, strolling. But come to a patch of shade, I'd take hold a little. You remember, Mac—how a feller does." And he grinned his corrupting grin at Ole Mac, then went on: "But just a little. I'd—"

"I do not want to hear it," Brother Sumpter said. "I want you to marry the girl."

Jack Harrick grinned. "I tell you, Mac," he said, "I swear I wasn't even really trying to love her up. She is the kind you

[86]

can't rush. I wasn't even prowling for a hand-holt. I wasn't even—"

"I do not want to hear it," Brother Sumpter said.

"—even holding her tight. I was holding her loose, and I wasn't doing nothing worse than counting her verti-bry a little and breathing in her hair, and she of a sudden said, oh, God, and give a moan-like, and it looked like a strut done busted in her. Her knees plain gave down and—"

"I do not want to hear it," Brother Sumpter said.

"She would of fallen in the road. If you can call that old grass track a road now. Yeah, if I hadn't held her up, she would of fallen and somebody coming along in the dark of night might of stepped on my bare ass. I didn't want nobody to do that and get embarrassed— Hey, Mac, how do you like that for a joke? You get it, Mac—*em-bare*—"

It was then that Brother Sumpter hit him.

The result was simple and predictable. Predictable, that is, for anybody short of Jack Johnson or Gentleman Jim Corbett. What happened to Brother Sumpter was what would have happened to any other citizen of Tennessee, since neither Jack Johnson nor Gentleman Jim was a citizen of Tennessee. Brother Sumpter went to sleep.

He went to sleep when the fist of Jack Harrick, who really wasn't, it seemed, the marrying kind, made contact with his chin. He slept there on his feet for a split second before he began to sink. But he sank so slowly that Jack Harrick helped him down with a clout to the side of the head and another to the pit of the stomach.

When Brother Sumpter woke up, the coal-oil lamp was burning low on the table in the house of Jack Harrick, but Jack Harrick was long gone. He had, it seemed, done one thing on his way out. He had put a pillow under Ole Mac's head.

That was the last Brother Sumpter heard of him for two months. Then a letter came, addressed in pencil, in a big scrawly hand, *Rev. "Ole Mac" Sumpter, Johntown, Tenn.* It said:

[87]

Dear Ole Mac:

I did not aim to hit you but one time, but I sort of slipped into the habit before you hit the floor. I am sorry but maybe it will learn you not to stick your you-know-what into my business, for no other son-a-bitch elst can.

Am well and hoping you are the same,

Your old friend,
Respectfully,
John T. Harrick

P.S. I am helping Uncle Sam kill Germans. Not because I got much agin Germans or much for Uncle Sam, but it is more fun than a bear hunt and the grub is plentiful. Don't bother to try to find me, because I got lots of helpers and we all dresses one like tother. Keep your pecker up. I'm sorry I hit you more than one time, like I aimed to, but you put your you-know-what into my business.

By the time the letter came, Brother Sumpter was more deeply involved than ever in what was, or at least had started out to be, Jack Harrick's business. Mary Tillyard was his wife.

The day after Brother Sumpter woke up on the floor of Jack Harrick's house, he sent a message to Mary Tillyard to ask her to meet him at the church. At first he had thought of asking her to come to his house—to the very room, that would have been, where now nearly forty years later he prayed for the soul of his son, Isaac. He had, however, discarded that thought as unworthy, realizing that it was motivated by shame at being seen on the street of Johntown with a cracked jaw and swollen head the very day when the dramatic absence of his old Hell-hopping crony and side-kick Jack Harrick would be the talk of the town. So he carried his marks of defeat—or victory?—down the street under all eyes, and entered the church and knelt before the pulpit. When Mary Tillyard entered, she found him there.

He was aware of her approach down the aisle, but did not lift

[88]

his head. When she stood beside him, he lifted it, and he saw her start and heard her gasp as she recognized his condition—and what, some hard small voice of unredeemed cynicism in his heart said, his condition probably meant for her condition, too.

"Kneel," he said. That was all he said.

She knelt beside him.

He prayed aloud: "Dear God, in Thy Mercy, I ask that Thou show us, Thy frail children, the way to redeem our corruption in an everlasting praise of Thy name. Lord, let Thy answer enter into our hearts."

He stopped and remained kneeling, hearing the girl's breath, hearing his own breath, hearing the watch in his pocket, hearing the whistle of a train that passed, far off down in the valley, toward Nashville, toward the world.

At last he rose. "Get up," he said.

She rose and looked at him.

"I say what is in my heart to say," he uttered. Then he waited, while she saw the Adam's apple twitch in his strong, corded throat. "If you will be my wife," he said, not looking at her, but up at a distance beyond the pulpit, "we might in humility live in such clearness before men that others may know the infinite mercy of God, seeing that mercy in our lives."

He did not look at her. He could hear his own breath, and his watch, but no breath from her. Then he heard a sort of gasp, a sound like a sob, and she sank down, and in that instant, even as he held his face away and did not look, he was hearing in his head Jack Harrick's lazy voice saying: *It looked like a strut done busted in her.* Saying: *Yeah, and if I hadn't held her up, she would of fallen and somebody coming along in the dark of night might of stepped on my—*

This was like that—oh, God, yes, like it—and if he looked it would be like it, and not even in the decency of dark, on grass, but in God's tabernacle, on the swept floor before the altar.

"Listen," he said, not looking, "weep if you must. Weep and pray. Then go to your father's house and pray again for God to

[89]

give guidance. You can send me word when you know God's will."

He walked down the aisle, not yet having looked at her. He was out in the sunlight, in the ordinary street, before he realized that the sound the girl had made in there this afternoon was not like the sound she had made in the spring night when the strut broke. She was weeping now, he realized, because she had lost forever what it was that had busted that strut, back on a night last April when dogwood was spook-white in the dark.

He had realized that, but then had put the realization away deeper than the dead cat in the bottom of the sinkhole, and had waited for the word he had known, somehow, would come.

She had sent the word. They had been married. He had held his head high. He had prayed in the church, thanking God for His goodness. And Johntown, not having all the facts, had seen the victory of light over darkness.

As for his plans, he would let things come to pass as God willed. Once or twice, as the months moved on, Mary timorously asked to go away, and MacCarland Sumpter felt a cold, clear, prophetic elation seize him—as though a great eagle had seized him in talons of ice to jerk him beyond sky—and had heard his voice saying distantly, far off, far down on earth where a poor woman wept: "No. We can at least be what we are. We can offer our filth on the altar in God's name and the name of Truth."

After such an occasion, when the poor woman, down on earth, had wept, but not with the moan and sweet sob of the time when the strut busted, something did bust. MacCarland Sumpter and Mary Tillyard were spared—or deprived of—whatever might have been the consequence of the birth of the son of Jack Harrick.

Now, nearly forty years later, standing in the water-green glimmer of vine-light which filled the boxlike room, MacCarland Sumpter realized that that night when Mary Tillyard had suddenly seized her middle and fallen to the floor, and brought forth the dead child, his heart had leaped with joy. It was not

[90]

joy that he was to be spared shame. He could have stood up before the eyes of men, in the arrogance of a man who would move in God's eye. No, it had been joy, he now knew, in the fact that what would have been the son of Jack Harrick was dead, was nothing, nothing but a bloody package of offal, and would never stand before him to remind him.

That leap of the heart which was joy had passed so quickly into the leap of heart which was alarm that he had never had the need to recognize it as joy. And if all was God's will—if God had struck out that foulness from the body of Mary Tillyard— why should he question God's will? But whose will had conformed to whose? MacCarland Sumpter's, to God's? Or God's, to MacCarland Sumpter's?

Now, standing in the water-green glimmer of vine-light, Mac-Carland Sumpter shook with his first knowledge of the dark deviousness of that God Who knows how to wait. The terror of God is that God conforms His will to man's will. The terror of God is that He bends ear to man's prayer. Knock, and it shall be opened unto you. And when it is opened, who can withstand the horror of that vision of prayer fulfilled?

Now, nearly forty years after, MacCarland Sumpter shook, knowing that God had answered his every prayer. God had answered the unspoken prayer that the white body of the girl whose arm Jack Harrick had secretly rubbed in church would be laid before him and opened to him, to MacCarland Sumpter, who had swapped bottle-spit with Hell's high-stepper.

God had answered the unspoken prayer that the son of Jack Harrick should be cast forth as filth and not offend the eyes of MacCarland Sumpter.

God had answered the prayer—this prayer a prayer spoken, over and over in the dead of night—that a son of MacCarland Sumpter's seed might rise up, to redeem all.

To redeem what?

To redeem the fact that MacCarland Sumpter lived in the knowledge deeper than any acknowledged knowledge that he had never truly had that white body that had lain down beside him for twenty years, a body that in some irony had remained white, firm, and shapely all those years till MacCarland Sumpter prayed that it should age, should fail, should go blotched and stale so that it might become more truly his, and then that prayer was answered, too, and the blood ran out of the white body, and it was for a moment whiter than ever, then blotched and stale forever, and irredeemably not his, forever. And now MacCarland Sumpter would never hear that sweet moan from the lips of Mary Tillyard when the strut busted. She was now removed from him, and he had never heard it.

No, that was not true. He had heard it always, ever since the moment Jack Harrick had said: ". . . and give a moan-like, and it looked like a strut done busted in her . . ."

He had heard it over and over in his head, when he lay by Mary Tillyard after he had had her in the way that he might have her, when he walked down a sun-baked street, when he stood in the pulpit, when he heard the peepers far off on an April night, or had the vision, in the darkness of his mind, whatever the season, of dogwood spook-white in darkness. Yes, he had heard that moan a million times. But he had never heard it uttered for him.

He swung now to the picture, stared at the face with its mortician's frivolity of color, uttered a groan of anger and deprivation, and lifted his right arm as though to strike.

But there was nothing to strike. Mary Tillyard was not here.

"I don't know what's wrong with me," he said, whispering. And he didn't know. He honestly didn't. For suddenly, all that had just now passed in his soul was not there. It had simply been blotted out.

Then he heard the movement upstairs.

He went out of the study, down the pine floor of the hall.

At the foot of the stairs he stopped. In a calm distant voice,

he said: " 'Thy sons and thy daughters shall be given unto an-
other people, and thine eyes shall look, and fail with longing for
them all the day long: and there shall be no might in thy hand.' "
Then he managed to pull himself together.
"God help me," he said. "I love my son."
And he mounted the hollow stairs.

Propped on the bed, Isaac Sumpter held a second-hand copy
of the Cambridge edition of *The Complete Poetical Works and
Letters of John Keats* in his hand, the cover an ugly pebbled red
with gold stamping flaking off, the paper of the page the color
of cheap hygienic tissue, the format double column, with an
offensive, blurred, too small type face like deploying ants, and a
glory showed through it all, for the immortal Bird was not born
for death, even though sick for home, here on a June afternoon
in Johntown while sunlight hit the tin roof above the room like a
hail of fire and the locusts frazzled away in the white oak beyond
the window and farther off filled the sky to distraction over every
ridge east to the Smokies and west to the soot-crusted limestone
window ledges of hotels, the soot-streaked Parthenon, the gas-
choked and flesh-crammed streets, the gilt flash of the Capitol
on its hummock of prinky grass, the glittering approaches where
chrome flashed and tires screamed and where, after dark, there
would be a hysteria of neon ablaze from a thousand highway
diners—west, that is, to Nashville, Tennessee, a city stuck in the
bend of a beautiful river in the middle of a patch of country
once beautiful with grass, stone, beech and cedar but no longer
beautiful, the city which Isaac Sumpter, now propped on the
bed on a summer afternoon, mumbling the poetry of Keats,
could not bear to think about. But the sound of his father's step
on the hollow stair made him think about it.
He knows, Isaac Sumpter thought. *He has found out,* he
thought. *He is coming up the stairs,* he thought.

[93]

The steps stopped outside the door, but the knock did not come.

He has found out, Isaac Sumpter thought, *and now—he's afraid to knock.*

With that thought what was his own fear became, all at once, an elation, as though bright-edged steel had been laid in his hand and the haft felt good.

Then the knock came.

"Come in," Isaac said.

The door opened slowly, and the old man entered, tall and big-boned but gaunt now so that the white shirt hung off his shoulders and the black trousers hung like a sack from the white elastic of the suspenders. The old man didn't seem to be able to speak, staring at the boy on the bed.

"Yes?" the boy said, distantly.

"I'm sorry," the man said, "I didn't realize—realize you were studying."

"I wasn't. I was reading."

"Well—reading."

"There's not much to do," the boy said, getting up from the bed, on the farther side, as though putting it between him and the visitor. And added: "Except read—this—"

He flung the book to the bed, and looked down at it. "This shit," he finished.

He had not indulged himself with even the most covert glance at the man's face when he said the word. He kept his eyes down, waiting with a thinly growing excitement for what the man might say.

After a moment he heard the man saying: "I didn't realize—I'm sorry I disturbed you, Isaac."

And for an instant, hearing that voice, the boy thought he was going to cry, he thought he was going to fall face down across the bed and cry, and everything in the world might be different. But then the possibility was gone. He felt suddenly shaky and

[94]

thankful, like that time when he had almost lost his footing and gone over the cliff over at Elkhorn Mountain. "You didn't disturb me," he said, almost gently.

"It's just I am going out," the man said. "I wanted to tell you."

"All right," the boy said, and then let the man wait in the silence.

Then the man said: "I am going to the Harricks'."

At that name something flickered in the boy's being. He had the impulse to say yes, yes, he and Jasper Harrick had found a cave, they would develop the cave, they would be rich, they—

They, what? He cut off the impulse, the innocent, natural impulse of hope, life, and outwardness, to tell the old man, who was his father. He cut it off with the words in his mind: *It is my cave. It is my land.*

"He is worse," the old man was saying. "The pain is getting worse."

And the boy was thinking: *I shall have money, and I will go out of this room, out of this house, out of this state, and never come back.*

He came out of his thought to find the old man looking humbly at him. The old man said: "It's just I thought I'd tell you where I'd be, Isaac."

The boy came around to the foot of the bed, and looked at the old man with a calm inquisitorial air, the air of the inquisitor who by calmness will trap the deadly admission. "Why did you name me that?" he asked.

"What?" the father said.

"You know what," he said softly. "Isaac—why did you name me Isaac?" And added, as the old man looked at him: "There wasn't any reason to. There wasn't any Isaac in the family, ever. I have looked at the family Bible."

"No, there wasn't any," the old man said.

"Well, just out of curiosity—you know"—he came closer, grew calmer, and more gracious—"why did you do it?"

After a moment, looking at the boy as though seeing him emerge from haze and distance, speaking as though to no one, not even to himself, the man said: " 'For Sarah conceived, and bare Abraham a son in his old age.' "

"You weren't so bloody old," the boy said.

"The years were long. For all those years I had prayed for a son."

"Well," the boy said, "you weren't so old it was such a bloody miracle you had to go and name me Isaac."

"You are my son," the man said calmly, "and that is a miracle of the mercy of God. What more—what less—can any man say of his son?"

The man turned slowly, and started toward the door.

As Isaac watched his father go, the impulse to burst into tears, to fling himself across the bed and cry, the blind hope that things might be different in that act, hit him again. If his father had gone out the door, it might even have come to pass. But his father turned, and said: "Yes, you are my son. And I praise God for that mercy."

"Yes," the boy said, taking a step closer, a little glint of excitement and power stirring in the darkness, "and Abraham was so glad that he took the bloody little miracle out in the country and tied him up and was going to cut his bloody little miraculous throat."

He paused, scrutinizing the man's face for the response, but there wasn't any.

So he said: "Oh, nothing personal. I was just remembering how the story goes. I was just wondering. Wondering how you'd do. Personally, I don't think you'd be up to it."

He laughed, ending the laugh with a charming, rueful smile. "You know," he said, "it makes a fellow feel a little bit safer to reflect that his old man isn't quite up to it."

"God in his mercy put the ram in the bushes," the old man said, "caught in a thicket by his horns."

[96]

"Yeah," the boy said, "but there might be a snafu in the celestial bureaucracy and somebody might not deliver that miraculous ram in time to save bloody little miraculous Isaac's little neck."

"Son," the old man said, "I know that some of your friends—the people you run with down at the university and on the newspaper—I know some of them talk like that. I know some of them are smart people. I know some are good people, better than they would admit maybe. But, son, it is cynical talk. I can't learn to appreciate it, son."

"You'll have to admit it's an interesting question, won't you? Just for the sake of argument. Yes, let's put it. Assuming that you really heard the voice of God putting the bee on you, would you really cut my throat? Assuming of course"—and he smiled the charming, pitying smile—"that there had been the little aforementioned snafu about the ram and you got stuck with it."

The old man stared at him, and his lips, ever so little, moved drily, without sound.

"Oh, it's a tough one," the boy said sympathetically. "I guess it takes time to say it. Whatever you're going to say."

"There are some things a man can't say."

"Yes, of course," the boy murmured, sympathetically.

"They aren't sayable, son," the old man said. "You just have to live into them. And pray."

"Little Ikey is the one better pray hard for that ram," Isaac Sumpter said, deprecatingly.

"Listen," the old man said, "what would you have me say? I can say only one thing. I believe that the Lord my God is a just God, and I believe that He is a merciful God." He turned to the door, laid his hand on the knob, turned back over his shoulder for an instant, saying: "Else how could I live?"

Then he went out.

For a moment Isaac Sumpter looked at the closed door, in a calm joy past triumph, like the general who sits his horse on the knoll, in gathering dusk, and sees, beyond the litter of carnage, the last stand of the enemy broken, and sees them scatter into darkness. Then the moment was dust in Isaac Sumpter's mouth. He turned, with an irritable, twitching motion of the shoulders, like a man who itches where he can't scratch, and went toward the bed.

He picked up the book with the ugly red pebbled cover and flaking gold letters, propped himself on the bed, found his place and began to read aloud, in the heat, while the locusts frazzled away in the big white oak beyond the window.

" 'Thou wast not born for death, immortal Bird!' " he said aloud.

" 'No hungry generations tread thee down,' " he said.

" 'The voice I hear this passing night was heard,' " he said, and stopped.

Then added: " 'In ancient days by emperor and clown.' "

He stopped again. He closed his eyes. A cool sweetness was dewing into the darkness of his breast. It was as though something that had mattered was, slowly, not mattering. He did not know what it was that was not mattering, because the cool dew fell in his darkness, or what made that cool dew suddenly begin to fall so sweet, but he did know that if he stirred, if he even drew a single breath, the dew might cease to fall, the *not-mattering* would again be that dark, grinding *mattering* which was every breath you drew. So he held his breath, as long as he could, letting himself slip loose into the coolness of that dark dewfall.

Then he had to breathe. But he did not open his eyes. He said aloud: " 'Thou wast not born for death, immortal Bird!' " And felt, in a kind of shyness and wonder, as tears grew under his closed lids, that something stirred now in his dew-dark inwardness. It was as though the bird woke in that inner darkness, as in a dark glade, and stirred, preparing the first note.

No, it couldn't be the bird stirring in that sweet, leafy dewdarkness. But it was something like the bird. It was something which, he suddenly felt, was free and immortal, like the bird,

[98]

and when its utterance came in that darkness it would be sweet to break the heart. But it wasn't the bird. It was his self.

No, it couldn't be his self, for his self was the self that knew that this being now stirred in the dew-darkness. But it had to be a self, for it was contained in the darkness which was himself. It was, he knew in a knowledge that was not quite knowledge, at least not quite words, a self of the self, a free, immortal self, ready for song, being born this instant in the darkness of the self that suffered and was not free.

He waited, again without breathing, until he had to breathe. Then he said: " 'No hungry generations tread—' "

He jerked up from the bed. *Oh, yes they do! They tread you down.*

He saw the blaze of sunlight out the window, heard the frazzle and grind of the locusts over the whole God-damned Sovereign State of Tennessee, and flung his gaze about the bare box room. It was as though he were trapped in a box, an animal, as though the gaze itself were claws scraping the wood walls, witlessly trying to claw out.

His gaze found the mirror of the marble-topped walnut dresser. He went toward it, stopped, leaned, and looked at himself in the mirror. He studied the face, with clinical detachment, trying to think what the world saw when the world saw that face.

He saw a handsome aquiline face, under dark, straight hair that lay to the well-shaped skull—the brow straight, the eyebrows straight and as cleanly marked as though plucked, the aquiline nose strong and driving, but with finely flanged nostrils, the mouth a trifle heavy—no, not heavy, but mobile, plastic, ready to curl back with a hint of sardonic incisiveness, or quiver into a pitying, distant smile, or go lax with some moment of self-indulgent apathy. The blue eyes were pale and sudden in the brown, lacquer-smooth skin.

Isaac Sumpter drew himself up to his height, which was five feet, nine inches, straightened his good shoulders, curled his lip with the sardonic incisiveness, and with a tone that seemed to say that now he had, indeed, discovered all, said: "Isaac Sumpter."

Then added, in a conniving whisper, with the pitying smile into the glass: "Ikey—Little Ikey."

He shrugged, dropped his hands, palms outward, in a parody of the classic gesture of the Jew's resignation and irony, and repeated, in the accent of the stage Jew: "Ikey—Little Ikey."

Isaac Sumpter was a good boy. He was strong and active, quick at games if not excelling, and got along well enough with the boys even if he never took part in their more rowdy or reprehensible activities—such as hitchhiking down to Sewanee to rock out the window lights at 2 A.M. in one of the dormitories where those stuck-up little horses' asses went to school at the University of the South, or pushing over privies on Hallowe'en, or putting roofing nails on the highway, or going out with some of the guys and looser girls on a blanket picnic, going up the mountain to the woods in a truck, or drinking rum and Coca-Cola, or even red likker, straight out of the bottle. He didn't snitch on anybody who did these things, but he stayed out of it all. He went home to his father, and his father came to his bedroom, knelt for a short prayer, kissed him on the brow, and said: "Good night, Isaac—God bless you."

The fact that Isaac Sumpter was going to be a preacher didn't make him unpopular with the boys. It gave him a sort of alibi for studying hard, for you were a horse's ass if you studied hard just for no reason. It also gave him a good scholarship when he went to college, down in Nashville.

In Nashville he studied hard. He didn't know anybody. He was lonely. He had to work in a restaurant to supplement his scholarship, and that meant that there wasn't any extra time after his studying. So the studying became obsessive. It was his only life, except the life of the classroom, the moment when he might answer the question, calmly, precisely, almost contemptuously, or sit in the quiz and see his pen move steadily ahead,

[100]

saying what he knew, arraying the data, summing the argument. If the grade came right, if there was the A, he felt an icy joy that, for the moment, justified all. If the grade was not an A, he received the information with an equally icy detachment, but under that icy surface he would begin to feel a slow coil and dark eddying and would know that in a few hours he would fall through into that black despair. So he would lie on a bed and stare at the ceiling. And then out of that blankness would come a new, grimmer energy. When the last semester of the year was over he had four A's and one B.

Meanwhile, he had lost the habit of prayer. He still went to church, simply because he had to keep up some kind of form for the scholarship. Nothing about this was reasoned out. Simply, he was different now. He was himself, and there was no God. No, he was not himself. There was no God and there was no self.

There was no reality but the icy joy in the moment of achievement. There was not even fatigue, or hunger, or sleepiness, or pain. There was not even hope. He had no plan, no ambition—nothing to hope for, or about.

So he came back to Johntown for the summer when he was eighteen, got a job in a filling station, and studied ferociously every night, leaning over a deal table in his hot-box of a room, with the sweat streaking down his naked chest and belly. When his father would come for the evening prayer, he went through with it. The first night he had almost refused. But he had said to himself: "Oh, what the hell," and knelt down. He found his lips drawn back in a secret sardonic grin. He began to wait for the moment of the prayer, and his secret joy.

During the summer a letter came, notifying him that, for academic excellence, he had been awarded one of the five full fellowships for sophomores. He had not even known such fellowships existed. There was the moment of icy joy, and he had the strange impulse to run into the house—he had read the letter walking back from the post office—and tell his father. Then suddenly he knew that he would not. His triumphs had always been secret. He knew that always when he had stood before a bulletin board where the grades were posted, and had seen the A, his face, as he turned away, had worn only a distant contempt. He would let no one see his pleasure. It would be the less his.

Or was that the reason for the contempt? Now he stopped in the blaze of midmorning, in Johntown, and wondered. He saw his own face as clearly as though in a mirror, saw the tight, controlled, masklike handsomeness, with the lip slightly drawing back in the controlled, scarcely revealed contempt. And with a cold slight thrill of agony, cold and thrilling as a bead of sweat dropping from your hot armpit, in the dark of your clothes, to run down your unfended side, he wondered if the contempt was for himself, for the self that had only the private joy of an A posted on a bulletin board, and nothing, nothing—desolately nothing—else.

In any case, he did not tell his father. He canceled his Religious Foundation scholarship, went back to Nashville, did not have to hash any more, had more time for study now, and two years later was standing before the bulletin board, wearing his contempt as he looked at an expected A, when the Jew Girl spoke.

The Jew Girl—that was not what she was then, when she spoke. It was what, long after, she was to become, and, after a certain moment, was to be, forever: the Jew Girl.

"Gosh," the voice said, a brightening, vibrant voice, a little husky, like the start of a cold, just a little frog in the throat, just a little golden frog on a golden lily pad in a dark-sparkling pool. "Gosh," the voice said, "it looks like we hung it on those dumb schmucks."

He hadn't known she was there. He had thought he was alone. Alone with the A—and his self-contempt.

He turned, to find himself looking directly into her eyes. They were large, dark-brown eyes, very bright and clear and directly innocent, sparkling with a merriment that somehow involved

[102]

him, and the world around, and they were right there, close and level, for she was a tall girl, almost as tall as he, and she was standing close. The suddenness of the voice had surprised him, the levelness of the eyes surprised him, and the closeness surprised him—even if the closeness, in a way, seemed to deny his presence rather than recognize it, for she stood so straight and casual, as though he weren't there, or if he was there, as though he were an old friend, a little brother, or a post.

He was about to utter something, to ask what she had said, for the words had been lost in his surprise, when he caught a full whiff of her perfume, and the words simply wouldn't come. He found himself swallowing hard, trying to pull back from her. He did manage to pull back, a little, and then was sick with desire.

Her eyes were merrier than before, merry at him, but also with him and for him, and he was vaguely aware of an impulse to smile, to grin, then aware of some mysterious danger in the impulse, the terror of falling.

"I said we hung it on those dumb schmucks," she said, and laughed. Before he could say something, she flicked a quizzical look at his face, and said: "I haven't gone crazy, have I? You are Sumpter, aren't you?"

He managed to nod miserably, as though caught in a humiliating offense.

"And that's yours?" she continued her gay inquisition, and stabbed a finger at his A on the bulletin board.

Again, he nodded.

"Good boy," she laughed; "'fess up and tell Mommy and you'll feel better."

Then she pointed farther up the alphabetical list. "That's me," she said.

He looked. The name was Rachel Goldstein. So that was her name. After it there was an A.

"Hims didn't even know my name," she said woefully. "Did hims?"

He couldn't answer.

[103]

"I knew hims'es name," she said, and pulled a long face, took on a voice of professorial mimicry, and said: "Mr. Sumpter, will you please give me a brief account of the rise of Greek Pyrrhonism?"

Then she lifted her head, turned it in profile to him, in a posture which he instinctively recognized as his own when he answered a question in class, turning his head slightly away from the questioner, finding a spot on the wall to stare at, rather high, curling his lips in contempt as he uttered the words.

She's been watching me, he thought, *she's been watching me.*

And in that thought he felt a sudden terror at being spied on, as though he were spinning away, down and down, into the depths of an astronomical telescope and a great eye were watching him from the wrong end as he spun away, getting smaller and smaller, forever.

Then, as he thought again: *She's been watching me,* the terror merged into something else—an indefinable shift in the chemistry of his being. He felt able to look at her.

In a voice which had something of his own dry detachment of tone, which, with a twinge of guilt, he recognized, she was saying: "The school is named for Pyrrho, but other names are important, such as Arcesilaus and Carneades. To take Pyrrho first, he was born in three fifty B.C. and—"

"Three sixty-five," Isaac Sumpter quietly corrected. He hadn't meant to.

"Oh, gosh," she said in wild distress, "oh, dear, oh, dear, alack, and damn it to hell—how did I ever make my *A*?" She flung an arm out despairingly, so that the gray wool cape with astrakhan collar flew wide in histrionic grandeur. A heavy gold bracelet clanked on her wrist.

When the cape flew back he saw how slim her waist was, how straight and supple from the hips. She was wearing a black wool dress, close-fitting, and when the cape flew back, the black-sheathed stem of her waist was suddenly, shockingly silhouetted

[104]

against the pale-gray lining of the cape. Then the cape fell back into place, and he knew that he was flushing.

"We ought to celebrate," she said. "We made the only two *A*'s —out of forty. That's pretty good, even if they are schmucks. Buy me a Coke"—she indicated the machine at the end of the hall—"and we'll celebrate."

So he followed her down to the Coke machine. There was a moment of panic that he didn't have any money. Then he found the coins, got the bottles, opened them, handed her one, and watched her as she tossed her head back for a big enthusiastic unashamed gulp, and saw the astonishing whiteness of her throat work and slide and readjust as she drank.

She lowered the bottle and looked right at him, with a sudden comradely grin. He could really see her face now, now that she grinned that way. He saw the big eyes glinting at him, saw that the face was rather broad, but the nose cleanly modeled and set, the chin short but well modeled, the mouth with its scarlet lips and perfect glittering teeth rather wide in the infectious grin. The cheeks were apple-bright, and just as you knew those scarlet lips were unnatural and were meant to be unnatural, you knew that the color of the cheeks was natural, the flush of high blood and gaiety. Isaac Sumpter was aware of that contrast, that disturbing contrast between the color of lips and cheeks, even as the lips gave their simple ingratiating grin—the grin of a child who trusts everybody.

He saw, too, the little saddle of delicate gold freckles across her nose, very gold on the whiteness of skin.

"Well," she said, "I drank to your *A*—aren't you going to drink to mine?"

He drank.

She was looking quizzically at him now. "Don't you like to make *A*'s?" she asked.

He hesitated, then said: "Yes—I guess so."

"You sure didn't look it," she said. "You looked like you hated

[105]

it. You just stood there and stared at that *A* and looked like you hated it and the whole bloody world. I looked at you about a minute and you were so busy hating that *A* you never even saw me. Take me, now," she was saying, after snatching a quick gulp, "I just love to make *A*'s. I make plenty of 'em, too. I was at Radcliffe two years, and I made plenty of *A*'s. I made a few *F*'s, too. When something bores me it's just to hell with it. Sometimes I get bored crapless, then I crave the *F*—I just crave it—it sort of keeps you clean inside to get that *F* when you know that even if you are bored crapless you could make an *A* if you were that kind of a bloody little sharp-kneed case of walking constipation with that kind of a myopic dandruff-trap on your shoulders. But, in a way, being bored is sort of fun too. I guess I even like being bored. F⸱⸱en if you are bored crapless, you—"

"What's Radcliffe?" he said.

She stared at him a split second, then grinned again. "Gosh," she said, "I'd give a cookie if Dean Sherman, Mildred P., could hear that." She let out a whoop, which she quickly controlled. "Gosh—did little hims know all about Pyrrho and never heard of Radcliffe?"

"What's Radcliffe?" he repeated, distant and steady.

"Do you know what Harvard is?" she asked.

"Yes."

"Well," she said, "Radcliffe is a place where girls go who wish they were built so they could go to Harvard. And you know, I don't wish I was built so I could go to Harvard. You know I am built the way that I think will best suit my purposes."

"Radcliffe—" he said, "it's a school?"

"You got it," she said. "It is a school where girls go who wish they were built so they could go to Harvard but have to settle for preparing themselves to be worthy helpmeets for Harvard boys who will teach at Harvard. Or at the University of Illinois." She threw back her head with the air of one whose work is well done, and took another drag of the Coke. She threw her head back so far that the astrakhan cap, perched perilously on the

[106]

tousle of dark curls, slipped suddenly and completely off and hit the floor.

He recovered it, and rose holding it awkwardly in his hand, looking at its shape, feeling the crinkly texture, forgetting for an instant that he was offering it to her.

"Do you like it?" she said.

He didn't know what to say. He managed to nod.

"I like it, too," she said.

"In fact," she continued, "I just love clothes. I like this dress. Don't you?" She opened the cape, fleetingly, to exhibit herself. "Yes," she said, "it's a nice dress, and if some of those bleeding coeds came by right now and saw me they'd say I was over-dressed. They'd say, 'Look at that Goldstein creature again, just look, how overdressed.' Well, I am not a bleeding coed, I am a special, and I don't care if they do say I am not wearing what *Mademoiselle* or *Seventeen* says the campus cutie should be wearing in the middle of the afternoon when she is admiring her *A* on the bulletin board, and they would be right. I am over-dressed, but I won't be overdressed at the party where I am go-ing in thirty minutes. Gosh, you ought to see the expensive Jew dry goods I am going to be in the midst of. I'll just be dowdy."

She paused, reached out and lifted the hat from his hand, and said wistfully: "But I do like my hat." With a forefinger she prodded a tight little curl of fur. "It's a Cossack cap," she said, staring down at it, prodding the curl. She looked up at him: "You know, back in Russia, in a village called Viminsk, right in the mud street, the Cossacks knouted, kicked, sabered, cuffed, clobbered and generally chivvied my great-grandfather to death. So—"

She stopped, set the Coke bottle on a window ledge, and elaborately placed the cap on her curls and lifted her head with the imperious swan-necked grace of a model showing off a crea-tion. "So," she repeated, "little Goldie Goldstein stuns Nashville, Tennessee, the Athens of the South, with a Cossack cap." She touched the cap into a more fetching tilt. "It's not quite as nice," she said, "as if a Cossack were a fur-bearing animal and I had treed, shot, and skinned me a Cossack and made a cap like you do with a coon, but still, it's sort of nice."

She stopped, suddenly. "I don't think that's very funny," she said.

She looked at him searchingly. "Did you think it was funny?" she asked soberly.

"Sort of," he said. "I guess."

"Well, it's not," she said, with authority. "I talk too much, sometimes," she said. "I just rattle on, like I was five feet two with eyes of blue and going to the sophomore prom. Which, by the way, nobody has ever asked me to, and which I would not go to anyway and be stepped on and rubbed by a bunch of delinquent babies who think they are Clark Gable. I talk too much," she said, and recovered her Coke bottle from the window ledge and took a drink.

Letting the bottle sink, she demanded: "So you think I talk too much?"

"No," he said, "I guess not."

"Yes, you do, you think I talk too much," she asserted, almost gaily. "But do you know why I talk too much?" she demanded.

"No."

"Because I'm alone so much."

He looked at her with a strange, almost painful feeling. "Are you studying?" he asked, leaning at her slightly, or so it seemed, leaning at her for some answer. "Is that why you're alone?" he asked.

"Some," she said. "But not mostly. I study fast. It's mostly working that I'm alone so much."

"Working?" He looked at the fur cap, at the heavy gold bracelet, then at her face. He saw she had followed his eyes, and read his thought.

"You're right," she said, and he flushed, and she grinned at his embarrassment. "I don't have to work. Not for money. My father has got more money than you can count and I am the

[108]

only child and the apple of his wise old Hebraic eye. He likes for me to make A's and study, for he is a very brainy guy, even if he didn't go to Harvard. You know what? Back then Harvard wouldn't take him. Yes," she said, "the quota or what you call it. But you know what my old man did?"

"No."

"My old man said that if the fake Cambridge wouldn't take him he'd have to go to the real one, so he went to England—his old man was rich—to the real Cambridge, and you know what he did?"

"No."

"He took two firsts."

"What's that?"

"He took high honors in Greek and Latin, and then he turned around and took high honors in mathematics. He's the only man in Nashville, Tennessee, who ever went to Cambridge, much less took two firsts. He was there seven years in England. He can act like an English gentleman when he wants to. It would slay you. He did know some lords and baronets and things, and went to their stately homes. He goes back to see them now and then, when he's abroad on business. He even took me once, and we stayed at a castle in Scotland. But you know what he says?"

"No."

"He says the only reason they were his friends was that one was a Jew lord, one was brainy, and one was a practicing Christian and—"

"What do you work at?" Isaac Sumpter said.

"Me?" She pulled herself up, went suddenly sober, and said: "Sculpture. I want to be a sculptor. I mean to be a real good one. I mean a good one. I work my tail off. I worked my tail off in Paris two years. Before Radcliffe, we lived in Paris. My father has built me the best studio you ever saw, really beautiful, over the old carriage house. When Daddy got his heart attack, I left Radcliffe and came home to be with him. He's so sick he can't see anybody, except the nurses, and me. And not too much of me, so

[109]

I'm in the studio nearly all the time. I'm just a special student here at the university, just two courses. I just work my tail off making mud pies and chopping rock. I work my hands off. Look!" she commanded, and thrust her hands out for his inspection.

He looked down at the hands, held forth primly side by side for his inspection—the gesture of a well-brought-up little girl holding hands out for the nurse to inspect. They were not too big, the hands—not for a girl of her height. In fact, the wrist bones were smallish, rather than large. But the fingers, he saw, came out strongly from the hand, and looked somewhat short. He realized that they looked short because the nails were cut brutally back, rather square. One, he noticed, was broken.

Suddenly, she thrust her right hand toward him, for a hand-shake. "Good-bye," she said, and gave him the comradely grin. "Thanks for the Coke. And listen, you better stop hating those A's you make. You better get used to 'em. You look like the sort of schmuck will be making A's all his life. It is kismet."

She looked down at her own hand, still outthrust and still not taken. He had been staring into her face, caught by her words, torn painfully, feeling terror at a fate being pronounced and a glacial thrill of joy at the promise of infinite triumph.

"Hey," she said, "aren't you even going to shake hands with a gal?"

He took her hand, aware that, somehow, it felt smaller than he had expected.

"Good-bye," she said, gave him a grin, wheeled, and with the flaunt and swing of the cape was gone down the hall, and down the stairs. He stared after her, trying to put himself, and the world he knew, back together, aware of the scent of her presence.

He looked down at his right hand, aware too, suddenly, of the strength—not so much the strength used as the strength un-used—of that hand she said she just worked off making mud pies and chopping rock, rapt, as it were, in an intimation of the thrill of fear, quickly overpassed and absorbed into blind excitement, that he was to feel, two months later, when, in the beautiful high studio, designed by the eminent New York architect who was Daddy's friend, surrounded by the mud and rock, she was to adjust herself and, with gentle decisiveness, lay her right hand to his readied member and conduct it to its proper path.

That spring it was as though he had entered a dream. Or, perhaps, had left the dream and, at last, entered reality.

On Monday, Wednesday and Friday the philosophy class which he and Goldie took was over at eleven, but he had Victorian literature just after; so Goldie would wait in the library till he was out. Rather, she would go to the library, concentrate for forty minutes, then go out and be sitting in the red Mercedes convertible, with the motor running, when he got to the parking area. She would rip out of the area with the tire-punishing start of a patrol car taking up chase.

When the car skidded to a stop, spraying gravel in front of the old stables, she would go up to the house, an enormous and enormously ugly heap of early Tennessee Tudor, to see how her father was, and Isaac would go up, alone, to the studio, to wait for her, standing motionless and incredulous among the finished and the unfinished pieces of sculpture, the wet-shrouded clay, the hacked stone, hearing the birds stir and chitter in the big maples beyond the glass of the great north window or a jay scream across the lawn, feeling desire grow in its strange balance of sweet nausea and brute glory. Then, she would come, fling her books down, give him a smack of a kiss, and jerk away from him to cook lunch in the kitchenette off the studio, or perhaps not jerk away and not cook lunch till after.

They always studied for a while in the afternoon. Or at least he always studied, and she sometimes worked on the head she was doing of him. "I have to do it, Ikey," she had said. "You see, your head is so bloody beautiful, it is the only thing I can think about, and if I don't do your head I won't be able to do

[111]

anything, and I've got to do something, so it's your head. Hold still, you idiot."

Or: "If I weren't doing your beautiful old head I would just be holding on to it all the time. My hands just have to do things. I would just always be holding your head in my hands. I would just"—and she ran over to him—"I would just hold your beautiful head between my big soft white pneumatic blisses and run my fingers over your head, the way it is shaped, and"—she had pressed his head, flatwise between her breasts, running her fingers, even if there was a little clay on them, over his head and cheek—"and never, never let you go. Oh, Ikey!"

They were going to be married. That, somehow, had got settled long back. It was settled for Goldie Goldstein because she could not think of life without Isaac Sumpter, and it was settled for Isaac Sumpter because he had not yet been able to think of the sensations Goldie Goldstein gave him without thinking of Goldie Goldstein. And he could not think of red Mercedes convertibles without thinking of Goldie Goldstein. And he could not think of artichoke hearts glittering with beads of oil and laced with red wine vinegar without thinking of Goldie Goldstein. There were many things he could not think about without thinking of Goldie Goldstein.

He could not think of a party in the high studio—the only parties he had ever been to, parties with expensive drink, parties with girls, not college girls, and young men, not college boys, and older men, men who made him talk and listened with respect—without thinking of Goldie Goldstein. And he could not think of his head being laid on a nameless bosom-softness, with his eyes shut and a feeling coming over him like tears for something, something missed—missed forever!—without thinking of Goldie Goldstein.

Also, as the son of MacCarland Sumpter, by whose side night after night, he, a little boy and then a big boy, had knelt in prayer, he could not think of doing to the body of Goldie Goldstein those things which he was accustomed to do, without thinking of marriage. Not that he put it that way to himself. He thought of those things which he did to that body. Then he thought of marriage. There was a blankness between the thoughts, but something was in the blankness, not discernible, but there.

He could not know whether marriage meant, simply, the comfortable guarantee that that very white-skinned, long-thighed, lissom-waisted, soft-sided, high-bosomed body would never, for eternity, be withdrawn from him—and that marriage, therefore, was something which he desired. Nor could he know whether marriage meant, again simply, the inevitable punishment for the sin of having performed certain operations upon that body—and therefore was a doom he was damned to. He could not know which of these things was true—or if both were. He could not even put the questions to himself. But the questions were there.

They were going to be married when he finished college—no, after his M.A. She had sent her other suitors packing—a broker from New York who had been flying down every other week-end to see her, a rich, worldly sportsman, half Jewish, and a young professor at the medical school, brilliant, handsome, driving, ambitious, Jewish. She simply sent them packing, and explained nothing. To Isaac she said: "I don't want them. I want you, just you, and you will give me everything I want. I don't want you just because you are going to be a great man, Ikey. I don't know what kind of great, but you smell that way. But that's not it. I want you because you are you."

Then after a long pause, she added: "I don't want anything they can give me. I want what you can give me."

Hearing her say that, he felt suddenly overcome with a sense of his poverty, his unkemptness, a mysterious weakness, and the blind malignancy of time which, he knew, would never, never, keep its promises. "I can't give you anything," he said, in grinding misery, the words wrenching out of him. "I haven't got anything to give."

They were lying on a couch in the studio, as the May dusk

came on, and the robins shifted in the maples, letting drop an occasional shy, liquid, dreamlike note. She didn't answer him for a time. Despair was growing in him. She was betraying him. Her silence was confirming all, in betrayal.

Then she said, very slowly, very calmly: "Ikey, you give me the only thing I want." She paused, then: "You give me, me, Ikey. I wasn't ever myself before. You give myself to me, Ikey."

He lay without moving, not knowing what he felt—or perhaps feeling the first dawn of a kind of awe, as though a mystery were about to be divulged. He could hear her breathing.

Then she said: "Kiss me, Ikey."

He rose on his elbow, leaned over, laid his hand on her breast and started to kiss her.

"No," she said, "not that way. I don't mean that. Just once, and gently, Ikey—please, gently."

He kissed her carefully, once, as directed. Her eyes were closed. He lay back down. The awe had left him. He felt disturbed, defrauded.

"Ikey," she said, after a while, still not opening her eyes, "don't be sore at me. I just want to lie here and try to think what love is. I just want to try to think what loving you is, Ikey."

He didn't say anything. He began to feel calm now, too.

After a while, her eyes still shut in the now thickening dusk, she said: "Listen to the robins, Ikey. They are almost ready to go to sleep, Ikey. They will put their heads under their wings, and go to sleep."

That was the summer he took his B.A., and that summer, except for two week-ends to see his father, Isaac did not go back to Johntown. He had a job in a bookstore, a temporary job, enough to keep him going. The owner of the store was a friend of Goldie

[114]

Goldstein's. There had been a party at Goldie's studio, and the woman who owned the bookstore was there.

So the summer was like spring. With one difference—the red Mercedes waited at the curb in front of the bookstore instead of in the university parking lot. That was the difference.

Shortly after term opened in the fall—he was now doing graduate work—he got another job. There was another party. There was another friend of Goldie's, the editor of one of the local papers, a man named Smathers, a red-whiskered, brawny, sportsmanly kind of a man, middle-aged, who wore tattersall waistcoats, in his drink quoted the verse of Byron and Robert Graves, and liked to suggest that he had, in his youth, been a great hand with the girls. He had a chronically sick wife who always stayed at home, and he liked to hang around pretty girls now—that was why he hung around Goldie Goldstein.

This man knew he would never get a finger on Goldie Goldstein, but he felt, in some obscure way, that doing something to please her made the impossible seem somewhat less impossible. He had a pretty good idea that that little Sumpter squirt was getting the guided tour and the view from the tower after the elevator ride—but he couldn't for the life of him tell why a big juicy round-bottomed piece like Goldstein would pick up that object, even if he was mean-smart, he had to admit that much about the squirt, and maybe good-looking in a kind of a way, if you ever got him hosed down, holystoned, and curried, but Jesus, it was funny, even if some of the juicy ones did seem to go best for the tight little bastards.

Anyway, when it dawned on him that he was going to hire that Sumpter squirt—not that Goldie ever outright asked him, but it just dawned on him he was going to do it—he got some kind of peculiar satisfaction, which he didn't quite acknowledge because it was somehow shameful, a satisfaction as though by hiring the squirt and pleasing Goldie Goldstein he somehow got a keyhole look at the goings on which he was pretty damned

[115]

sure took place on that couch where right this minute Goldie was sitting and telling, with gestures wider than Sarah Bernhardt's and a voice like Duse's in a death scene, some crazy tale that had a half-dozen citizens of Tennessee draped around her and whooping and hollering in high glee.

He felt sick about something. His bum knee began to ache, just a little. He hated everybody, most of all Goldie Goldstein. He never had been too hot on Hebrews anyway, he suddenly said to himself, and felt hard and clean in his candor. He didn't know where all this liberalism and such was leading. Well, a man got trapped. A man had to think of advertisers, for one thing. But a man didn't have to hang around on his own time and eat the sweet-smelling. He got his hat, and not saying a word to anybody, left.

But Isaac Sumpter got the job.

It wasn't much of a job, just to do a column about college and university goings on. Within a month the editor was preening himself on his perspicacity. People read the column. They wrote letters about it. That squirt Sumpter was, the editor had to admit, funny. He had a trick in his funniness—he could make somebody who had never been to college and hated everybody who ever went feel damned superior. That Sumpter could make all the Joe College stuff sound just a little bit silly. He could really goof it up. But he could do it with a straight face, so even the pea-brained and pussel-gutted alumni who boozed up in frat houses after the annual defeat at the Home-coming Game didn't take offense. Somehow the pussel-gut ended up feeling charming, whimsical, privileged and slightly tragic, like a French aristocrat cracking a joke in the tumbrel on his way to inspect Dr. Guillotine's recent invention.

That Sumpter, he could make other things funny, too. If a young geneticist got a Guggenheim, somehow that got to sound a little funny, too.

Yes, the editor knew that that squirt was pretty good. What he didn't know was that if you laughed at Goldie Goldstein when

[116]

she laid into a tale, you were very apt to laugh when you read a column by Isaac Sumpter. But Isaac Sumpter didn't know this, either.

Isaac Sumpter did know, however, that he was known now. He was the guy who, when the prof—after ten others had fluffed it—asked him the question, looked contemptuously at the hypothetical spot on the wall and gave the answer. He was the guy you might talk about behind his back, he was such a son-of-a-bitch, but you better be polite to his face, for he could set a barb in you right where you had the sore spot and your best friend would be ganging up in the laugh. He was the guy who wrote that column, the little louse, but it was funny, even if he was a louse, and even if you didn't know why he was a louse. He was the guy who walked right past you and got in that red Mercedes convertible with that stuck-up Pride-of-Jerusalem sex-box and you bet in half an hour was laying out his work kit to tune up her Pride-of-Jerusalem motor, right in the middle of the day. And seeing him whisk off, you suddenly felt raw, deprived, and lonely, even if you were a big man on campus and everybody liked you, and you stood there and hated your sixty-five-dollar roll-lapel sports jacket from the College Sport Shoppe which looked just like the Ivy League issue of *Esquire* and which today you were wearing for the first time to give 'em a treat.

Isaac Sumpter was, in fact, the guy you handled with respect. You knew he probably didn't know your name, or care, but you met him on the walk as he was headed downtown to the paper or toward the parking lot where the red Mercedes was waiting, with the motor already revving up, and you said: "Hello, Ikey." That was what you called him, and he looked at you and said: "Oh, hello."

You did not fall into step with him for a chat.

But the tall boy, a senior philosophy major with bifocals, curly black hair smelling of tonic, and a face scraped to hamburger texture from hacking away with a dull razor at his tough black rabbinical beard set in a thin, waxy-white skin, did fall into step

[117]

with Isaac Sumpter one morning. He did not, however, say: "Hello, Ikey."

He said: "Hello, Sumpter." He said it in a very mature, man-to-man tone.

"Hello," Isaac said. He did not know the boy's name, though he had been in several classes with him for two years. The boy was one of the bright ones. He made very good grades. He was a Jew, but he was not the kind of Jew you ever saw at Goldie Goldstein's. For one thing she just didn't fool around with college boys with sweet-smelling tonic on curly black hair.

The boy walked along soberly beside Isaac, under the unleafing trees. It was fall, and their feet shuffled the colored leaves on the campus walk. The boy was clearly getting ready to say something. Isaac did not help him any. Isaac was clearly not getting ready to say anything to the boy whose name he couldn't, and never had tried to, remember.

"You know," the boy managed, "you know, Sumpter, the men over at the house, they—" He fumbled a second, then resumed: "They would like it mighty well if you would drop over to the house for dinner. They're a fine group—quite a fine group, you know. Real intellectual interest—lots of them have. Now, any night you wanted. You just pick the night. You know where the house is. On Trowbridge Avenue—" and he gestured over to the north of the campus.

"The house—" Isaac Sumpter said out loud, honestly puzzled.

"Yes," the senior philosophy major said, "on Trowbridge Avenue. You know, we've been wanting to do this for some time. Really years, you might say—for a fact. But I guess some of the boys were just too shy, but I said to them—I said, gentlemen, if you just knew Sumpter the way I know him, being in so many classes with him and being good friends, you'd understand him and know he'd take things in the spirit in which they are sincerely meant, and—"

Isaac Sumpter had stopped and was standing stock-still, his

feet in the colored leaves. A couple of other students, a boy and a girl holding hands, passed by and looked curiously at him. But he did not see them. The senior philosophy major was staring into his face, anxious behind the bifocals.

"The house," Isaac Sumpter said again, but almost in a whisper now, caught in an inner process, a strange sense of floating, of disorientation. And then he saw the house over on Trowbridge Avenue as clearly as though it were, this instant, solidly before his physical eyes, a squarish, limestone house, the gray limestone streaked with soot, two soot-dappled umbrella trees mathematically placed on the patch of lawn, once the house of a solid merchant or lawyer, now with a hi-fi blatting away sixteen hours a day inside, and the Greek letters over the doorway.

And years ago—four years ago—when he, Isaac Sumpter, was a freshman in the fall, when he knew nobody, when he was nobody, one evening when he was out walking in the full pain of autumn loneliness, he had passed down this street and had stopped under the shadow of a tree, hearing the hi-fi blat, hearing voices through open windows, seeing the Greek letters ritually illuminated by a bulb concealed in the eaves of the porch. As he stood there in his shadow, two boys passed, then were arrested a few paces on by the hi-fi blat and glanced up at the Greek letters and one of the boys said them aloud, proud, no doubt, of the Greek alphabet he had learned to go with his pledge pin. And the second boy said: "Greek, for Christ's sake. They better get Yiddish. They better hang it up in Yiddish, like the synagogue!"

The first boy had snickered his appreciation, and they had gone on, happy, down Trowbridge Avenue in the sweet-smelling autumn dark, leaving the hi-fi blatting away, and Isaac Sumpter secret in his tree-shadow.

Now, in autumn noontide, colored leaves at his feet, a good coat on his back, the red Mercedes waiting, Isaac Sumpter turned slowly to look, as though for the first time, at the tall young man

[119]

with the peeled face who was **staring** so humbly at him from the drowned distance of thick bifocals, and thought: *He thinks I'm a Jew. The son-of-a-bitch thinks I am a Jew like him.*

"We hope you'll come," the senior philosophy major was saying. "We really do."

"It's very kind of you," Isaac Sumpter murmured.

"You just name the time," the senior philosophy major said, leaning at him relieved, happier now.

"There just isn't any time I can name," Isaac Sumpter said, sadly. "That's the whole trouble. There just isn't any time I can name." Then, all at once, he smiled charmingly and thrust out his hand.

He held the smile steady, steady and compelling, until the senior philosophy major had groped out from his befuddlement to take the hand. Then Isaac Sumpter chopped off the smile, the way you take a hatchet and chop off against the gunwale a taut painter you can't untie, withdrew his hand from the befuddled grip, said: "Thank you very much, thank all of you very much," and turned away.

When he got to the parking lot, the motor was running. "Hello, Ikey-Baby," Goldie said, "I love you."

"Hello," he said, and got into the car.

She slipped the car into gear, and even jabbed the accelerator a couple of quick jabs, but kept the clutch down. She was looking at his face. Suddenly she leaned and laid a hand on his knee. "Got the grumps?" she asked, grinning. "Has Ikey-Baby got the grumps?"

"No," he said, and managed to smile. The fact of the smile hurt him in some deep, grinding way. Not because the smile was a lie, but because it was a lie he had to tell, a pretense he was compelled to make, and if he didn't there would be a punishment, undefined but awful.

"I don't want Ikey-Baby to ever get the grumps," Goldie Goldstein said, and with her hand still on his knee she let her head drop a little to one side, and what had been her comradely

[120]

grin was, for an instant, a smile of such shy, naked, defenseless sweetness that he couldn't bear it.

She lifted her hand from his knee. He felt that act, not seeing it, and felt the car move forward. He was surprised that there wasn't the usual patrol-car start. He could almost see, on the face he would not turn to look at, the shadow of puzzled sadness. He had never, never, seen that expression on her face, but now, without looking, he knew that that expression was on her face, and knew what it was like. Knowing this, he was thinking: *She is the first person who ever called me Ikey.*

The car was moving out into the traffic now. But it was moving in a sad, legalistic precision, far to right. And he thought: *If she had never called me Ikey, nobody would ever have called me Ikey.*

He knew he was going to think something soon, but he couldn't bear to think it yet. Instead, he thought: *She is a Jew. Everybody knows she is a Jew.*

Then: *Now everybody calls me Ikey.*

Then, there it was: *Everybody thinks I am a Jew.*

When they got to the Goldstein place, she, as usual, went into the house to see her father, and Isaac went up to the studio. As soon as she came back, he went to her, seized her, and began kissing and caressing her. For an instant she responded, then drew away. She made a comic gesture of despair—or one that tried to be comic—and said: "Oh, Ikey-Baby, there just isn't time—not with my quiz tomorrow to study for and to get ready for this dratted party tonight. I haven't done a thing yet for it—and—"

He approached her. "Well," he said, laying hand to her, feeling a dusty anger rise in him as though you had tried to shift things around in an abandoned storeroom and the dust rose in a choking cloud. "Well," he said raspingly, "we can just do it quick. Quick as hell."

She was resisting him, still keeping a kind of comic grin on her face, or what tried to be a grin, saying: "No, Ikey-Baby—no."

[121]

"All right," he said, somehow aware that he didn't quite recognize his own voice, the raspingness, "all right, you haven't got time—well, we won't take any time—you won't even have to take any valuable time to lie down, if you're so pressed for time—we'll just—"

She had jerked away from him. "What's come over you?" she was demanding angrily. "Just what the hell has come over you?" Then: "You're all fussed up, Ikey-Baby. I don't know what it's about, but I'm sorry, I really am. I love you and I'm sorry, but I'm not going to let you just use me some way because you're all fussed up. I'm just not going to let you use me for some kind of Grade-A masturbation—or whatever the hell it amounts to that you were trying to use me for, and—"

He sat down in one of the chairs by the table. He felt dry and drained, nothing else now.

Goldie crossed to him, and laid a hand on his shoulder. "It's all right," she said quietly. "Everybody gets fussed up some time. But we love each other. That's why I don't want to do anything with you when anybody's fussed up. It wouldn't be right. Not when we love each other. And, oh"—she ran her hand over his hair, smoothing it—"we do love each other, and everything will be all right, Ikey-Baby."

"Don't call me that," he said.

"Don't call you what?"

"Oh, nothing," he said, and love for her gushed up in him. He suddenly thought that he had never really loved her before. He felt his eyes swim with tears, felt what seemed to be a purity of love beyond desire, and put his arms around her waist. She laid his head against her bosom, and continued to run her hand gently over his hair, murmuring: "Everything will be all right, Ikey-Baby. It will be all right."

But it wasn't. Late that afternoon, after she had finished her studying for the quiz and was busy about the studio arranging

[122]

things for her party, he looked up from his book, and said: "You remember the first time you ever talked to me?"

"Yes," she said, and paused in the act of putting some boughs of colored leaves in a big earthen vase, holding a sweet-gum bough in her hands and looking at him across the red and gold.

"When you spoke to me that day," he said quietly, studying her, "did you think I was a Jew?"

For a moment she regarded him over the leaves, then said, very quietly, too: "You know, I guess I always knew you were going to ask me that someday. I guess I knew there was something in you that would make you ask me that question."

"Well, did you think so?"

"I'm glad you're asking me," she said, looking level at him. "I guess I'm glad because now I don't have to wait any longer for you to do it."

"Well, did you think so?"

"Yes, I did," she said.

He felt anger, like the morning's anger, come back in him. Somehow, he had hoped she would lie. By telling the truth—just telling it so calmly and sweetly, looking at him over the red-and-gold gum leaves with sad, sweet love in her eyes, and the eyes glinting a little too bright as though tears might come—by telling him the truth, she had somehow betrayed him. Even the love in her eyes was some kind of a betrayal. That was what was funny. He was aware that that was strange, even in that moment.

"Well, I'm not," he said.

"Oh, yes, you are," she said and giggled, and dropped the leaves, and came quickly toward him. "Oh, yes, you are, Ikey-Baby, for I've made you one—I've made you an Honorary Jew and that's the very best kind. You're the honorablest Honorary Jew that ever was, and I love you to total distraction and there—"

With that she kissed him a whack of a kiss, and then jerked back, continuing, as though in the same breath: "—and if there really were a darn bit of time to spare from getting ready for this party I'd pop right into the hay with old sweet Ikey-Baby right this minute and show him how much I love him, I'd just wrap all around him, for I really do love him, and I'm just storing up love inside of me right now, and all for Ikey-Baby to let loose—oh, sweet Ikey-Baby!"

And she ran back to her task with the colored leaves.

That was that, but it definitely was not all right. That night at the party he found himself carefully sorting out the Jews from the non-Jews, then counting them very carefully. There were twelve Jews, and seven non-Jews. Eight, if he counted himself. *Yes,* he thought, *if I count myself.*

Then he found himself carefully inspecting the non-Jews. He was inspecting them to find out what was wrong with them.

Among the guests at the party was a girl named Eustacia Pinckney Johnson, a friend of Goldie's, one of the eight Gentiles present, about twenty-five years old but looking a good deal younger, for she was a small girl, with rich, curly auburn hair worn long and loose about her soft face, a trim little figure not yet plump but definitely promising plumpness, and greenish eyes that she could open to wide, hopeful, sad trustingness or draw to mysterious slits through which she peered out and assessed the world. Just before the party she had telephoned to say that her date—an intern at the hospital—couldn't come until late, maybe not at all; he had been caught in some extra duty. Goldie said not to worry, if the date didn't show up, she and Ikey would drive her home and then she'd drop Ikey off at the university. No, it wouldn't be any trouble.

Just as the party was breaking up, the nurse who lived in the house to keep an eye on Mr. Goldstein's condition telephoned the studio to say that Mr. Goldstein wasn't too well, and she, the nurse, thought it might be a good idea if Miss Goldstein came up and sat with him a little. No, it wasn't serious, but this might do him good. So Goldie asked Isaac to drive Eustacia home. He could take the car and park it at the university. She kissed him good night, in a hasty and preoccupied way, switched off the studio lights, and ran toward the house through the slight drizzle that had just begun.

The girl gave him directions and curled up in the seat, watching him through her assessing eyes. Caught up in his musings of the evening, Isaac didn't try to make any conversation. He really didn't know what to say to her, anyway. He scarcely knew her. He had never thought her particularly attractive. So the thoughts went on in his head, reliving the day, the peel-faced philosophy major, the fact that Goldie had refused him his will, the fact she had once thought he was a Jew.

Then new thoughts came—not even thoughts at first, merely a sense of entrapment, a sense of weakness, a sense that he was paying a price for something, for the red Mercedes, for the job he had at the paper, for the likker he had drunk too much of that very evening, for the tail he got. Yes, he was paying for everything. Yes, he had sold out and he was paying the piper and he wasn't calling the tune. It was a hell of a price to pay for tail.

With that he thought again how Goldie had refused him, and thought, angrily, that he wished he had taken it away from her. Then, with sickening candor, he wondered if he could have done it, a husky girl like Goldie. Not without clubbing her or socking her. Even if he was strong, maybe he couldn't have just wrestled it off her. Unwittingly, in time to his dragging thought, he had let the car slow down to some fifteen miles an hour or less, a mere crawl.

"Can you give me a light?" the girl said.

When she spoke he was actually startled. He had actually forgotten she was there. Now he turned to her. He saw her curled up on the seat, half facing him, her feet back under her, her knees, round and slick with pale silk, showing under the twisted edge of her dark-green dress, a cigarette held almost to her slightly parted lips but not touching them, her eyes looking at him through their slits. *I could handle her,* he thought. *I could*

[125]

just wrestle it off her. And the thought of that smallness, that plain manageability, paralyzed him so that he couldn't even speak.

"Can you give me a light?" she asked again.

The car was barely drifting now. His hand was fumbling in his pocket for matches, but he couldn't seem to find any. He couldn't take his eyes off her face, still trapped by that plain fact of manageability, something to be twisted, turned, adapted. At that moment the Eustacia Pinckney Johnson who stared out at the world, including Isaac Sumpter, from the assessing slits became the Eustacia Pinckney Johnson who, all at once, opened her eyes to their wide, hopeful, sad trustingness, and the hand that held the cigarette to her lips sank down slowly.

"All right," she said, the huskiness barely a whisper now.

He was still fumbling for the matches, not finding them. He didn't really understand. He didn't understand till he saw that her face was inclining bit by bit toward his own.

"There's a lane right there," she said.

He let the car drift into the lane. It had begun to rain now.

"It's raining," he said dully, for an instant almost grateful for rain, for something, anything, that might prevent him from doing what he now knew he would do.

"Well, this isn't the Ritz," she said, "but it's bigger than a telephone booth," and she gave a harsh little vulgar incongruous laugh, a quick brittle laugh which he couldn't quite believe, like an obscenity, a laugh that outraged some secret prudery of his nature, and at the same instant inflamed him.

"Yeah," she said, and laughed that brittle laugh, reaching out to him, "it's big enough—if you aren't built big as a horse." And added, with a snatch of that laugh: "Like some people."

So that was it, in Goldie Goldstein's red Mercedes, which wasn't the Ritz, but was bigger than a telephone booth, and in the course of the process Eustacia Pinckney Johnson had said, whispering huskily: "Goldie Goldstein—that Goldie Goldstein— she's stuck up—for a Jew—isn't she—isn't she?"

He had heard the words, far off, not meaningful.

But the whisper, in its huskiness, was insisting: "Isn't she?—isn't she?—say she is—say she is—say she is, or I'll stop—I swear to Christ I'll stop."

He thought he could prevent that all right. But he said yes, anyway.

Isaac Sumpter spent a miserable night, torn by conscience, agitated by excitement, salved in vanity, fortified in confidence, exulting in new vistas of infinite freedom, torn again by conscience, saying to himself that he loved Goldie Goldstein, he truly loved her, feeling a gush of pitiful love for what seemed suddenly her sweet defenselessness, but seeking even in that instant to justify what had happened. It all seemed like a trap, and he couldn't have helped it. That fool intern who was Eustacia Johnson's date and for whom she had apparently come armed and ready—he, Isaac Sumpter, hadn't made him get extra duty and not show up. He hadn't made old Mr. Goldstein get his death fears and want his daughter by his side in the middle of the night. He hadn't made that peel-faced, tonic-smelling philosophy major come up to him that morning.

No, he hadn't caused any of that, and why—for God's sake why?—had Goldie pushed him off that afternoon when they got to the studio? Couldn't she have seen that he needed her? It wasn't fair, what she had done, to refuse him, reject him, when he needed her most. Not knowing why he needed her, not trying to know, he thought of laying his head on her bosom while her hand stroked his hair and joy and innocence came flooding back, like sunshine.

He finally fell into a fitful sleep, to be wakened about ten o'clock by his landlady saying there was a call. He put on his robe and went down. It was Goldie. Could he come right out, she said, couldn't he cut his psychology at eleven and come right out?

[127]

The misery of the night hadn't yet risen into his befogged mind. So he asked if it was her father, was he bad?

Then he heard her voice, muffled, saying: "No—no—" Then there was an indecipherable sound, and the words: "Oh, you know—you know what it is!"

Then he heard the distant sob—it was clearly sobbing—and the click of the phone. He stood there, holding the instrument in his hand, while the brute fact dawned on him that she knew about last night. But how—how in God's name—could she know? He felt a surge of anger at being wakened to this, to the complication of life. He felt anger at that Eustacia Johnson for getting him into it, for merely existing. He felt anger at Goldie for finding out. Why did she have to find out? If she hadn't, he thought with a sudden comforting revelation, he could have gone to her and told her everything, then everything would have been all right in the sweetness of forgiveness and deeper understanding. Yes, he would have done that.

But, it developed, that was exactly what Eustacia had done—come dashing over immediately after breakfast, full of contrition, tears in her sad, trustful, wide eyes, to have the sweet joy of confession, which, as she made confession to that stuck-up Goldstein, who was big as a horse and thought she was so bright and beautiful and talented, was a deeper and more lasting satisfaction than the act confessed, or any act similar to what she confessed, had ever been.

She didn't care if Goldie didn't exactly forgive her, Goldie having, in fact, almost ignored her in the distress of something going on inside of her big-as-a-horse self. Eustacia Pinckney Johnson didn't care a bit. She came down the steps, got into her two-and-one-half-year-old blue Chevrolet convertible, which was not a red Mercedes, and feeling gay as a kitten that had just eaten a cricket, tooled off down the drive. She had a right to feel pretty good. It was her masterpiece, to date.

Nor did Goldie forgive Ikey-Baby, even though he tried to explain how everything had happened, in so far as he could bring himself to do that, told her how he would have confessed as soon as he had a chance, and was altogether quite abject and suffering. It was perfectly sincere. When she sent him away, he had to stop at the foot of the drive and sit down, he was so weak and shaken. On the bus going back to town—the bus he had so infrequently had to ride—he shivered and sweated, as though with a chill.

After three days of misery, he wrote her a letter. It was, also, perfectly sincere. He said that he guessed he somehow resented the fact that he owed everything to her, that he took it out on her in the meanest way possible, that, as she knew, she was the first girl he had even been with and he guessed he had sort of resented that too, and he wanted to die, he hated himself so. But he loved her. He felt like a son-of-a-bitch, but he loved her. Perhaps she could come to love him again.

There was only one thing in the letter which was not sincere —or at least not uncalculated. He hesitated quite a bit in choosing between *Isaac* and *Ikey*. With a sense of cunning, he finally wrote down *Ikey*. Then, after a moment, he put a hyphen and added *Baby*.

Two days later, Goldie replied:

Dear Ikey-Baby,
   Come to see me. I miss you, and we will love each other, forever.
                                                     Goldie
P.S. Come at six o'clock and I'll cook a nice little supper for you. I love to cook a nice little supper for my Ikey-Baby.

On his arrival, they kissed, held each other for a moment, tenderly, even cautiously, as though something might get broken, and by a mutual shyness, separated. He noticed that she was pale, the clear natural red of her cheeks quite gone, and somehow this seemed to make her more his own, and more beautiful.

In this paleness the little saddle of gold freckles across her nose stood out quite clearly. It made her look like a child, like a girl not quite grown-up. In a sweet, almost awed, hush, they went about their little tasks, he setting the table and mixing the highballs and opening the claret to breathe, while she did the cooking. They drank their drinks, kissing now and then, very decorously, not talking. They ate the meal, and drank all the claret. After the coffee, she lay on the couch and put her head on his knee. When she took off her clothes, he saw that she was thinner, and that fact profoundly stirred him; it was like a perfect gift she was making him, and his heart filled with gratitude for her, for life, for all the future.

But it was a great sell. It was a mess. There he was, and there she was, and just at the moment of his kiss she jerked away, crying out: "I can't—I just can't!" She sat up, and tried to jerk the cover of the couch up around her, as though she had been suddenly surprised by an intruder, and from modesty, or shame, sought to cover her breasts and body. He tried to put his arm around her, to soothe her, to placate her—or what? He didn't know what. But she again jerked away, again drew up more of the cover, and said: "I just can't—don't you understand? Don't you see what you've done to me?"

And as, in his confusion, he tried to embrace her, she was saying: "Oh, what have you done? I don't want to be this way—oh, Ikey, I don't want to be this way. But you did it, you did—"

"I'm sorry," he said, aware, even as he spoke, of the comic ineffectuality of his words, "I'm sorry—about that—that business. I told you I was."

"Oh, I don't care what you did with that fool," she said, jerking back, and her eyes began to go bright with unsheddable tears. "It's what you did to me—oh, what did you do to me, Ikey? Get back—don't touch me, don't ever touch me!"

Then, as he retreated, she cried out: "Oh, Ikey, it was going to be so wonderful. I was going to love you all my life, Ikey. I was just going to wrap my arms and my legs and myself all around

[130]

you, Ikey, and love you all my life. And I was going to have babies hanging off me like grapes on a grapevine. I just dreamed of babies and they were all your babies and beautiful like you, and I didn't care if some day a million years off I was a big fat mamma with a million grandchildren and you wouldn't care if I was big and fat for I would have loved you so good a million years, but, oh!—"

She cried out in grief, waving her right arm free of the inadequate huddle of the couch cover, exposing her right breast as she made her tragic gesture.

"Oh," she cried out, "and look what you have done! You and your crazy goy awfulness, you and your God-damned bleeding Campbellite awfulness, and—"

He heard his voice, far-off, in a tone of academic correction, saying: "No—no—not Campbellite—"

"Well, Baptist, then!" she cried out. "Or whatever kind of bleeding, clod-hopping, Honorary-Jew Bible-thumper you are. Go away—just get your clothes on and go away and you'll be great— yes, you're so bleeding smart and you'll be great, but remember—"

She straightened up, her gaze flung wide about the studio, on the swathed pieces of clay, on the hacked stone. "But just remember," she said, "I'll be throwing rocks at you all the way. I'll be hacking out great big beautiful rocks and people will pay a million dollars for 'em, and I'll be throwing them at you all the way. But, oh!—that wasn't what I wanted. Get out!"

She flung herself face down on the couch, her white shoulders shaking with sobs, and as quickly as possible he got out, and caught the bus.

By summer Isaac Sumpter had been dropped from the university, and had lost his job with the paper. After the business with Goldie Goldstein, he had been absolutely demoralized. For a time he had felt that a chunk had literally been hacked out of his vitals. He could think of nothing but Goldie, in grief, and then of Goldie, in fear, fear of some mysterious threat in their parting. He suffered anew the loneliness of his first months at the university. But worse now, loneliness coupled with sexual deprivation. He even called up Eustacia Pinckney Johnson, the person he had decided he hated most in the world, and tried to make a date with her, but she laughed into the phone. He took up with one of the middle-aged reporters, a lush and a tart-chaser, who fixed him up. He was fixed up with some cheesy little tarts whom he couldn't bear. Until he got drunk. Then, while drunk, he felt Byronic and tragic, and next morning vomited more at recollection of himself than at the likker.

By the end of the first semester he had fallen so far behind in his studies that he was on probation in the graduate school and would have been dropped had it not been for his previous record. By late April he was involved in a sordid affair on the campus with one of the tarts whom, in drunken bravado, he had brought into campus shrubbery. That finished him at the university. Two weeks later he was dropped from the paper for drunkenness and undependability. He stayed in Nashville until commencement time, to deceive his father, and then went to Johntown. He had nowhere else to go.

Now, in the wooden room in Johntown, under the blazing tin roof, he stared at himself in the mirror and, with the classic palms-out gesture of the stage Jew, said: "Ikey—Little Ikey." Then he stood there and thought that he had to leave, and never come back. But money—he had to have some money. He thought how maybe the cave might pay off. But that would take time. And it meant associating with that Jasper Harrick. Suddenly he couldn't bear the thought of Jasper Harrick.

He couldn't bear the thought because yesterday morning he had gone with Jasper into the cave, had crawled down crawl-ways and seen great galleries of onyx, stalactites like pipe organs, and crawled again through a passage like a dry, black gullet, and had come, in the end, to a greater gallery, high, almost beyond

[132]

the beam of the flashlight, populated with the monster statuary of a dream, stalactite and stalagmite, the high ceiling studded with gypsum flowers. Jasper went to one of the great columns and inspected it with his flashlight. It had a pale, brownish cast, but with an inner brightness. He rubbed his hand down it, then picked up a stone from the floor and tapped the stalagmite. It rang like a great bell and the bell-tone echoed up into the dome.

"Iron," Jasper said. "That gypsum has got enough iron in it to ring like a bell. Yeah, and you got something here. Listen to that echo. It's music."

He struck again, more sharply, and the full bell-tone unfolded, filled the dome and came back from below, deep down. Jasper threw his beam in that direction and stepped forward. "Look," he said. "Look!"

There was the pit. It blocked the far end of the chamber. From its blackness, deep down, came the sound of water.

"We can make it," Jasper said, flashing his light along a narrow ledge at the edge of the pit. "Yeah, we can make it. And Great God, look yonder!" Beyond the pit the light showed a gallery, grander, higher. "Come on!" Jasper said, and moved forward to the ledge that skirted the pit on the right.

But Isaac had not been able to make it. He simply hadn't been able to face that ledge and the sound of water from the deep dark.

"Can't make it, huh?" Jasper had said softly. Then shrugging his shoulders, he had said, with a calmness not quite contempt: "Well, some folks is made that way." He again considered the ledge. "I could get on," he said, "and you could wait for me here."

To that prospect, Isaac Sumpter simply could not answer a word. He thought he detected a satiric grin playing at the corners of Jasper Harrick's mouth, but he couldn't be sure.

Then Jasper said: "Or you could crawl on back out, and wait for me outside."

Again, Isaac couldn't quite answer.

"Well, pal," Jasper said, and gave what seemed to be a real grin of friendliness, but you couldn't be sure, "we can go out now before we catch pneumonia and get the papers fixed up with old Bingham at the bank, and I'll come on back and take a crack by myself. Come on, son, let's crawl."

They had crawled out, into the sun. There, under the beech tree, they had sat while Jasper transferred to a little notebook the compass readings and distances he had scribbled on the back of an envelope. "Without measuring off," he said, "that last place would be up the ridge a little. Off your land, I reckon. But there's not any other opening nigh. So it's your cave, pal." He had wadded up the envelope and idly tossed it behind a rock.

Then they had gone to the bank.

And now Isaac stood here in his room and hated Jasper and hated the thought of having to see that smile on Jasper's face. He wanted to flee, to go far away, forever.

He went to the window and looked out into the sun-dazzling street. Into his range of vision a girl came running. Rather, she was trying to run, exhausted and stumbling. She was, as well as he could tell, a pretty girl. Pretty, but she was certainly messed up now with running and sweating. All at once she stumbled again, and before she caught herself, he sensed, under their cloth, the weight of her breasts.

"Jesus," he breathed, "Jesus Christ," and went sick with longing and deprivation.

IV

Old Jack Harrick, old heller of high coves and hoot-owl hollows, stared out the window at the big white oak from which hung the piece of rotting rope he had put there for a swing for his older son when that son was a little squirt, stared at his wife's flower bed even now full of red and yellow nasturtiums, giddy and jimcrack as the toy counter of a dime store, stared at the fence beyond the flower bed and felt sorry that he had not replaced the rotted palings as his wife had asked him, and tears came to his eyes at that regret. For he loved his wife.

That was the awful thing, he loved her right now as she set the glass of iced tea on the little table beside him and laid her cheek against his hair and murmured: "John T.—dear John T."

God damn it, why did she talk that way now, for he could love her a lot easier if she didn't. It would be a lot easier to love her if she were dead and six feet under like some of those other round-bottomed contraptions that he hadn't loved but had shore-God taught the meaning of the word to so they could spell it backwards and forwards for anybody's benefit afterwards, including their own, and had something to remember for those long, dark winter nights in the graveyard.

It would be a lot easier to love Celia Hornby Harrick if everything, and all the honest work he had done on her in a love-way, were all tidy and tied up in a package for good and the lid clamped down.

But no, God damn it, she had to be alive. She had to put her cheek against his hair. And not only alive but twenty-five years younger than he, than Old Jack Harrick, the cancer-bit heller and beauty-boy of the wheel chair. Right now, as she leaned her cheek against his hair, he couldn't bear to look round at her. If he did he would see a woman who didn't even look her years and tears and time, just a little gray in the yellow hair, like it wasn't gray but the light just struck it slantwise to silver, and some pink left in her cheeks, if her blood got up, and her breath sweet-smelling enough, and her body, you get her stripped down and the light gentle, shaped all ripe and ready for hand-holt.

Thinking that way, he was suddenly blind-mad like he had caught somebody peeking on his wife, on Celia Hornby Harrick, on Mrs. John T. Harrick, and her getting ready for bed or bathtub, and his hands clenched tight like he would break the bastard's back, like a piece of too long kindling over his knee. But there wasn't any bastard peeking out of the dark under the old green window shade. It was just himself, and he was sick at the thought.

If only she were dead, then everything would be as it had been and not as it was now, and he would not be like an old tramp sneaking up in the dark cold night to a crack in a window to peek in. If she were dead then he would be for always the man who lived in that house. Things would seem like long back when he used to lock the kitchen door, and bank the fire in the cook stove so she wouldn't have any trouble in the morning—oh, yeah, he always was careful to make things easy for her, and he knew all about fires, being the best blacksmith between Blue Ridge and Rocky Mountains—and wind the kitchen clock, and get himself a drag of buttermilk out of the icebox to sweeten his digestion, and go down the hall toward the bedroom.

He used to stop just outside the door, and smile to himself in the dark. Standing in the dark hall he wouldn't have to peek. He had always been able to see it so well, in his head. He had done his peeking long back. He would know how she was putting on her nightgown, standing with her arms over her head for a second, with that position lifting her whole body up like it was a Christmas present and glad to be one, letting the gown slip down over her arms, then over her, and her head coming through the collar.

It would be a flannel nightgown, white with tiny little blue flowers, or some such thing, and it would reach nigh the floor so you couldn't see her feet. The collar would be sort of high, and after it got settled down over her head she would tie the little white, or maybe blue, ribbon that closed the collar. Standing there in the dark hall, he could see in his mind's eye how she would tie that little ribbon, how her lips would purse a little, the way women's lips purse when they do some little thing. He would grin to himself in the dark, thinking how she was tying that ribbon. He always waited till he was sure she had tied it. For he wanted it tied for him to untie.

Then he would come in the door, and she would look up at him over the ribbon, for a split second, as though he had surprised her. Then her smile would begin, and for another split second it always looked like the smile of a little girl who didn't know what the world was like but loved it all because it was so dew-bright and sweet-smelling. Then that little-girl smile, which was as teetery and shy as a lady wren balanced on a bent stalk of wild parsnip, and which a thousand years ago when she wasn't much more than a little girl was what he had first noticed about Celia Hornby, would be gone.

[137]

It would be changed into another kind of smile, the smile of Celia Hornby Harrick, a grown woman standing very still in a blue-flowered nightgown, who might not know all about the world but didn't have to, and didn't want to, because she knew quite a lot about Jack Harrick in general and what he had in mind in particular, for her health, benefit and instruction, and standing there with the ribbon tied prim under her chin, she didn't mind a bit. She didn't mind, that is, unless one of the young ones was croupy, or it was a season with money tight and grub scant.

That sort of thing sort of dried the juice up in a woman, he knew. In a man too, sometimes, if the worriment got too deep. Like that time after he had run off to the army to fight Germans and was in the AEF and doing fine, whether it was crawling through barbed wire or kicking off covers, and the word finally got to him how Ole Mac Sumpter, his old Hell-hopping side-kick now turned Bible-beater, had married Tillie Tillyard and they were about to have a baby but she had a fall or something and spilled the works right on the floor.

When Sergeant John T. Harrick, who had got a ribbon for German-killing and got himself called Jumping Jack Harrick because of devoted activities over and above the call of duty when he was sent out of the line to rest up from killing Germans, heard about Tillie and Ole Mac, it looked like something drew the pith. He knew, God damn it, it wasn't his fault, except maybe hitting Ole Mac those two extra times to help him lie down quicker. Anyway, he had listened to Ole Mac's heart to be sure he was all right, had put a pillow under his head, and had sent a written-out apology. What the hell more did you expect a man to do? Was it his fault that that Tillie Tillyard, that night when the dogwood was spook-pale, had sort of had a strut bust in her?

He couldn't figure out what it was, what the worriment was. But it preyed on his mind, and the more he figured out how it wasn't his fault the more it drained him, like he was nothing but a big fat hen in a dark hen house and couldn't even kick

[138]

when the weasel was drawing the blood out of his throat. He couldn't bear to think about it, and he couldn't think of anything else. It looked like there was a big black hole right in the middle of him where a man's thinking and feeling and living ought to be, and he was going to fall into the hole and fall forever into black nothing. He nigh got himself killed, his mind wandering that way. He was on night patrol and nigh got himself killed. He did lose some weight, whatever about a quart and a half of blood weighs which came out through a couple of holes made by a Mauser 7.98 mm. But the Mauser 7.98 mm. didn't kill him. In fact, he figured it saved his life, for it took his mind off whatever worriment it was he couldn't bear to think about.

As for that other time, long after, when the other worriment got on his mind—the time he ran off blind to Chattanooga and caught the clapp and got put in jail—he never could figure out what pulled his mind off the worriment. But, then, just like before, he had not been able to figure out what the worriment was, either. Maybe what pulled him back into shape that time was just loving Celia Hornby Harrick, who forgave him. No, she hadn't even found it necessary to forgive him. She had simply fallen on her knees beside the chair he sank into, and hugged his knees and closed her eyes and lifted up her head and, weeping, had cried out: "God, dear God, I thank Thee, for Thou has brought back to me what is dearest to my heart."

That was enough, he reckoned, to sort of bust something in a man, especially when six weeks of likker has gone bad on your stomach and you've got the clapp and the place on your head isn't yet healed where they clubbed you and you've been thrown in jail like a hog in a pen and you're forty-five and your name's been in the paper. It had busted something in him, all right. He had joined the Baptist Church of Johntown. The Reverend Mac-Carland Sumpter had baptized him in Elk Creek, in the big still pool below where the creek came boiling white over the gray limestone of Beecham's Bluff Falls. Ole Mac had dunked him good.

[139]

For one black instant, bent over backward in the water, with Ole Mac pushing him down, he had had the sudden terror that Ole Mac—Ole Mac whom he had knocked in the head all those years ago—was going to drown him. Then the flicker of terror had passed, and the peace of God came into his soul.

Ole Mac lifted him up into sunlight. The ladies' choir, ranged on the limestone shelf above the pool, under the shadow of gray bluff and the dappling green glimmer of June leafage, was singing "Bringing in the Sheaves." The Reverend MacCarland Sumpter lifted up his hand in blessing. Celia Hornby Harrick, with tears running down her cheeks and blue eyes bright as glory, threw her arms around his body and pressed her face against his chest, no matter if he was sopping wet and all Johntown goggle-eyed. And he stood there, with water squishing in his shoes as he shifted his weight from side to side, and patted her on the head, saying: "Baby—now Honey-Baby—don't take on, Baby."

He was glad he had been dunked good and well. With all that water coming out of his thick head of hair, folks couldn't tell whether it was creek water or tears running down his own cheeks, as he stood there patting the head of Celia Hornby Harrick.

Later, he felt a little ashamed of having suspected that Ole Mac was trying to drown him. Then the shame turned into a wry, secret joke. He reckoned that Ole Mac, knowing all he did about him, had to give him a little deeper dunking than the ordinary sinner needed. Once, meeting Ole Mac on the street, he even had the impulse to tell him the joke. Ole Mac had liked a joke in the old days. But now, giving Ole Mac's face a preliminary survey, he decided against it. He reckoned it was a sort of pride, just plain ornery human man-pride in sinfulness, that made him want to tell the joke in the first place. So he made another joke to himself. He reckoned since even if he was saved he still had such a bait of sin-pride, he might take longer than most to build up saint-pride.

Then, grinning to himself, he reckoned maybe it might take

him less time since he was naturally just proud as pus, and all his pride had to do was just switch sides from Old Nick to God-a-mighty and never miss beat or breakfast in the process. Maybe he ought to get dunked again, he thought. No, maybe Elk Creek wasn't enough. Maybe they'd have to put him in a big wash kettle and build a fire under it and render the pride out like fat for making soap.

Jack Harrick might make jokes secretly to, and about, himself and his salvation, but nobody else did. No doubt, some of the un-regenerate made such jokes, but they made them in scrupulous privacy. Jack Harrick might have been moving on fifty and have a skull cracked by a cop's night stick, but when he walked down the street nobody mentioned either Chattanooga or Jesus Christ, either baptizing or bottle-fighting. Anybody who thought he might spring a joke the next time Jack Harrick walked down the street could just listen for a second to the song that anvil was singing in the heat of a summer afternoon, way over yonder on the other side of town, and dream up a mode of entertainment that might cost his insurance company less. The Baptists believed that once in grace always in grace, but nobody wanted to push Jack Harrick too far to find out if he had really been in grace at the time of his dunking. His daily progress down the street of Johntown was greeted by respectful salutation or discreet silence.

So whatever worriment had driven him off to Chattanooga that time had long since been washed away in the waters of Elk Creek, just as the other nameless worriment had been knocked out of him by the Mauser 7.98 mm. He knew enough, however, about worriment, and what worriment might do to dry up your juices, to respect Celia Hornby Harrick's occasional worriments over croup or short cash when he would come in the bedroom door and find her standing in her nightgown and the smile didn't come. Or tried to come, and couldn't quite make it.

No, it wasn't just her worriments he had had to respect. There was something else in her. There were just certain things you felt you couldn't do to Celia Hornby Harrick—even back yonder

[141]

when she was just Celia Hornby, hardly twenty years old and teaching the third grade. There had been a time when he had Celia Hornby out in the dark in dogwood time, and the peepers down in the valley had been making their sound like opening and closing squeaky little silver hinges. He hadn't crowded her, even if he did guess she had kind thoughts and curious curiosities about Jack Harrick.

If she didn't have very kind thoughts and specially curious curiosities, why was she here and not off with some snotnose sitting in a movie with the feature Lassie the Dog We Love, or maybe in a Chevrolet with the feature Snotnose Tries to Come of Age? Why wasn't she in the Chevrolet with Snotnose, whom any healthy girl of a hundred ten pounds could keep out of the bureau of vital statistics with her left hand, and not spooking along in the dark under the dogwoods, with nobody to yell to if your foot slipped, spooking along beside a man old as your father and one who by public report had never fought in the snotnose class since he took off short pants?

There was only one answer, as Jack Harrick, forty-five years old but not yet Old Jack, said to himself under the dogwood-darkness. A girl didn't go out with a man that age and reputation unless she harbored kind thoughts, even if the man didn't look fifteen years of his age, didn't have more gray hairs in his black sideburns than you could count on your fingers, two hands to the side to be fair, and, even if he did have a little more girth than once, still had a belly flat as a washboard and with corrugations hard enough to scrub clothes on.

Jack Harrick sucked his belly in as he walked beside her in the dark, and felt pretty good. He knew things were going to roll his way. But there was something about that Celia Hornby you had to respect. He reckoned it was because she was sure of herself. He could never abide a man who wasn't sure of himself, but had never had to give the topic a thought in so far as women were concerned, for simple instinct had led him to close in fast on those that weren't sure. He didn't have any impulse to close in fast on Celia Hornby. He didn't crowd her, even when she breathed shallow.

He walked along, with his gut sucked in, and felt twenty-five years old, which he reckoned was a man's best time for performance in most lines of worth-while endeavor even if by then a man hasn't had time to build a universal reputation to bask in between efforts. They were moving quiet as a dream together on the soft grass by the dogwoods, in the dark. They were dreaming the same dream no doubt, but not dreaming it in the head, just letting their bodies dream it until their bodies felt so light and drifty they didn't feel like bodies at all, and wouldn't until the dream suddenly came true.

But it didn't come true that way. It wasn't because of that self-sureness she had. Or because of the respect, or whatever it was she inspired. It was because of something that happened inside of Jack Harrick.

He was drifting along in that communal dream, feeling better than he ever had in his life. As his body was dreaming that communal dream, the bodies drifted along with considerable space between them. His hand reached out in the dark to hold her hand. They weren't even looking at each other, drifting along. His hand held hers very lightly, just barely holding, aware of its softness in his, of its smallness but good strength.

Occasionally he would put the slightest pressure on her hand, not looking, and then wait for an answering pressure. He figured that there was an answering pressure, but only after he had let up and so slight you couldn't be really sure there had been anything at all. She could certainly micrometer that pressure down till it would take jewelry-store scales to tell it. So he tried cutting his down, down to the barest, the barest you could with a hand like his.

So they drifted along, playing that game in their dream, and his mind went emptier and emptier as the dream grew and seemed not only to fill up his body, but the dark trees and the dark, barely star-teased sky above the trees, and included not

[143]

only now, this minute, but all the times he had ever lived and walked in the dark. He found himself sucking in his guts tighter and tighter and wasn't even sure he felt the soft sod under his feet. Then clear as a bell, a voice seemed to say in his head: *I'm not ever going to die.*

That was a moment of perfect joy. He had found the great secret that everybody had always hunted for. He, Jack Harrick, had found it. Then, suddenly, he didn't know whose hand it was he held.

That was the terror. It was like waking up in the dark and not knowing who you are. Yet he was afraid to look and find out who was there, and therefore who he himself was. His head spun, as in a kind of vertigo of all the past times he had walked in the dark. He was afraid that if he turned his head to look he might find nobody, nothing there at all, nothing because everything, all the past there, which was nothing, nothing but whirling blankness. This moment was only a dream of the past, and it was about to whirl away into the dark and he would be alone on a mountain side, in the night-shadow of trees, with the last dogwood petals about to drop in the dark. He was shaking—like malaria in dog days and the quinine not taking hold.

Then he felt the pressure on his hand.

Thinking about it afterwards, many nights, lying in the dark with Celia Hornby's sleeping head on his arm and her breath gentle and steady, he figured that in that instant of terror his hand must have tightened on her hand, not playing the dream-game any more, just twitching like a frog leg dropped in the hot fry-fat in the skillet. And the girl, not knowing the reason why his grip came suddenly stronger, must have come back herself with just a little more juice.

Why wouldn't she have come back with a little more juice? If she was drifting along in the dream-game, feeling the dream grow? She couldn't know, he was damned glad to reflect, that he had been hit like a field mouse by a hoot owl and snatched into the dark sky. He was ashamed, plain puke-ashamed, sometimes lying in his bed, to remember how he had been snatched, like he wasn't a man sure of himself. It was a comfort, particularly since she had that self-sureness, drifting along in her own sure dream, that she couldn't have known what was happening to him when she came back a little stronger.

Or had she really come back at all? It was a long time, many nights of figuring, before that doubt struck him. Perhaps in that moment of terror and disorientation on the mountain he had had to have the feeling that whoever's hand was there was holding on to him.

But he always decided that maybe that didn't matter too much. Supposing she hadn't come back at all that time when his hand had gripped hers, not knowing whose hand it was, she had come back plenty since. He reckoned he was on firm ground there, and, by God, it was ground he himself, and no other God-durn man, had bought and paid for, cleared, broke, seeded, weeded, laid by, and brought to harvest.

Yes, on the whole, he figured he had no gripe about the way the cards had fallen. But he still hadn't been able to figure out the reason they fell the way they did that night on the mountain. When her fingers had returned the pressure—or when, in his need, he had thought they did—he had turned toward her, and grabbed her hand in both of his, and fallen right on his knees in the dark, on the soft grass, under the dogwoods. Yes, right on his knees, in the way they said fellows used to propose, the way they showed it in cartoons and in the funny paper, some simp kneeling down and an expression on his face like waiting for castor oil to show the first signs. Long later, thinking about it, he had had to grin in the dark, at his own expense and the strangeness of it, to think of Jack Harrick coming down on his knees like a stunned beef—him, Jack Harrick.

But the funniest part was that when he swung around and grabbed her hand with both his and cried out and fell to his knees like the stunned beef, he still didn't really know what woman it was he was falling down to. It was a light-colored

[145]

shape there in the woods-dark, real, yes, but which shape, with what color eyes and waist-feel and name and address, he would have had to be damned from hell to bell-time if he had to say that minute. Anyway, he cried out, or rather, croaked out: "Marry me, marry me!—You got to marry me!"

She had married him. She had stood there a moment—or a thousand years—after he croaked his croak, as calm as though she were alone and listening for somebody to call from way down the valley. Then, in her calmness, she had laid her free hand—her left hand it would have been—on his thick head of hair, and roughed the hair just a little, like recognizing a dog or kid that's got its head against your knee, and said: "Yes, John T. Harrick. Yes, I will marry you, John T."

Even in that moment, he was aware, below the level of other, more urgent, awarenesses, of how strange it was to be called "John T." Nobody had ever called him John T. He was Jack, he was Jack Harrick. Hearing that other name, even as it answered his need and desire, he knew that something was happening to Jack Harrick. What, he didn't know. He had turned and fallen on his knees and cried out because, for that one terrible instant, he had felt that he, Jack Harrick, was being snatched up into darkness like the field mouse by the hoot owl. Now as that hand drew him back to reality, he wasn't Jack Harrick after all. He was John T.

So she had married him, him, John T.—who, however, remained Jack in the salutations of Johntown and in the tales told, gradually becoming Old Jack in the tales, but remaining Jack, not John T. or Old Jack, in his own thoughts, except now and then when, as she called him John T., some vague half-humorous but discomfiting wonderment started up as to where Jack Harrick had gone, or worse, who he had been, after all.

She became Mrs. John T. Harrick, and he called her Ceeley. Ceeley, or Baby, or Honey-Baby—or even Doll-Baby, for her smallness, in comparison with him anyway, when he took her on his knee. In their bed-passages, however, he never, or practically never. called her anything, anything, that is, when the water got rough. Even if things were just drifting along, especially if the light was out, he was, for some years, pretty guarded about that *Ceeley*. No, to be more precise, as he observed to himself, with some sense of exculpation, it was not he himself, Jack Harrick, who was guarded about that *Ceeley*. For he loved Ceeley, and wasn't boasting or kidding himself when he said he damned well would run through fire for her. It wasn't himself that put the clamp on that *Ceeley*, it was something, but God knew what, inside himself.

The reason, as he told himself, wasn't simply that he was afraid of making a slip and hurting her feelings. Naturally, it would hurt any lady's feelings, but with Celia Hornby, with her sureness of self, it wouldn't be more than a flesh wound. She would know who she was, no matter what you called her.

And she certainly knew that Jack Harrick had voted in more than one precinct, and even if she, to his certain knowledge, was a lady who had done God's little ballot counting, she had common sense enough to guess that a man might develop certain work habits and enough sense of humor to realize that it took time to develop new ones. Not that he wouldn't have tapped himself over the left knuckles with a ten-inch monkey wrench before he'd hurt her feelings, or that he, Jack Harrick, wouldn't have undertaken to avoid reference in close discourse, to some Annie Laurie or Sara Lou, or such. It was simply that he never had to undertake to avoid them. That something inside himself always clamped down on easy name calling, long before he ever had to.

It took him some years to guess what that something inside himself was. He guessed it some time after Celia had ceased to be Ceeley, or even Baby or Doll-Baby, and was only Momma, even when lights were out, or Sunday breakfast was late. By that time what he guessed didn't seem very relevant to the course of life, and he even sort of guessed that was why he managed to guess it.

[147]

What he guessed was that the something inside himself that kept such a close watch on name calling after lights-out was not something different from himself. It was, simply, that part of himself that knew that if a wrong name got called in the dark the danger was not in the fact that Jack Harrick didn't know the name of who was there in the dark with him. The danger was in the fact that Jack Harrick might not know that Jack Harrick himself was there, might not, in fact, know who Jack Harrick was, or if Jack Harrick had ever existed. If Jack Harrick called the wrong name, that hoot owl might swoop down again, and snatch all to blackness.

For now Jack Harrick didn't say to himself any more that he wasn't ever going to die. He even mentioned that fact of his death to other people, quite casually and with a certain pride in so doing, the kind of pride, he thought in rueful midnight humor, with which, a thousand years ago, he had tossed off some information to a just-voice-changed compeer about his first piece. He took some pride in talking about his insurance. He bought a lot in the cemetery, and paid more than it was worth.

He himself wouldn't have given two whoops and a hog-holler where they dumped his two twenty just so the drainage was reasonable good, for a man didn't want to lie soggy. And the drainage was good in the old Harrick burying ground. Even if the family burying ground was gone to wrack and ruin for the most part, those old homemade stones down, and blackberry bushes and passion flower and second growth and saw-briar taking the place, it would still have been good enough for him, for he wasn't any fancier than the old-timers who had beat him in the door and to bed by more than a hundred years, and tucked the covers tight.

But he had some hesitation about sticking Celia Hornby off there in the whippoorwill and possum-trot territory. She had been raised with sterling silver and Haviland china, down in the valley, where the railroad ran, and she had been educated. She had been off to the normal, and who wasn't educated if a schoolteacher wasn't? So he bought the lot from the Johntown Ever Watchful Memorial Company, of which Mr. Timothy Bingham had been the organizer. So, in an offhand way, he would mention the lot now and then. That, too, was a little bit like mentioning his first piece, long back, a mark of age and distinction.

The satisfaction he got now by a casual mention of dying was also a little like the satisfaction he had got when he noticed—or rather allowed himself to notice—that his wife's figure wasn't as good as it had been. Her waist was thickening, and to tell the truth there was some danger that she, being a short woman, might go dumpy on him, something he had never been able to abide. But one morning when he had really brought himself to look right at her, as she was leaning over to put on her stockings, and honestly looked at what was happening to her, he felt a sudden wave of tenderness. He felt warm and tender about her all day, and could not wait for night. He was as excited as a honeymooner.

Even if Jack Harrick had bought a cemetery lot, he had no intention of dying for quite a spell. There was gray in his hair, as time ambled on, but you could hear that anvil ring. If you didn't hear it ringing that was because Jack Harrick was probably doing some mechanical work on a tractor or pay-loader or even a car, for a good many folks, especially farmers, not the corn-patch-and-shack hill-scratchers who wouldn't know what to do with a tractor if they had one, but the fellows who had the creek bottoms and the white weather-boarding, asseverated with heat that Jack Harrick was a lot better mechanic than that pimply squirt down at the Chevrolet agency with a cigarette hanging out the corner of his mouth.

The anvil rang, but less often. The gray in the hair got grayer. They put in the state-highway slab through Johntown, heading over the mountains. Two new agency garages came to town, and had neon out front. Cars got longer and shinier and three-toned, and who the hell was going to drive his floating juke box and casket of the heart's desire around to a broke-down blacksmith

[149]

shop? A Greek came to town with a yellow-headed wife who looked like the kind that used to come to town with the street carnival and would merchandise it to the boys back of the tent when the show was over. People ate waffles at the Greek's restaurant.

Celia Hornby Harrick had, as a matter of fact, kept her shape pretty well, but her step slowed down some. The boy Jasper damned near had to duck for the door lintel, and did shore-God not look like he was suffering from consumption. He was clever with his hands but didn't seem to settle down. He went to Korea, and got him a ribbon, but not as good as his old man's. They said he was a chip off the old block. They said he might never make a living but he shore-God made life worth living for some of the opposite sex. A chip off the old block. Well, let him be, by God! He was a Harrick. His daddy was Old Jack. Recollect Old Jack?

Even Monty was stringing out, after a slow start.

Then the anvil didn't ring any more. The wheel chair creaked, even if the weight in it wasn't two twenty. Celia Hornby Harrick set the glass of iced tea on the little table, and laid her cheek against the grizzled head, and Old Jack Harrick wished she were dead, dead so he could love her, and not hate her as he did when he thought of her lying alone in her bed on a June night with moon coming in the window, and staring up at the ceiling to the dark above the moon ray and fighting off the wish for a man there. He hated her as he thought of her struggling against the need for a man-shape, simply a man-shape in the dark, not him, not Jack Harrick, just a nameless, faceless shape like a cloud coming over to darken the moonlight. If she let that nameless, faceless shape come into her mind, he knew he would be dead, and he knew she knew he would be dead.

He hated her because, in his mind, she struggled against the shape. Let it come. Let Jack Harrick die.

"John T.," she was saying, leaning over the wheel chair, and laid her cheek against his hair. "Darling John T.," she said, and he wished she were dead and six feet under so he could love her. So he could be the man in the house, even as he was dying. His hands clenched the wheel chair as hard as he could. He knew that she could see his right hand, and that she thought it was the pain. He knew, without looking, that she was going to push the little pill bottle closer, and say nothing, and go out so he would not have the shame of taking a pill in front of her.

But he was not going to take any pill.

"Dear John T.," she whispered, and roughed up his hair, ever so lightly, with her hand, the way you rough up a dog's head or a kid's, and went soft-footed out of the room, hoping he would take the pill he would not take.

He wanted her to be dead, for she had roughed up his hair that way, the way she had done in the dogwood-dark on the mountain when he had been on his knees before her, and he thought, with a burst of elation, that if then, that instant, long back on the mountain, he had turned and seized her, not falling on his knees, and ripped her, and ripped out of her what he wanted, and flung her aside on the grass and run on over the mountain, his feet scarcely touching the rocks as he ran under the dark, barely star-teased sky, then nothing would ever have happened like this. All would be different, he would not be dying in a wheel chair. He would have run on forever, over the mountain, under the dark sky.

Then the elation was gone. The tears came into his eyes, for he was ashamed of himself, and he truly loved Celia Hornby Harrick. He thought maybe he was going crazy, the way his mind ran off in all directions.

Then, in the cold distance, he thought how he had never really taken it away from anybody, just ripped it off 'em. He had seen it done, in the AEF, long back. Many a girl he had walked out in places so woods-dark and private and quiet you could have heard a goat cough two pistol shots down the mountain, and with him as strong as he had been in his days and time of strength a girl would have had about as much chance

[151]

with him as a moon-bemused crawfish on a sand bar with a hungry he-coon waiting in the willow-shade. But he never wanted any partaking that way. He had reckoned he was too proud. He never had to rip it off anybody. A little squeally scuffle maybe, but just in friend-fun, everybody knowing how it would come out and not even a thumb mark to show.

Then he thought he would never know how it was that way.

"Am I going crazy?" he demanded inside.

He heard somebody in the hall. Then somebody knocked. He could hear their breath.

Celia Hornby Harrick stood in the bare hall outside the door which she had just closed and wondered if he had taken the pill. She wondered how bad it would have to get before he would take a pill. Everybody had a cracking point, she reckoned. But she did not want to be around when Jack Harrick reached his. Some people knew they had a cracking point and they lived their whole lives knowing it and waiting for it; she supposed that was one way to live. But it was not Jack Harrick's way, and Jack Harrick was what she loved.

She leaned her forehead against the wall, where the wallpaper was faded and the canvas sustaining it hung loose off the wood wall to which it was tacked—the wallpaper put on for her, just after she had married Jack Harrick—and knew that his not knowing he had a cracking point was what had made her marry Jack Harrick. It had made her put her hand on his head in the dogwood-dark and rough his thick hair up, like roughing up the head of a dog or kid that leans against you. If somebody does not know that he has a cracking point, and you are the person who finds out he does not know that, then you have got to be the person who is on hand to hold his hand when he finds out. Somebody has to do that. If you do not want to do certain things you should not find out certain things.

She had married him for that strength-which-is-weakness, and

[152]

now, as a consequence, in that dim hall where the heat of summer had not yet begun to penetrate, she leaned her head against
the wallpaper put up there to make things worthy of her Haviland china and sterling silver, put up in loving tenderness by the
very hands of the man who had led her down this hall to put her
upon a bed and legally, respectably, and with consideration de-
flower her; and now, with her head against the wall, she prayed.
She prayed that her weakness might become enough of that
weakness-which-is-strength to permit her to hold Jack Harrick's
hand when the time came. She did not think she could stand to
be there when Jack Harrick found Jack Harrick had a cracking
point. But somebody had to be there. So she prayed: "Dear God,
I can't stand it, but when the time comes I want to hold his
hand."

She felt better, and lifted her head. As she moved down the
hall to the kitchen, she was whispering, not as a prayer now but
in some other way, the words: "I want to hold his hand." She was
aware of a strangeness in those words said not as prayer but as
if she were sleep-walking and sleep-talking, and then was aware
that the strangeness was shot through with some excitement like
guilt.

By this time she had reached the kitchen, the old part of the
house where the walls were chinked log. She stood in the middle
of the floor and experienced a nameless yearning. She was sick
with yearning, as she whispered again: "I want to hold his hand."

The yearning was so strong she knew it must be guilty.

She looked around the kitchen to find some extenuation in that
scene of her common life. There was the electric stove, still
good, which he had bought her when TVA came in, to replace
the wood range of his mother. There were the chinked logs
which she hadn't let him cover. There was the big old stone fireplace, with the cooking crane and pot, which she had made him
knock the boards off, saying to him: "No—no, John T.—whatever
made you want to cover that beautiful old fireplace? Why, it's
just like a magazine, John T.!" And he had grumbled in man-

heartiness, out of some duty to something, then grinned, and pinched her bottom, and knocked the boards off.

Later he had bought an old-timey bear-grease lamp somewhere, and cleaned it and stuck it on the stone chimney for her, to make it more like a magazine, he said, if you had to look like a durn-fool magazine. She had kissed him for thanks, and he had chased her three times around the kitchen table, like when they were first married, but she was nimble and got away. She had always been nimble-footed. And two twenty is wide on the turns.

She looked now at that grease lamp stuck in the stone, and it was suddenly as though somebody had hit her back of the knees with the heavy end, and narrow edge, of a pick handle. They just gave down, with no warning. But she managed to get hold of a chair back, and sit down before the tears came.

Then, with a start, she was aware of the tall shadow, black against the afternoon light, standing outside the open kitchen door, beyond the hooked screen. Even as the chill of surprise still tingled her nerves, she recognized the outline of the shape, and in the recognition, her shock turned into a guilty wonderment as to how long he might have been there, to see her, to hear her.

"I just got here," Brother Sumpter said, as though he read her mind, or her face. But she had decided already, putting away her unacknowledged apprehension, that Brother Sumpter, who tried as hard as any man she had ever known to walk as Christ would have him walk, was not going to hang around kitchen doors, spying on folks who suffered there in the afternoon shadow inside. She got up from her chair, trusting her knees now, but not yet, somehow, her tongue.

"I didn't want to knock up front," Brother Sumpter said. "I was afraid somebody might be asleep."

"He slept pretty well last night," she said, unlatching the screen door.

"I thought you might be getting a little rest, too," he said.

[154]

"I'm making out all right," she said, and by way of thanks gave a sort of smile. At least, she tried to and hoped she had.

He had entered the kitchen, and stood there holding in his hand his old Panama hat, planter type. He had on a black alpaca coat now, over the white shirt and white elastic suspenders, and a black tie. If you went to visit the sick, grief-bowed, or afflicted, no matter how hot it was, you wore a coat and tie. "What kind of day's he having?" he asked.

"Not to brag on, it looks like," she said.

Brother Sumpter almost imperceptibly shook his head, and made the almost inaudible little clicking, tut-tuting sound of fatalistic regret.

"He won't take his pills," she said, "I don't think."

"The doctor told him, didn't he?"

"Yes," she said scornfully, "that doctor! He told him." Then added, with a crazy little flicker of pridefulness: "And a lot of folks have tried telling John T. Harrick things!"

"Yes," said Brother Sumpter, who had been Ole Mac, and who had once tried to tell Jack Harrick something.

"That doctor, he might try putting a gun on John T. to make him take 'em," she said, "and maybe John T. would rise right out of that wheel chair, sick as he is, and take that gun away from him. It wouldn't surprise me to see him hit him on the head with that gun. You know John T."

"Yes," Brother Sumpter said.

"I can't make him eat right, either," she said. "Look how his weight's gone down, a big man like him."

"Yes," Brother Sumpter said, "he's lost weight all right."

"Only one thing I don't have to struggle to get down him."

"What's that?"

"You wouldn't guess, John T. not ordinarily being a fancy eater."

"I wouldn't guess," Brother Sumpter said.

"Waffles," she said, with a fleeting, deprecatory smile, apolo-

[155]

gizing for John T. "But ever since that Greek fellow came to town he has liked waffles. Looks like he ate 'em the first time by a sort of accident, when I was in Tracy City when my aunt died, and he ate at the Greek's once for supper. Looks like he got a taste for them. After I came home he said he had a treat for me, and after church one Sunday night he took me down to the Greek's for a surprise and we ate waffles. It is not much of a treat to me to eat waffles, we had them at home when I was little. My mother had a waffle iron like a chafing dish thing, with a lamp under, and she would make them for Sunday-morning breakfast, if we had company. But somehow I never got a taste for them. But I wasn't going to tell John T., when he had thought up a surprise. I told a white lie, and it got so he took me many a Sunday night, after church, to eat waffles. He said a good sermon built a man's appetite."

"He always had a good appetite," Brother Sumpter said.

"I can't get anything down him except waffles," she said, "and not too much of them. Not the kind I can make. So I went to the Greek and—"

"He is not a bad man, the Greek," Brother Sumpter said.

"He and John T. got on," she said. "They would jolly one another some, and long back they would hand-wrestle on the counter, both of them being so strong. The truck drivers started to make bets then, and John T. said he wasn't going to strive and strain just so some damn fool could lose his money and peril to perdition his immortal soul to boot, but he would hand-wrestle anybody that took offense, and break his wrist off. He said it laughing, but one driver did not laugh and said he would break his wrist if he wasn't an old man. John T. laughed and said he was old but still eating, and said come on, son. John T. bent his wrist back, but not to hurt him, and won, and they all laughed that fellow out of the diner. John T. and the Greek, they—"

"He comes some to church, now," Brother Sumpter said. "It was funny, the first time, seeing somebody that dark-com-

[156]

plected come into church. He has not been baptized, but he is a good man. I reckon he got to coming to seek strength in trouble, his wife sick so long and—"

"Oh, I can't make him eat," she broke in. Then she sat down in the chair, and pulled herself together. "I went to the Greek, and told him about the waffles. He asked what kind of iron I had. I had got an electric iron at the hardware, but Mr. Papdou—the Greek, he sort of laughed and said it was no good. I was near crying, it looked like all of a sudden—you know, no money coming in and sickness, not just the amount I paid for it, but the feeling. I didn't want to show how I felt, not before him, a Greek and all."

"He is a good man," Brother Sumpter said.

"Maybe he guessed how I felt," she said. "He said to me, 'Mrs. Harrick, I will come to your house and bring you a decent iron that I don't need and show you what I know and we will make the best batch of waffles Old Jack ever tasted and after he gets them down him, me and him will go a brisk round of hand-wrestling. Now, how is that, Mrs. Harrick?'"

"Baptized or not," Brother Sumpter said, "he is a good man."

"I almost cried," she said, "right on the spot. Him doing that, and a Greek, and all. He's coming this afternoon, to show me."

"God bless him," Brother Sumpter said.

"If he'd only eat—John T., I mean. If he'd keep up his strength."

She stopped, then suddenly rose from the chair. "But the pills," she cried out. "He won't take the pills. If he keeps up his strength, it's just strength to suffer. If he won't take the pills. Oh, he won't ever take not even one," she cried. "I see the sweat coming down his temples and his hand gripping in secret. I tried for a time to make him take them. But I learned better."

After a long pause, Brother Sumpter said: "What did he do?"

"Do?" she echoed. Then said: "He didn't do anything. John T. doesn't have to do anything sometimes. He just looked. He looked at me like I had made something else, and worse, hap-

[157]

pen inside him. He looked at me like because of it he hated me."

"He loves you," Brother Sumpter said, from his height, and distance. "He has to love you, for you are a good Christian woman and a good and loving wife to him, who loves him in Christ."

"I try to be a Christian," she said forlornly, feeling even more what she had felt as he spoke from his distance, that she was dwindling away to nothing, "and I love him, but—"

He waited there, his eyes coming to focus on her.

"I love him," she said desolately, her hands making a small gesture of appeal, to make him understand something.

"You've got to hold on," he said.

"Oh, I want to hold his hand!" she cried out irrelevantly.

He studied her, her arms held out from the elbows to him, the palms cupped upward in timid supplication. "Sister Celia," he said. "It is not easy. It is harder for you because it is harder for Jack Harrick. It is harder for some than others. Jack Harrick is a Christian man, but he had to come a long hard way to live in Christ. That is his glory, we got to remember, and the glory of Christ. It is harder for a man like Jack Harrick to die than some, and it is harder for him to die in Christ. But he will have his glory. We have got to—"

"Oh, I want to hold his hand," she cried out in the smallest voice, supplicating against whatever was being said, and did not know what was happening to her, in the middle of a June afternoon, there in her own kitchen, with the old-timey fireplace and pot crane and grease lamp, like a magazine. But she didn't fall down, even if for a second she had felt she might.

"Do you want to pray?" Brother Sumpter asked her. "Before I go in to see him? We can pray together."

Things seemed back in place now. The room was steady. This would not be the first time she had knelt with her pastor in prayer, for herself and for John T. The first time had been long ago, when John T. had run off to Chattanooga, and they didn't know where he was. The last time was just day before yesterday, in the front parlor, after Brother Sumpter had come out from John T.'s room.

But now she heard herself saying: "No." Saying: "No thanks," politely as though somebody had offered her a second helping of chicken, with a politeness that sounded simpering and awful in her own ears this minute, but was the only way she could say it, until, all at once, she burst out: "Oh, I can't—not right now! Oh, please don't make me!"

She was caught in the infantile terror of her refusal, as though the ceiling might split open to let her punishment come through from On High. And when she saw Brother Sumpter lift up his hand, she had the crazy notion he, in the will of God, was going to strike her. He didn't, of course, and his face looking down at her was wearing, as she now saw, a kind of yearning pity, the usual hardness of his face, the far-offness, breaking like ice on water in the first spring sun.

Then he closed his eyes, the folds of flesh on each side of his mouth settled into the old severe pattern, and the lifted hand stretched out over her head, not quite touching her. "Father in Heaven," his voice said, "bless this woman in her pain and striving, who is Thy daughter in Christ. Amen."

She wanted to say thank you, as he turned away and went down the familiar hall to John T.'s room. But she knew that that would sound too silly, even sillier than when she had said it before.

She didn't know what she could have said, really, she decided when, after she had heard the door of John T.'s room closed with that deferential caution due to doors concealing the sick or the dead, she went up to her own room and lay down. For a moment she had been thankful, and had felt safer, standing there in the kitchen under the bony hand, which had once been strong.

But she wasn't thankful now. She was, rather, resentful, as though Brother Sumpter had practiced a fraud upon her, resentful as a person is who goes to a doctor and does not get a cure. Then that resentment slipped over into another kind of resentment.

Naturally, over the years, they had been together a lot. Often she had sat with them. She had not thought much of it, had not felt cut off by the fact they were old friends—and old enough to be her father. But since John T.'s sickness, Brother Sumpter had been over almost every day, and it had got so she couldn't bear to be with them together more than a minute.

It wasn't that she was, exactly, jealous, she decided, as she lay down on her bed in the room she now occupied by herself, to get a little rest before the Greek came. She looked over at the alarm clock. She would have a little time, for it was now half-past two, and he had said he wouldn't come till three, in the afternoon slowdown.

It wasn't jealousy, it was just that he was going to die. He had lived forty-five years before she had ever laid eyes on him. It was all so far back she had forgotten, or might as well have forgotten, how she, just a young girl then, did come to lay eyes on him—on a bright winter afternoon, snow on the street, the Ford pickup slithering in the snow despite chains, a tall man standing in the back of the truck, riding the sway like a sailor on a tossing deck, hatless, wearing a red-plaid mackinaw and cowhide boots, waving a rifle easy as a bookkeeper waves a lead pencil, yelling like a kid to some crony, yelling: "Yeah, got two!" then tossing the rifle down, on a tarpaulin-covered heap in the truck, and leaning over to come up with a fresh bearskin, holding the big head high above his own head, the bear-jaw open in a last white-tusk-studded rage, the eyes staring, fixed and unrelenting under the blood-streaked spot where the 30.30 had gone in, the big hide, fur-side and blood-side, trailing down half over the red mackinaw, and the man's face, with a blood-streak now on it from the hide, grinning with teeth as white as the bear's.

She was twenty then, just that fall come up from the valley, leaving her mother with the genteel chafing dish and Haviland china and the father with his wax-colored hands and consumptive cough and county-seat law practice and tidy bank account, leaving normal and, she suddenly knew, the silly girls with their silly engagements and the pimply boys, to any number of whom she could have been engaged, too, if she hadn't been honest enough with herself to know that if their hands ever got into her dress she would just be stiff as a board. But she hadn't been willing to fake things up, and it had been on a winter afternoon, as she stood beside one of the other teachers in whose house she had a room and kitchenette, an older woman, a native of John-town, daughter of a physician now deceased, named Abernathy, and heard the woman sniff.

"Who's that?" she asked the woman.

"Just another hillbilly that thinks he is Daniel Boone," the woman said, and curled her lip in the expression which was the terror of the Latin class.

"He killed the bear," Celia Hornby said, uttering the super-fluous words half as though talking to herself. She had never seen a bear, except in a zoo, at the Glendale Park in Nashville, long back.

"He'll probably claim he choked it to death," the woman said. "Without gloves on."

"Did he?" the girl asked. "Did he choke one—not this one—but did he ever choke one to death?"

"No," the woman said, with bitterness, staring unforgivingly at the unforgiving bear-jaws and the blood-streaked face of the man peeking from around the hide, "he stood a long distance away, a perfectly safe distance mind you, and murdered the defenseless animal with a rifle. But now that hillbilly stands up there yelling like an idiot, and thinks he's a hero, and by tomorrow night some other fool hillbilly will be telling how Jack Harrick strangled the creature with his hands. Oh, yes," she said, with a last climactic flourish of the bitterness, "that is Jack Harrick, the hero of all the hillbillies! The tales they tell about him—just so they themselves can feel big."

[161]

The girl found herself looking at the woman, at the bitter gaze now following mercilessly, and unconsciously, the swaying idiot on the retreating pickup, and found herself desperately saying inside herself, as she stared at the woman's face: *I don't want to be like that, like Miss Abernathy, oh, God, don't let me be like that!*

She wasn't prepared to say exactly what "that" was that she did not, suddenly, want to be like, but no prayer she had ever uttered—and she was a sincerely religious girl—had been so urgent. Then, she turned her eyes after the truck, which was just then slithering around a corner, and in that last glimpse it seemed almost as though her prayer had been answered. As she and Miss Abernathy moved on down the street, she felt warm and soft inside. She felt calmly happy, and the sun fell bright over everything, even the churned-up, mud-streaked snow of the street of Johntown.

With a start, she heard the woman saying, not in bitterness now, but in some sad, fatalistic explanation as it were: "He's a blacksmith."

For a moment Celia Hornby didn't quite connect the remark with the man on the pickup truck. It didn't seem, somehow, that that man had ever had to earn any living, in any way, just flashing through the world, holding up a bloody bearskin, and yelling in good humor and joy.

"Blacksmith?" she echoed, pulling herself back to things like earning livings, and how you did it.

"Yes," the woman said, "a blacksmith!" Then, as though apologizing for some edge that had been now added to the word, she said: "Oh, I don't mean it's not a decent, honorable livelihood. If it's all you can do. It's just—"

She stopped suddenly, there on the slushy pavement, like a person who stops on the brink.

Celia Hornby looked at her: "The tales, you said. You said they tell tales about him."

The woman leaped at the idea. "Yes," she exclaimed, "yes—

that's it. It's not just being a blacksmith. It's the things he does—the tales."

"You said he never really strangled a bear," the girl said, honestly puzzled.

"Oh, don't be a ninny!" the woman said in ferocious contempt, hidden anger flashing between the words, like the hot molten inwardness showing when the crust cracks on the slow-moving lava field. Then seeing the girl's shocked, hurt face, she controlled herself, tried to patch things up. "You are young," she said, "but you know. It's the things he does."

"I suppose he drinks," musingly said Celia Hornby, in whose father's house that word had seemed the synonym for all unnamable depravities.

"Drinks!" Miss Abernathy snorted, the ferocity and contempt glinting out anew. "You could float *Old Ironsides* in the amount of illegal and poisonous moonshine whisky that man has drunk. Drink! Oh, the drinking and brawling. But—"

She stopped, and scanned the girl's face, till the face flushed with the guilt of unacknowledged speculations stirring deep down. Then, as though satisfied with what she saw on the face, she leaned closer, almost whispering, darkening the bright winter sunshine of the street to a sudden preternatural twilight full of a close, musky odor, and said: "You know what! He is shameless. It is the shameless—it is the shameful things he does to—to women."

Well, he was never to do anything to Celia Hornby that she thought was shameful. Except, of course, the first thing.

It was that time in the post office, the first time he had ever spoken to her. She supposed it wasn't more his fault than hers, if it was anybody's and not just a plain accident. She had been in a hurry to get her mail one morning, one Sunday morning. With her key in her hand, she had made a little dive toward the lock of her box at the post office, just as a man, stooping with back toward her to open a box next to hers, moved a little bit. She bumped him. He swung around, straightening up, swinging

[163]

away on the ball of his right foot, with a lightness that, even then in her confusion, she was aware of as incongruous to his size. "Oh," she cried out, "oh, I'm so sorry!"

Then she saw that, despite blue serge and white shirt, and no bearskin, the man was the man of the pickup truck, and he was looking right at her.

"Oh, I'm sorry," she repeated, more flustered.

"Well, lady," he said, and his bright blue glance was flickering on her, "you just be sorry to your little heart's content. But"—and the bright glance was flickering all over her—"I'm not. And don't aim to be."

She wasn't wearing any low-neck dress, even if spring had just begun to come on, but his eyes, she knew, were looking right there just as though she did have on one. And then, as she recognized that fact, it was as shameful as though right there in broad daylight he had snapped off a button and run his hand in. He was grinning at her, just as though he had, and didn't intend to take it out quick. But that wasn't the shameful thing. The shameful thing was that, even that second in the midst of being ashamed, she was happy there was something there worth his trouble to be putting his hand on. She felt full—and in a funny way, almost sleepy.

It was that feeling that made her have to say: "What—I beg your pardon?" when he said something she hadn't heard a word of.

"I said," he said, "you look like you're going to church. All dressed up."

She nodded.

"Well," he said, "would it discombobulate or embarrass you if I walked you as far as the door?"

If he had been a young man, near her own age, looking down at her like that, where he had looked, and then asking her to walk to church, she might very well have refused him curtly, as fresh. But this man was, she knew, as old as her father, and she was saying that deep down in herself: *Why, he's old as my father,* and mixed with that, too, was a sudden, quickly blacked-out vision of her father's waxy hand reaching for the bottle of cough medicine, or some other God-damned thing.

Some other God-damned thing—yes, those words had actually been in her, as part of the vision, and it was the awareness of their sinful blasphemy, words she had never in her life uttered, that made her black it out.

But no, maybe it was something else, for she had, in the same flash, done something worse, not only taking the name of the Lord God in vain, but knocking twin dents in the Decalogue at the same time. For in that instant, she had been far from honoring her father. She had hated him, as cleanly as a sizzling, ammoniac flash of lightning in the dark. She hated him, simply, because he was the way he, so awfully and without being able to help himself, was. He had never ridden on a slithering truck, yelling like an idiot as he held up a bloody bear-head.

The vision was over in a flash, like the lightning flash leaving only the tingling ammoniac smell as the dark closed again in her inner night. But it had unsettled her so that she wasn't able to answer until he spoke again: "Little lady, how about it. I'll just walk you to the door."

Then he laughed: "You know, they mightn't let me in the door. Even if Ole Mac—he's the preacher—used to be a side-kick of mine. Before he took scairt of weather signs and ran for cover. Come on—let me walk you to the door."

"Yes," she said.

His being an older man, even if he didn't exactly look it, that made it all right. Or made it so much worse that it was hopeless anyway, or something.

The next two or three times they met on the street, he spoke politely and passed on. Certainly that was all she herself intended to do, but when it was what he did, she was a little nettled, then ashamed of herself. Then she realized that each of those times he had been wearing his work clothes; and she explained to herself that he had had the delicacy not to embarrass a lady by stopping to speak with her under those circumstances.

The next time she met him, he was in shirt sleeves—the spring had begun to show real signs—but he had on dark trousers with a crease, and the shirt was white. It was after supper, with a little light in the sky still toward seven, and she had walked downtown to the post office, to mail a letter, this time to one of those silly engaged girls from normal. He was lounging down the street in his clean shirt sleeves—what he put on, she reckoned—after work. That thought was prim, decent, and comforting.

He stopped, and bowed. He didn't have any hat on to take off, but she saw that his thick, somewhat unruly black hair had been thoroughly wetted and brushed ferociously into submission. "Good evening," he said, and added in a sly way, as though it were some joke he had on her: "—Miss Hornby." No names had passed between them on the previous encounters, not even on the walk to the door of the Baptist Church.

"Good evening," she now said, and lifting her head with a little air of defiance—defiance of what, she didn't quite know—added: "Mr. Harrick."

She was wearing a low-necked dress, her first of the season, in honor of the mild evening, with a blue cashmere cardigan around her shoulders, blue in honor of her eyes. He looked into her eyes, but only for a second, and not at all down at the low neck of the dress, at the place where he had made her feel shameful, and shamefully happy, in the post office. Now, in fact, he looked off down the street, as he began to speak. "If you've got a minute, Miss Hornby," he began.

She said she did, but looked, not too secretly, at her watch.

"That moving picture, *The Big Parade*," he said, "the one everybody is so het up about. It is coming to Knoxville again." He stopped; then, with a tone of apology proceeded. "It's not I'm one for moving pictures," he said, "and I missed it then, four

[166]

years ago when it came. But I had the notion—" And he stopped again, then picked up: "But it's about the war. About the AEF, and over there in France. Well—well, I was sort of—over there, and—"

Yes, she knew he had been there, though she didn't say so, letting him suffer it out. She knew he had been there and had the Congressional Medal to prove it. She knew the Governor of the state had met him at the train when he got to Nashville on the way home.

"You know, a fellow likes to see some place he's been, and how it was. I thought I'd go, and—" He hesitated, then plunged on. "Mr. and Mrs. Blunden, and Mrs. Blunden's mother, she's an old lady"—emphasizing the word *old*—"and it's in their car"—emphasizing the word *their*—"and I sort of had the notion, it being a fine picture and sort of educational, they say—"

He stopped dead. He brought his eyes back to her, and looked at her face, with a saddening lack of expectation.

Oh, the big fake! she was thinking, with all his fake hemming and hawing and stammering. Did he think she didn't see through him? Did he take her for a fool? What kind of fool girls were deceived by him and led off into the dark where he seized them and practiced some shameful thing on them that made them cry out. Well, she'd show him!

But she heard herself saying, as calm as the evening sky: "Why, Mr. Harrick, I'd love to see it."

He was hanging on to that sad unexpectant expression on his face as long as possible, she was sure of that, just to let her see the innocent joy slowly dawn there. "Would you, really?" he was saying. "Would you, Miss Hornby?"

"Of course, I would," she said briskly, eying him as though he were in the third grade. "For I didn't see it either; when it first came out, you see, my mother thought I was too young." Then she added, with even more cheerful malice: "I'd love to go if old Mrs. Blunden's old, old mother is really going. And if asking me

[167]

is what you had in mind with all that hemming and hawing."

"Lady," he said, grinning, "that was what had crossed my mind."

"Don't think I don't see through you," she said, in her newly acquired schoolroom air of having caught out the culprit who threw the spitball.

"Lady," he said, soberly, "I promise you one thing. I promise you I don't see through you."

She was so startled, she couldn't reply.

"Lady," he said, and as he stared down into her face she saw his head outlined against the pink-paling sky of evening, "I bet if I threw a rock down your well, I'd be listening down in the dark a long time before it hit water."

The Latin teacher, Miss Abernathy, was waiting up for her when she got in from Knoxville, long after midnight. She had not told Miss Abernathy where, or with whom, she was going, but Miss Abernathy, she was sure, had her own sources of information and had been on the wire before the sound of the strange car had died away from her front gate. "You've been to Knoxville," Miss Abernathy announced.

"Yes," the girl said, and peeled off her black gloves.

"You have been to that moving picture that glorifies lust and violence."

"They were in love," the girl said. "That was all. And I don't guess there was any more fighting and all than in the *Birth of a Nation,* and you said you liked that."

"That was different," Miss Abernathy said.

"This is supposed to be educational, too," the girl said. "It is historical, in its way. I found it educational."

"Presumably," Miss Abernathy said, and curled her lip.

"I went to the movie with Mr. Harrick," the girl announced sweetly, stealing what she knew was the thunder Miss Abernathy held in reserve, and before Miss Abernathy could reply, added, "and with Mr. and Mrs. Blunden, who are quite respectable, and with Mrs. Blunden's old, old mother."

She was proud of that last touch. She didn't know what had got into her, but she felt like riding it out.

Miss Abernathy got up to her scantling-thin height. "You know my views," she said. "You have rented a room in my house, and as long as you remain under this roof I expect conduct that will not reflect discredit on this house or the name of my father who built it."

"Miss Abernathy," the girl said, "I know that your father was a very respectable physician."

"He was indeed," Miss Abernathy said.

"Well, mine is a very able lawyer, and has won cases in front of the Supreme Court of this state. He knows all about the laws of libel, and if anything should be insinuated about his daughter which would not stand up in court, he would make it cost very, very dear."

"Well, you'd never get another job teaching," Miss Abernathy said, leaning viperously. "Not at Johntown, or anywhere else!"

"But you see," Celia Hornby said, gay and surprised at what she was going to say, "I'm not going to teach any more. I'm going to get married!"

"To—to that—"

"Yes, of course," she said. "To that blacksmith! Only he hasn't proposed. He doesn't even know it yet, but he will."

"Ah," Miss Abernathy breathed, eyes glittering, "so you're—"

The girl shook her head, laughing. She had never had so much fun even if she didn't know where it might end, like a roller coaster going too fast. "No," she said, and had to stop for the giggles, "it's not that. You know, from what I hear, that might not be the best way with Mr. Harrick. Besides, I really am a virgin. I haven't been loved up much even, not even after dances in the back of a car. I never even let a hand get between my legs, the way some nice girls do—yes, they do, they've told me—"

[169]

"Hush, hush!" Miss Abernathy cried out. "I won't hear this in this house!"

But she did, for Celia Hornby was whirling right on, her head spinning like stars, in the run-away roller coaster, saying: "I really am a virgin—just like you are—or aren't you, Miss Abernathy?"

"Hush, hush!" Miss Abernathy implored, but it was no use, for Celia Hornby hadn't really hesitated for an answer to her question, whirling on: "And when Mr. Harrick does to me whatever he does to stop me from being á virgin, I want—"

"Shameful—oh, it will be shameful!" Miss Abernathy cried out, wringing her hands, or seeming about to. "You're only a young girl, and you don't know Jack Harrick—what he will do—how shameful!"

"Yes, shameful, just like what your father did to your mother was shameful," the girl rebutted, thoroughly delighted with that flourish.

"But, oh—it wasn't like that!" Miss Abernathy cried, in her last despair, "not like Jack Harrick! Oh, you are vile!"

"Well, whatever he does," Celia Hornby said, "to make me stop being a virgin, I want to be perfectly comfortable. I don't want to be in the back seat of any old car. I want to be in a big comfortable bed, as big as the state of Kansas and dark as pitch, so I could just sink back forever and be comfortable and get the most out of whatever he is going to do. Wouldn't you want it that way, Miss Abernathy? Wouldn't you? And that's why I'm going to wait till Mr. Harrick takes me to a bed as big as the state of Kansas and dark as pitch, and—"

Her words trailed off. There really wasn't any use talking any more, for Miss Abernathy wasn't there. She had managed to go out, to totter out, propping herself from one chair to the table, from the table to another chair, from that chair to the doorjamb, thence into the dark hall. "Remember about libel suits!" Celia Hornby called gaily after her.

Celia Hornby went upstairs to her room. She was terribly excited, excited with herself, for being the way she was, the new

[170]

way she had never expected. It was like getting a present. She looked in the mirror at her still flushed cheeks and brightened eyes, and said; "Gosh," in a kind of awe. "Gosh, Celia Hornby," she repeated, peering more closely at the face in the mirror, and she was a little appalled, and afraid, too. And she was sorry, a little, about Miss Abernathy.

In a kind of muted way, carefully getting out of range of the mirror, she got undressed, and into her nightgown. She didn't want to brush her teeth, or comb her hair. She liked the faint sense of escape, rebellion, untidiness, frowsiness. But she came back to the mirror and looked at herself standing there in her nightgown. She wanted to lift up her nightgown and see her whole self, as she might be seen. But that didn't seem decent. She thought that it might, somehow, be really shameful.

So she got into bed, still in that strange muted way, which was really, she knew, just another kind of excitement. She lay in the dark, and thought that she didn't care what Mr. Harrick might do to her. She didn't care if he bit her till she bled. She wondered where he might bite her.

She was just about to drift off to sleep, wondering, when she remembered she had not said her prayers. She got up, and knelt by the bed and said them, as she always did, and was surprised, after she got back into bed, how her prayers and her wondering about Mr. Harrick was all part of the same nice warmness of things.

She thought of Mr. Harrick, fully dressed somehow, kneeling beside the bed with her. She would teach him to pray, to get on his knees and pray with her to God, and then she would lie in his arms all night. No, she revised that, he would be asleep and she would watch over him. Like praying for him.

She had watched over him, and prayed for him, a good many nights, she thought, as she lay on her bed, an aging woman now on a June afternoon, before it did any good. Before, that is, he ever got down on his knees beside her. He had cracked that much, John T. Harrick had, and she imagined now that he had never thought he could come to it. How sweet it had been, she thought, when he had been lifted, saved in Glory, from the water of Elk Creek, and she had laid her head on his sopping chest. Some longing stirred in her again for the moment when he would really crack and take the pill and she might hold his hand. And again the yearning was touched by some guilty excitement.

Now she thought of the two old men downstairs in the room where John T. sat with his cancer, and suddenly saw them, quite literally in time, as old. It wasn't that she was jealous of them, of some past they shared, but she was glad they were old. The older John T. was, the sooner he would come to the cracking time, and she could hold his hand. There would be none of those others to hold his hand— Who were they? What were their names? Had he walked with them in the dark? Had they just lain down on the dark grass for him, right in the dark, because they couldn't wait? Had they cried out?

She felt, for the first time, somehow deprived, cheated. She suddenly saw the face of Miss Abernathy, not the face of the old doddering fool living yet in the absurd little house that was paintless and falling apart now and still trying to be grand with its jimcrack scrollery and stained glass, but the face of Miss Abernathy that night after the trip to Knoxville to see the movie —what movie was it?—oh, yes—the face of Miss Abernathy contorting in desperation, uttering the words: *Shameful—oh, it will be shameful.* And now, at that recollection, with its dire prophecy, or promise, Celia Hornby Harrick, in a kind of grim unwittingness, pushed up the half-sleeve on her left arm and bit the flesh on the biceps.

She looked at the place where the two half-moons of tooth marks showed blue with blood about to burst through.

Suddenly she rose from the bed and stood in the middle of the floor, pulling her sleeve down as far as it would come to hide the place, rubbing the place, which really hurt now, or which she now knew really hurt. "Gosh," she said. "Gosh, that was stupid, to hurt myself. How stupid can you get?"

Then she wondered about anybody seeing the place. No, nobody would see it. There was no reason now for even John T. to see it.

She was still standing there, rubbing her arm, and thinking maybe she ought to put iodine on it, for the skin might be broken and they said human teeth are more poisonous than an animal's, for man is a carnivore, too, when she heard the knock at the front door, and glanced at the clock.

She knew it was the Greek.

Nick Pappy had eased the Cad right down Main Street, past the bank, not giving a damn, and proceeded at the same pace, which had been contemptuous and was now meditative, toward the shotgun bungalow he called home. He got out, passed the paling gate that was hanging off its hinges, climbed the board steps that creaked with his weight, entered the living room and saw Miss Whatever-the-Hell-Her-Name-Was wearing her white nurse uniform and sitting with her fat behind on the sofa propped with the tapestry harem-scene cushions, reading *True Confessions*.

He mumbled something, passed under her superior nod, and went into his wife's room and closed the door.

"She is sitting on her fat behind out there, reading a magazine," he said.

Giselle, propped on pillows, wearing a pink silk real imported French nightgown, looked up from *True Confessions,* looked right at him and didn't say anything. She glanced over at the TV that was going.

"She is sitting on her ass," he said. "At ten dollars a day."

"She can't work all the time," Giselle said.

"I can," Nick Pappy said.

"It's not my fault," Giselle said. "You got me like I am, so I

[173]

got to have a nurse, and you won't even get a trained nurse. You just got a practical nurse."

"I could get a girl or something just to wait on you," he said. "I am going to go broke."

"Suppose I had a hemorrhage," she said, "and you want to get a girl or something because it is cheaper."

"It is over a year and a half. The doctor says you are not going to have none now. I owe the bank four thousand dollars."

"You got me like I am. I think you are crazy, treating a girl the way you treated me."

"That Bingham just called me over to the bank today."

"Tell him I am sick. It is hot and I ought to have a air-conditioner set."

"I owe four thousand dollars."

"It is hot and I don't feel like talking about it."

"You could talk a lot better if you turned this God-damned thing off," Nick Pappy said, and stepped over to the TV, where a man in a striped blazer and a walking cane was singing about his love life, and turned it off.

"I want it on."

"I paid four hundred ninety-one dollars for it."

"Well, you ought to let me get the good out of it."

"I paid seventy-nine dollars and ninety cents for that nightgown you are wearing. I didn't have it in my pocket and had to go back and get it out of the cash register, when it came C.O.D. at the post office and you never told me you ordered it."

"A girl has got to have something. She has got to have something to live for."

"Listen," Nick Pappy said, "that bastard Bingham called me over to the bank."

"It is hot," she said.

"He wants to get an abortion."

"Christ," she said, after a second, and gave a quick, hacking laugh, "who knocked him up?"

[174]

Nick Pappy did not grin, even wanly. "It is not him knocked up," he said. "It is a girl. It is odds on win, and forget place or show, it is that girl in the bank."

She gave the quick, hacking laugh again. "The one used to hash for you?" she said.

He nodded.

"The one used to get on her back for you?"

When he heard those words, Nick Pappy felt, all of a sudden, weak and dizzy. Things got out of focus.

Now he stood, sick with despair at the way the world was. He was sick at the lie he would have to tell now. He wet his lips. "Somebody has been lying to you," he said.

"I didn't need anybody to tell me nothing," she said. "Them nights when you come in on tiptoe and patted the pillow and couldn't you get me a cool glass of milk or maybe give me a back rub with alcohol—yeah, I didn't need nobody to tell you had slipped some tramp the meat."

She stopped, and was staring at him. He could see the beads of perspiration on her temples. Then with a thin wailing sound, she burst out: "But not to me—but not to me."

He had to get a grip on things. He had to get a grip on himself. There was no telling what might happen. "Listen," he said, his voice going dry and grating.

Then as she looked up at that new tone, he asked: "You can do an abortion, can't you?"

She studied him a little, her lips twisting in some sad, mean irony. Then, after the silence, she demanded: "And now what made you think I could?"

Way off on the highway a truck was barreling down the mountain. You could hear the *boom-boom* of the Diesel backfire, soft and heavy, each explosion like a .45 fired in a shoe box of cotton batting. You could hear the catbird giving off a few trills in the hydrangea bush under the window, sweet as a canary, and then bursting into a squawk like a scalded tom cat. Nick Pappy wished the world were different. He wished he could kneel by the side of the bed and take her hand and say: *I have loved you forever.*

And he thought: *Forever.*

But *forever* was time, and somehow she hadn't belonged in time. He saw in his mind the way she had looked, long ago before she put on the blubber, when she had stood in the middle of the Indianapolis honky-tonk, her white nakedness wreathed in blue shifting veils of cigarette smoke, and how with her finger tips she had lifted her breasts, and had closed her eyes, and had jerked her head so that the pale hair snatched with every beat of the tom-tom. That had not belonged in Time. It was as though she had risen there, pure as foam, out of some timelessness like the sea. Being out of Time, she had had no past, glimmering like a dream, too beautiful to be real.

But she was real enough now—if she was that bloat of blubber on the bed. Well, anyway, something, whether it was the same thing or not, was on the bed in a $79.90 pink nightgown, and was real, and being real, was in Time, and being in Time, had a past and he bet knew how to do an abortion. In that knowledge, and in the knowledge that he had said what he did, some last something had been taken from him. He closed his eyes, hoping to see what? Some last vision of the glimmer of dream veiled in blue smoke?

"So you just worked it out I'm the kind would know," her voice was saying.

He opened his eyes.

"Well, I do," she said.

His mind went hard. Sure, she knew. "All right," he said. "All right. And you are going to do what I say. When I say."

She was looking at him in a kind of tired, dazed way, as though she didn't quite get it that he was there.

"You better," he said, "or you will be laying up in the poor house without no pink nightgown or TV."

[176]

He did not turn the TV back on. He walked past it to the door, his shoes creaking with his weight. As he laid his hand to the doorknob, he heard her voice.

"Listen here, Mr. Big," she was saying.

He turned.

"I know how to do lots of things I never told you about," she said. "And never told you how I learned 'em either."

He was staring at her, trying to make sense of what was real and what was not real. She gave her quick, hacking laugh. Then said: "And how does that make you feel, Mr. Big?"

He went out of the house, and did not know what he felt. He stood there in the blaze of sun—and in the blaze of reality, where Giselle Fontaine knew all those things, and where she would do that to Dorothy Cutlick and he hoped to God would not kill her, and where he had a note for near $4,000 at the bank, but would not have long, and he did not know what he felt. So he heaved himself into the yellow Cad and cut out across town, with a speed like flight, toward the Harrick house, out yonder under the cool cedars.

When the knock came at the front door—the knock of Nick Pappy—Brother Sumpter had already risen from his chair, about to go. He had done the things he could do. He had asked Jack Harrick how he was today, he had told how they were broadening the highway over toward Athens, he had told how Mr. Broadus had sold the hundred head of short horns he had brought in to feed for Chicago, he had read a chapter in the Bible, he had prayed. He had sat in his chair in the silence that, sometimes, in its sense of communion, had nourished his soul by the thought that, even through pain and sorrow, life drew to its glory.

But today that silence had not been one of communion. He had not even been able to think of the pain of the dying man.

[177]

He had been able to think of nothing but his own isolation in pain. Now he stood ready to go, but afraid to go, to face what he had to face.

The knock came at the front door, the feet passed down the hall toward the kitchen, silence settled again. Brother Sumpter turned toward Jack Harrick, and in a tight voice wrenched out of him, said: "I am in great distress."

Jack Harrick turned his heavy, grizzled head toward him, with an expression of incomprehension, or even resentment, that another's pain should intrude upon his world of pain, and stared at him.

"I am in such distress," Brother Sumpter said, "that I can look at you sitting there in your pain, and want to change places. I know you cannot appreciate my saying that, but it is true. I know that I sin against God in questioning His will, but it is true."

The face of Jack Harrick was staring up at him. He leaned toward it. "Pray for me," he besought. "If in your pain you can pray for me, I feel that God may hear."

He reached down and took one of Jack Harrick's hands, and clutched it saying: "Pray for me, Jack. Pray for me, Jack!"

Jack Harrick, feeling a sad stirring in his heart, almost sweet, was about to say yes, he would pray, when there came the sound in the hall. Somebody was running, or trying to run but stumbling, down the hall. Somebody was hanging on the doorknob a second, getting strength to push it open. You could hear their breath.

V

When Isaac Sumpter got his father's telephone call saying for
him to hurry over to the Harrick house, he said he would, and
went out. He saw that his father hadn't taken the car, the broken-
down Studebaker—walking to save gas money, he reckoned—
and it was just as well that he, Isaac, now had the car. For he
wasn't going to run, in that heat, he said to himself, even if, as he
supposed, that old burst bellows of a windbag of a blacksmith
was dying, or dead.

He didn't feel any particular guilt in not being sorry about
what had happened, whatever it was. He found himself, instead,
being sorry that whatever the hell it was it might very well hold
Jasper up for a time from their cave business. He took a relish, as
he drove the half-mile to the Harrick house, just outside of the
town, in his virtue of candor. He wanted to get out of Johntown.
He wanted to get out of the damned state of Tennessee. He

wanted to get out and never come back, and yesterday would not be too soon to leave. But he had to have the money. If, he thought bitterly, there was any money in that hole.

Isaac Sumpter drove up the lane to the Harrick house, a one-story structure that, over the years, had sprawled out farther and farther from the original two-room cabin of hickory and walnut logs. The growth along the lane gave him a bit of coolness, and the house itself, set on rich grass and flanked by the great cedars that must have been big when the first Harrick ax blade rang in the cove there, looked deep and cool. *Damn it,* he thought, *I hope they've got some ice water.* He then thought of beer, ice-cold beer, but a hell of a chance there was of any beer there, now that that Old Harrick, who, they said, had drunk all the moonshine off Skunk Tail Mountain, had long back turned into such a teetotaling Christer. *Yes, Old Jack Harrick,* he thought, *stuffed bull-moose head number one in the Come-to-Jesus Trophy Room of the Reverend MacCarland Sumpter.*

He turned off the lane into the yard; the drive was gravel, marked off on each side, in country ostentation, by old truck tires half buried in the ground and the loop above ground pridefully painted with aluminum paint.

He noticed two cars out in the yard, on the grass, an old but carefully tended Chevrolet, the Harrick car he guessed, and the big yellow Cadillac convertible. *Pill-pushing must be picking up in Johntown,* he thought, then thought the car might belong to some specialist from Nashville.

He started up the steps to the porch, then noticed that a kind of board ramp had been laid there. *For a wheel chair,* he thought, *yeah, for a wheel chair,* and despite the heat, with a sudden alacrity, an exultation that he was not in a wheel chair and would never, never be in one, he bounded up the steps. The screen door, he noticed, was open, just the way somebody had flung it back getting into that house in a hurry. He closed the door carefully after him, and took a step into the dark hall, dark now after the blaze of sunlight. Then he saw that patch of white down the hall

[180]

that was, as his vision got adjusted, the white shirt and white apron on that Greek standing there staring into an open door, but what the hell would he be way back up here in the cedars for, wearing a white apron in the middle of this accursed hell's-hinges of an afternoon and holding an iron mixing spoon, to boot? Well, the Greek accounted for the yellow Cadillac, anyway. But then, where the hell was the doctor?

He approached the Greek. The Greek peered at him a moment, trying, no doubt, to identify him against the light; then recognized him, and nodded with mournful significance into the room, as though speech would violate the decencies of the occasion, whatever the hell the occasion was. Isaac peered around the jamb of the door.

Old Jack Harrick was not dead, and gave no sign of immediate demise. He sat in his wheel chair—the bright chromium of the slick modern contraption striking Isaac Sumpter as incongruous in that room—with Brother Sumpter standing just beyond, leaning a little, Mrs. Harrick bent over, too, but closer, and that girl with the bouncing bubbies, whom he had seen running in front of his house, now flung down against the knees of Old Harrick, as though she had managed that far before taking her last tumble, with the bubbies pressed against Old Harrick's right knee—and wasn't that a waste of good material?—and her face lifted as she babbled something between the breaths that it looked like she still had to fight a little to get. She had one of Old Harrick's hands.

What she was managing to get out, between breaths, was, Isaac figured out, that Old Harrick had to do something, whatever it was she figured the old crock was capable of doing. She was saying: "Do something—do something—you've got to do something!" And jerking the hand.

But Old Harrick wasn't giving a sign. He simply stared out the window, gaze rigid and fixed, as though he had had a stroke, while Mrs. Harrick leaned over the girl, saying: "Honey—but, honey—he'll be here in a minute—he'll know, honey—we can't

[181]

do anything till we know—Brother Mac has called him, honey—"

Then, as Isaac, having sized things up, entered the room, Mrs. Harrick was saying: "And Monty—he'll know something—he'll—"

But with that, Mrs. Harrick suddenly jerked up straight, losing for a moment whatever grip she had had on herself, and looked wildly around and cried out: "Oh, Monty!—Where's Monty?—Oh, Monty, why don't you come?"

She saw Isaac.

She ran toward him, past the wheel chair and the girl, almost stumbling over the girl. "It's Jasper," she said, gripping his arm, shaking him, "it's Jasper!"

Then, all at once, she had hold of herself again, took a deep breath, and said, almost calmly: "Jo-Lea and Monty, they were up on your property. They saw Jasper's boots. And his guitar. She says you and Jasper found a cave. She says you and Jasper started exploring. She thinks Jasper is lost in the cave."

She stopped, abruptly, and her eyes fixed on his face with their question. As his mind raced around, figuring things out, he told her. Yes, they had found a cave. They had broken in, and explored it. They had made a deal, and got Mr. Bingham to draw papers. Yes, Jasper had said he was going back in again. He hadn't felt like it himself, having a summer cold coming on. But didn't Jasper go in caves sometimes and stay a couple of days? Didn't he go off down the river or into the mountains and just not say anything? Didn't he do that? Didn't he?

And for an instant, Isaac didn't know whether he was really asking her, the mother, that last question over and over or whether he was just asking it over and over inside his head to tell himself that everything would be all right, he would get the cave fixed, he would get the money to blow, blow away from here, from Johntown, the ass hole of Tennessee, and Tennessee, the ass hole of the universe, blow far away and quite forget the weariness, the fever and the fret, here where men sit and shake a few sad last gray hairs, as they gawk deathward from chromium-plated wheel chairs—

He brought himself up short from that crap in his head.

"Mrs. Harrick," he began a question which he never got framed even in his own mind, for a car had just pulled into the yard, and Monty Harrick had jumped from it, leaving a man to climb out with the help of some boy, and Mrs. Harrick was turning toward the door even as her son came pounding up the hall.

As he stopped on the sill, grabbing his breath to speak, she was at him, clutching his arm, trying to make him speak. Then he managed. "I went in," he said. "I went in far as I could. I—"

"Tell me, tell me!" she cried, shaking his arm, drawing him into the room.

Behind him, in the door, Mr. Bingham appeared, hanging on the jamb on one side and supported on the other by the hard-faced boy who, back on Main Street, in Johntown, had offered to run his daughter down for him and whom he had asked to get his car for him. Indifferently holding Mr. Bingham up, with the grip of one strong brown hand that must make his poor left biceps blue, the boy was chewing his gum with a slow, remorseless motion, while he flicked his assessing gaze over the whole durn business going on here.

Mrs. Harrick hadn't even managed a glance of recognition at Mr. Bingham. All she could do was jerk on Monty's arm, saying: "Tell me!"

"I was coming home—running and they—" Monty indicated Mr. Bingham, "they picked me up—in town—"

"Tell me!" his mother cried out.

"I went in," he said, "but I didn't have a light, and—"

The old man in the wheel chair jerked one of the wheels and turned himself to face the boy, leaving the girl crouched there on the floor. "You went in?" he said. Perhaps it wasn't a question, perhaps a statement.

Mr. Bingham, at this point, managed to stagger from the sup-

[183]

port of doorjamb and the boy's grip, and made it to his daughter, to lean over her, and then to crouch beside her, patting her shoulder, murmuring: "Baby, Honey-Baby," trying to catch her attention as she stared at Old Harrick, seeming about to call out to him again, in appeal.

"You went in?" Old Harrick was saying to Monty.

"In the first chamber I yelled but I didn't hear a thing. Then I got in the crawlway. I crawled—heck, I don't know how far—but I couldn't turn. It was a crawlway and I didn't have any light—"

His mother was holding him tighter by the arm now, looking up into his face, the face blotched by red dust that was rivered by sweat, murmuring: "Son—oh, son—and no light—"

She was crying now.

"I got through the crawlway," he said, "and I yelled. I yelled and listened. I didn't hear a thing. I thought once I heard water, but—"

"There's no water in the second chamber," Isaac Sumpter said. "It's the fourth chamber where—" And he stopped, remembering suddenly what the flashlight beam had showed then, the great cathedral pillars rising to the arches of ceiling, the dome beyond studded, in the light, with ghostly gypsum flowers, under that dome the black pit with the narrow shelf along the pit; and what he had heard, the sound of water from the deep blackness. His mind, then, simply refused the vision.

But Mrs. Harrick was jerking her son's arm, saying: "Tell—tell me!"

And he said, miserably it seemed: "I—I didn't go on. I just didn't go on. I didn't have any light. I was just afraid to leave the mouth of the crawlway."

For a second, there wasn't a sound, except the old man's hard breath.

Then the boy burst out: "All right, God damn it, I was afraid! Say it, somebody—I was afraid!"

[184]

He glowered around. "All right," he challenged, "I was afraid —and my Brother—my Big Brother, he's in there!"

"Oh, son!" his mother said, "you weren't afraid. You had to come out. And tell us. So we can—"

Abruptly, she stopped patting his arm, and drew away.

"No," she said, "we don't have to save him." Her voice became quiet and factual. "You see, he's just in there and he has plenty of light with him, and he will come out. Like he always does."

She stopped, and smiled calmly around, as though she had just settled a small difficulty among children and restored good humor. Her eyes fell on Mr. Bingham. "Oh, Mr. Bingham," she said, smiling brightly at him with no amazement at discovering him. "I must get you a chair. Imagine me letting you stay there on the floor, and—"

Mr. Bingham managed some kind of deprecatory smile, waving a hand to indicate that he was perfectly and naturally all right, there on the floor, patting his daughter's head and shoulder, murmuring to her, trying to attract her attention; and his pince-nez slipped off his nose, for with all the excitement and running around and it being such a hot afternoon, the bridge of Mr. Bingham's nose had got quite damp with perspiration, although he, ordinarily, was not a man who perspired very freely.

When the pince-nez fell off, Mr. Bingham's inexpert attempt to recapture and readjust them seemed magically to release Mrs. Harrick from the obligations of hospitality. She was again carefully explaining to children something they seemed to forget, that her son Jasper often went into caves and always came out, though it was very inconsiderate of him not to leave word and therefore to cause so much excitement and inconvenience to so many people, who, she hoped, would excuse him, and she would certainly give him a piece of her mind when he did come out.

She certainly would.

But Old Harrick, staring at her from his wheel chair, from his grizzled leonine head, croaked: "But my box!"

"Oh, your old box!" she exclaimed, with patronizing, wifely irritation. "What do you care about that old box?"

"But my box!" he croaked.

"Oh, that box," she said, "you haven't touched it in years. You haven't touched it since—since—" she hesitated, thinking, then turned with a triumph of memory toward Brother Sumpter, "since you baptized him! Don't you remember, Brother Mac? How you said playing the box didn't have to be sinful, but John T., he laughed and said since he was washed in the Blood and was giving up drinking and dancing and gallivanting and carrying a pearl-handled pistol, he might as well give up the box too, for he had it so mixed up with so many other things he didn't know whether he could ever unscramble that bait of scrambled eggs. Those were his very words, and he wanted to bust the box. That night, after we got home, he wanted to break it over his knee, and I wouldn't let him. I said it might be sinful for him but not necessarily for somebody else, for I am not superstitious, and anyway I don't like to see property destroyed. So I put it in the attic, and Jasper, he found it long after, and because it was his father's—you know how he always admired his father, Jasper—he—"

She stopped. She stood perfectly still, and was suddenly aware, it seemed, how all the eyes had been on her all the time, watching her as the words kept on coming out from her mouth, in the hot June afternoon.

"My box," the old man said. "If he left it—"

"Oh, I hate your box," she managed, rallying to a burst of weak strength.

"It was my box," the old man said, "and Jasper, he wouldn't ever leave it out all night for the dew to ruin!"

"I hope it's ruined—oh, I hope so!" she cried. "You just think of your old box, while your son, he's—"

And with that word, she could not go on. In her mind she saw the guitar, glinting in mountain moonlight, bright and slick with dew, ruined or near, and then she knew. She knew that Jasper

[186]

would never willingly have left it there. She fumbled for a chair, and as she sank down, Monty's hands were holding her. "I'm sorry, John T.," she said. "I didn't mean a thing. It's just I didn't realize—"

She couldn't bring herself to say what it was she hadn't realized.

"Mammy, Mammy," Monty was saying, gripping her shoulders, "I'll get him!"

"I was just talking," she said weakly. "I was just standing there rattling on like I didn't have good sense, and my boy—my Jasper—" she turned slowly around to look at them all, and continued with a strange, detached calm, "he is down in that cave, in the cold ground, and he wants to get out. He wants to come home —he—"

Monty, as though his mother's shoulders had got, all at once, intolerably hot to him, snatched his supporting hands away, and dashed from the room.

"Do something—somebody do something," Mrs. Harrick suddenly cried out, and her husband's eyes stared at her, and his hands clenched the bright chromium of the chair.

"Yes," Mr. Bingham said, "yes, indeed," and rose from the floor, with an air of authority adjusting his glasses. "Something must be done. I shall drive into town and collect help. I'll inquire who best knows the situation in caves and who—"

"Oh, do something!" Mrs. Harrick cried.

Monty was back in the room, dragging a pair of coveralls, carrying a pair of sneakers in one hand, holding a flashlight and a miner's lamp in the other. He ran to his mother, grabbed her awkwardly around the shoulders, still hanging on to his paraphernalia, and kissed her, saying: "Mammy—don't worry, Mammy—I'll get him—"

He was trying to pull away now, to go. She was holding on to his arm with both hands and staring at the objects he held. He had kissed her on the cheek and the red dust and sweat from his face had rubbed off there to give the impression of rouge

[187]

smeared crazily, drunkenly, on one cheek in wanton dissymmetry. "No," she was saying, "no—"

"But, Mammy—" he protested, and pulled harder.

She was clutching him now, with both hands. "You can't go," she said. "If you go, I'll die. Jasper is in the ground, and if you go too I'll die."

"But he's my Brother," Monty was saying, pulling.

She wouldn't let go.

"Let him go," the old man croaked.

"I can't—oh, I can't," she wailed, and clung to him as he stood there in his misery.

"Let him loose," the old man commanded.

"Oh, I can't—he's my boy, he's my baby—"

"He's a man," the old man said. His hands clenched the sides of the chair. His breath drew hard, clearly audible in the afternoon, as he seemed to be waiting for something. Then it burst out of him: "God damn it—let him be a man. A man, do you hear!"

"A man," she repeated, then seemed to gather force. "Oh, that's all you think about—a man, a man—oh, a man—oh, if you—" whatever it was, she couldn't go on. The force was gone. One hand, her left hand, yet clung weakly to the boy's sleeve, but with the other she covered her face. You expected the sound of sobs, but it didn't come. The old man's breathing was what you did hear.

Brother Sumpter had gone behind Jack Harrick's chair. He had laid his hands on his shoulders, one on each shoulder, and his fingers gripped into the faded blue cloth of the old work shirt. As he stood there he did not know what he felt. He wanted to pray. He wanted to help the old man whose body seemed tightening, tightening intolerably, under his very fingers with its last terrible strength until something was bound to break. But he didn't know what to pray for. He found himself thinking: *If he would die, if he would just die, then it would be over.*

Though he didn't quite know what he meant to be over.

Then he realized that what he was really praying for—if it was a prayer and not the last blasphemy that was wrenching him at the bottom of his being—was that he himself might die, for there was something in the world he did not think he could bear. He did not think he could bear it.

At that moment he became aware of what Mr. Bingham was saying. Mr. Bingham must have been saying something before this, for he was now saying: "—and he was there yesterday, and he knows what it is like inside. And he has the right build, I assume, for a—a what do you call it?—a caver. I mean he is slender and not heavy-built. Yes, I am sure a cave is no place for a fat man. Not that I mean to make a joke. Now if Mr. Sumpter"—he bowed with a hint of formality toward the boy—"if you, Mr. Sumpter, could see your way to go in. I didn't mean to make a joke. It was just another slip of the tongue. You would have proper light, of course. I mean if you could bring yourself to go into the cave and relieve Mrs. Harrick's quite natural anxiety. Even if you have got a summer cold coming on, and—"

"Rock me to sleep," the hard-faced boy in the door said as though in appalled prayer, but quite audibly. "Him—" and then gulped, and suppressed what might have developed into a snicker.

Mr. Bingham's voice was continuing: "—and in case things are —are not exactly what we hope and—"

Brother Sumpter was watching his son's face, straining toward it over the head of the old man, trying to read it, while deep in him an indeterminate hope and happiness was tremulously unfolding, as though God might be about to divulge Himself in answer to the anguish of prayer. Straining there, Brother Sumpter was aware, in some perspective of his being, of how this moment was like the moment long ago when, after all his sweating for salvation, he had had the sweet, simple call as the night fell, like a bird far away, in a leafy valley at twilight. It was as though he, again, might hear God's voice.

Mr. Bingham's voice was saying: "—of course, you have no

[189]

obligation—but since the young man in the cave is your friend and since he is your—your business associate, we might say—perhaps you—"

Brother Sumpter strained toward that smooth, clean-modeled, almost olive-colored face, from which the blue eyes looked out so bright and divulged nothing, and was saying, or feeling, or hearing: *He is my son, and he is beautiful, and God will give him back to me.*

He saw the lips of the handsome face open ever so little. He saw the tongue tip delicately obtrude, touch the lips with moisture so that the light now picked up the slightest glint there. The lips moved with a stiff minimal motion to make the words: "Yes. Yes. Yes, of course—I'll go."

Isaac Sumpter lay back in the Cadillac, as it took the ruts in the lane down from the Harrick house. He had never ridden in a Cadillac before.

"It's tough," the Greek was saying.

But Isaac scarcely heard. He was thinking how he had never ridden in a Cadillac before.

"It's tough," the Greek said. "On her. Her big boy in the ground, and her not knowing how permanent. And her old man on the way there. Permanent."

Isaac was thinking.

"Her old man," the Greek said, "he was strong now. I have gripped with him. Did you ever grip with him?"

"No."

"He was a man," the Greek said. He drove on a moment in silence, nursing the Cadillac over the ruts. Then he said: "He must of give her what she wanted."

"Yeah."

"She is a nice lady," the Greek said. "I hope he give her which*ever* and when*ever* she wanted."

"Yeah."

The Greek gave special attention to the car, then, staring off down the lane, said: "It is a pleasure to do something for a nice lady like her."

Then, after a moment: "I was up to her house showing her to make waffles for the old man. But it happened before I got a good chance."

Isaac Sumpter felt the massy, casual certitude with which the Cadillac angled over the culvert at the bottom of the lane. He lay lax in that cradle-like motion, and thought how he had never ridden in a Cadillac before.

Well, what of it, he thought bitterly. There has to be a first time for everything, and damn it, was it his fault that he had to be born in Johntown, got by a Bible-thumper out of some woman who, no doubt, was the kind would marry a Bible-thumper, and the Bible-thumper, no doubt, had had to work his way past eight or nine yards of the dry goods such a woman would swathe herself in and call a nightgown, and when he got there, he and his partner in the crime of begetting Little Ikey Sumpter had, no doubt, pretended they were doing something quite different from what they were doing, even pretending they were sound asleep so that everything was merely a guiltless and pleasureless somnambulism and—

No, he brought himself up, not somnambulism, for they hadn't been ambulating when they were working on Little Ikey. It would have to be *somni*—*somni*-what? Somnifornicating, you might say, and so Little Ikey, Little Ikey the Jew Boy, prize product of somniconception, was sort of first cousin to an Immaculate Conception, first cousin being probably as good as the Baptists could do in a place like Johntown.

Well, what about Virgin Birth? Twilight Sleep with Baptist Patent, None Genuine without This Label, Jew Boy Won't Hurt, You Won't Know a Thing till You Hear His First Coo—and then he thought of the picture on the bookcase in his father's study,

[191]

the photograph tinted with the gay, though now fading, mortician's tints. He thought of a woman bleeding to death in a bed. *Damn it,* he thought, *it's not my fault.*

If it was anybody's fault, it was that Bible-thumper's fault. He was the one that had put it to her—and, oh, he had no mother, he had no mother, Little Ikey the Jew Boy, he had no mother.

Christ, he thought, and his mind made a motion like slamming a drawer shut, and the Cadillac took a nice luxurious wallow at the turn into Main Street.

Johntown, Isaac Sumpter thought, *the town where Ikey gets his first ride in a Cadillac, and it's the only Cadillac in town, and the Cadillac belongs to a bald-headed Greek who sweats through his seersucker coat and smells like a place where a dray horse stood too long, and who buys the superoctane with proceeds from a hash-haven for truck-shovers.* And, stealing a look at the Greek, he thought that the Greek was exactly the kind of guy you would expect to have to have a Cadillac so he would feel like a big shot—or maybe even half human.

"It's a nice car you've got," he said.

"It'll have to do," the Greek said, and you felt that a muted, rich satisfaction was beginning to glow discreetly deep in his being, like the filaments in a vacuum tube.

"You must feel pretty good, having such a car," Isaac Sumpter said, excessively innocent.

"It's good enough," the Greek said, and if the filament in the tube started to glow again, the glow flickered quickly out. Ikey studied his face and guessed that the dray horse maybe wasn't as dumb as he smelled.

Then, just at that instant, Isaac Sumpter, riding in a yellow Cadillac, thought of the kind of car that didn't have the aroma of this hash-heaver's conception of the Good Life, a car that was light, shrewd, prancing, and slick as the silk sheen on the shrewd, long, prancy legs reaching down to tickle the accelerator, juggle the clutch, and then drive the accelerator to the floor as they burst into the open and roared away.

He thought of those legs working softly under the dash of the red Mercedes, and how they—Little Ikey, and the Jew Girl—had broken every speed and traffic regulation ever devised by the Police Department of Nashville, Tennessee, to get out to the couch in that slick studio, on a hot May afternoon, or a June afternoon as hot as this one, when the fleshed but not yet summer-hardened leaves would be hanging motionless on the trees visible beyond the studio north-glass, and the very heat would be a kind of suffocating medium into which bodies could sink to plumb a new absoluteness and animality.

"Let's turn the air-conditioner off," the Jew Girl had said one afternoon. "Let's just turn it off and we'll get all slick and soaked and just sort of float away with ourselves. We'll just float away in our own metaphysical joy-juice, oh, Ikey!"

She had turned it off, and he thought now he would die remembering it. Remembering it and choking on the dry, grinding misery of deprivation, he didn't see how he could live.

Then, with a jerk, as though somebody had slapped him, he thought that maybe he wouldn't live. Maybe he would go into that cave and not come out. He shut his eyes and he heard the cold, deep sound of water from the pit in the cave, in the fourth chamber. In the absolute darkness of his head—and the pit—he saw a body in the absolute darkness of the roiling water, and even wondered how he could see it, in absolute darkness.

Whether it was his own body, or Jasper Harrick's, he couldn't tell. No, it was not Jasper's, it had to be his own, for if you couldn't see anything, you could still feel things, and if he knew that the body was there, it would have to be because he himself was the body in that water, and he himself was that knowledge in that absolute darkness.

He opened his eyes to the blaze of sunlight, and Main Street of Johntown. No, he, Little Ikey, was easing down the street in a

[193]

yellow Cadillac belonging to the Greek with the dream of the Good Life. It was Jasper Harrick who lay in the pit.

Yes, he thought, *yes, that is where he must be.*

Then he thought that if Jasper Harrick was in the bottom of that pit where the water made that sound, Little Ikey was in the soup. How the hell now would he get the cave going?

He saw the drugstore, coming up. "Listen," he said to the Greek, "I got to get a new battery. For the flashlight. Stop just a minute, please."

The Greek pulled over, and as Isaac started to run across the street to the drugstore, he saw the other car coming, and flagged it down, right in the middle of the street. "Listen," he explained to Mr. Bingham. "It's the flashlight battery. I want a battery. I'll be right on."

Mr. Bingham nodded, and looked out from behind his pince-nez. He was sitting in the back seat of his own car, Jo-Lea, the Bubbie Queen, Junior Division, was leaning against him, and he held her hand. The slick-faced boy was driving, with Monty Harrick, white behind the streaks of sweat and red dust, in front beside him.

"I'll be right on," Isaac said, and waved the car on its way. He dashed into the store, asked for the battery and got change for a five-dollar bill. *Damned near the last Little Ikey's got,* he thought. *Dear God of the Baptists, let Little Ikey use it wisely.*

"Break me two bucks," he said to the sad fat man, soft as a pale cloud of tallow gone ectoplasmic, who was waiting on him. The man, with his white cloudy finger, seemed to have great trouble with the cash register, but at last it worked. Isaac glanced out the door, to check on the Greek, who was now surrounded by the midafternoon shade-snoozers and no-goods. Getting the scuttlebutt on Death Underground, Ikey figured; then he went into the telephone booth.

He asked for Mr. James Haworth, city desk of the Nashville *Press-Clarion,* put the money in for the person-to-person, and braced himself to hear that voice. It came.

[194]

"This is Ikey," Isaac said to the voice in Nashville.

"Why, good afternoon, Mr. Tittlebum," the voice said from its godlike desk in Nashville. "What have I done, Mr. Tittlebum, to merit this honor?"

"I've got something for you," the boy said.

The voice seemed to hesitate a second, as though taking time to discard the dreary banter for a grim factuality. "I'm not sure I want anything you've got," the voice then said.

"It might be big," the boy said, trying to keep appeal out of his tone.

"What is it?"

"Listen, I am calling from Johntown. There is a guy caught in a cave up here. He is a sort of romantic and colorful guy, half-ass war hero, etcetera. I know the cave. It is my cave. I went in with him, and—"

"Christ," the voice said dolefully, "they caught the wrong one."

"Come off it," the boy said, "I was in there. I will write it. You know I can write it. It might be big."

"Listen," the voice said, "I don't care—and the whole bleeding world waiting for the sunrise does not care—if half the hillbillies in East Tennessee get stuck in caves. You included. From now on out till the time Republicans love niggers. I will give you rural correspondent rates. And make it brief."

"It might be big—" and damn it, despite all he could do, the appeal was coming into his voice.

"You heard me," the voice said.

"Did you ever hear of Floyd Collins?" Isaac Sumpter demanded.

"Did you ever hear of Quentin Reynolds?" the voice from Nashville said. "Did you ever hear of John Hersey? Did you ever hear of Richard Harding Davis? Did you ever hear of John Gunther?"

And hung up.

Isaac made it back to the car, and the no-goods around it gave back respectfully. One of them even opened the car door for

[195]

him, with the awkward deference ritually paid in Johntown to the crippled or sick. Isaac didn't quite comprehend.

Then one of the men, an older man, gaunt, malarial and be-gallused with one gallus over faded blue shirting, and with an Adam's apple like a jumping frog, managed a sepulchral tone of cheer: "Good luck to you, and God bless you."

Ikey comprehended.

"Yeah, good luck," a younger no-good managed, leaving God out.

Isaac comprehended, amply. He comprehended, in a cold flicker down his spine, even as he said: "Thanks, men." And then, turning to the Greek, added calmly: "All right."

Under the respectful gaze of no-goods, the Greek eased the Cadillac out into the street, and Isaac sank back into his inward cursing of that voice from Nashville. Who did he think he was? A tin-horn city-desk bully on a fifth-rate sheet. A lousy Yankee from Jersey City who had come down here because he couldn't make good up there, and hadn't made good here either. And he thought with self-contempt how he himself had once yearned for, and been grateful for, the approval of that same tin-horn bully. He thought how even the *Tittlebum*—"And how is Mr. Tittlebum tittling this fine day, sir?"—had come like balm to his soul, for that had been, he knew and all hearers had known, the tin-horn bully's tribute of middle-aged and scarcely solvent envy to Little Ikey who was, it was tacitly assumed, getting it off that rich Jew Girl with the snappy red foreign crate and legs like a race horse. He put away the twinge of pain at deprivation—the twinge he had come almost to treasure as a sensual thrill. He damned the tin-horn bully on cold, practical grounds, in cold, savage inner iteration.

"Did you get it?" the Greek was saying.

"No," the boy said.

"If you'd told me, we could of stopped at the hardware," the Greek said. "They carry 'em. You don't want to be going in the ground with bum batteries."

[196]

"Oh, I got the batteries," Isaac said, snapping back to the world of brilliant, factual sunshine which soon, soon, in a few minutes, he would not be seeing.

They were going up the old road up the mountain now, back of the old Sumpter farm. Yes, the Sumpters' had sure been pickers, Isaac Sumpter thought, shifting his mind from thought of the brilliance of sunshine and the darkness of dark. They had sure had a genius for picking land with a perpendicular bias, and a flourishing stand of post oak and copperheads. Even the post oak was long cut off for crossties for the railroad in the valley, second-growth left, and it was a low market this year on copperheads.

Yeah, how many rich Baptists do you know? Isaac thought, and the Cadillac crept up the grade like a luxuriously rising tide, lolling up the rise with a cradle-roll.

"Listen," Isaac Sumpter said, sitting up straight in the soft wide seat of the Cadillac, but not looking at the Greek. "Do you want to make some dough?"

At that question, in some faint subliminal way, in the dark inwardness where the tears fell, Nick Pappy felt discovered and defenseless. He stole a look at Isaac Sumpter. The fact that Isaac Sumpter was staring straight ahead, not looking at him for the answer, seemed sinister. Isaac Sumpter must know. He must know about that note at the bank.

"Dough," Isaac Sumpter said, then suddenly swung his gaze directly on Nick Pappy, staring right into his eyes, right into his guts it seemed. "Now tell me," he said, his voice sinking almost like a whisper, in a way that made the sweat suddenly feel cold under your armpits, "yeah, tell me, couldn't you use some dough?"

He must know. Nick Pappy saw that fellow looking him right in the eyes now. He knew that he had been to college. He knew that at college you studied psychology and hypnotism and things. He wondered if this guy had studied those things.

That guy must know that no matter how hard Nick Pappy worked, nothing ever stuck. He must know that Nick Pappy was

[197]

unlucky, and when he got his Heart's Desire with the beautiful hair as pale as taffy, whom he had dealt with across the foot of the bed and backed into closets and adjusted on the bathroom floor, she had to go and get TB and swell the size of a two-door, ten-cubic-foot de luxe Frigidaire, restaurant model, and you couldn't reach your arms around it, or her, even if you had wanted to.

He must know that Nick Pappy's Heart's Desire now had hair the color of river mud, for the white cotton-candy effect was gone, gone, gone. He must know that Nick Pappy's Heart's Desire had to have new silk bed jackets and imported French lace nightgowns, the size of circus tents now, and super de luxe TV sets, with hotel-size screens, for a girl had to have something to live for.

He must know that Nick Pappy was going broke. For he must know that Nick Pappy could not now deny anything which his Heart's Desire happened to desire, he was so caught in a sense of guilt and self-betrayal because he had slipped it to that Cutlick.

No, he thought, it wasn't any one thing, it was everything that ever was and ever would be, the way the world was, and at that something compelling and unspecified welled up in him for utterance, like a gas pain. He let the Cad drift. He leaned at the boy. "Listen," he said, "you just don't know. You just don't know how it is, how things look one way for you and come out another."

He had forgotten the wheel, leaning at the boy. He recovered the wheel barely in time. It would have been six feet on the low side there before you fetched up against a post oak. Nick Pappy was sweating, but not because of what he had nearly let happen to the Cad.

It was Isaac Sumpter's voice that brought him back. "But couldn't you use some dough?" he was asking quietly, as though nothing had happened, or nothing had been said.

"Dough," Nick Pappy repeated, and suddenly thought: *Jeez, I can get all the dough in Johntown. It is in the bank and I can get it. If I play it right with that bastard Bingham. I can get dough.* He sat up straight in the car. He pulled out his handkerchief and wiped the sweat off his face.

Then, all of a sudden, he remembered how everything was different now. He—Nick Pappy—was not like he had been. It was just that you had been a certain way for a long time and you forgot you ain't any more and don't have to be, and nothing was like it looked. He felt his lips lifting in a grin.

"Son," he said, "if it is dough you got on your mind, I can use it." The grin went deep and secret, so that he felt as though the skin and flesh of his face were grinning inwardly, knowingly, back into the inside dark which was himself. So he said: "Yeah, I can use all they is."

"It's worth the gamble," the boy was saying.

"What?" Nick Pappy said, coming out of himself and the inward-turning grin.

"What I'm going to propose."

"What?" Nick Pappy asked, and thought: *He's about to slip it to me now.* And he thought, with a strange detachment and sweetness, how he didn't feel that flicker of panic he used to feel when somebody, it didn't matter who it was or about what, was coming to the point, and was going to gig him. *Maybe it'll be me gig him,* he thought.

"This is my land," the boy was saying. "It came from my grandmother. The cave where Jasper is caught is on my land." He stopped, as though to let Nick Pappy's mind work on that.

Nick Pappy said nothing. He let the car barely crawl now, the engine laboring softly.

"There will be people here," the boy was saying softly. "There may be a million."

Nick Pappy looked straight ahead, feeling the deep reserve of power under his toe.

"People have to eat," the boy was saying. Then, suddenly, he straightened himself, and said briskly: "But the thing is to get old Jasper out."

"Yeah," the Greek said. Then: "I will say you got the guts, going in. I am not one for caves and submarines and such."

"Jasper Harrick is my friend," Isaac said. *Jasper Harrick is my friend,* he said, simply, to himself, hearing the words, caught by the rhythm.

"Whatever, you are being a friend to him, crawling in there," Nick Pappy said. "In the dark."

Isaac Sumpter suddenly had a vision of breaking through the brush near the cave to see Jasper sitting in the cave mouth, strumming a tune on the box, smoking a cigarette in the sunshine —and his heart leaped, and filled with gratitude, gratitude to Jasper for coming out and not making him go in, gratitude for the sunshine, for everything.

But just as suddenly then, that vision startled him like a blow across the back of the neck: deprivation, defeat. He turned to the Greek. "Listen," he said, speaking fast. "If he is caught in the ground there will be general hell to pay. There will be a million people here. They will be coming from all over, the vultures. They will have to be fed. It will be big. It will stay big. There is a cave here about like Mammoth or something. This is a scenic location. There is the falls. There will be a tourist hotel, a nice one, a nice little gold mine. But—"

He stopped, watching Nick Pappy's face. "But," he resumed, "I am not in that line. There will be need for someone—someone to take over. Besides, I have no capital."

"Yeah," the Greek said. He thought of all that money in the bank. He thought: *Bingham will have to invest, the bastard.*

"It will require something right away," Isaac said. "Immediately. To get things in motion. Say, five hundred dollars."

"Yeah."

"Perhaps something more," Isaac said, speaking even more rapidly, more matter-of-factly. "What I need is a line strung down to the telephone office. If Jasper is stuck in there, I need it immediately. I shall need to call for help, to get information, and

[200]

so on. There will be inquiries. As soon as I get out of this car, you get into town and get things set up. Then get back up here, and if I report that Jasper is really stuck, you get that line run up. Time is of the essence."

"What's that? Time is what?"

"It means," Isaac said, "to kick out of the asses of whoever is putting the line up whatever is in their asses."

"Yeah," the Greek said.

"Pull in here," Isaac ordered, looking up the lane, the track to where the Bingham Buick was waiting. "We have to walk some here. I guess they've gone on."

The Cadillac stopped and he got out. "That is," he said, off-hand, leaning into the back to get his equipment, "I have to walk. If you are going back down to the heart of Johntown to see about that line."

The Greek did not answer. Isaac rose from the back, with his equipment, and said, in the very act of turning away, almost in a whisper: "Or are you?"

"Yeah," the Greek said, wetting his lips. "Yeah."

Isaac, who was two steps away now, heard. He looked back over his shoulder. "Time is of the essence," he called gaily, and plunged into the greenery.

Nick Pappy sat there a moment, before he turned the car. He thought of all that money in the bank. He thought how Mr. Bingham would be glad to back a hotel, and would not own all the stock either. He thought of how performing an abortion can get you into the pen. He thought how Mr. Bingham might say, hell, if you got something on me, then I got something on you, and what I got on you you can go to the pen for. Then he thought that Mr. Bingham was not the kind would make any trouble for nobody.

But he did not know how that made him feel.

Even if he did not know, he closed his mind so as not to know, and swung the car.

[201]

Isaac Sumpter, well down the grade now toward the cave, heard the motor of the Cadillac. To nobody, to the green woods, with sudden ferocity, he said: "Kick it out of their asses!"

He didn't think whose asses he was thinking of. He was not thinking of anything. He was suddenly almost light-headed with elation. He simply was not going to think of what it would be like in the fourth chamber. Not yet.

"'Unto thee, O Lord, do I lift up my soul,'" Brother Sumpter read. He stood by the window, not looking at them, not even facing toward them, but in black profile to them against the appalling brightness of light out there in the yard where the rotten rope hung down from the white oak where Jasper's swing had been.

Somehow Celia Hornby Harrick knew that Jasper would be swinging there right this minute if the rope weren't rotten, if only John T. hadn't put up a rotten rope, and if only those nasturtiums didn't make those bright colors out there which, all at once, she could not bear. She hated nasturtiums, she decided. Why had she had to take all these years to find out she hated nasturtiums? She would just get up and go out there and dig them all up. She would spit on the ground. She would throw salt on the ground. That was what they did in the Bible, they sowed salt on the ground and then no fool nasturtiums would ever—

"'Show me thy ways, O Lord,'" Brother Sumpter's voice was saying, and was saying that so she, she and John T., poor old, dear old John T., who sat there dying, would believe it all to be God's will that—

That what? She couldn't say it. Oh, that couldn't be God's will—not if He were God.

"'—teach me thy paths,'" the voice was saying, but no, no, His path would not run down, down, down, to a hole in the ground, down, down, down, to a hole in the ground, and the fish down there didn't have any eyes, and the crawfish down there didn't have any eyes, and the crawfish down there were pale as

[202]

water, pale as water with a little ghostlike milk in it, and you could see right through them like glass, and the cave crickets hopped, they hopped in the dark, and didn't have any song. They hopped on your face in the dark, and, oh God, can you breathe darkness instead of air?

" '—for thou art the God of my salvation,' " the voice was saying; " 'on thee do I wait all the day.' "

She jumped out of her chair. She ran to John T. and leaned over him. She jerked him by the arm. "I can't wait," she cried out. "I just can't wait. You know I can't wait. You know I never could bear to wait. You always wanted me to wait. You know how I get all worked up, how quick, and you want me to wait, you want me to hold on, you say, Baby, now wait—just hold on, Baby—"

She was clutching his arm, shaking him, and he was staring up into her face.

She felt a hand grip her own shoulder, and looked up. It was Brother Sumpter. "You've got to hold on," he said.

So she sat down again.

And the voice said to remember the tender mercies of the Lord and His loving kindnesses, for they had ever been of old. She tried to remember them.

" 'Remember not the sins of my youth,' " the voice was saying, " 'nor my transgressions.' "

But what had she done, she tried to remember, that was so awful bad? Bad enough to make her feel so awful right now? It was so long back since she was young, but she had tried to be good, and do what her mother said, and she had studied her lessons and said her prayers and never let any boy put his hand under her dress in the back seat of a car after a party, and she had tried to honor her father, even if his hand did reach for the medicine.

And in that instant, as she, in her mind's eye, after all those years, saw her father's hand reach for the medicine bottle, she also saw the man in the red mackinaw standing in the back of a lurching Ford pickup truck, slithering down a snowy street,

[203]

holding up the angry, staring head of a bear above his own, with the hide hanging down, fur-side and blood-side, and a smear of blood on the man's face as the man yelled in joy and grinned with teeth as big and white as the bear's. And she remembered how, that instant all those years ago, she had not honored her father, hating him because his hand trembled toward the medicine and he had never swayed and yelled for joy with bear-blood on his face.

Was that the sin of her youth? Was that why she was so unhappy now—even as her mind refused to give the definition of this grinding pain?

She looked at the old man in the wheel chair, and suddenly saw that face, not as the staring, ruined, massive old face of the moment, but as a face yelling for joy and smeared with bear-blood. And she thought: *It is his sin.*

She thought: *He was young all those years before I was born, and he sinned. Oh, it's not fair, for I wasn't even born, and I have to suffer for the sins of his youth and—*

But the words gave out. If they came they would be too awful, and would shrivel up everything that her life had been. She knew that much, somehow, or something in her knew that and would not let the words come. There was the feeling behind the words, the feeling about John T. it was too awful to give the name to, and—

So she leaped from the chair and ran toward John T. and dropped on the floor by his chair and seized his hand, and stared up into his ruined old-lion face, and said, over and over: "I love you, John T.—I love you, John T.—"

Brother Sumpter was leaning over her. "Let us pray together," he was saying. "It will help you to hold on."

She stood up. In a very small voice, she said: "Not now. I simply can't pray right now."

She went back to her chair. Looking across to Brother Sumpter, she said: "I couldn't pray in the kitchen either. When you asked me to. I just couldn't."

[204]

"We are all human," Brother Sumpter said. "We are all human and weak."

"Because I couldn't pray in the kitchen," she asked, beseechingly, "because I couldn't pray then, do you think that's why—why this had to happen?"

"You must hold on," he said. "We don't know yet what has happened. We can pray that it will be all right when we know."

"Do you think that's why this happened?" she demanded. "Because I couldn't pray?"

"Whatever it was," he said, "it was before you couldn't pray."

He went back across the room, toward the window, and picked up the book from the chair where he had laid it. He began to read, in that distant voice, not looking at them: " 'Mine eyes are ever toward the Lord; for he shall pluck my feet out of the net.' "

"Look," Celia Hornby Harrick cried out. "Look at John T.! He just sits there and doesn't say a thing. Make him say something—make him say something! Make John T. say what it is he won't say!"

That was why they got into the old Studebaker, which was the Sumpter car. They had managed the wheel chair out the hall, across the porch, and down the ramp, which was there in the first place because before he began to feel so bad Old Jack Harrick had liked to sit under the trees. It had been hard to get him into the car, but they had managed. They then had folded the chair, and started out, the old man and his wife in the back seat, Brother Sumpter driving.

They had started out, because when Celia Hornby Harrick had cried out what she did, the old man had turned slowly toward her, had stared at her, and had said: "I am going to go."

They had told him he couldn't go.

He had said that he would go. If they did not help him, he would go alone. And he began to rise in the chair. By a frightening strength he was rising up in the chair.

[205]

So they took him.

The car proceeded down Main Street, and the fact that Old Jack Harrick was in a car going up the mountain to where they said they reckoned that not-much-account Jasper Harrick was stuck in a cave was observed by several respectable storekeepers and such of the no-goods as had lacked energy or opportunity to get up the mountain to see what the hell was really going on.

Going up the mountain, Celia Hornby Harrick was in perfect control of herself. She asserted that it was a good thing they had got out of the house. Things always seemed worse when you were stuck in a house, and now she was pretty sure nothing serious was involved. She said she was glad that John T. had the good sense to get them out of the house, even if it was hard on John T., and she appreciated it. She appreciated, too, all that Brother Sumpter was doing for them. She appreciated what Brother Sumpter's son was doing for their son. If it wasn't necessary to save Jasper, and he was just being foolish and staying down too long, it was mighty nice of Isaac to take the trouble. And if, as she didn't believe to be the case, Jasper was having a little trouble, it was mighty nice of Isaac to save her son.

Brother Sumpter drove the car up the rutted lane without saying a word for some minutes after she got through. Then without turning his head, speaking without seeming to realize that they were there, Brother Sumpter said the most peculiar thing.

He said: "It is my son who will be saved."

VI

The boy, Monty Harrick, with the red-check gingham shirt, and straw hat, with the gallant drake feathers, unfarmerishly canted to one side, sat apart, at the edge of the shade of the biggest beech tree. Beside him were the boots, propped carefully erect now, not sagging, the same kind of boots he himself had on, number X-362 in the Monkey-Ward catalogue, genuine cowhide, prime leather, expertly tanned, but his were new, disgracefully new, without careful resolings and loving applications of saddle soap to give the dim, rich, experienced feel to the leather. The boy, secretly, ran his finger along the side of one of the empty boots.

Then he returned again to his occupation of polishing the guitar, which lay across his knees. He polished it with a red bandana handkerchief, in a slow, finicking motion. Now and then, bending his face low so that the hat completely concealed it, he plucked a string, muting it.

The locusts were grinding away, on the ridge, and far away, over all the ridges, caves, corn bottoms, cow pastures, golf courses, tobacco patches, split-level developments, cemeteries, beautiful country homes, and hunt clubs of Tennessee.

Deeper in the shade of another beech tree, some thirty feet from the boy, the old man sat in the wheel chair, the bright chromium glinting even in that recessed light, and stared at the fern-fringed mouth of the cave flanked by the great humping gray roots of the biggest beech. Beside the wheel chair, the woman crouched on the deep grass, one hand on the old man's right knee, supporting herself, comforting him, in that contact defining their oneness in the moment of sad expectancy and tremulous hope after all the onenesses of all their years.

This is my life, the woman was thinking. *I can live it if he puts his hand on my head.*

He laid his hand on her head. She had been staring toward the cave mouth and that touch on her head was a complete surprise. The tears were suddenly swimming in her eyes, so that the sunlight striking down between her shade and the shade of the cave mouth now dazzled, and she could distinguish nothing clearly.

Beyond the man in the wheel chair and the woman were the other people, spread in a rough semicircle. There were now some forty-five people, mostly the Main Street loafers who had hooked rides up the ridge, and some half-grown boys. One of them had a catcher's mitt, on which he sat for a cushion. The baseball game —the game for which Monty Harrick had not pitched—had been given up, because it wasn't every day somebody got stuck in the ground. Jo-Lea sat on the grass beside her father, who had spread a handkerchief on a rock so as not to get the seat of his blue serge trousers dusty.

Brother Sumpter stood not far from the cave mouth, just at the edge of the biggest beech. His lips, now and then, seemed to be moving, but no sound was audible. Once or twice he came to stand behind the wheel chair, saying nothing; but always, after a little, he withdrew, closer to the cave, and his lips began, again, to move.

The afternoon was wearing on: four thirty. The jay came back and screamed in the beech tree. Many eyes looked up at him, and then returned to the cave mouth. The locusts stopped. That is, the local ones stopped, their sound dribbling off into silence. Then you could hear all the other locusts in Tennessee ringing off the hills and hollows like an electric razor God-size and for eternity, or like some recollection all at once gone short-circuited and significantly blazing inside your head.

Monty Harrick, sitting over yonder with his brother's box across his knee, struck a muted chord; waited, struck another chord. The girl rose from beside her father and moved toward the boy.

She leaned over him. "It didn't ruin his box, did it?" she asked. "Did the dew ruin Jasper's box?"

"No," the boy said, not looking up, studying the box.

She sat on the grass a little way from him, but she kept staring at the cave mouth.

The father seemed nervous and looked at his watch.

Some of the boys began to rustle and titter. Neither the old man in the wheel chair, nor the woman crouching by him, seemed to notice. Nor did Brother Sumpter, standing over yonder, with his lips moving soundlessly. But Mr. Bingham noticed. He looked at the boys with a disapproving glitter of his pince-nez.

Then Mr. Bingham thought: *It's one of them. Or somebody like them.*

It was somebody like that who had done what they had done to Jo-Lea. He couldn't stare at them any more. He couldn't bear to face them. He got up and moved toward his daughter, trying to move soundlessly, holding his gaze on them by a last courageous act of will. He leaned over her, whispering, "Honey, Honey-Baby —don't you think we ought—"

[209]

"No," she said, "no," not taking her eyes off the cave mouth. "I can't, I just can't go now. Oh, please, Daddy!"

He stood leaning above her. It seemed he would be like this forever. He wanted to reach down and enfold her in a cloud of comforting darkness, like a magic cloak, and protect her forever.

But he couldn't. He had to lift up his head, and then he found himself again standing helpless in the world, caught in that communal stare. But he bravely met their eyes, and they dropped their gaze from his, flushing a little, almost as though in embarrassment for him. That is, they all dropped the gaze except the hard peel-faced boy who had offered to run his daughter down for him, on Main Street, in Johntown. That boy was now staring back at him with a blankness which was a wicked knowingness.

Oh, it couldn't be him, Mr. Bingham thought, in sick outrage. But he remembered, for the first time, that that boy had been to the house, to take his Honey-Baby to a high school dance. He had forgotten that till now.

The slick-faced boy held something wadded in his hand which he was showing to the other boys. It was the pair of drawers which Jo-Lea had worn, which Monty Harrick had been working on, which Jo-Lea, when she had started to run and found they hobbled her, had stepped out of and flung aside. Mr. Bingham, of course, could not see what the boy held.

At that instant Monty Harrick struck a muted chord, then another.

His head low over the box, his face screened by the hat brim, he began slowly and softly to pick the box. His head was still down and his face not visible when he began to sing. He was singing so softly the words were almost indistinguishable, even close up. Jo-Lea leaned at him, straining to hear. She rose to one knee, and hunched herself forward, listening, leaning her head toward him so that in that beech-shade her throat had a white, swanlike, yearning lift.

"It's him," she cried out. "It's him you're singing about!"

Mr. Bingham stood there, not knowing what to do.

[210]

The music stopped. But the boy did not lift up his head.

One of the men nearest Monty Harrick—some fifteen feet from him—had been straining, too, toward the music, his old red-weathered, gaunt face cocked sidewise, one eye squinted in puzzlement to work on the words he couldn't quite make out. It was old, beer-soaked Jim Duckett.

"Durn," he uttered, suddenly, all having come clear now in his mind, "he's a-singing about his Bubba!"

Jo-Lea leaned toward the boy. "Sing it," she said. "I want to hear."

With the face still not visible, he sang louder now, but not loud. The words came out from under the hat, over the box:

> " 'Twas a sad, sad word to hear,
> How war come in far Korea.
> My Big Brother, he was brave,
> And he would his country save,
> So he went away to fight with never a fear."

"That's right," one of the men allowed. "Nobody ever said no Harrick was scairt."

"Why that young'un ain't gone in the cave then?" somebody demanded.

"Shut up," somebody said.

The music resumed, from under the hat:

> "They shot him in the side,
> But he yelled, 'Boys, I ain't died,
> I will shoot 'em, I will stab 'em,
> If your bullets give out, just grab 'em!'
> When strife was o'er the enemy wished they hadn't tried."

"Singing about his Bubba," one of the men said, in the tone of a man in church.

"Yeah," another man said, then added with slow marveling:

[211]

"Yeah, singing, and on the self-same box belonged to his Bubba."

"Naw," Old Jim Duckett said. "Naw, it is not his Bubba's box. It is the box of Old Jack. It is the self-same box Old Jack used to tear the screaming guts out of. Way back yonder when he was helling and Hell-fahr gaped. Anybody who never heerd Jack Harrick in his day and time of strength rip off 'Turkey in the Straw' and whoop and click his heels in the air twi'est 'twixt verses, he ain't heerd—"

"Shut up, Pap," the other man commanded, and in dolorous significance nodded toward the load in the wheel chair.

The man in the wheel chair had, apparently, heard neither the music nor the conversation. He was staring toward the cave-mouth.

A couple of chords came from the guitar.

"He's gonna be singing," Old Jim Duckett, with his one gallus, out of his beer-depth, said.

> "My Big Brother, he was brave,
> But he is lying in a cave,
> He is lying in the ground
> And he cannot hear a sound—
> Oh, save my Brother who his country tried to save!
>
> "Oh, he's lying under the land,
> There's nobody to—"

The man in the wheel chair swung his heavy head toward the boy, and gripped the sides of the chair. "Stop it!" he commanded, with a throaty, strangled cry. "Stop it, God damn it," he cried, and seemed to be struggling to rise. "Don't you see you're making her cry? You're making your mother cry!"

The woman crouching beside him, clutched him, drawing him down, lifting her tear-wet face now for all to see. "Oh, John T.—John T.," she said, "let him play—let him play to make him feel better—oh, I want to cry, John T.!"

[212]

"Lady," Old Jim Duckett yelled with what voice was in him, "lady, we gonna save yore boy!"

"You and how many more, Pap?" a voice said, low but quite distinct from back in the crowd.

Then, after an instant, the same voice, aggrieved, in a higher key: "Durn it, that's my foot you—"

And another voice, sad and detached: "Lucky it ain't yore durn teeth drove down yore throat."

"Sing! Sing, boy," a voice called.

Monty Harrick remained motionless, bent over the box.

"Yeah, sing," another voice said. "Sing fer him to be saved."

The boy did not move.

"Singing is right pretty," a voice said, very soft, very slow and easy, from among the boys nearest Monty Harrick, under the edge of beech-shade. "But if hit was my brother—"

The voice stopped. Nothing had stopped it. It simply hung in the air, while those who hadn't made it out tried to make it out.

For a long moment, it didn't seem that Monty Harrick had made it out. He stayed as he had been, his head bowed, hat brim low, over the box. Then he slipped the box to the grass, very quietly, and rose. His face, visible now under the hat brim, didn't seem to be thinking about anything. He walked as slow and soft on the green grass as though he were just drifting and didn't care where he drifted, lost like he was. Then he was among the boys, but speaking so low nobody any distance could tell what.

"Jebb," he said, "Jebb Holloway, did you say something?"

"I might of," Jebb Holloway said, and elaborately stared away, across the glade, into the far greenery.

"He didn't say nothing, Monty," one of the boys said.

"I didn't say a thing," Jebb Holloway corroborated mildly, still looking elaborately away. "I was jes thinking out loud, you might say."

Monty Harrick went straight for his throat. He got it in both hands, as they turned over managed to get a scissors on his waist,

[213]

and ducked his own face as low as possible as they rolled over and Jebb Holloway beat hard at the sides of his head.

It was all so quiet and so fast, that it was over before most people there even knew anything was happening. The boys had pulled them apart, two of them holding Monty, still struggling, white in the face. Jebb Holloway, not being held, fingered his neck. "I'll fix you," he said.

"Listen," the slick-faced boy said, "he wanted to go in. He was going in the cave, but his mammy wouldn't let him."

"His mammy," Jebb Holloway began with a faint tone of mimicry, and Monty jerked and was almost loose and on him again.

"I was there," the slick-faced boy said. "I heerd it. She wouldn't."

"You ought to apoly-gize," one of the boys said, "and his brother in the ground."

Jebb Holloway looked at him. "I ought to fix you, too," he said.

"Jebb," another boy said, "you don't apoly-gize and if that Jasper comes out from that cave you might wish you had."

"I ain't afraid of no Jasper," Jebb Holloway said.

"You might not have time to be 'fraid," another boy said. "Not and him Jasper Harrick."

Then Old Jim Duckett was there. "Son," he said mournfully to Jebb Holloway, "you kin jes fergit about that Jasper. Fer listen, son, they's strong men walking the earth of Kobeck County today wouldn't be in yore shoes so long as Old Jack ain't yet laid out for burying. Certain kinds of talk Old Jack never favored none and—"

"What?—what's going on?" Old Jack called from his chair, but nobody was listening.

But a burly black-browed man standing behind Jebb Holloway, speaking with dour indifference, in a voice nicely calculated not to be heard by either of the ladies present, said: "Don't be a born turd. Apoly-gize to that boy or I'll kick yore ass in like a watermelon gone rain-rot."

[214]

"Monty!" Old Jack was calling.

Then somebody began explaining something to him.

"I apoly-gize," Jebb Holloway said, sullenly.

"You see," Old Jack Harrick was saying to Celia Hornby Harrick, "you see, you wouldn't let him go in. Not after his own brother, and—"

She bowed her face to his knee.

"Oh, John T.," she said. "Don't talk. Just love me. Love me," she said, "and help me to live."

Monty had crossed again to the patch of grass where the box lay, near the girl. He picked up the box, and stood there with his head bowed, the face again lost under the hat brim.

Mr. Bingham went back, and sat on the rock, on his handkerchief.

"Sing fer him, boy!" somebody called.

Monty jerked his head up, looking up into the braided beech boughs as though into infinite sky. Then his eyes closed, and the skin seemed to go tight and dry on his face, it suddenly looked so drawn. He hit the box with the palm of his hand across the strings, and let the clang come. Then he picked a chord, beginning:

> "Oh, he's lying under the land,
>   With nobody to take his hand.
>   He is lying in the ground,
>   And he cannot hear a sound.
>   Oh, bring him out and let him in the sunshine stand!"

They could see that Monty Harrick had his eyes tight shut and that tears were coming out from under the tight lids.

"Yeah, let him in the sunshine stand!" a voice yelled out.

The girl scrambled to her feet. She took a couple of uncertain steps toward the cave, staring at the opening so intently that for a couple of seconds people thought she saw something, even

[215]

thought that they saw something. But she turned and came back and sat down, nearer Monty now. "Monty," she whispered, "I'm trying to pray for him. I really am, Monty."

He looked at her from under the hat brim, then ducked his eyes down again. Looking at his eyes so bright with tears, she thought she herself might cry. She was afraid she might.

Over yonder the slick-faced boy was whispering to Jebb Holloway. "You know," he whispered, crouching down beside Jebb, fingering the nylon panties, or whatever they were, which he held tight rolled in his palm. "You know," he whispered, "I wonder if 'twas her hen house somebody pulled these here things off of."

"I would pull 'em off," Jebb Holloway asserted, staring at the girl.

"I aim to find out if these things was pulled off her hen house," the slick-faced boy said.

"Yeah, and I reckon you aim to ast her."

"Naw, but I bet I find out."

"Yeah," Jebb Holloway said in weary sarcasm, still staring at the girl.

"I bet 'twas off her," the slick-faced boy said, "but I bet it wasn't Monty done it." He looked appraisingly at the girl. "I bet it was that Jasper."

Jebb Holloway was looking at the girl.

"I bet it was Jasper," the other boy continued. "I bet he done it just afore he crawled in the ground."

"Well," Jebb Holloway said, with weary authority, "if he done it, he has sure got something to think about, laying down there in that hole."

"I bet it wasn't Monty," the slick-faced boy said.

"That Monty," Jebb Holloway said, sourly, "I bet he never pulled off nothing. Not even off'n no china doll."

It was then that Mrs. Timothy Bingham debouched from the brush.

Mrs. Bingham was a tall angular woman with no casual soft-
nesses to mark her sex, and the brown serge dress she wore, well
designed for a woman of mature years and high social position,
did nothing to conceal the lack of natural endowment. "That's
that Jo-Lea's old woman," the slick-faced boy confided to Jebb
Holloway, in that instant when Mrs. Bingham first broke from the
brush and stood there to get her bearings in the open.

"Naw," Jebb Holloway said, marveling, "naw."

"Hope to die," the slick-faced boy said, and was corroborated
that moment, for Mrs. Bingham, having sighted her prey, had
swooped down on Timothy Bingham, who, at that very instant,
having found his perch harder than before, was all unwitting as
he devoted his full attention to shifting his femurs.

"Well," Mrs. Bingham uttered. The pince-nez of Mr. Bingham,
who was, only that instant and by that word, apprised of her arrival, slipped off his nose, even though his afternoon perspiration
had long since dried.

Mr. Bingham got off the rock, got the glasses back on, and
said: "Well, Matilda, you see—"

"I see what I see," she said. "I see that this is how a leading
citizen elects to spend his afternoons, sitting on a rock and—"

Mr. Bingham leaned and quickly retrieved his handkerchief
from the rock, as though to destroy evidence.

"—and I see that his own wife has to get this information from
strangers—"

"Now, Matilda," he tried, "in Johntown you can't exactly say
there're any strangers, and—"

"There are strangers to me," she declared, "and I take relish in
the fact, and I only wish there were more strangers to my daughter—" She suddenly, with a sharp, covert snatch of the thumb,
indicated Jo-Lea. "I can wish the whole town and the whole Harrick family were strangers to her, but you, you even have to go

with her to their house—oh, yes, I have been informed—you bring her up here in a public place, and—"

Mr. Bingham took his pince-nez off and wiped them. "Matilda," he said, with a change of tone that, for a moment at least, commanded her attention, "do you realize that a young man is, in all probability, trapped underground?"

"A Harrick," she rallied to retort, "one of the precious Harricks, and may I say that I, for one, would not mind if they all were."

"You are speaking too loud," he said. "Somebody might hear you."

She glanced around. "Your friends," she said, and turned toward her daughter, who, crouching on the grass across the glade, watched her, not moving, gaze fixed.

As she approached the girl, setting her brown kid oxfords firmly on the grass, the girl remained crouching, looking up at her. "Get up, Jo-Lea," Mrs. Bingham said. "What are you doing humped that way on the ground? Do you think that is ladylike?"

"Mother," the girl said, shifting a little, but still crouching, not going on then with whatever she had been about to say.

"Get up," the mother commanded. "We are going home."

"Oh, Mother," the girl said, and stretched out a hand to her, appealing. "We don't know what's happened. I've got to know what's happened. I've—"

"You've got to know," Mrs. Bingham said, in an appalled voice. "And why, pray, do you have to know?"

Mr. Bingham had approached, and was standing just behind his wife.

"Daddy—oh, Daddy," the girl said, "oh, let me stay!"

Mrs. Bingham leaned and seized the girl's arm. "Get up," she said.

"I see no harm in her staying," Mr. Bingham said. "Till we know. It strikes me as a normal, human, Christian impulse."

"It strikes *you!*" Mrs. Bingham retorted, as soon as she had recovered from surprise.

[218]

"Yes," Mr. Bingham said. He took off his pince-nez and began to polish them. As he polished the glasses, carefully inspecting the process, he distinctly heard his own voice saying: "Matilda, sometimes I think that you lack dignity."

At first he didn't believe what he seemed to hear, that it was his voice. He thought it was a thought in his head that had slipped out of some dark place, and would go right back. Then he saw Matilda Bingham's face, long and sallow and sharp-nosed, looking much longer even than common, because the jaw had dropped open and was, apparently, going to stay open.

Mr. Bingham had the thought that that was the way they said a dead person's jaw was, and they had to tie the jaw up to let it set. *Somebody ought to tie her jaw up*, he thought. *It's not decent to let it hang that way.*

Then under its own power the jaw closed, and he knew that he must have said what he had been afraid he had said. Her jaw had dropped because she was stunned. But he was stunned, too. He knew he was, as his fingers, without sensation, kept polishing the glasses. He was stunned, and thought, wondering: *Something has happened to me. I don't know what's happened to me today.*

Then he saw that Matilda Bollin Bingham's face had assumed a calm, a detachment, a dignity. The twisted strain seemed to have gone off it, it was smooth as evening water, and he thought, with a strange fleeting twinge of the heart, that her face would look this way when she was dead and there was the smell of flowers and everything was quiet in the house. Then he thought: *Yes, after they have tied the jaw up to set.*

Then he knew, viewing the face in that instant of calm and dignity, which seemed so long, that what he was looking at was the face of Matilda Bollin when she was a girl, a sickly girl who had quoted poetry to him and held hands with him in the leafy side streets of the West End section of Nashville, Tennessee, as they moved through the serenity of twilight and he thought how beautiful and serene their life would be. Looking at her now, he

[219]

felt time flee away from him, and for one split second he thought that they might now take hands again, before all these people, and enter upon their serene happiness, as had been foretold.

But then, from that face, even in its serene dignity, words were coming. She was saying: "Oh, I forgot to say how I learned all about this in the first place. You had left your place of business and responsibility, without deigning to post word of your movements—even with the examiner there. But he could not wait, it seems. So he called on the road to Knoxville—called the house because there was no answer at the bank. Your Miss Cutlick, it seems, had closed the bank. When the cat's away—who knows? The examiner was very courteous to me, but I could read between the lines. No"—she interrupted herself, as he seemed about to speak—"no, he wouldn't tell me. He did not want to trouble me, he said. Oh, he was the pink of courtesy!"

"The examiner," Mr. Bingham managed to begin the question, "you say he—"

"Yes," Matilda Bingham said, and smiled serenely, with great dignity. "Couldn't it be," she asked, "that he has found some flaw?"

That dark, gnawing guilt that had been at work in the dark bottom of Mr. Timothy Bingham's mind that day in the bank as he listened to the click of Dorothy Cutlick's posting machine and thought of the examiner examining books back in the board room where he, Timothy Bingham, had so often passed judgment, flooded back into his being, like dark, filthy water rising in the cellarage. He started to explain to his wife that his books were in order. They were in apple-pie order.

But he saw that serene dignity on her face, lighted ever so little by a victorious smile.

"Come, daughter," he said to Jo-Lea, and reached down to take her hand, for there seemed, suddenly, nothing else to do.

"Oh, Daddy—" she began. But she saw his face, and rose quietly. She held his hand tight as they walked across the glade behind Mrs. Bingham. As they approached the greenery Mrs.

Bingham stopped. "Here is the taxi man," she said, indicating a young man at the edge of the brush. "He has been most helpful and gracious," she added. She smiled briefly on the young man, and said: "My husband will pay you."

"Good afternoon, William," Mr. Bingham said.

"The damage is two bucks," the young man said apologetically. "You see, Mr. Bingham, I had to go out to the house, then I—"

"That's fine, William," Mr. Bingham said. "Thank you, very much." He put two bills and a half-dollar in the young man's hand.

"Thanks, Mr. Bingham," he said. Then added: "Things is beginning to boil downtown. Strangers coming in. The word has got out. Johntown is gitting on the map."

"Yes," Mr. Bingham said, and turned to his daughter, who had stood quietly waiting during the transaction. She took his hand again, and they went up the ridge through the brush that now was getting beat back and the grass that was getting beat down by the passage of many people. They met some people coming down from the track, strangers. They met the Greek. They met two state patrolmen. They couldn't see Mrs. Bingham up ahead for the brush, but they knew she was there. She would be waiting by the Buick.

Just before they got to the Buick and found her, they heard a burst of singing from below, the words indistinguishable. He felt his daughter's hand tighten on his. "Oh," she cried out, "Oh, they've found him—they must have found him! Oh, I want to go —I've got to go—I've—"

She had pulled away from him.

"Come, daughter," he said. "Your mother is waiting."

He had a peculiar complication of feeling then, something emerging, as things had a way of doing today, into a new light. He tried to decide whether he had commanded his daughter to come because of the mother or because he himself had to flee from the eyes of those terrible boys. Had he just blamed it on the mother?

It was the sort of question he had known, instinctively, all his life, a man had better not be asking. It impaired a man's apple-pie efficiency.

Jebb Holloway watched the Bingham family disappear into the brush, then turned to the slick-faced boy. "There she goes," he said, "and you found out like fun."

"I'll find out," the slick-faced boy said, and spread the drawers out to admire on the grass. "Ain't they pretty?" he said.

"It ain't the wrapping you eat on no two-dollar-and-a-half box of Whitman's chocolate candy," Jebb Holloway said.

The boy wadded the garment up and stuck it into his hip pocket.

"You might as well keep on admiring and mirating," Jebb Holloway said. "The wrappings is all you got."

The Greek came out of the brush, and moved toward Jack Harrick and his wife.

"There is that Greek," Jebb Holloway said.

"I bet it was that Jasper pulled them things off her hen house," the slick-faced boy said.

"He is shore dark-complected," Jebb Holloway said.

"He ain't dark-complected," the boy said.

"The hell he ain't. He is nigh nigger-complected. Jes you look at him."

"You durn fool, how can I look at him when he is stuck in the ground?"

"Who is stuck in the ground, you durn fool?"

"Jasper Harrick is stuck in the ground, and I bet it was him pulled them things off'n that—"

"Durn," interrupted Jebb Holloway, with high contempt, "if you'd jes git yore mind out of that hen house, you could follow a conversation and a man's line of thinking and know I was talking about that Greek."

[222]

"He is talking to Mrs. Harrick."

"You fool, anybody could see he is leaning over and talking to Mrs. Harrick. I ain't blind."

"I jes said it, to be noticing."

"He has shore got a funny build."

"It is a Greek build. He is still leaning over and talking to Mrs. Harrick."

"Durn, I can see. Me, I wouldn't want no Greek build."

"He could bust yore ass," the slick-faced boy said.

"I would bust him one in the gut. He has got lot of gut."

"You would bark yore knucks on his gut. It ain't soft gut."

"There come them highway cops."

"The tall one is Lieutenant Scrogg. He is the one shot and killed that fellow held up the filling station in McMinnville. Between the eyes. He is a friend of the Greek. He eats there a lot. He is getting introduced to Mrs. Harrick by the Greek."

"I got eyes," Jebb Holloway said.

"Well, you ain't using 'em, or you would see what I see, and shet up."

"What do you see, pretty boy?"

"I see that pretty boy Isaac Sumpter, who has been to college to get knowledge, coming crawling out of that hole in the ground."

It was true. Jebb Holloway looked, and saw. Isaac Sumpter was crawling out of that hole. He seemed to be having a little difficulty getting to his feet, or perhaps Monty Harrick was grabbing him not so much to help him as to make him say whatever it was he had to say. But he was, apparently, holding back what he had to say.

"Look," the slick-faced boy said, "he is jest standing there. He ain't saying a thing."

"Maybe he got so scairt in that cave he can't say nuthin."

"I bet you would be, too."

"Shet up, he is saying something."

Monty Harrick was running toward his mother, yelling. He seized her, jerked her to her feet, and began kissing her. People near the cave were yelling.

"He is kissing his old woman," the slick-faced boy said, "because I bet they found that Jasper."

"Naw," breathed Jebb Holloway reverently. "You don't say! You mean you got it all figgered out."

Somebody near the cave mouth threw up his hat and yelled: "Found him! Found him alive!"

Several men were pounding Isaac Sumpter on the back. One was offering him a drink from a bottle of whisky, miraculously produced from a hip pocket in the middle of the afternoon, but he waved it away. He came over to the Harricks, and with careful attention answered their questions. Old Jack Harrick reached up from the wheel chair and shook his hand four or five times, and with a voice choking up said: "Son, you're a man."

At that somebody yelled. "Hurray fer Isaac Sumpter!" Several voices echoed the words.

"He jes crawled in a cave," Jebb Holloway said, who last season had scored thirty-one points in the basketball game against Tracy City High, in the state-wide tournament.

MacCarland Sumpter stood behind his son and laid a hand on his shoulder. "Thank God," he said, and his heart was, at the moment, too full for more.

"You are Ole Mac's boy," Jack Harrick said. "You will save my boy."

Mrs. Harrick suddenly threw her arms around him and kissed him several times.

"She is kissing him," the slick-faced boy said.

Isaac Sumpter managed to detach himself a short distance and was talking earnestly with the Greek.

Monty Harrick had gone back to pick up the guitar. He stood apart, his hat brim, as before, hiding his face bent over the box.

"It is Ole Jack's box," yelled the old man with one gallus, in his cracked voice, "and time was I hear'd hit ring fer carnal flesh and jubilation. But, son—but, son," he yelled, "you let her ring fer glory!"

"Sing!" somebody else yelled. "Sing fer him to be saved!"

Monty Harrick laid the box across his body, thrust his right knee a little out, lifted his right heel from the grass, struck a chord, and, under the big beech tree, threw back his head, shut his eyes and sang till the stiff leaves above him shivered. He sang:

> "All the bullets in Korea
> Couldn't make my Brother fear.
> My Big Brother, he was brave,
> But he's lying in the cave—
> Oh, God, bring him out to daylight bright and clear!"

Somebody's voice picked up the last line, breaking out wild and pure.

> "Oh, God, bring him out to daylight bright and clear!"

Monty cut back into his tune, not singing himself now. But many voices were singing:

> "My Big Brother, he was brave,
> But he's lying in the cave—
> Oh, God, bring him out to daylight bright and clear!"

Then they sang it again, Brother Sumpter singing with tears on his cheeks and arms lifted to heaven, out in the open, beyond the beech tree where he could stare up into the gathering glory of the evening sky.

The slick-faced boy was standing now, singing. Suddenly, he stopped, kicked Jebb Holloway, who was still on the ground, solidly in the rump, and said: "Sing, God-durn you—get up and sing!"

Jebb Holloway got up, and sang.

VII

Jasper Harrick, according to Isaac Sumpter's report, was trapped just beyond the fourth chamber, beyond the shelf leading around the pit. He had been coming back through a very constricted crawlway, and a stone caught in a fault in the ceiling, a big one, really a thin section of the ceiling, like a bulkhead door, Jasper said, had settled just enough to pin his leg below the waist. There was some injury to the right leg, but Jasper, according to Isaac's report, did not think it too serious.

Jasper wasn't in too much discomfort, literally speaking, Isaac Sumpter said. "Food," he said, "that's the important thing. And coffee. Black, Jasper said, and he wants ham sandwiches on rye, no mustard. And a Hershey bar—almond—and water."

"I'll go," a boy said. "Lemme go get it!"

"I'll run you down," a man volunteered, "in my car."

"Listen," the Greek said, "you tell 'em at my place—tell 'em to rush it!"

Lieutenant Scrogg kept breaking in, asking questions and writing stuff in his notebook, getting the picture clear. They had to organize some rescue teams to go in, he said. He clapped Isaac on the shoulder and said: "Son, you've done your part."

"But you can't do anything going in," Isaac said, and despite the singing, which had just started, Mrs. Harrick heard this, and leaped up, crying out that somebody had to go in and get that rock off Jasper.

The lieutenant nodded vigorously.

"Yes, yes," Isaac was saying, "yes," and put his arm around Mrs. Harrick's shoulder. Then he jerked away from her, as though, very suddenly, he couldn't bear to have his arm there.

"Listen," he said, speaking very fast, addressing the lieutenant, carefully not looking at Mrs. Harrick, "It has to be done from the other side. Jasper's body fills up the crawlway. Absolutely. He says, however, that behind him there is plenty of space. A big chamber. Very big. You couldn't miss it."

"But you can't get there—oh, you said you can't—" Mrs. Harrick wailed.

"Drill," Isaac said, fast, to the lieutenant. "You have to drill in. That's what Jasper says and he knows more about caves and caving than anybody in Tennessee."

The lieutenant seemed to hesitate.

"Dig!" Old Jack Harrick said, from his chair. "Do it."

"We can investigate," the lieutenant said, "and the—"

"Investigate!" the old man cried, with a new strength in his voice. "We've done investigated. That boy there—the boy-son of my friend, the boy of Brother Sumpter—he's investigated. What more do you want?"

"Well—" the lieutenant hesitated.

"Well, I'll dig," Old Jack said. "You expect me to sit here while you talk? I'll dig for my boy—" He was struggling up in the chair, lifting up his great unkempt head, crying out in the cracked, croaking, suddenly powerful old voice: "Dig! Who'll help me dig for my boy!"

There was sudden silence. The singing stopped. People looked at the old man. Then somebody yelled: "I'll dig!"

"We'll dig—you're tootin, we'll dig," somebody else yelled.

"Ole Jack—dig fer Ole Jack!" It was the voice of Old Jim Duckett.

Then another voice, crying out, high above the others: "Dig fer daylight bright and clear!"

The crowd began to press around, milling, demanding.

The lieutenant waved his arms. "Quiet! Quiet!" he commanded.

They were, for an instant, quiet.

Then somebody, quiet and aggrieved, said: "I ain't got no pick and shovel." And his words stirred immediately the milling and demanding.

"Quiet!" the lieutenant yelled. "We have to organize."

"Where we gonna dig?" somebody demanded. "How we know where to dig?"

"Survey," the lieutenant said, with authority. "You survey."

"Yeah, survey," somebody said. "But how survey? Survey from nothing to nothing?"

The lieutenant was turning to Isaac Sumpter.

But Isaac Sumpter had withdrawn, murmuring: "Excuse me, excuse me," as he pushed his way through the crowd, no longer the forty-five or so, but a real crowd now. He passed beyond the crowd, beyond the big beech. He stopped, looked back over his shoulder, moved on a pace or so, leaned over once or twice, stopped with his back to the crowd and stood. The lieutenant was staring at him, as well as he could over the heads of the people. Then he said something to the patrolman, who headed up the ridge on the double.

Then Isacc Sumpter was coming back, slowly, apparently adjusting his dress. He came back through the crowd murmuring his excuses, and slipped back into his old place.

"I wanted to ask you something," the lieutenant began, eying him.

"Yes, yes," the boy said, still murmuring, "I'm sorry, but you see I—" He cast a significant glance at Mrs. Harrick, as though he was too diffident and polite to explain, and then reached down to tighten the zipper of his fly.

"Yes," the lieutenant agreed, hastily, giving a kind of side glance of country politeness toward Mrs. Harrick, as though even harboring a certain thought made apology in order. She, anyway, was now occupied with her husband.

"What I wanted to say is—" the lieutenant said, "is we got to get surveying in that cave. I got my man talking in to headquarters now. They'll be getting surveyors out here, and such, and tools and maybe a rig. Those crawlways now—or whatever you call 'em—how tight and all are—"

Isaac Sumpter gave him a soft, pitying smile. "Tight," he said quietly. "But you know," he said, "nobody will have to go in to survey."

"Look here," the lieutenant said, "you can't expect folks to go digging by guess and by God. I'm no surveyor—or cave-crawler either, thank God—but I know enough to know—"

Isaac was holding out to him a piece of paper. It was an old envelope. Puzzled, the lieutenant took it. He looked at it. Then he looked up. "It's addressed to Jasper Harrick—*Mr. Jasper Harrick, Johntown, Tennessee*—it's addressed to him, all right, but—"

He stopped, and glared at the boy with the dawning anger of a man of place and importance who thinks he has been made a public fool of.

"Turn it over, Lieutenant," Isaac Sumpter said, more quietly than ever.

The lieutenant obeyed.

"It's figures," he said. And began to puzzle them out: "N. 4—40 —N.E. 7—21—N. 3—" He stopped. "What the hell?" he demanded.

[229]

"That's the survey," Isaac said, with an air of finality. "The twelfth entry is where he is. There's no inclination, not to speak of. That's what Jasper says." And he added: "Distance is in feet."

"Where did you get it?" the lieutenant demanded.

"Jasper wrote it," Isaac said steadily.

"Look here," the lieutenant said, "you mean to say he figured he was going to get trapped, and so he was so darn beforehanded that he—"

"Officer," Isaac said, "my friend wasn't—isn't—a cave-crawler. He's an explorer. He always kept such records. He—"

"That's right," Mrs. Harrick broke in. "He has got little pocket notebooks full of figures."

Old Jack Harrick's hand, big, gnarled, veined, but with the skin slack and pale now over the bone and under the blotching, reached out. "Give it here," he commanded, "give that thing here."

The officer gave him the envelope.

The old man studied it, peering at it, twisting his brows as though light were bad. He looked up, straight at the lieutenant. "It's his writing," he said. "It's my boy's writing, and if it's his—by God—" He hesitated, gathered force: "Then, by God, you dig by it!"

The lieutenant took the paper, and put it into his wallet.

Old Jack Harrick turned his face painfully around and up toward Brother Sumpter, who now stood behind his chair. "Mac," he said, "Mac—I didn't mean to swear and blaspheme. I pray to be forgiven."

"You didn't blaspheme," Brother Sumpter said. "It was a kind of praying."

With the Greek, Isaac Sumpter's conversation was brief. The Greek said that things were beginning to boil downtown. People from other towns and settlements were beginning to come in. The Greek had hired him three more cooks, a fellow who had been a cook in the army and two others all right. He had laid in supplies. He had sent to Knoxville for supplies.

"You had better arrange to feed here on the ridge," Isaac said. "There will be the diggers, and if things break—" He paused, and began again: "If things develop in a certain way, there will be a large number of people up here. They can best be fed up here if you set up some kind of outdoor rig. Not too close to the cave mouth. It would not look good. You know, it would seem undignified."

"Yeah," said the Greek, "I get you. It ain't respectful, and him laying in the ground."

"But get it near enough," Isaac said. "And one more thing. That cop Scrogg is a friend of yours, isn't he?"

"Yes," the Greek said. "We get along."

"Can you call him over here?"

The Greek got the lieutenant.

"Lieutenant," Isaac Sumpter said. "I'm a little worried about something. I—we—my friend here"—indicating the Greek—"we need your advice. When the rescue work starts, and when the crowds come in—"

"Son, you leave the crowds to me," the lieutenant said.

"Naturally, naturally," Isaac murmured, "but Nick here has much on his mind the problem of feeding people up here. He is equipped to feed rescue crews. But there will be others to feed. Nick is bringing in a big outdoor rig to feed right here. Nick has got public spirit and he is a great friend of the trapped boy's family. He wants things to go smoothly. And as for me—my father being a preacher and all—I am worried about drinking and confusion, when strangers come in. When people try to exploit this—commercialize it." He paused, then said: "This is, after all, my land. You know what I mean."

The lieutenant looked at him, then at the Greek.

"Yeah," he said. "Yeah. I get you."

To the Greek he said: "Nick, I'll kick anybody's ass off this hill who tries to sell a frankfurter. Is that it?"

[231]

The Greek seemed to be suffering. He couldn't manage to say anything.

"So that is it," the lieutenant said. Then he turned back to the boy. "I don't know what the hell you want, but if you are running on the Prohibition ticket, OK by me. I'll say you had some guts, anyway. Going in that hole."

The lieutenant went away. The Greek and the boy were silent for a moment, not looking at each other. Then Isaac looked calmly at the Greek. "I guess you have the arrangements made for the telephone line to come up."

The Greek nodded.

"Well," the boy said, "start getting some power up here. We may get it paid for some way—public appeal—but we'll need it. Get me some electric pads. And more flashlights. And—" he stopped, ticking over a list in his head. "And a sleeping bag."

"A sleeping bag?" the Greek wondered.

"Of course," the boy said. "Somebody has to stay in control. And get me—oh, yes," he continued, picking up his train of thought, "some typing paper, carbon paper, a portable type-writer—one at my house, in my room, and—now get this straight, a first-rate tape recorder—either a Morton-Smith or an Acme, large size, field type, play-back, and about twenty spools of tape, small spools. You better write that down."

"But ain't no store in Johntown—" the Greek began.

"To hell with Johntown," the boy said. "You get on the phone to Nashville, Tetford's Supply Company, and get it."

"Tomorrow—it's past store time now and—"

"Now," Isaac Sumpter said. "Get a person-to-person to Milton Tetford, get it sent out by car now, to Johntown, up here to the cave, in fact. C.O.D."

"What do them things cost?" the Greek began. "We are sort of piling up stuff, and—"

Isaac gave him a slow, assessing look, and the Greek flushed under his complexion.

"Greek," Isaac said, very softly, "if you don't want in—"

Nick Pappy stared at him. He felt the old, sad, almost sweet sense of entrapment, the old certainty that things would always be a certain way. That bastard had been to college and studied mind reading and psychology and such and had said *Greek* to him in just that way.

And was saying: "Yes, if you don't want in, you want out—Greek."

But all at once the sweet weakness was gone. Nick Pappy—Nicholas Papadoupalous, who was not Nick Pappy—was on the verge of striking Isaac Sumpter. For a split second he thought he might kill him. Kill him and go to the electric chair. He even had the split second of wondering if he would be man enough to take the chair—let them put on the headpiece and strap the electrodes on your legs—without yelling or crying, or struggling like a hog before being jerked up to have the throat slit.

The hands of Nick Pappy, which had clenched to fists, relaxed. It was not because he had decided he couldn't take the chair. It wasn't that he was afraid of that. He was afraid, if of anything, of the blaze of that impulse. He had better watch it, he thought.

"OK," he said. "OK, I'm in. I said I was in."

Isaac Sumpter was looking at him. Suddenly he laid a hand on Nick Pappy's shoulder. "Nick," he said, "we're going to get that Jasper boy out. Aren't we?"

Nick nodded. That Isaac Sumpter sure kept switching things. You had to watch to know under which shell the pea was.

"Yeah," Isaac Sumpter was saying, "he's a good old boy, that Jasper. And he's my friend. We'll get him out."

All at once the Greek felt a lot better.

Not long after the Greek had gone down the ridge the food came for Jasper. Jebb Holloway volunteered to take it in, but Isaac insisted. Jebb then demanded to take it in. He said that Jasper was his friend, too, and everybody knew it, and it wasn't fair for Isaac Sumpter to—

"Fair?" Isaac Sumpter demanded quietly. In exactly what way was Jebb Holloway being deprived of something.

Jebb Holloway flushed, then got belligerent. "I'm a-going to take it in," he said, "and ain't nobody going to stop me just because he has been to college and thinks he can run things."

Isaac said, very coolly, that he intended to be quite sure that the trapped man got the food, and that the best way was to do it himself. At this Jebb Holloway again flushed up, and demanded an explanation of the implied opinion of his reliability. When, wordlessly, Isaac turned his back on him, and started to walk away, he grabbed him by the shoulder, and lifted a threatening fist. Lieutenant Scrogg was standing nearby.

"Boy," the lieutenant said, "if you aren't careful you'll be ordered off this mountain. In fact, boy," he said, "if you aren't very careful you'll be under arrest. You get me?"

Jebb Holloway got him.

"Go ahead, son," Lieutenant Scrogg said to Isaac, nodding.

Isaac was in the cave quite a long time. When he got out, he found that a couple of experts had arrived, a professor of geology from the University of Tennessee, at Knoxville, and a mine superintendent. The question of the survey was again raised. The superintendent was rather insistent, but the professor finally said: "Look here, Mr. Corwin, we know these figures are vouched for. The fellow's own father vouches for them. And you know as well as I do that you can run a cave this way, by compass. And a lot of these hillbillies are pretty good. Up in Kentucky, I remember, we had the figures and drawing done by some kid, and when we went in—a cave as complicated as a pretzel, mind you—and ran the map and checked closure and all, by God, that kid wasn't off enough to worry about. Some of these hillbilly cave-crawlers, they can sense distance from compass station to compass station as close as machine calipers. You'd almost say some of 'em have

[234]

built-in clinometers in their heads, too. But we, we don't have to worry about inclination, anyway. When we dig, we'll be striking down. Near vertical, I imagine, till we hit the cave system."

"Yes," the superintendent said.

"Anyway," the professor said, "there wouldn't be much inclination in the cave itself. I know these formations pretty well. Nearly horizontal. Now at the mouth, no doubt surface debris has been in effect, and done some choking, and maybe there's a breakdown inside. Now if you'll look yonder up the ridge, you'll see—"

In the upshot, they had run the surface survey from Jasper's figures. By four in the morning the digging had begun. With first sun, the locusts picked up again, and as an undertone to their zing and whir and grind, you could catch the distant nerve-wracking racket of the air drill, biting down into rock. If the locusts trailed off for a minute, and the crowd fell still, the drill was all you heard, off yonder, northeast.

The operation was far out of sight of the cave mouth, northeast, and slightly up the ridge, beyond the spot where the official cars and service cars and trucks were parked by the track. The highway police had long since blocked off the track to general passage. The curiosity-seekers had to come up through the woods now. By noon the next day they had beaten tracks down as though a bulldozer had been through. Up by the cave mouth, the crowds knelt in prayer.

By the time Isaac had come out of the cave from that first trip to take food in, the Greek had sent up the tape recorder, and other supplies, and the telephone line was in. By the light of a carbide mining lamp—the standard equipment for cave-crawling—Isaac Sumpter propped the portable typewriter on its case, put two sheets, with carbon, into it, and began to write. He wrote steadily at first, gradually slowing; then he snatched the sheets out and tore them to bits. He lay back on the ground, on top of the sleeping bag he had rigged up back in the cave mouth. He was very tired, he discovered. But, all at once, he did not feel tired. "Ah," he breathed, "ah," in a luxurious exhalation.

He picked up the telephone. When the operator actually answered, he experienced a lift of the heart, out of all proportion to that commonplace and predictable event. He put in a call, person-to-person, to Jack Blakely, in Nashville, and gave his father's number for the charge.

Blakely answered. When Isaac had identified himself, Blakely said: "You'll have to hurry, whatever it is you've got to say. I'm on the air in ten minutes."

"Do you still have your morning broadcast?" Isaac asked.

Blakely said yes.

"I've got something for you," Isaac said. "It's hot and will be hotter. Furthermore it will not be in the morning paper. You'd like that, wouldn't you?"

"What is it?"

"We've got a man in a cave up here in Johntown," Isaac said. "He is a war hero, a damned colorful character. His father won the Congressional Medal in nineteen eighteen. That old one is dying of cancer. He sits in a wheel chair at the cave mouth. There is a mob here. They have been singing and praying. By tomorrow there will be a million people here, singing and praying. Do you want it?"

"Yes, it sounds OK."

"OK. But one thing. I'm sending the tapes in. You play my tapes. Reasonable editing. OK?"

"Your tapes?"

"I am the guy went in. I am the guy found him. I am the guy with the face-to-face."

Isaac Sumpter hung up. He got out the recorder, thought a moment, leaning over by the light of the carbide flame.

"A man is in the ground," he began to speak to the tape.

A man is in the ground. He is a young man. He is a brave man. He has been decorated for valor, in the Korean War. Wounded, he rallied a platoon, and hung on to a shell-swept, hell-swept hill-side. This afternoon, he looked into my face, deep underground, trapped in the crawlway of a cave, a stone on his leg, and said, "This is tougher than Korea. But I'm going to make it," he said.

His father, an old man, a brave man, a man who has a Con-gressional Medal dating back to an old war—nineteen eighteen, how long ago it seems?—sits in front of the cave, in a wheel chair, dying of cancer. He wants his son to come out so that he can die happy. His mother waits, and prays. The crowd prays with her. They are singing now. Do you hear them?

The crowd had begun to sing:

> "All the bullets in Korea
>   Could not make my Brother fear,
>   My Big Brother, he was brave,
>   But he's lying in a cave—
>   Oh, God, bring him out to daylight bright and clear!"

He had taken the recorder out into the open, and set up the receiver. Then he carried it back into the protection of the cave mouth. "Edit sound as necessary," he said. And resumed:

His brother composed that ballad. No, it is not a ballad, it is a prayer. We might all pray for Jasper Harrick of Johntown, Ten-nessee. And I pray for him. For I asked him to go into that cave to explore it for me, for it is my cave. It was on my responsibility. And I ask you to help me pull for Jasper. Pull for those good peo-ple here who are praying and digging. Tonight, wherever you are, remember Jasper. This is Isaac Sumpter. No, Ikey Sumpter. Good-night. Good-bye. Let us pray.

He came out of the cave mouth. The Greek had arrived. He gave the Greek the spool of tape. He scribbled on a piece of pa-per. "This has got to get to Jack Blakely, at the Sam Davis Hotel, in Nashville. Pull him out from between whatever pair of legs it is on that Beautyrest, and give it to him personally," he said. "It goes on the air, at eight."

[237]

"I'll get somebody," the Greek said. "Somebody to drive down."

"You are reliable," Isaac Sumpter said. "A Cadillac is very reliable. I elect you."

"I have had a day," the Greek said.

"I have, too," Isaac said, "but at least you'll sleep in a bed. I won't."

The Greek seemed to hesitate.

"Do you read your Bible?" Isaac asked him.

The Greek didn't answer.

"My father is a preacher," Isaac said, "so I have read my Bible. I remember about the miracle of the loaves and fishes. Did you ever hear about it?"

For a moment the Greek was blank, then nodded with difficulty.

"Well," Isaac said, "you have got the loaves and fishes. All you need is a multitude."

The Greek looked at him, figuring it all out.

"Tomorrow," Isaac said, "you might spare some time to look around for a nice hotel site, for a nice little hotel."

As the Greek, with the tape, crossed the glade beyond the crowd, the singing stopped. He turned and looked back. Brother Sumpter was speaking: "Dear people, our stricken friends here, Mr. and Mrs. Harrick, are going to their home, and wait. Let them take our prayers with them. Let us pray."

People knelt, waiting. Brother Sumpter lifted his arms, lifted his face, closed his eyes.

"Oh, God," he said, "we pray unto Thee. We pray unto Thee in our affliction, for we know, oh, God, that Thy afflictions are Thy last mercy. Oh, Thou Who hast in darkness and the dark ground laid the stone on the leg of Jasper Harrick, lift him up in Thy glorious light. Lift up our hearts that lie under the stone of darkness. Oh, God, let us in our striving to lift the stone from our hearts help lift that stone from Jasper Harrick, in the dark ground. Oh, God, bring all forth!"

[238]

The Greek had waited for the prayer to finish. Now he plunged up the ridge. He heard the singing begin again. He almost went back and offered the Harricks a ride down in the Cadillac, but he knew a million people were helping them. So he didn't. A Cad, however, would give them the softest ride down, the old man like he was, and Mrs. Harrick, that nice lady, all worn out. He wished he could take 'em down. He felt sad and deprived.

But all at once, hearing the singing, the words about coming into the daylight bright and clear, his heart flooded with a tearful joy, like a busted hot-water pipe in a basement. Then he went on up the ridge. "We'll get him out," he was saying to himself, promising himself something.

The old man sat in the wheel chair, in his room, under the nakedness of the hanging electric light. His wife was unbuttoning his shirt. The night insects of summer, drawn by the light, thumped with soft, sad, fatalistic bluntness against the screen. You knew that they knew they couldn't get in. But they thumped against the screen.

The woman went to the washstand, got a toothbrush and a tube of toothpaste, and squeezed a not too parsimonious strip out on the brush. She poured a glass of water, and brought the things to the old man. He held them, while she went for a basin that he could lean over. While he washed his teeth she patiently held the basin, but did not know she was holding it, for she stared into the warm, leaf-fleshed, throbbing dark beyond the screen and wondered what it would be like to be in the ground.

Once, long back, she had asked Jasper what made him want to crawl in caves. What had he said?

"It's not what you'd expect, down there," he had said. "It's not like above-ground folks would expect."

"What's it like?" she had asked.

[239]

"It's a nice temperature down there," he had said. "It is not summer and it is not winter. There aren't any seasons to bother about down there," he had said, and laughed.

"Well," she had retorted, laughing too, for Jasper always made you feel good and about to run off into laughing, whatever the subject you were off on. "Well, what's so wonderful about that? Up here you can always stir up the fire or pick up a palm-leaf fan, come blizzard or hot spell."

"Blizzard or hot spell," he said, "a lot of things don't matter down there."

This had been at a time when she was worrying most about Jasper, after he had been home from the war quite a spell and had time, you'd think, to take hold. But he didn't. She was wishing he'd get married, for that might help. Girls just threw themselves at him, she knew, and even though she closed her mind she knew the kind of talk.

But she couldn't quite close her ears to the jokes John T. would make to Jasper. It seemed just too awful, in a way she couldn't quite say, to think of John T. making that kind of joke to Jasper, his boy, her boy, their son. She even had the more awful notion that those jokes and winks and leers didn't happen, except when she was present. But that suspicion was too awful, somehow, to hold on to.

After a while, however, the jokes had stopped. It got so Jasper would get sort of white in the face under his brown, and his skin would look tight over the jawbone. It got so he stayed away more and more from them, from the house. That was the time when things were worst, she reckoned, the tales about his carryings on and his disappearings.

So when he had said that a lot of things didn't matter under the ground, she had just burst out. "Well, it seems a lot of things don't matter above the ground, either," she had said. And had added with an irony so unaccustomed to her nature, that later she was simply sick: "At least to certain people."

The words weren't out of her mouth before she had the desperate hope that he'd take it as a sort of joke, and she put a smile on her face to cover what she knew had been there. But even as she put on the smile she knew it would be about as much good as the veil she had once seen on the face of a woman on a bus passing through Johntown—a woman who had a great purple swelling thing, grainy and knotted, on her cheek, the color of an overripe plum.

No, the smile had done no good, for Jasper, looking steadily down into her face, had said in the quietest voice: "No, Mammy, to certain people they don't."

And he had gone on with whatever life it was he was living, working a little for just enough money for shotgun shells, sitting alone and singing his songs, drifting down the river for days and nights, off into the mountains, in winter, alone, with or without a rifle, hunting or not hunting, crawling into the caves, off and gone, without ever a word.

Just after he had said what he did that day—"No, Mammy, to certain people they don't"—he had kept on looking down at her in the strangest way, as if he wanted to say something to her, to tell her something, cry out to her. And at that moment, she had been absolutely terrified of what he might say, whatever mysterious thing it might be. She had not had the slightest notion of what it might be, but she was so afraid that she hadn't even been able to reach out and touch him.

If only she had touched him.

If only she had been able to reach out and touch him, then everything might have been different. He might be right here now, asleep in his room.

But she hadn't touched him, and what had he said then?

He had looked down at her with that strange look as though he were about to cry out to her, and then—she was almost sure of it, or was it just the way she felt it had to be?—he had shrugged. He had said: "Well, in the ground at least a fellow has a chance of knowing who he is."

Oh, it was too awful! Standing there under the electric bulb, while the fleshy-hot, quivering June darkness thumped at the window screen, she cried out in her heart that it was too awful to think that you had to go down into the ground, where the seasons never came and a lot of things didn't matter, and lie there in the earth-dark before you could know who you are.

"John T.—John T.," she cried out, holding the basin while the old man let the pure white foam of dentifrice fall into it, "oh, I didn't reach out and touch him!"

"What? What?" the old man demanded from the white-foamed lips.

"Rinse your mouth, John T.," she said, as though to a child. But he wasn't childish.

He rinsed his mouth, and spat into the basin.

She felt she couldn't stand there any longer. She just sank down by his knee, and set the basin on the floor. "I didn't reach out and touch him, John T.," she said. "But you—you can save him, John T.!"

"Me—" the old man said, "me—" and made a grinding, strangled exhalation in his throat, two or three times, as though he were trying to raise something out of it.

"You could pray," she said. "Oh, John T. you haven't prayed for him!"

"Pray," he said, as though the word were a sound with no meaning.

"You could pray, and God wouldn't let it happen."

"Happen?" he demanded. "Happen?"

"Oh, He wouldn't let it happen," she cried out.

"Well, He let the world happen," he said. "He let the world happen, didn't He?"

And sitting in the chair, a toothbrush clenched in one hand, a glass of bedimmed water in the other, under the naked electric light, the old man made a sound in his throat, over and over again, that bore some resemblance to laughter.

VIII

Mr. James Haworth, city editor of the Nashville *Press-Clarion,* sat alone in the living room of his split-level in a new development out beyond the Hillsboro section, and let the sadnesses which were what his life had, it seemed, become, rise in his mind like miasma. He was worried about the fact that the plumbing was already rotten in the house and the place only four years old with the mortgage scarcely dented. He had hoped to pay out just in time to retire, but now as he worried about the plumbing he sort of hoped he would die, quietly in his sleep of course, before too long and not have to think any more about the rotten deal they had handed him on this lemon of a tepee, or the fact he couldn't ever get ahead financially speaking, or even at the paper where they should have made him assistant managing editor instead of that s.o.b. Smather when Sarton became vice president. They would have promoted him, too, he was damned sure, if he hadn't been a Yankee, which was one of the things they did not let you forget, even after twenty-five years and you married to a Southern belle, even if she was third-string. He wished he had stayed in Jersey City, where maybe he would have made out, and never come to the Athens of the South, the capital of the Buttermilk Belt, and never—

He hoped he would die, and that would fix Louise, who was out right now with the League of Women Voters and would soon come in and give him hell and what-for for drinking the bourbon he was now drinking as he watched TV. She was right, he reflected bitterly, for he would have acid stomach by 2 A.M. and be getting up and ruining her sleep.

Yes, it was her sleep she was worried about, the cow. If she had slept less and eaten less and taken some exercise, like even dusting that hell hole of an apartment over on Ellison, or now even dusting this lemon of a tepee she had made him get because she said the stairs at Ellison gave her varicose veins, she would not now be in the shape she was in and a man might look forward to some pleasure in life beyond drinking bourbon, even on a June night, temperature a Middle-Tennessee 97 at 8:45 P.M., humidity 87 per cent, but as it was, when that cow came lowing home across the lea there would be no joy and her side of the bed sagged so a man had to claw all night to hang on to the hillside and not fall down there and be drowned, suffocated, or reviled. After all she was only forty-five and he bet that that Sally Suffolk, of whose décolletage he was at that moment acutely conscious on the TV screen, was not a day younger but she had everything and not too much of anything and she would not make her side of the bed sag unless she got co-operation.

Mr. Haworth thought he was going to cry. He thought of his daughter and wished she had not died when she was fourteen and promising to be pretty and well stacked. Then he felt ashamed, not saying to himself what exactly he was ashamed of, and thought of his boy who was not dead but might as well be, and that too after all the money they had spent sending him to the University of Virginia, which was where Louise had wanted him to go to be a gentleman.

He was wondering why these days he so often thought he might start crying when the phone rang. And suddenly the phone rang and he thought, God Almighty, he bet that call was trouble and then there might really be something to cry about.

He took a morbid satisfaction when he heard the voice of Joel Sarton. He took the morbid satisfaction even before the s.o.b. got unlimbered and delivered.

"What are you doing?" Sarton demanded, without even a *how-do-you-do.*

James Haworth said he was watching TV.

"That's nice," Joel Sarton said. Then asked, solicitously, what program. When Haworth told him, he paused a minute and then switched the subject. "You fired that college wonder, Ikey Sumpter, didn't you?"

Haworth, with a sudden nausea of apprehension, said yes, he had fired the *Kollege Kutie.* He put the capital *K*'s in, in his mind. Defensively, he added that Mr. Smather had OK'd the firing, and that he, James Haworth, had been the last to fire Mr. Tittlebum, for Mr. Tittlebum had been fired out of whatever he had been into with that round-butted Pride of Jerusalem with the red German buggy and a million bucks, who, as he understood, was the only reason Mr. Tittlebum had been hired by Mr. Smather in the first place. And Tittlebum had been fired out of college too. He drank, he added.

"To excess?" Joel Sarton breathed horror into the other end of the telephone.

"Yes," James Haworth said.

"It seems to me," Joel Sarton said, "that, to judge from the way you are gargling, you yourself must even now be drinking to excess."

"I am watching TV," James Haworth said stubbornly, and tried to control his breathing. He found that he was even trying not to breathe at all so the odor would not go over the line ten miles out

[245]

to where Joel Sarton, no doubt holding a Scotch and soda bubbling in crystal with the patrician paleness of champagne, stood in the den of his beautiful country home, which had cost six times what James Haworth's lemon of a tepee had cost and where cool night breezes would comfort a man's brow even on a hell-broth night like this and where the cans flushed properly with a quiet satisfying authoritative swirl and where no mortgage lay down to breathe in a man's ear on his midnight pillow. James Haworth thought he was going to cry. He almost missed what that s.ȯ.b. Sarton was saying.

The s.o.b. was saying: "Didn't that Sumpter boy call in about what was happening at Johntown?"

"Yes," Haworth said, "he called yesterday afternoon, and you would have thought it was John Gunther trying to do us a favor. I offered him county correspondent space rate and said make it short and he hung up. So I got the guy at Rutledge to get the facts. And," he added with the tone of a man virtuously winding up a subject, but not believing in his own tone, "the story is in tonight's edition."

"I must indeed take a look at it," Joel Sarton said softly. "And while I am informing myself I suggest that you, for your information—that is, if you feel information is still a commodity in your profession—I suggest that you switch your TV set from the charms of that big-titted nightingale who is promoting lung cancer, to a simple, homey, wholesome Tennessee story which you will find on station LSXU. And"—Joel Sarton's voice went velvety in the velvet night out at his beautiful country home, merely a velvet whisper now—"may I suggest that, when you have informed yourself, you call me back? I sit up late. Don't hesitate to call. After you have decided what to say."

Mr. Haworth knew for some seconds that he was holding a dead receiver, but it seemed that he couldn't put it down. As soon as he put it down he would have to do certain other things. Then he thought that he might, before doing anything else, freshen his drink. Fortified by that thought, he managed to cradle the receiver.

He thought again of his dead daughter, and how they had muffled the phone during her illness. He thought now that everything might have been all right tonight if he had just muffled the phone so it wouldn't disturb him.

He got the new drink, took a sip, and approached the TV set, where now the nightingale had ceased to sing and was promoting lung cancer. He took one more look at her, felt that his viscera were, suddenly and inexplicably, falling away from their moorings, and reached numbly, fatalistically, for the button. It was LSXU, he remembered with an effort.

Then, all at once, he remembered what the program would be. It would be "The Land We Live in."

My God, he thought, *my God, that's national.*

Then he managed to turn the control.

But what he first saw soothed his apprehension. It was simply the famous face of Wes Williams, a good handsome American face, clear-eyed, earnest, direct, a face with a wry humor barely masking the depth of feeling, a young-looking face with the youth scarcely belied by the heaviness of the clean-scraped, glistening jowls. It was a good face, and if the tailoring on the good shoulders was perhaps excessively good, it was casual; and the face was a face that loved the land we live in and loved you, the face of the American boy coming home, home to Mom, home to the old swimming hole where that delicious mud got between the toes, home to apple pie, home to a man-to-man talk with the soda jerk he used to go to school with, home to remember how he had held hands with Sukie Morgan—or Bildshoff, or what the crap was her name?—under the maples, or elms, or cottonwoods, or chinaberries, or long-leaf pines, or maybe under the water tower by the railroad track, but now he'd have to hurry, darn it all, for he had to make a plane into New York tomorrow morning.

The face of Wes Williams comforted Mr. Haworth. Until he

[247]

gradually comprehended what Wes Williams was so earnestly saying out of the twenty-one-inch screen.

"—and as we have heard these good people praying for the safety of Jasper Harrick, and singing for him to be saved, we have felt how much they love and admire him. It is not merely because he is a suffering human being, deep in the ground, a boy they knew and watched growing up in little Johntown. It is not merely because Jasper Harrick fought for his country and holds a medal for heroism on a shell-swept, hell-swept Korean hillside. It is also because he embodies one of the deepest American traits, the courage to plunge into the unknown. Jasper Harrick is the descendant of frontiersmen. He himself is a frontiersman. Not blazing new trails to lead men into this green country of Tennessee. Not fighting the savage Cherokee. But plunging into the earth itself, seeking the new, the unknown. It is because he embodies that trait that opened America, that is why we honor him. But that, too, is why tonight he lies deep under—"

Why?

The word hung in Celia Hornby Harrick's mind, as that man went on talking, telling about Jasper. But what could that man know about Jasper? That man didn't know that it was a nice temperature down there, and not summer and not winter. He didn't know that there weren't any seasons down there. He didn't know that a lot of things didn't matter down there.

He didn't know that she, Celia Hornby Harrick, had not reached out her hand to touch her son.

If that man knew that would he tell all the people? Would they turn that camera on her so that all the people in the world would suddenly see her face on their little gray flickering screens and see the face of a mother who had not saved her son? And all the people in the world would look at her face and say: *Yes, yes, look at that face, that is the unnatural mother who would not—*

That man was going to do it. She knew he was going to point

[248]

the thing at her face. So she covered her face with both hands and sat there sweating.

They'll think I'm praying, she thought. She even tried to pray. But pray for what? To be hidden? Then, as she prayed, the Bible words came into her head—*for the rocks and the mountains to fall on them.*

She stopped the prayer, in terror. If she prayed to be hidden, the rocks and the mountains might really fall on her. Then it would be dark. It would be dark and she couldn't breathe. With her hands on her face, she made a gasp for air.

So she couldn't pray.

Then she thought that if she had been able to pray and the rocks and the mountains had really fallen on her, that would mean she had taken Jasper's place and he would be saved. So she tried to pray, but the words wouldn't come. She would die for Jasper, she knew that, and the Lord God, Who saw into the innermost recesses of her soul, knew it. She would lie down and die in pain to save Jasper, but she could not die that way, with the rocks and the mountains suffocating her with darkness.

But all at once her guilt in the fact of that refusal overwhelmed her, and it was suffocating her in the dark behind her squinched eyelids and spread hands. So she jerked her hands away.

The glaring lights were there. The trees rose beyond the light, and the leaves that that light hit had the incandescent sick green of the light before a storm. The trees out of the light rose up blacker than black. The ridge was black above them. The man had Monty up there in the light with him. Monty blinked into the light, holding his brother's box, and he looked sick. She wanted to yell out to the men to leave Monty alone, to please, dear God, leave him alone.

But she was afraid to. If she did, the man might show her face to all the people in the world.

The man was making Monty say how they found the boots and box at the cave. Then the man took the box out of Monty's hands, just took it out of them, and held it up. He said it was the guitar which the famous father of Jasper Harrick had once used to make mountain merriment and bring happiness to his neighbors. He said it was the box on which the trapped boy had composed his lonely songs that had the joy and heartbreak of the American Highlands. With a sad sweet smile, he thrust the box back at Monty.

"Play one," he said, softly, "play one of your brother's songs. I know—we know—you can play. We know, Monty, how you love your brother. How you borrowed his songs in secret. But don't be ashamed that we know. It was human, you loved him—"

In that terrible light Monty looked sick. Celia Harrick knew he was sick. But she couldn't call out.

"Play for Jasper," the man was saying, leaning toward Monty, bending a sad look on him. "Sing—sing for your Big Brother."

The boy gave him one murderous glare, looked widely around as though in appeal, then shut his eyes, swung the box into position, lifted his right heel, and struck the strings:

> "Mist on the mountain
> Fog round the hill,
> I'll still be loving,
> Do what you will:
> Do what you—"

The man had touched Monty on the arm. "Thank you, Monty," he said to the boy. Then into the thing he talked at: "That is one of the songs of Jasper Harrick. Let us all pray that he may bring that talent back to us in the light of day. The world can't afford to lose such talent. And now—" He was moving toward the spot where Monty now sat near his parents, and Celia Harrick knew that man was going to come to her, so she shut her eyes.

She wished John T. would put his hand out to her. She wanted to ask him to, but some dark resentment made her refuse. *He ought to know, she thought. He ought to know. Without my touching him or telling him.* But she desperately wanted him to put out his hand and save her. He would save her from that man, from her guilt.

And then she thought: *He wouldn't save Jasper and he won't save me. He let Jasper go down and lie in the ground.*

Somehow, in some awful way, that made her feel better. Yes, if John T. had refused to pray to save Jasper from the dark ground, then it wasn't her fault, it wasn't hers, no, not hers.

As that Monty stood up there and played on that box, the slick-faced boy, sitting over at one side of the crowd reached into his pocket and drew out the wadded panties. Covertly he showed the wad to Jebb Holloway. "Do you reckin it could of been that Monty?" he demanded. "You reckin he jerked 'em?"

"That Monty," Jebb Holloway said. Then added: "That boog-ger said he was gonna TV me tonight. Like they done that time I made thirty-one points in the basketball turna-mint fer my Alma Modder, the Johntown High—they said I come out well on TV. That boogger said he was gonna TV me tonight fer going in the cave."

"When you crawled in you ought to of ast Jasper if it was him jerked these-here things off that Jo-Lea."

"He wasn't of no mind to talk about jerking things off no hen house," Jebb Holloway said.

"He said what he said about his girl," the slick-faced boy said stubbornly.

"That was talking serious," Jebb Holloway said. "It was not talking about no drawers-pulling. He did not say who his girl is."

"Next time you ast him."

Jebb Holloway fell thoughtful.

"They said they was gonna TV me," Jebb Holloway said. "And now he's wasting time on that Monty."

"You reckin it was really Monty jerked 'em off her?"

"You make me sick," Jebb Holloway said. "They might of been jerked off your old lady for all you know."

[251]

"Ain't nobody gonna talk like that about my mother," the slick-faced boy affirmed.

"I ain't saying nothing special against your old lady. Maybe was your old man done it," Jebb Holloway said. "I am just saying you don't know."

"I'm a-going to find out," the slick-faced boy said, stubbornly, half to himself.

"Well, why don't you ask her?" Jebb Holloway jeered.

"Maybe I will," the slick-faced boy said.

"Maybe you will git religion, too," Jebb Holloway said. "Like all them others done tonight. Maybe you will confess your sins."

"Maybe you won't never git on TV if you don't pick your ears and listen," the slick-faced boy said.

"Jesus," Jebb Holloway breathed, scrambling to his feet. "Jesus, he was calling me—"

Wes Williams, as he stretched out his hand toward him, looked astonishingly like Jebb Holloway, a Jebb Holloway who had, however, been to college, had money in the bank, admitted to no self-doubts, and had twenty-five more points of intelligence quotient and a considerably better tailor than the present Jebb Holloway. They might, in that moment, have posed as brothers, or as a before-and-after-taking ad for success. Wes smiled benignly on the self he had been, and with an old yearning stretched forth his hand toward that innocence. "Let me call you Jebb," he said to Jebb Holloway. "I would feel honored to be on first names with a man who did what you did today. Folks," he said turning from the handshake toward the great world, "this is Jebb Holloway. He is the man who—"

Jebb clasped his hands above his head like a champion and gave a champion's smile to this side and that.

"—went into the cave today to take light and warmth to his dear friend Jasper Harrick. It is not strangers who take comfort to the trapped youth, but old friends, Isaac Sumpter and Jebb Holloway. They will permit no others. 'I asked Jasper to go into

[252]

this cave,' says Isaac Sumpter, haggard and worn, 'and I am going to do what I can to expiate.'

"Yes," continued Wes Williams, as the champion's smile began to fade from the face of Jebb Holloway, "Isaac Sumpter, who is in the ground this very minute, would let no one else go in—not the stout-hearted sons of Johntown, nor the newsmen, like myself—and this community of individualists understands and backs him up. Only Jebb Holloway may go in with Sumpter to carry into the dark ground not only what is needed for survival, but the warm clasp of an old comrade who will risk all."

He turned to Jebb, who had recovered his smile. "Jebb," he said, "have you been in many caves? Are you—to use the local expression—a caver?"

"I crawled a few," Jebb said, brightening, "yeah, I crawled some, and—" Then he stopped, reassessing the situation. "Naw, I wasn't never a caver. I just crawled a few, like a kid will. I never took to going in the ground. Now, me—what I take to, it's basketball. Yeah, now—"

"Yes, yes," Wes Williams interrupted, with a slight firmness, then turning hastily to the world beyond, "Jebb here is a well-known basketball star. In the state high-school tournament last season, in one game, he ran up twenty-one points." Then back to Jebb: "Now, Jebb, if you aren't a caver—"

"It was thirty-one points," Jebb Holloway said.

"Yes, yes, of course," Wes Williams said, managing one of his smiles, but then moving in swiftly, "but, Jebb, if you aren't a caver, I just want to say it was even more courageous of you to go in the ground."

At this, Jebb visibly relaxed, and smiled the champion's smile. Wes Williams fixed him with a deep, manly gaze and asked earnestly: "Why did you go in?"

Jebb began to writhe in embarrassment. "It was just—" he hesitated. "Aw, heck," he said then.

Jebb writhed again, trying to remember exactly how that

[253]

bastard Isaac Sumpter had said it, sort of straight out and quiet. The bastard, just because he had been to college, he figured he was smarter than anybody. Then he remembered exactly how Isaac had done, before he went in the ground tonight, so he lifted his head and sort of looked off yonder in the dark beyond the lights, and began over. "Jasper Harrick is my friend," he said quietly.

Wes Williams held it a couple of seconds. Then, even more quietly, he said: "And how did he seem, Jebb?"

"He's making out," Jebb said. "But he was right glad for the heat pad. He said, 'Thanks.' Just, 'Thanks, kid.' Jasper, he never was one to take on and mirate much."

"Now, Jebb," Wes said, "I know you have delivered the messages Jasper sent out from his Golgotha—I mean out of the cave where he is stuck—but tell all the people everywhere who are looking and listening and praying for Jasper—who, I bet, are pulling for you too—tell them what Jasper said."

"He said—" Jebb began. "Well, he sort of grinned and said, 'You tell 'em out there to do the digging and I'll do the grunting.'"

"That's spirit," Wes Williams allowed, and shook his head in grim admiration.

"I give him them pills," Jebb said.

"Yes," Wes said, "tranquilizers."

"He wouldn't take 'em," Jebb said. "He said he could hold on."

"That's spirit," Wes Williams said again, and compressed his lips to master his feelings.

"He said, 'Tell 'em I'm holding on,'" Jebb elaborated, "'but it's tougher than Korea.'"

"Jasper held on in Korea," Wes said, then turned to Jebb, his voice going soft: "What else did he say, Jebb?"

"He said tell his mammy and p-p—his mother and father—to pull for him but not to worry."

"Thinking of those he loved," Wes said quietly, as though to himself. Then to Jebb: "Was that all, Jebb?"

[254]

"Naw," Jebb said, getting an expression of grave sweetness on his face, an expression strangely similar to that on the face of Wes Williams. "Naw," he repeated, "he said something else. He said, 'Tell my girl I'm holding on, but if I don't make it, not to grieve. Tell her I got her in my heart.'"

Wes Williams held it. Then he laid a hand on Jebb Holloway's shoulder, gripped it firmly once in unspoken understanding, shook his head, and said, almost in a whisper: "Thank you, Jebb."

As Jebb Holloway stood there in that splendid second, the tears rising in his heart and wetting his eyes, with the beauty of the words Jasper had spoken, he felt a strong grip on his shoulder, the comradely hand of Wes Williams tightening secretly to revolve him away from the microphones, away from the lights, away from all the eyes all over the whole God-damned country that had been staring at Jebb Holloway, God-durn it, looking right at him.

But now all those eyes all over the whole country were not seeing Jebb Holloway, but just Wes Williams, who had never been in a cave or run up thirty-one points against Tracy City, who was saying: "I hold here in my hand the latest report from the rescue digging. It has just been handed to me. They are working heroically, those volunteers of this Volunteer State. They are driving a shaft through soft limestone to strike into the cave beyond Jasper and lift the stone that pins him. Eighteen hours now, they have been striking down. The shaft is now down seventy-four feet, the report says, but for the last two hours they have had to give up the air drill. The experts fear the percussion will jar rock loose in the cave below. It is man-work now, back-breaking, man-killing work. It is the old pick and shovel, deep in the rock, in rapid relays, for a man can just take so much. The buckets of muck come up by hand-hoist. Those heroes are sweating for Jasper. They come up from the hole and lie panting on the grass, heaving for breath. I have seen them. But a man lies there happy, for he

[255]

knows he is playing a man's part, he knows that deep in the ground another man, trapped and waiting trusts him. He knows that here tonight the heart of a young girl is—"

Standing there, looking at Wes Williams, whom nobody, nobody, could shove away from those mikes and cameras, Jebb Holloway felt a murderous, sick rage growing in him against those fingers that had so secretly and firmly revolved him away from that glare of happiness toward the darkness that was himself.

For he knew now that as soon as he was away from the lights all things would be as they had been that afternoon when he was in the ground and as tonight, while he was waiting for the man to call him up to the mikes and cameras, they had, somehow, not seemed to be.

He made his way numbly back to the spot where he had sat before. The slick-faced boy leaned at him and said: "You done all right. You done better than Monty."

"Shut up," Jebb said, and pretended to be listening to what that Williams bastard was saying. But he was not really listening, for what he heard was what Isaac Sumpter had said that afternoon, deep in the ground, and what he was, this minute, saying deep in the darkness which was the suffering self of Jebb Holloway.

Yes, everything began to happen again.

It began happening again just as it had happened late that morning when Isaac had come to him in front of the cave and said: "Jebb, I'm sorry I blocked you from going in—when you were with those reporters. To let you go would just have complicated things about them. But you're a friend of Jasper's, and I'm going in now, and if you want to come, fine. The power line's about here, and we'll run the line for the heat pad and light."

So Jebb had put on coveralls, feeling very much, as people stood around looking respectfully at him, like one of those jet

[256]

flyers in Korea who had gone up, like you could see in the movies, and knocked down them Commy-nist fellows and saved America. He was almost surprised when he turned around to see nothing but a hole in the ground.

It was nothing but a hole in the ground.

Heck, he thought, and saw himself swinging up to a cockpit.

Nothing but a hole in the ground, he thought, feeling letdown and contemptuous, and then, in the same instant, feeling a tightening of the chest.

God, he thought, *God*, and thought how a fellow up in a plane could breathe—it wouldn't be nothing to have to go up in that there wild blue yonder and slug it out. A fellow could breathe.

Then Isaac was crawling in. Somebody put the miner's lamp on Jebb, and lit the carbide. He got down and got ready to start.

"Good luck," somebody said.

He wished to Christ they hadn't said that.

Monty and two other fellows got in the entry to feed the line in—light, stout, plastic-covered line. Jebb looked back at them once, then he was in the hole. He was pulling the line. It was tied to him. He could hear Isaac up ahead, scratching along. It wasn't nothing, he figured, for that durn smart aleck of a Isaac Sumpter to go crawling around in the ground, him thin-built like he was, but when you had you a pair of shoulders like him, like Jebb Holloway, it was different, a fellow taking more risk and all to get stuck. Folks ought to realize how it was different for a Isaac Sumpter, being built about as thin and slick as a rat tail, durn him. He began to feel the anger grow against Isaac Sumpter for getting him into this.

Then he was entering the first chamber, and felt better. A feller could breathe here.

"You stay here," Isaac Sumpter was saying, and Jebb felt a deep, unacknowledged relief and, suddenly, a liking for that Isaac Sumpter.

But he was going on: "—and when we get enough line

pulled in, then I'll crawl through the next crawlway. I'll take the end through and you can feed it all in to me."

"Yeah," Jebb said, "yeah."

"Then you crawl on to me," that bastard said, "and we'll repeat. One thing, though—this crawlway is tougher. Just take it easy, and you'll make it."

Isaac Sumpter was studying him by the carbide flare. "You aren't any bigger than Jasper," he said quietly. And added: "And he made it." And added softly: "Through here, I mean."

"Yeah," Jebb said, "yeah," and saw that little rat-tail bastard go slicking into that crawlway, leaving him, leaving him alone by himself, with the small steady hiss of the carbide flame. He crouched there and fed the line in. A fellow had to keep his mind on it, to keep the line clear, even if they had got it all laid smooth and ready. He kept his mind on it.

When no more slack got pulled, he waited. He waited to be sure. There was a little line left, and maybe Isaac was just resting. He had to wait to be sure. Then he couldn't wait any more.

Isaac was right. This crawlway was tougher than the other. It was real tough.

When Jebb got into the next chamber, he was panting. It seemed he couldn't make his heart settle down. That slick rat-tail bastard was looking at him. "Good boy," the bastard said, "you made it."

"Yeah," Jebb said, and felt himself grinning at Isaac Sumpter. He even felt himself feeling grateful to him for saying that— "Good boy."

"I expect you learned something on that one," the bastard was saying. "I know I did, the first time I came through. About hunching your shoulders to help crawl. There where the roof gets so damned low."

"Yeah," Jebb said, remembering how the roof came down and scraped right on a fellow's shoulder blades. It was like somebody

[258]

was about to put a great big hand between your shoulder blades and just press down.

"It's good you learned," Isaac Sumpter said. "The next one gets a little tighter."

"Yeah," Jebb said.

"Let's get the line straight," Isaac Sumpter said indifferently. He turned his back on Jebb and began straightening line. Even when he had to turn again, straightening line, he didn't look in Jebb's face.

It was funny, Jebb began to feel, a feller not ever looking at you in the face, just sorting out line and not acting like you were even there. Jebb began to feel funny. He wanted to say something, but he couldn't figure out a thing to say. Also he was afraid he might say something and there wouldn't be any sound to come. It was almost like you couldn't risk it.

But why didn't that bastard say something?

And the bastard did. The bastard said: "Look—cave crickets."

Jebb stared at the insect there on the floor beside the wire.

"Plenty of them in the next crawlway," Isaac Sumpter said. "Get on your face sometimes, when you're crawling. You can't brush them off." Then added, after a moment: "Your hands aren't free, of course."

They finished sorting the line. Isaac Sumpter went and peered into the mouth of the next crawlway. He came back to where Jebb squatted beside a big stalagmite, his hands dropping over his hunched-up knees.

"I been thinking," Isaac Sumpter said.

"Yeah?" Jebb said.

Isaac waited, not looking at him. Then he said: "I think one man ought to stay in this chamber. The other—"

The other, Jebb Holloway echoed in his mind.

"—he can take the line into chamber three, sort it by himself. You see, there won't be much length then left. Then he can get on through the real tough gut of a crawlway. To Jasper. That gut isn't long, it's just tough. What do you think of that arrangement, Jebb?"

"Sounds all right," Jebb said finally.

"Oh, I didn't explain my reasoning," Isaac said. "If anything goes wrong—I mean if I got stuck or something—you wouldn't have so far to crawl out by yourself. And easier ground."

Jebb didn't say anything.

Isaac Sumpter continued to squat there, eight feet away from the big stalagmite by which Jebb was now propping himself as he squatted. It was so big, it felt like a tree trunk, when you leaned sideways against it. It felt like a tree trunk, he was saying to himself. He was not looking up at Isaac now.

"Oh, one more thing," Isaac Sumpter was saying. "You know, I sort of feel bad about one thing."

"Yeah?" Jebb said, not looking up, knowing, somehow, that the eyes under the flare over there were looking at him.

"You've come in a long way. And I know you like Jasper."

The voice hesitated, and Jebb felt a cold clutch of apprehension in his belly. He didn't know what it was about. But he knew it was there.

And the voice coming out of the face which he would not look at over there under the flare was saying: "I don't want you to think I'm trying to get into the limelight myself. Trying to hog the credit. You know why I've been coming in here. To make it up to Jasper. But I want you to feel free to go on. I'll stay here."

The voice stopped. Jebb didn't look up to meet the eyes under the flare. He leaned against the rough surface of the stalagmite. He felt its roughness, but its funny sort of smoothness too, through the coveralls. It was like a beech, that was what it was feeling like. If you leaned up against this thing in the dark, durn it, you'd think it was a beech. *Yeah, if in the dark, you—*

His mind stopped right there.

It stopped in time for him to hear Isaac Sumpter saying, very softly: "You feel free, Jebb, to carry on. To go on to your—your friend."

[260]

"He's yore friend," Jebb burst out. "Jasper—he is crazy about you—he was telling me, he was saying—"

"Yes, he is my friend," Isaac said, slowly rose, and stood looking down at the crouching Jebb. "Feed the line slow," he said. "It's better to keep a little tension."

Then he entered the crawlway.

Jebb Holloway never knew how long it was. In a way it seemed like forever, as he watched the line crawling, crawling inch by inch away, into the crawlway. Then suddenly, as he saw how little line was left, he felt time racing away, and the line was racing away, leaving him, Jebb Holloway, here alone, by that piece of rock that felt like a beech tree if you leaned against it and didn't look. In the dark, if your light went out, it would feel like a beech tree.

Then the slack was all gone, and he held his breath. As long as the line was moving it was like somebody with you. It was alive. But now he was so lonesome he thought he would cry.

As he held his breath, it seemed like forever, as though all time had stopped. In a funny way it was like bleeding to death. It was like blood running out of him from a secret wound and being soaked up by all the earth around him, and by the absolutely motionless air, and nothing could staunch the wound. He was just bleeding away into the dark beyond the edge of the light made by his carbide lamp.

When a cave cricket jumped into the light, right there on the red-brown dust of the floor, he almost cried, he was so happy. Something had stopped the wound. He wasn't bleeding to death any more. What he thought of, then, was how much he loved his mother. He thought of all the things he hadn't done that she wanted him to do and all the things he had done she didn't want him to do. He wanted to lay his head on her breast and tell her how it was going to be from now on.

It was just about then, in the midst of this sense of purification and new beginnings, that Isaac Sumpter emerged from the crawlway. Thinking of it afterwards, Jebb couldn't understand why he hadn't heard anything. It was almost as though he had been asleep and had dreamed about laying his head on his mother's breast and feeling how everything would be different, and Isaac Sumpter had interrupted the dream.

But, no, he didn't interrupt it, he entered it. That is, he entered the feeling of happiness, and was part of the feeling of happiness, as Jebb ran to him, helped him get up, and said, over and over again: "Jesus—Jesus—Jesus," and tried to dust the dirt off of Isaac Sumpter's coveralls.

"Thanks," Isaac Sumpter said, when he had his breath. Then he looked at the boy.

"Jesus," Jebb Holloway breathed. That word, too, was part of his happiness.

"He is worse off," Isaac said.

That statement, for some reason, struck Jebb with terror. The happiness was gone.

"But he is holding on," Isaac said.

"Yeah?" Jebb felt better again.

"He said, 'Thanks,' just that, when I gave him the heat pad. He just said, 'Thanks, kid.' Just like that. Then you know what he did?"

"Naw," Jebb Holloway said. "Naw."

"He wouldn't take those pills, those tranquilizers the doctor sent in. He said he would hold on. Then you know what he said?"

"Naw."

"He said tell his mother and father to pull for him, but not to worry," Isaac said.

"Yeah?"

"Yes," Isaac Sumpter said. "But there is something else," Isaac said.

"Yeah?"

"Yes," Isaac Sumpter said. "There is something else. He said these very words. He said, 'Tell my girl I'm holding on. Tell her not to grieve. Tell her I got her in my heart.' "

At that, Jebb Holloway again thought he was going to cry. As though to himself, he repeated the words: "Tell her I got her in my heart." It was about the sweetest feeling Jebb Holloway had ever had. The strange thing was, the feeling was a little bit like he himself was lying in the dark and bleeding to death, but not caring, it was so sweet. He didn't know a feeling could be so sweet. To tell a girl that.

Then something crossed his mind. He leaned at Isaac Sumpter. "Listen," he demanded, "was it that-air Jo-Lea Bingham? Is it that-air Jo-Lea he is talking about?"

Then Jebb continued: "You know what?" He leaned closer at him. "You know what, we found that-air Jo-Lea's drawers in front of the cave. Hit's a fack. Bet he give her the meat before he crawled in. She was the one figured out he was in here, wasn't she? Ain't that a fack?"

"Yes," Isaac Sumpter said. Then said: "She has sure got the biscuits. She has got the self-rising biscuits."

"I bet it was him and not that Monty took them things off her hen house," Jebb said, hunching closer.

But Isaac Sumpter was not listening. "It's just come to me," he said.

"Huh?"

"Listen, Jebb," Isaac Sumpter said, and laid his hand on Jebb's shoulder. "You took your risks, you crawled in here. And it's not right—"

"What's not right, huh?"

Isaac Sumpter removed the hand, and said: "Just—just that you mightn't get credit—full credit, I mean."

"Yeah?" Jebb said. He sank back down by the stalagmite.

"They're doing a big TV tonight," Isaac said, squatting too, a little way off, leaning over to try to capture a cave cricket, failing, but still not looking at Jebb. "I just got the call from Nashville before we came in. National. This news about poor Jasper, it's getting big."

[263]

"Yeah? Yeah?"

"I'm sorry, Jebb," Isaac Sumpter said, seeming about to shake his head in sad regret.

"Huh?"

"Yes, Jebb, you see I ought not to have let you hang back. I ought to have let you go on in—in to Jasper."

Jebb was sinking deep into thought.

"Yes," Isaac continued, speaking as though in a sad soliloquy, "then you could be the one to stand up and tell everybody— everybody on all those TV sets all over the country—what Jasper said."

"I was on TV—one time, last year," Jebb said, musingly, almost whispering. "That time I run up thirty-one points and—"

"I saw you," Isaac Sumpter said. "You were good." He hesitated. "Yes," he said, "it was you being so good—that was what made me think how tonight it would be a shame for you not to—"

He stopped, turned away as though about to drop a fruitless subject. Suddenly, he seemed to reach a decision. He rose abruptly to his feet. "Damn it," he said, "it's not fair. It simply isn't fair. It was just for my sake you didn't go on in to Jasper, tonight."

"Yeah," Jebb breathed, staring at him.

Isaac Sumpter took two decisive strides over to the crouching boy. He laid a firm hand on his shoulder. The boy looked up, but he couldn't see Isaac Sumpter's face. "Damn it," Isaac Sumpter was saying softly, "you know what Jasper said. I told you what he said. You know it as well as I do."

"Yeah," Jebb Holloway breathed, with what little breath there was available, his heart was pounding so. His breath was barely there. "Yeah," he breathed.

That was the way it had been, down in the ground, and that was the thing, the voice and the weight of shadow pressing all around beyond the carbide flare, that now came again in the darkness of Jebb Holloway's self as he squatted on the grass at the edge of the crowd, after the strong fingers of that bastard Wes Williams had revolved him away from the mikes and the lights.

Now he was alone inside himself with what had happened under the ground. But it wasn't fair. Nothing was fair. It could have been real different. If that bastard Isaac Sumpter had just let him go on in to Jasper. The way he had really wanted to go.

Then the thought came into his head. At first it came in so quietly, he just didn't get the full sense of it. It was the fact his breath just stopped that gave him the full sense of it.

He thought: *If they get that Jasper out—*

He thought that, but he couldn't go on with the thought. He just couldn't.

But the thought went on with itself, independently and cruelly inside his head: *If they get him out he'll say I never come in there to him.*

It was too horrible.

Durn him, durn him, he thought in anguish, but didn't know whether he was durning Isaac Sumpter, who had led him into the ground, or Jasper Harrick, who might come out.

Then, with a stir of relief, he thought that there was one thing. He could go in yet. He could go in to Jasper.

But then the thought of crawling in, in there in the dark where the hand pressed down on you between the shoulder blades, into that last gut where he hadn't been—that thought took on a new terror.

Then he thought no, no, even if he went in, that durn Jasper would remember it wasn't him he told that to about holding his durn girl in his heart.

But that thought, even in its new desperation, was a kind of relief. Now he wouldn't have to go into the ground, down that last gut, because it wouldn't do any good anyway.

But Jasper would come out. In despair, he thought that.

Then, with tears of hope, a tremulous lift of joy in the heart, he thought: *Maybe—God, maybe—maybe he—*

That thought, too, he couldn't quite finish.

Then the slick-faced boy was nudging him, whispering something. "Shut up!" Jebb Holloway hissed at him in righteous outrage. "Shut up—can't you see I'm thinking?"

The singing stopped. They had been singing:

> Rock of Ages, cleft for me,
> Let me hide myself in Thee,

and the rest of it, about the water and the blood, and Nick Papadoupalous had had a deep mysterious impulse to sing too, but hadn't never got the words straight in his mind except at the beginning. He could not quite make out what the other words meant, about the water and the blood stuff, no matter how hard he puzzled them. He was puzzled, too, and wrinkled his big sweat-slick, bowling-ball-slick, brown forehead about why they were singing even those first lines, anyway. Who wanted to hide in a rock?

Tonight of all times, that was. That guy was stuck down in the ground in a rock, and Brother Sumpter, he was making 'em sing about how they all wanted a Rock of Ages, which must be an awful old and big rock, to crack open and let them all fall down in and get caught in the crack too, worse than Jasper, or as bad, anyway.

He looked over at that nice Mrs. Harrick, whose head was so bowed down, with the sadness and worry, and the bright TV lights shining on her yellow hair, which he knew had some gray in it, if you looked close, but that didn't matter, it was pretty anyway, especially at a little distance, and he thought it was not nice and considerate of them to be singing that song to remind her

[266]

of being stuck in a rock. She was worried enough as it was.

He wished they would not sing and worry her about it. They ought to sing about asking God to take people out of trouble, not put 'em in it. That song Monty Harrick made up, it made more sense. It made more sense to ask God to bring Jasper Harrick out to the daylight bright and clear than to sing about that Rock of Ages. But they had stopped singing now anyway, and Brother Sumpter was preaching again. He was asking people to come up and confess to Jesus the things they oughtn't to have done.

Nick Papadoupalous knew that for one thing he ought not to be here right this minute. He ought to be down there seeing to things in the restaurant, where hell was breaking loose with a million people trying to get fed, or he ought to be down the hill here where he had the outdoor rig. He ought to be seeing if that strange nigger he had brought in from all the way to McMinnville they said could barbecue so good was attending to his business with them young goats and that hog meat.

That nigger looked like a drinking nigger to him. He did not claim to be no authority about niggers, but this one with them red-shot eyes, he looked like a lush. A lot of good cooks drank, he knew that, but he did not want any drunk nigger to be burning up all that expensive meat that was hard enough to bring up a mountain anyway. And he did not want any drunk nigger falling in the barbecue pit and barbecuing himself to death. You could not sell barbecue of that type and description even at half-price and with cole slaw, dessert, and choice of drinks for free.

He knew he had better go see about that colored man. He knew he ought to see if the supplies were coming through. He knew he ought to go check receipts, before somebody stole a million dollars off him. He knew somebody was going to steal off him. It looked like a man could not help things slipping away, and as he sat there thinking that thought in general, about nothing in particular, it was funny how he felt like he was bleeding away in weakness and in a minute would be too weak to move.

[267]

He was just tired, he decided. He had not had any sleep it looked like in forty-eight hours. He ought to go down and check the receipts now, but he was too tired to move.

The receipts: if they did not steal 'em off him he might make a little. He had not raised prices down in the diner, but there was a million people and they lined up to eat. But he had a right to double up price and more on the mountain, with the trouble of setting up rig and getting supplies in. And it saved people going down to eat. That Lieutenant Scrogg, he had done like he said, he had to say that. He had knocked off the mountain those chiselers who tried to come in and pick up a fast buck after he had taken all the big risk and trouble. Lieutenant Scrogg could not knock 'em off the highway, but he had kept 'em off the track up the mountain. That was for officials and the car taking up the family and guys at the digging. And supplies for Nick Papadoupalous.

He had to say that that Isaac Sumpter, who had been to college and studied psychology and mind reading and such, was smart. He had fixed it up with Lieutenant Scrogg. Easy, and not really sounding like nothing crude.

He had to say that that Isaac Sumpter was right about things being big. It was big and getting bigger. Now with what he figured he had got in today, if things held up—

But his mind veered away from what it meant if things did hold up, and seized on the words of Brother Sumpter.

Brother Sumpter was saying how God knows everything, and even a sparrow falling down. God knew Jasper Harrick was in the cave.

Nick Pappy wrinkled the big bowling-ball-slick brow. *If God makes everything happen,* he thought, *then God certain would know about that rock on Jasper Harrick's leg, for He had put it there on that leg.* So what was the use of harking on God knowing?

It didn't do a man any good to keep harking on God.

It was God, he thought, Who was making Nick Pappy have

[268]

that funny light-headed feeling. It was God making Nick Pappy not be able to go down and attend to business and check the receipts before somebody stole a million dollars off him, like they would anyway, and it would be God's fault.

Brother Sumpter was saying that not only did God know everything and make everything, but He never wasted anything. Nick Pappy thought about how everything had to be on a purpose. It was not a harry-scarry, or a random-scandom, or whatever it was Brother Sumpter said it was not.

I wonder what God is making me feel this way for, Nick Pappy thought.

I never done nothing to Him, Nick Pappy thought.

Nick Pappy thought he had better go down and check the receipts, but Brother Sumpter was saying that if God did not waste anything, then Jasper Harrick getting stuck down in that rock was some use, but Nick Pappy did not see how it would be much use to Nick Pappy if Nick Pappy got caught in a rock in the ground. The notion of it being some sort of use to him to get caught was more than he could understand, and it was scarier than just being scared of being caught in the dark ground. For one thing, it made it seem more likely you might get caught, for God might drop a rock on you because He figured He was doing you a favor. Nick Pappy sat there and sweated.

"Nothing is wasted from God's hand," Brother Sumpter was saying, "and if Jasper Harrick suffers—"

Suffers: that word just hung in Nick Pappy's head. It was not a word like just getting hurt, or getting hit, or being sick, or even dying. It was a bigger kind of word, and he wished he could get it out of his head. It made you feel like they were tying you up with lengths of clothesline, or something more like silk-insulated electric house wire, the soft kind, but tighter and tighter and around and around, and you couldn't move, or breathe. It was an awful word for a man to get in his head. He wished Brother Sumpter had not mentioned it.

He wished Brother Sumpter would not hark on *suffer*. For one thing it must make that nice Mrs. Harrick feel worse, and her feeling so bad and fagged-down, you might say, already.

"Oh, he is suffering for us all," Brother Sumpter was saying. "He lies in the dark and suffers to remind you that you lie under the burden of your sin in the dark. Oh, cry out to Jesus! The stone is lifted off your leg. It is lifted off your neck. It is lifted off your chest and you can breathe. Oh, come forth into the light and—"

For a second Nick Pappy felt better. He took a deep breath. He felt a flood of sweet gratefulness in his heart and chest. He thought: *He is suffering for me. Jasper Harrick, he is in the ground suffering for me.*

He thought how he, Nick Pappy, would not have to go into the ground and suffer. Because Jasper would be doing it for him.

"Oh, come forth into the light!" Brother Sumpter cried out, and lifted up his arms. Then Old Mr. Duckett, with the peg leg and beer breath, he was managing to stand up. He was hobbling down to Brother Sumpter. He was crying and the tears were on his face. He made out to the rock Brother Sumpter stood on, and reached up his hand.

It was then he fell down.

Nick Pappy bet it was too much beer. Then he remembered there was no beer on the mountain. Lieutenant Scrogg and his patrol boys, they were keeping likker off the mountain, even beer, like Isaac Sumpter had said. There was guys with heads broke who had tried to sneak some up to sell on the sly.

Then that Old Mr. Duckett was yelling. Lying on the ground, he was lifting up his head and yelling: "Oh, God, the things I done! God! I can't stand them things I done!"

Brother Sumpter was picking him up. Old Mr. Duckett was crying and yelling out the things he had done. But Brother Sumpter's voice, it was louder. It yelled to God for salvation. "Lord God," Brother Sumpter cried out, holding up Mr. Duckett, "let us hear Thy voice!"

Then he stopped. Everything was quiet, except the little burr-

[270]

ing sound of the cameras. It was quiet like after thunder you did not expect.

Old Mr. Duckett lifted up his face. "Oh, God," he yelled, in feebleness, "I feel the breath of Jesus!"

Then he went all to pieces, and hung there with Brother Sumpter's arm holding him up like a rag doll with a peg leg. Then Brother Sumpter laid him on the grass and said: "God, in Thy mercy, this man is saved."

In the quiet, Mr. Duckett was crying very gentle, for being saved.

He is saved, thought Nick Pappy, in a deep-dawning relief.

Then he thought: *Saved from what?*

And because he didn't know, that was worse than before. So he sat there, and his breath came hard, and other people got up and got saved, and fell on the ground or knelt down, and Nick Pappy's breath came hard, or some fell down and cried out the things they had done and named them, and Nick Pappy's breath came hard, for what they had done was not what he had done, at least not what it was that was making his breath come hard. His breath was coming harder and harder because he did not know what it was he had to be saved from.

Brother Sumpter reared up tall as a tree and lifted his arms to the sky and his face looked wild and his eyes squinched shut, and he cried out toward the sky, which was black up there beyond the lights: "Oh, God, all pain will end in Glory! Oh, God, we thank Thee for Jasper Harrick."

And Old Jack Harrick, who had been staring up at him from his savage, leonine distance, suddenly spoke, in his strong, grating voice, like moving a heavy barn door on rusty iron hinges that had not been moved in so long they had almost rusted tight, saying: "He will die."

All the people turned at him. But he was not looking at them. He was staring out beyond the people and the lights into the dark sky over the trees and the valley far off down yonder. His

[271]

big hands gripped the sides of the wheel chair. The veins on his hands stood corded out. His eyes were wide and they glittered.

"He will die," he said. "He will die. In the ground."

Celia Hornby Harrick uttered a groan, and slumped forward almost out of her chair.

He had said it. He had had to say it.

The people had begun to sing. They were singing:

> "Oh, he's lying under the land,
> With nobody to take his hand.
> He is lying in the ground,
> And he cannot hear a sound.
> Oh, bring him out and let him in the sunshine stand!"

Nobody had told them to sing. Simply, somebody standing near the wheel chair had begun to sing. And now voices filled the mountain side, people close and people far off, in the dark of the trees down the mountain.

Brother Sumpter, standing beyond the wheel chair, heard the singing all around him, and the voices from down the mountain. His lips tried to move with the song, but the sound would not come.

He thought: *I cannot sing.*

He thought: *I was glad he is in the ground.*

He could not sing.

He thought: *It was for the hope there would be salvation.*

He could not sing.

He thought: *It was for Thy glory, God.*

They were singing down the mountain. They were ending on the line:

> "Oh, God, bring him out to daylight bright and clear!"

[272]

But he had not sung it. He felt too weak to sing now.

He thought: *No, it was for my son.*

The song had begun again. It sounded, somehow, very far away.

He thought: *Is it wicked to love my son?*

They sang.

He thought: *It was only for the hope, God, that Thou hadst moved in this way for the salvation of his soul.*

At that moment Isaac Sumpter emerged from the cave.

James Haworth was sitting on the floor of the living room of his lemon of a tepee, where, with his last drink, he had stopped for convenience on the way back to his chair from the kitchen, when he saw, somewhat dimly and small on the TV screen, the figure of that little bastard Ikey Tittlebum come crawling out of the mouth of the cave where, for all of him, that is, for all of James Haworth, the bastard could have stayed. Mr. Haworth did not pay much attention, at first. Everything had got sort of blurred, anyway. Then he caught on again.

Wes Williams was talking to Mr. Tittlebum. The camera came close up to their faces as they talked. Mr. Tittlebum's face was streaked with sweat and dirt. *Mr. Tittlebum,* James Haworth thought, *you look like hell.* That struck him as very funny, so he giggled. *Mr. Tittlebum,* he thought, *I do hope you have not over-exerted your sweet self.*

At that he laughed out loud.

He laughed so hard he almost missed what was going on. Wes Williams had asked Mr. Tittlebum something, you could tell that from the way he leaned for the answer, with that polite seriousness. James Haworth caught on just as Mr. Tittlebum was saying: "—somewhat weaker but holding on. There is one message."

"Yes?" Wes Williams demanded soberly, and leaned a shade closer.

"He sends his love to his girl—" Mr. Tittlebum said, and stopped. "He says he hopes she will forgive him for—for—"

Mr. Tittlebum stopped again.

"Yes?" Wes Williams breathed encouragingly, leaning closer.

Mr. Tittlebum looked soberly down toward the ground. "I'll just give it in his words," he said softly.

"Yes," Wes Williams said.

Mr. Tittlebum raised his head and looked straight into the camera: "Jasper just said, 'Tell my girl I love her and would have loved the baby. Tell her I was not going to run out on her. Tell her I was exploring this cave hoping to make a little money for her and the baby. If I don't hold on till they get to me, tell her not to think too hard of me.'"

For a moment there was silence. Mr. Tittlebum dropped his eyes again. Then the camera closed in a little on Wes Williams.

"Folks," he said, straight out of the little screen, "good people, everywhere—in little Johntown there is tonight a sweet young girl whose heart is bleeding. In these hills of Tennessee there is a girl who, this very night—"

Mr. Tittlebum reached and touched, almost timidly, the sleeve of Wes Williams. "Just one thing, one more thing Jasper said," he said.

"Yes?" Wes Williams said.

"Jasper said, 'If I don't make it—tell her to kiss the baby for me,'" Mr. Tittlebum said.

Staring out of the screen, through what seemed the gray flow, flicker, and vibration of a million midges, the face of Wes Williams grew larger. His eyes seemed to be about to fill with tears, but his voice was under control as he echoed, almost whispering: "Tell her to kiss the baby for me."

Perhaps it was not, Mr. Haworth discovered, the plague of vibrating gray midges raised to the millionth power that afflicted the TV screen and made Wes Williams' good American face so hard to see clearly. Perhaps, Mr. Haworth discovered, it was the tears in his own eyes.

[274]

He found himself thinking of his daughter who had died when she was fourteen and had promised to be pretty and well stacked, and he could not keep back the tears. He didn't bother even to wipe them.

After a moment he got carefully up from the floor, went to the telephone, took a steady drag of his drink, and dialed a number. It was a long time before there was an answer.

When the answer came, he said as crisply as he could manage: "Jim Haworth."

When the outrage at the other end of the line had died away, Jim Haworth summoned up dignity and said: "Mr. Sarton, you suggested that I call when I had finished the program, and I have taken you at your word. In any case, I have a suggestion which cannot wait."

There was another outburst, through which Jim Haworth waited patiently, holding the instrument at some distance from his ear to let it run down. Then he resumed, with careful diction: "The trapped man sent word out of the cave that he has knocked up some—I mean has left his sweetheart going to have a little baby. I suggest that the *Clarion* raise a fund to take care of this poor sweet young girl and the child of the hero. That is, of course, if he is not saved—as now looks damned unlikely. I suggest that we announce this by morning radio. Before those—those bastards at the *News* cook up something."

There was a long silence. Then the voice from ten miles away, at the beautiful country home, said: "Haworth, you are tighter than a tick in the navel of the fat lady of the circus."

"I have been watching TV," Jim Haworth said, grim and stubborn.

Then the voice said: "The *Clarion* will announce for five thousand dollars, on the morning radio. I will call Skidmore now. I will get my wife on it first thing in the morning to organize a committee. We will bully and blackmail twenty thousand dollars out of the biddies, babes, bags, broads, dowagers and assorted lastex-stretchers of Belle Meade by sundown. They will love to

[275]

write the checks. They will cry over that poor innocent child of the hills. Each will wipe away a tear and be half convinced that the handsome hero has entrusted the precious keepsake to her own sweet belly. Now you get to bed before you fall on the floor."

"I have been watching TV," James Haworth affirmed stoutly.

"You are drunk as General Grant at Vicksburg," the voice said.

"I am not," James Haworth said.

"I don't give a damn," the voice said. "I begin to like the brand you drink."

The voice hung up. James Haworth could hear the click. But the last words echoed in his ear. He felt a gracious sweetness rising in his heart, a grudging, manly affection for Joel Sarton, the old bastard.

He thought he would fix himself a nightcap. He had earned it. As he fixed it, he was anxious for Louise to come on home. He wanted to tell her all about it. Maybe she would like to be on the committee. He could fix that for her.

As he thought about that, he began to look forward with a new excitement to her return. Yes, it was a hot night and all, but maybe if she wasn't too tired, maybe if her feet didn't hurt, maybe if the resolution she was trying to put through the League of Women Voters had been well received, maybe if he told her about that little girl in Johntown in just the right way, and it sort of softened her, well—

He strode into the living room feeling very brisk and competent. He could not know, of course, that when Louise did get home he would be out cold on the divan.

IX

Isaac Sumpter crouched by the stalagmite, which would, he knew, ring like a bell if he struck it, and shut his eyes, and heard the small unrelenting hiss of the carbide blaze. He could reach up, he knew, and shut off the little valve, and then it would be dark forever. He could throw the matches away, the extra flash away, and just sit here forever. He did not do that, but he shut his eyes, and it was almost as though he were in another place, and in another time, and nothing had happened yet or perhaps nothing might ever happen and he would not have to suffer. He thought: *Other people don't have to go through this.*

So he, Isaac Sumpter, shut his eyes and thought of being in a warm, comforting darkness, where he would be outside of what he had to go through, in a darkness which had none of the deep, twisting strain of life, and yet was life, a state of being which was, at the same time, both peace and achievement, both non-life and life. He let his mind flow into that state, with a sweet, tearful yearning. He felt the tightness begin to go out of his muscles and nerves. The trouble was just that he was plain tired. God knows, he had been through enough in two days.

But he knew it wasn't just that. He knew, with a sad dawning certainty, like dawn coming up through autumn rain, that somehow it had been like this all his life. The thought came to him with a slow, cold revelation, like a hand opening with perfect indifference under your eyes to show the painful little secret hidden there: your life.

He thought: *If I were just somebody else.*

The mere thought, merely by being a thought, carried with it the faintest flicker of possibility, like a hope. But the very possibility, in that instant, was a terror. And the words were there: *But I wouldn't be me—I wouldn't be me!*

He had said the words out loud. And with the words his eyes had opened to the cave, the motionless air, the forest of statuary looming like a dream in the shadows beyond the power of the carbide flame.

Well, there was one consolation. Jebb Holloway, in the chamber where he had been left, just before this one, would be crouching by a stalagmite, too, breathing hard, listening to the carbide flame. *The fool,* Isaac thought, and thought how that fool had just been aching to step into the trouble he was now in, just because he wanted to stand up before a microphone and feel the cameras grinding away on him for two minutes. *Well, Jebbie-Webbie,* Isaac thought, *you have sure bought an assful of trouble for just two little minutes of pleasure.*

A kind of gaiety took him. "Yes, Jebbie-Webbie," he said out loud, to the figures of stone fantasy that leaned, in rigid attention, toward him from the shadows, "what price man will pay for just a little ego satisfaction."

He felt, all at once, full of energy, as though by his words he had been magically released from his own distress. "Yes,

[278]

Jebbie-Boy," he said, in patronizing gaiety, "that's what we call it—ego satisfaction."

Then the cold thought came: *How am I different from that turd?*

But he had to be different. A man could not live if he were like Jebb Holloway. Then his mind fell like a flash on a little stir of thought, like a hawk thunderbolting down from the empty blue at the white flicker of a rabbit's tail. Yes, that was it: Jebb Holloway had done only and exactly what he, Isaac Sumpter, had determined. Jebb Holloway hung at the end of a piece of string, and was, therefore, a thing. Isaac Sumpter pulled the string and was, therefore, a man.

Isaac Sumpter thought: *Nobody is pulling the string on me.*

All at once, as though he himself had been jerked up, he rose to his feet.

I am myself, he thought, and his breath came shallow.

He stood there for a moment while the breathing subsided. Then he decided he had better do what he had come to do.

Over to one side, in the shadow, well hidden behind a stone, lay the accumulated packages of food which, presumably, he had brought in for Jasper Harrick, and the vacuum bottle of coffee which was always supposed to be left with him. Over to the other side, with the electric cord neatly coiled, was the heating pad, turned on, where he had placed it some thirty-odd hours back, warming the base of the stalagmite against which it was propped. He looked at it and wondered, with a feeling of childish innocence, why he hadn't simply laid the pad down and been done with it? Why had he taken all the trouble to prop it against the stone?

Then he burst out laughing. "For Christ's sake," he said, "I sure must have been in a state when I did that. That's a symbolic action if I ever saw one. Can't warm Jasper, then warm a rock."

He wanted to stop talking, but he didn't want to, either. It made him feel good to talk. Nobody could hear you talk here. He realized that, and again laughed out loud.

[279]

"Yep, Little Ikey," he said, out loud, "you are human, after all. I am glad to see you have a sympathetic nature. You will warm even the cold stone. Though of course, Little Ikey, I suspect that you were trying to dodge some irrational sense of guilt. Now you knew perfectly well that Jasper Harrick was down in that pit and had no use whatsoever for that heat pad, but you made the irrational motions."

He wished he could stop talking. If he could just stop talking, he could go on and get it over with.

"Yep," he said, "you are perfect, you are out of a textbook, Little Ikey. If you made the motions you were not guilty."

But he thought: *Guilty of what?*

He walked over to the place where the food was hidden. He gathered up the packages, counted them to be sure, and picked up the vacuum bottle. He brought the stuff back near the stalagmite where he had been crouching. Standing there, he carefully undid the top of the bottle and began to pour out the coffee onto the red dust. Some coffee splashed on his hand. It was fairly hot.

Feeling the heat of the coffee, he had the overwhelming desire to have a drink of it. Quickly, almost surreptitiously, he poured some into the top of the vacuum bottle for a cup, and began to drink it. He had about half of it down, in quick gulps as though to finish before detection, when, all at once, he thought he was going to vomit. He mastered himself, and sank back down by the stalagmite. "Jesus," he said, "Jesus."

He knew he had to get hold of himself. He knew he would get hold in just a minute. *All I need to do is just be rational,* he said to himself.

So he told himself, quite carefully, that Jasper Harrick was down in that pit, where he had fallen more than, no doubt, seventy-two hours earlier, and, being deader than mackerel, had had no use for that coffee.

And he said to himself that it was all an accident, that he Isaac Sumpter, had not planned it that way and could not be blamed.

For he had planned nothing. That thought began to grow in him. It was all, in a way, an accident. It was an accident that Mrs. Harrick had not been willing for Monty Harrick to go in. Damn it, she ought to have let him go in. He was the brother, wasn't he? Isaac Sumpter was not the brother of Jasper Harrick.

And it was an accident that that self-important, pasty-faced busybody of a cretin Bingham had suggested that he, Isaac Sumpter, should go in. Just for something to say to feel important, just because he, Isaac Sumpter was, by accident, standing there.

And he, Isaac Sumpter, had had every intention of going in. Damn it, he had gone in. Nobody could deny that. And he had meant to go all the way, into that last gut of a crawlway, at which he now stared, a black low slit of a hole over yonder, just at the edge of the light of the carbide blaze. He had gone to the very entrance, and leaned his head in. If there had been an answer he would have gone in. He had called out, "Jasper—Jasper—Jasper!"

But there had been no answer. That crawlway was not long. He was sure that his voice would have carried through. But he had been sure, too—as sure as death and taxes, he now said to himself, with a sardonic twist of the mind, and lip—that the body of Jasper Harrick was in the bottom of that black pit, deep down there where the black water ran and the ray of the flashlight had not reached.

Nobody could say that it was because he was afraid to go through that last gut to the fourth chamber. He had gone through it with Jasper Harrick, so he had known he could do it again. He was going to go through it again, now, in a few minutes. He would have to go to—to arrange things. It could not, therefore, be said that he was afraid.

It had only been that he had known back then that there was no need to go.

But he had planned nothing. He honestly hadn't. That first afternoon, when he had crawled out of the cave to face the people, he had not had the slightest notion, not the foggiest

[281]

notion, of what he was going to say. He had, of course, meant merely to say exactly what had happened—or merely that he had gone into the fourth chamber and found nothing. That would have been merely a slight extension of the truth.

Damn it, he had not even been going to say that he had gone into the fourth chamber. He was going to say, simply, that he had gone into the third chamber, and had called, and had had no answer.

If only those people waiting for him to come out had not looked at him that way.

Then he had heard his own voice saying what it had said.

It was an accident, his words just popping out that way.

Well, God damn it, he had deserved something. It was just plain bad luck, when he had a chance to make a little money out of this cave, the only asset he had, so he could get the hell out of here, for that Jasper Harrick to go and let himself fall into the pit and ruin everything. Coming out of the cave, he had not said that to himself. There had been no need to. His mind did not have to say it in words. It had merely felt the truth, the deep, clear abiding conviction.

And from those words which, upon coming out of the cave, he had heard his own voice, from no intention of his own, saying to the assembled people, all else had followed, step by step, by its own logic. He had planned nothing. And if he had not planned anything—any more than he had planned for Jasper Harrick to be fool enough to fall into that pit—then what fault was his? God damn it, he hadn't pushed that Jasper Harrick off the shelf.

He sat there, holding the bottle top with the coffee he had not managed to get down, and felt the sense of cleansing grow in him.

He would get up in a minute and crawl into that gut and throw that grub into the pit and carry the electric line farther with the pad. That was as far as he could think ahead.

But what would happen if the drillers broke through and

found nobody? He had had to think about that. He had even thought he might go across the shelf—yes, if he just had to— and carry the electric line and try to arrange some stones at the far end of the next passage, and get an old sneaker of Jasper's and leave it caught in the stones to make it appear that he had somehow pulled free and, abandoning the heat pad and vacuum bottle and old sandwich papers, had crawled back to the fourth chamber. Something might be done to indicate that he had then slipped off the shelf, trying to get back across. You could mess up the shelf, someway—making it look like a piece of rotten rock had cracked. The body, of course, could never be found.

But that would be very complicated. He would have to get that cretin Jebb Holloway to get hold of a sneaker, an old one that could pass for Jasper's. He could, of course, get that cretin so deeply involved he would have to co-operate. Just tell him the truth, and put him on the spot about his stupid lies. Yes, there would be a certain morbid pleasure in watching his face when he got the truth stuck up his ass.

But the whole bloody thing was too much like Rube Goldberg. He had better apply the principle of Occam's razor—make it simple. Make it simple, like the song says.

It would be simpler just to kill off Jasper, and trust to luck. *My dear friends, I regret to inform you that Jasper Harrick is dead. He is, in fact, very, very dead.* Nunc in pulvere dormio. *That packet of worm seed, that sack of stercory, that semi-fluid mechanism which was the handsome and generally admired carnal envelope of Jasper Harrick is, even this instant, as certain chemical changes begin, entering the great anonymous economy of nature. His soul, assuming that he ever had one, has flowed back to that burning fountain whence it came. So don't bother your pretty heads further. Back to your lasts—oh, ye pismire-brained, pussel-gutted sons of Johntown!*

He wished that that crap would stop coming into his head. What he meant was simply to report the death of Jasper. Would they continue the drilling and try to recover the body?

[283]

He crouched there, holding the bottle top of coffee, letting his mind go blank. You really couldn't plan. You just had to trust for the logic of things to work out. He made his mind blank.

So far he hadn't had to plan anything, and everything had worked out. Even when one of those cretin reporters, that skinny red-headed one who had flown down from New York, had insisted on going into the cave to interview Jasper, things had worked out. Folks had backed him up, had backed Isaac Sumpter up, Mrs. Harrick had backed him up, and—that Bible-thumping Old Sumpter the Baptist Prophet had backed him up. *Why should a man lying in pain and in anguish of spirit, in the dark of the ground—why should he suffer your vanity, and the vain things of the world?*

The old boy had waved his skinny old arms, and yammered his stuff, and the people had said amen, and he, Isaac Sumpter, would not have taken a fin, hard up as he was, thank you, for the look on the face of Pinky the Yank when confronted by the rhetoric of Old Sumpter in full bloom. Also, when the people said amen, and looked at Pinky, Pinky looked around and seemed to recollect things he had heard about hillbillies and extralegal operations.

Pinky had talked to Lieutenant Scrogg. Lieutenant Scrogg had said: "Pinky, you are lucky to be on this mountain at all." Looking down at the build of Pinky, Lieutenant Scrogg, who had once given a very good account of himself as bucking back on the football team of the University of Tennessee at a period when the Volunteers were unaccustomed to losses, added: "As a matter of fact, Pinky, come a fair puff of wind and you might get blown off this mountain."

Yes, you had to trust to the logic of things. You had to read the flight of birds in the heavens. You had to follow your star. And things were working out.

That thing he had dictated into the tape recorder was being printed, this very night, in half the newspapers in the country. *By Isaac Sumpter.* Another spool of tape was even now flying

[284]

somewhere through the night sky, toward New York, toward the office of the syndicate. The deposit had been made for him in the Manhattan Dutch Trust. In the name: Isaac Sumpter. Philadelphia had called him that afternoon. It was the *Saturday Evening Post*. They would use six thousand words, at the earliest possible moment. They asked instructions for deposit. He had said: "The Manhattan Dutch Trust."

Now, crouching in the cave, he thought with a passing pang of condescending pity of that callow youth who had thought to get a few bucks out of hick tourism to a hole in the ground.

Yes, you had to trust the logic of things, Isaac Sumpter reasserted to himself as he crouched by the stalagmite, and the coffee grew colder in the bottle top.

The inner logic, he thought. He seemed on the verge of the unveiling of truth. He felt a power grow in him. But it did not feel like his own power. It was as though forces beyond him were filling him, possessing him. It was like destiny. He felt like a crap shooter riding it out, knowing that when the bones turn all will again be well, again and again, and he can say: "I let it ride."

He crouched there, with that strange paradoxical sense of powerlessness in power. He was nothing, merely the guiltless instrument of a power, but that power, which was not himself, somehow conformed to his will, so that his will was, guiltlessly, achieved and he was filled with the exultation of power. It was like the time when—at least now the image sprang into his mind —he had first been alone with Goldie Goldstein in her studio where they had stopped for only a moment on the way to dinner at the house of a friend of hers, and they had started kissing, standing in the middle of the room as dusk drew on, and he had felt the change come over her, and had heard her say breathlessly, to herself as though he were not there: "I can't stand it," and then, after what seemed forever, with a weak awkward movement she had disengaged herself from him, saying in strained embarrassment as though to a stranger: "It's all right—excuse me—excuse me just a minute," and had gone out of the room, and he, with

[285]

his heart beating to strangle him, had known perfectly well that when she came back she would be moving in naked whiteness through the dusk, sorrowful and slow, with her long, rather thin white arms hanging limp by her sides, the palms outward toward him in humility. He had known, too, as all conformed to his desire, that in the end it would be her hand that would be laid on his member to control it, and all, all, should be no guilt of his.

So, crouching now in the cave, he suddenly felt that all would be achieved. And the thought came to him: *The last request of Jasper Harrick is that his body be sealed in the crawlway where it lies. He requests that his friends Jebb Holloway and Isaac Sumpter fulfill this wish, while above ground a simple ceremony be performed by the family pastor.*

He crouched there, letting his mind be blank, feeling the idea run through his nerves, like an electric current. With dry lips, he whispered: "I believe it will stick."

He rose to his feet. "It has merit," he said gaily, and took a drink of the coffee.

Then he decided that he would let Jebb carry the ball. He would let Jebb carry the last words out to the multitude. *Old Jebbie,* he thought, *you will love it. And after all, my boy, you have labored long and faithfully.*

He laughed loud, drained the coffee, picked up the packages of food, and the heat pad, bowed himself down, and entered the crawlway to the fourth chamber.

When he had reached the very end of the gut, and could see the darkness of the fourth chamber expanding enormously beyond, he lay there for a moment, letting his head sink down, his cheek actually lie against the silky dust. He felt that he could not go on. The joke would be too horrible if now he got through and if—

He couldn't bring himself to frame the thought.

Then he tensed himself, and pushed on through, and rose up.

There was nothing there.

Jasper Harrick was definitely not there.

So Isaac Sumpter sank to his knees. He simply could not stand up, he was shaking so. "Oh, Jasper," he was saying, shaking with joyful gratitude, "oh, Jasper, I knew you were dead. If you hadn't been dead, I wouldn't have done it to you, Jasper. No, I wouldn't, Jasper. You know I wouldn't have, Jasper."

The words just came out of him. He let himself go. He lay on the even, red velvety dust of the cave floor, and cried like a baby while the darkness stretched away among the looming forms, and water murmured in the depth of the pit. The tears were tears of joy, after all the pain. He thought of those people outside, before the cave mouth, who, last night, had fallen on the ground and wept in the joy of salvation.

I'm saved, he thought, and his heart overflowed with gratitude to Jasper Harrick, who had saved him.

For Isaac Sumpter wanted to be innocent. He wanted to be good. He had always wanted to be good. And now, in some dark recess of the self where all bargains are debated, and all transactions are made, and all potions brewed and mysteries performed, he was promising—promising whom, what power: his father, himself, the dead face of Jasper Harrick white under water in the dark of earth?—that he would be good for always.

He could be good now forever, for he was, he knew, entering upon that success which was his due, and for which the price had been paid. He could afford to be good now.

Mrs. Harrick stood at the front door and spoke to the man and woman on the porch. "Thank you," she said. "It was sweet you came. It was real sweet. I can't tell you how sweet it was of you to come and bring us our supper."

"You're welcome," the woman said. She lingered a moment, while the man stood beyond her in the immemorial stance of a man waiting while women say good-bye. "You are sure," the woman asked, "sure you don't want us to drive you up—up there?"

"Yes, thank you," Mrs. Harrick said, wishing they would go. It was sweet, the way people did things, but she just couldn't talk now. She just couldn't. Sooner or later the woman would want to talk about that baby of Jasper's some girl was going to have. No, she'd be too polite to talk about it. She would just be thinking about it, and she, Celia Harrick, would, the first thing she knew, be talking about it. It would just be drawn out of her by the woman's thinking. She couldn't stand that.

"We'd love to drive you up there," the woman was saying. "Of course—I know Mr.—Mr.—the Greek gentleman, I mean—he has a big fine comfortable car and all. For Mr. Harrick. It's the finest car in Johntown. It is a Cadillac. But if we—"

"It's not that," Mrs. Harrick managed, looking past the woman, out where the evening light slanted beyond the trees, on the field. "It's just that he and John T. are sort of—friends, you know. They always got along, I mean. When we ate down at the diner." Then she added: "He's a nice man, I mean."

"Good-bye," the woman said.

Celia Hornby Harrick watched them get into their car and drive out of the yard, between the upward-scalloping rows of half-sunken truck tires John T. had put in and painted with aluminum paint to mark the drive, and on down the lane between the trees. John T. had put the tires in the ground as a surprise for her when she had gone down to the valley to visit her mother. Ten years ago, she guessed. No, more; for her mother had been dead eleven years.

He had put them in the ground to please her. To make things pretty. He had said: "I was lonesome when I got in from work, you not being here. If I was sort of doing something you might like, it was a little bit like talking to you."

"Oh, I love it, John T.!" she had exclaimed, and kissed him.

She had, of course, hated them. It was—the word had actually

[288]

crossed her mind—tacky. But the word had been quickly expunged. It was like the time she had come into the schoolroom one morning and noticed, just in time, before the children came in, that somebody, one of the bigger boys, had written a dirty word on the blackboard. She had grabbed so hard for the eraser, she had broken her fingernail on the blackboard. It had been like that when she expunged the word *tacky*. She had expunged the word with the act of flinging her arms around John T. and kissing his bristly old cheek.

She watched the car with Mr. and Mrs. Dawson go off down the lane. She wondered how it would be to drive off in the cool of the evening with your husband, just the two of you, not talking, going off home with the evening light calm and sweet across the fields, and go into your house, not saying anything, because you didn't have to. Somehow just being together, while the evening came on.

Many times, she and John T. had come home that way, the way married folks do. She pressed her forehead against the jamb of the front door, as though trying to remember how it had been. She stared out at the light lying sweet and calm across the field, and tried to remember.

She saw the double row of the aluminum-painted tires sticking up. *They are tacky, they are,* flared into her mind, and she felt dizzy and sick. It was because the words had flared up in her mind. She felt her face flushing for shame. *Me thinking something like that,* she thought, *with John T. about to die, and Jasper in the ground.*

She thought, *I am awful.* She didn't know what was wrong with her.

She felt so dizzy she simply had to sink down in the chair there in the hall. Then she thought she would soon go back up the ridge. She knew she could not bear to stay away. She had to go. But she did not see how she could bear to go and sit there with all the people looking at her and wondering which girl it was who was going to have Jasper's baby.

No, the worst was sitting there and herself looking around at the girls and wondering which one was the one had let Jasper do it to her. She found herself caught in a sudden spasm of hatred for that girl who had let Jasper do it and put that baby in her. It was as though that girl were responsible, as though, somehow, because she had got that baby inside her, Jasper had to go off in the ground and never come back. That seemed to make some awful sense to her—a sudden, frightening discovery that made her shake again, and worse, with the spasm of hate.

But how could you hate somebody if you didn't even know what their face was like? Didn't even know their name?

She looked out at the light on the field, beyond the shadow-thickening trees of the yard, and thought how Jasper had put that baby in that girl, and how John T. had put the baby who was to be Jasper in her, and how her father, that sickly man she could only remember reaching for a medicine bottle, had put the baby that was to be her inside the woman who was her mother, and how her mother once had been a baby inside somebody. The thought dissolved into a sense of shadowy concatenation of flesh reaching back into darkness—a sense not quite image, but heavy and ripe with the immanence of imagery pulsing in the dark, straining to emerge. She didn't know why she couldn't stop this shaky and dizzy feeling.

She kept looking out at the light on the field, beyond the trees—looking out from the shadow of the hall, then out under the deepening shadow of the maple boughs in the yard and the big cedars, out into the open where the light lay so sweet and far away like a place she would never come again. She could not take her eyes away. Spying out from the shadow of the hall like this, it was like looking back on the life she had lived and would not live again.

But what was the life she had lived? She was asking herself that question, not in words, but at the very feeling of dizziness she had as she stared at that light beyond her curtain of shadow. It seemed awful you might live and not know what kind of life

[290]

you had lived. She shut her eyes, and what she saw was something she had forgotten for so long, or at least had not chosen to think about for so long.

She saw, in the dark of her mind, like a movie suddenly coming on the screen in a dark theatre, big and sudden and shaking before it settles into focus, the face of John T. Harrick as she had first seen him all those years back, the bear-head held up above the man-head, the bear-eyes staring, the bear-jaws snarling in the unappeasable rage, the raw hide hanging down, fur-side and blood-side twisting and draped, John T. Harrick balancing in the back of the skidding pickup truck, yelling out his gay triumph, his teeth white and flashing, the blood-smear on his cheek. And the voice of that woman who that day had stood beside her on the pavement of the snowy street of Johntown was there in her mind, too. It wasn't even the image of the woman, of Miss Abernathy, just the voice coming in the dark of her now, over and over, as the face of John T. Harrick flickered big on the screen of darkness, grinning forever under the bear-head: *It is the shameful things he does—does to women!* And the voice was saying it again: *It is the shameful—it is the shameful—*

She didn't know what was the matter with her. She opened her eyes. She found she had been clutching the place on her upper arm where, two days back—could it have been then? it seemed like a million years—she had, in grim unwittingness, set her teeth into her own flesh.

I am awful, she thought, again, and rose abruptly, and shook her head with a quick motion, the motion of exorcism, and went down the hall to the room where John T. was. She stopped just outside the door, took a breath, and was about to go in.

Then she thought: *He said Jasper will die. He said Jasper will die in the ground.*

She stood there for a long moment before she could go in. She was afraid if she went in he would say it again. If he said that, she did not know what would happen.

John T. was sitting in the wheel chair, in black profile, like a silhouette cut from black paper, against the gold-green rectangle of evening light which was the window. For a second he didn't seem real, just a black paper cutout, two-dimensional. She went over and looked down at the tray on his lap.

"You haven't eaten a thing," she said.

"I ate some," he said.

"You just messed a little with it," she said, and she detected, with calm detachment, the little disciplinary edge in her tone, the way you speak to a child that is just doing it to aggravate you. She thought of Jasper, Jasper two years old or so, little enough to be yet in a high chair, just messing with his oatmeal, or his banana, throwing it on the floor and grinning joyfully at her, and knowing she wouldn't spank him, not if he grinned.

Oh, he had had that grin he always could throw at people, like throwing a lasso around you, and you couldn't spank him. *I ought to have spanked him,* she thought, and her voice, the voice of a thousand years ago, was saying to that grin there in the high chair, right now: *I'm going to spank you—I am really of a mind to spank you.*

Tears were coming up in her so full, she was afraid she would choke when she said: "But you've got to eat, John T. You need your strength, John T."

She sat down by the little table that held the tray Mrs. Dawson had fixed for her. She tasted the soup. It was good soup, and still hot. "Eat some soup, John T.," she said, but didn't even look to see if he did.

She worried down some soup. Then a few bites of chicken salad. Mrs. Dawson had a name for her chicken salad. Celia Hornby Harrick held another forkful of delicious chicken salad in the air, halfway to her mouth, but couldn't get it any farther.

"I didn't reach out and touch him," she said.

"What?" the old man said.

"It's Jasper, I mean," she said. "If I had just understood and reached out," she said, and stopped.

The old man made no answer.

"Eat some chicken salad," she said then.

But she did not bring her own fork any closer to her mouth.

"We did something wrong," she said. "We did something to unhand him for the world."

"I did what I could," he said, not looking at her.

"I'm not blaming you," she said.

He didn't answer.

"Take just a morsel of chicken salad," she said.

He did not even seem to have heard.

"We unhanded him," she said. "And he went in the ground."

"I did what I could," the old man said, from his distance.

"I didn't say *you*, John T. I said *we*. I said us both."

"I—I—" the old man uttered, in a husky, growling exhalation, "I tried."

"Oh, sure!" she exclaimed, impatience and despair in her voice. "Oh, sure, you tried."

His big head swung toward her for the first time. She saw his eyes glittering in the dusk, under the shaggy brows. It was as though you had thought the fire was out in the forge, and a breath of air stirred, as when she used to go to the shop, at the end of day, and watch him shut things up. His big hands would be black-dirty, and in hot weather his big arms, bare to the shoulder, all corded and twisted and bulging with muscle, all slick with sweat and streaked with dirt. His face even was so dirty sometimes that his teeth, when he smiled at her there in the gathering gloom of the shop, would flash whiter than white.

Standing there in the shop with him, as evening fell and he moved about in the gloom putting things away, with the clink of metal, with the smell of leather, with the clean, sharp smell of hot ash, waiting for him to turn toward her and flash the startling

[293]

white of his teeth, she had always felt caught in a thrill of strangeness tinged with guilt, in adventure about to be divulged, in an enchantment.

Once in that darkening shop, long ago, as a spring evening fell, she had moved to him, so soundlessly that he had not heard her foot on the earth floor, and had stood right behind him, and when he turned, not knowing she was there, she had put her hands up to his black-smudged face, pulling his face down to her, kissing him hard in the way he had taught her, not letting him go, getting her bare arms up around his dirty neck, thinking of her fresh-starched yellow dress getting all dirty against him, and thinking: *I'm glad of it, I'm glad of it*, suddenly thinking of herself, the dress gone, herself white, bare, distorted in the act of being possessed, there on the dirt floor, in all the dirt, with maybe some scrap of metal, a bolt or nut or some old discarded something, cutting into her intolerably, but perfectly and indispensably, from the dirt of the floor. Then just as that image was, for a second, in her mind, and just as she knew it was, somehow, flaring up in John Harrick's mind too, he had sort of let her go, saying: "Gosh, Baby—gosh."

As for a moment longer she hung there against him, he was saying: "Gosh, Baby—and me all dirty, like I am."

At that she had let her arms go loose. She had just slipped from him, like a dead weight, feeling some dullness of the world over her, some weight of encroaching time and sadness, a weariness of all the days and nights, and the rising and the lying down, and the putting of food into her mouth and the sight of her hands moving in their small tasks and the smiling at people, whom you liked or didn't like, loved or didn't love. She felt a thin, sharp sense of defraudment, like a tiny wound bleeding its single silky thread of blood on her white skin, a wound no bigger than a pin, but as deep as life, that wouldn't stop bleeding, in daytime under your nice starched underwear, at night on the clean white sheet, the tiny shameful hemorrhage which would be life—or at least her life.

[294]

She had seen the white-toothed grin fade from his puzzled face, as he stared at her in the gloom of the shop. It was a face that, for the moment, she had scarcely recognized, the face of a big, work-dirty man of early middle age, looking rather dull and confused—even, to tell the truth, not very bright.

She had turned listlessly away, looking out of the gloom of the shop into the pale green-gold evening light lying yonder across the field, like a dream. As it had lain across the field this evening, beyond the shadow of her hall from which she had stared out.

In the shop, that evening long ago, she had turned away from him, but within a couple of minutes she had been saying to herself that she had to expect things to be a little funny when you were pregnant. Everybody knew that you got a little upset, being pregnant. That was all it was, she knew, and she held John T.'s hand all the way to the house, and got hot water for him to wash up, and changed her yellow dress she had got dirty, and cooked him a good supper, and teased him and got him laughing.

She had been about four months pregnant with Jasper then, and now, so many years later, with Jasper stuck in a hole in the ground, the old man, sitting in the wheel chair, the tray on his knees, had, in some painful defensiveness, burst out: "I tried—I tried to do what I could for him. But me—I was just an old black-smith!"

And she said: "Oh—oh, that!"

And he turned his old, pain-banked eyes on her, and they suddenly gleamed up, through the pain, like coals in the forge you think is banked but a movement of air comes and they gleam in the darkening shop.

And he said: "Yes—yes, that—that's what you married. A blacksmith."

What was John T. trying to do, talking that way? It wasn't fair. That was what was awful, to have your whole life suddenly twisted out of shape. After you had lived it, to have somebody turn it upside down so it was all a dirty joke. So she cried out: "Oh, how can you say that?"

[295]

"Blacksmith," he said again. "But you knew what you were getting into."

"Oh, how can you be cruel like that!" she cried out.

"You talked like you were blaming me," he said. "For being what I am."

"You know that wasn't what I meant," she said.

But he was not even looking at her now. "I wanted him to be a better man than me," he said. Then he swung his head toward her, demanding with what old strength could stir: "Don't you know that?"

But in her own suffering, caught in the outrage at the injustice done her, she couldn't answer.

"Before Korea," he was saying now, "before then he was doing good. He was a good mechanic—he could have gone away to learn more'n I could teach him. But I couldn't teach him what I didn't know—I was just what I was and—"

"Korea," she said, as a new pain grew in her. She got up from her chair. "I almost died when he went to Korea," she said. "But you—"

In the failing light she was staring at him, trying to read his face.

"But you," she said, with a voice gone vibrant with a growing, marveling discovery, "you wanted him to go. Yes—"

"He had to go," he said, dully. "They would of come and took him."

"Oh, but you were glad," she cried out. "You said, 'You get some Chinks for me, son!' That's what you said."

He passed his tongue over his dry lips. "It was just a way of talking," he managed to say.

"He nearly got killed," she said. "You've seen those scars on him. They nearly killed my baby." She began to move around the room, her hands moving in an aimless weaving, a tangling and untangling.

"It was that medal," she said.

"Sure," he said. "They gave him a medal. He was brave."

[296]

"I mean the medal they gave you," she said.

"What?" he said.

"That's why he almost got killed. Because of you and that old medal."

"Did you want him a coward?" he demanded.

"Oh, it's not being a coward or not a coward," she said bitterly. "It's something else. They almost killed my baby, and you—it's like you had—"

"Like me what?"

"Oh, it's like you had made 'em!" she cried.

"I—I what?" he demanded, staring at her as she moved.

"It's like everybody made 'em," she said. "Everybody in Johntown made my baby get killed. He walked down the street in his uniform before he went to Korea and everybody stopped him. They would put their hands on him—that awful old drunk Mr. Duckett, he put his hands on him—and they said—"

Her face twisted in a mimicry which was, somehow, the only way the pain could get out of her.

"They said, 'A chip off the old block.' They said, 'Boy, you do like Old Jack would do.' They said, 'You're Old Jack's boy, you show 'em.' They said, 'Old Jack got him a medal, you git two.' And they—"

She stopped, then swung toward the old man.

"—they put their hands on him. They kept putting their filthy hands on him."

"It was just they knew he was brave," the old man said.

"Brave?" she demanded. Then cried out: "It was filthy! It was like—"

She couldn't go on.

"Like what?" he grated at her.

"—like when he came back—and the girls were all crazy about him—and the things they did—oh, you know the things they did!"

She came close, and leaned at him.

"Say it," she commanded. "Say you know the things they did!"

[297]

"All right," he said. "They did what folks do."

"You made jokes with him," she said. "You'd wink at him," she said. "I couldn't stand it when you were together!" she said. "The way it looked like you were about to get up from the table and go off in the dark with him, and—"

"Shut up," he said.

"And he couldn't stand it. Don't think he didn't get so he couldn't stand it either, and that's—that's why he kept staying away from home, and you'd sit here and wonder what he might be doing, wondering and wishing, and hating him because it was him—oh, yes—"

"Can't you shut up!" he said, in his grating, grinding voice.

She was quiet a moment, then said in a voice little more than a whisper. "Yes. Yes, that's why he'd go off in the woods by himself. That's why he crawled in the ground. To get away from everything. To get away from the hands on him. To get away from the jokes and the winks. To get away from the wishing and the hating. To get away from—"

She stopped, and walked over toward the window and looked out at the pale-green light on the grass and at the shadow gathering under the white oak. "From you," she said, not looking back.

She felt so weak all of a sudden, having said it, that she had to sit down. She sat in the chair and stared out the window. She heard his breath there in the room behind her.

"And now that girl," she said. "The one that got down in the dark and got Jasper's baby in her. You sit there and—and—"

"What did you want him to be?" he demanded. "Be a cut boar only good for grunting for slop?"

She heard his breathing.

Then he said: "Come here. Come here."

She turned, rose, took a couple of steps toward him.

"Yes," he said, "and was that what you wanted me to be? Yeah, and was that why you walked on the mountain with me in the dark? Oh, yeah, was that why you married me? Was that why you let me prop you and you bit your lip till it bled to keep from squalling like a cat?"

She stared at him, and thought that all the world was nothing.

"Yeah," he demanded, "was that what you wanted me to be?" And his face twisted in a painful grin, as he added: "Like fun it was."

She turned her eyes from him, leaving that face and its grin, and went back and sat in the chair. The light held on in the open. It was funny how it held on, so sweet and calm, even with the dark under the trees. She wondered if some people could look back on their life and it really was like light sweet and calm and pale on the evening grass. She wanted to cry.

"It's not me I'm thinking about," she said, not turning, speaking in a small voice that seemed to rise without will from the despair, almost sweet, that was in her. "It's not me," she said, "it's Jasper I'm thinking about."

She thought, for an instant, that if you really didn't have to think of yourself ever again, not what had happened or might ever happen, you could be happy.

"There was always something wrong about you and him," her voice was saying, a wispy, drifting voice, like the last little smoke rising from a fire almost out. It was more like a thought than a voice. It came like a new thought to her.

"Even when he was born," she said.

"You know I was sorry for what I did," his voice was saying sadly from the gloom and distance behind her.

"You ran away," she said, her voice yet quiet and small. "Off to Chattanooga. Leaving him and me here, and him just born."

"You know I was sorry," he said.

"He was just born—and so little—and you—you—"

"All right," he burst out, his voice grinding in anger and pain now. "All right, I don't deny it. I ran away, and I was drunk for three weeks, and I lay around with whores in alleys and hotels and whorehouses—yes, filthy, dirty whores, and it looked like they couldn't be dirty enough to suit me or act dirty enough—

[299]

yeah, I ought to tell you how dirty—and I picked fights in blind pigs and speakeasies, and I lay drunk on the floor, and I fought cops, and I got my head busted and got put in jail and got the clapp. All right," he said, breathing hard back there behind her. "All right."

He looked over at her, but she did not turn. Distantly, she said: "Don't think Jasper didn't know. He knows that you ran off and left him. And him a baby."

For a moment, he couldn't speak, it seemed. Then he said: "You —you didn't tell him. You wouldn't do that."

"This is Johntown," she said, wearily. "Somebody else would. They would tease him in school."

In his shadow he made some kind of exhalation, not quite a groan.

"So he crawled in the ground," she said.

He was silent a time. Then his voice, sad and weak now, said: "I wanted to be forgiven."

"You should have prayed to God," she said.

"I did," he said. "I got religion and prayed."

"Maybe He forgave you," she said.

"I wanted you to forgive me," he said. "I asked you to. And afterwards I swear I never laid a finger on any—"

"Oh, that," she said, with a strange, distant, shriveling contempt—but contempt for what? For him, for herself, for what things they had done together, for what he had done with those dirty-acting women in Chattanooga, for what all men and women did, for all past pain and pleasure? For the ignorance that set value on pain and pleasure?

She was staring out into the yard where that pale light hung on, and had been staring, it seemed, for a long time, when he said, quietly: "You said you forgave me."

She heard the words, merely heard them as words, for they seemed to have no meaning for her. But something about them, even in their meaninglessness, started an idea. It filled her head, like a burst of light.

"Listen," she said, "listen—lots of the time—for years now—when you've been up at the shop—up there by yourself—you haven't been working. There wasn't any work for a blacksmith."

"There was some," he said defensively.

"You would just beat the anvil," she said. "Just to make it ring. Oh, I know—just so people way off down there on the street would stop and say, 'Listen—it's Old Jack Harrick, he can still sure make that anvil ring.'"

He looked at her a time, out of the shadow. Then, even more gently than before, he said: "You never forgave me. Not for Chattanooga. Not for anything. Did you?"

She was again staring out into the yard, not having spoken, not knowing what to say, even inside herself, when she heard the steps on the porch, then the knock at the door.

He knew he ought to be back up there on the ridge, where he had just come from, and where that barbecuing nigger from McMinnville, who was sure a lush if he ever saw one, to judge from his red-shot eyes and the way he rolled on the outsides of his feet when he walked, like his feet weren't nothing but big wads of wet sponge, had not yet managed to fall into the barbecue pit and barbecue himself and sell the finished produce for seventy-five cents a sandwich to get the money to buy whisky. And where the two girls, one of them a towhead but she had a breaking-out on her face, were passing out the sandwiches so fast they didn't have time to wipe sweat, but the nervous, broke-out one spilling a sandwich now and then, which was going to cut down the profit, even at seventy-five cents and slicing the meat thin, like he couldn't get them two new boys to do, the hicks, trying to act like they knew how to act in town but their hands still crooked like when they took 'em off the handle of the plower, or whatever the hell it was you called those things you plowed up ground with to plant seed, not the tractor kind to ride on but the kind a *ani-mule*

[301]

pulled, he meant a mule, and you walked behind, with no socks on, and like as not no shoes. That was the kind of hicks, like you called 'em, a fellow running a restaurant in Johntown had to hire to work, and put up with and go broke with, and they thought they were the nuts, come to town, just getting away to where that *ani-mule* pulling the plower could not break wind in their faces.

He knew he ought to be up there on the ridge, before that new boy with the close-screwed eyes and the slick-down hair would rob him to death. He was taking in big money, if they just didn't rob him to death so he went bankrupt or something. Standing there on the porch, he felt like he was bleeding to death the way they robbed him and he would go bankrupt, even if he was taking in the big money. But it was funny, if he came up here to the Harricks, it was because he was taking in the big money, and things getting bigger and maybe a hotel with that Isaac Sumpter. But if that one with the close-screwed eyes would rob him or somebody else would rob him, and there wouldn't be any big money after all, then there wasn't any reason for him to be wasting time coming here to the Harricks, for he wouldn't have to be making something up to them.

It looked like whichever way it was, a man was set up and knocked down. A man was in the middle alley. He was behind the eight ball. He had his finger in the meat grinder.

Then he remembered about Mr. Bingham and all that money in the bank, and how maybe you could get your hands on some of it, and he felt better.

But what the hell was he doing here on the front porch of a log cabin? He wondered if cancer was catching.

At that moment that Mrs. Harrick came to the door. Rather, since the door was open except for the screen, he saw her moving up the hall toward him, her face pale in the shadow, and her hair.

"Come in," she said, and looked up at him, for she was not a tall woman, and gave him a thin sort of smile, sort of sweet because so thin, like she was lying down sick and he had handed her something.

[302]

No—no, he thought, it was not Mrs. Harrick who was lying in bed sick and you handed something to. It was Giselle Fontaine—that is, Sarah Pumfret Papadoupalous—who was lying on the bed up at his house, and her hair was not like Jean Harlow's silky platinum any more, but was the color of creek mud at low water, and if you closed your eyes and put your arms around her, which there was a natural disinclination to do, you would never think it was Jean Harlow any more, but more like a female walrus escaped from the Bronx Zoo, and fled to Johntown, Tennessee, to wear pink silk French nightgowns, and if you tossed this female walrus a dried fish or handed her a plate of ice cream, she would not give a thin, sweet smile by way of thanks. She would give a look like you had tracked in a bad smell, or would burst into tears because she was going to die and you had not bought her a new TV set.

"Come in," Mrs. Harrick repeated, for Nick Pappy hadn't moved. He was just standing there, as though, somehow, he could not yet enter that shadowy hall. He even looked back, with a quick, strange look, at the light still on the field beyond the cedars.

"I'm early," he said. He stood there embarrassed, then blurted out: "Mr. Harrick, did he eat anything for supper?"

"No," she said, "he just messed around some on his plate."

"I came early to make some waffles," he said. "If he didn't eat already."

"That's real nice," she said.

"I never had a chance to make 'em and show you how."

"That's a lot of trouble."

"I brought some real maple syrup," he said, exhibiting a paper-wrapped parcel. "It is from the State of Vermont. I thought maybe it would be good on his waffles."

"Thank you, Mr.—Mr.—" She didn't know how to say it. She had got started saying it without thinking, and you couldn't say *Mr. Pappy.* Not to his face.

He was staring down at her, but because his back was against

[303]

the light, what light there was, she couldn't make out the expression.

"Mrs. Harrick," he said, very quiet, "you know, I been in Johntown more'n six years, and nobody here, nor even in Kobeck County, has ever said my name. Except maybe that Mr. Bingham at the bank when I went to get my account opened. And he can't say it now."

She didn't know what to say.

"Mrs. Harrick," he said, "they got things they call you. Like Nick Pappy. But if it is not your right name, it looks like sometime you don't know who you are, maybe."

He paused, staring down at her from his shadowy face. It didn't help any to try to read his face in the shadow, it being so dark-complected anyway.

"You know what I mean, Mrs. Harrick?" he said.

"Yes," she said, and felt embarrassment flood over her, and knew that her cheeks were flushing. So, to escape the embarrassment, she said: "Yes," again, with sudden emphasis, and turned down the hall toward the kitchen.

Just as she had entered the kitchen, she heard the voice behind her: "Mrs. Harrick—if you didn't mind—if you'd do me a favor—"

She turned, and saw him standing there in the hall shadow, as though he had to say something before he could come on in.

"Just if you would," he said.

"Would what?" she asked.

"Would you," he said, hesitating, then going on, "would you mind trying to learn it right? So somebody can say it. In Johntown."

"It is Greek," she said. "I am not handy with Greek," she said, "but I'll try—Mr.—Mr.—"

"Pap-a-doup-a-lous," he said.

She did the best she could. She tried three times.

"That is all right," he said. "Thank you, Mrs. Harrick."

[304]

It was lighter in the kitchen than in that dark old hall. In the kitchen there were lots of windows—John T. had cut some extra in for her, she loved light so when she worked—and the big back door was open, and there were no trees close here, and the mowed grass seemed to reflect the last light. It was funny to come in here, after that dark hall. She went straight to the cabinet to take out the mixing bowl and spoon, and the waffle iron Mr.—Mr. Pap-a-doup-a-lous—had brought the other afternoon. The afternoon when—

Her mind couldn't go on, for what had stopped the waffles the other afternoon was too terrible. She laid the mixing bowl and spoon on the counter under the cabinet and was bending down to the lower cabinet to get the waffle iron. "It's just he won't eat," she was saying to the dark of the cabinet, reaching in there for the waffle iron.

He didn't say anything, over there behind her.

"He's got to keep his strength up," she said, fumbling for the heavy iron, her hands seeming too weak, somehow, to pick it up.

"It's a terrible thing," Mr. Papadoupalous' voice said, "sickness in the family. I know."

"I know you know," she said, into the cabinet, as she got the handle of the iron tight and dragged it out, and started to rise. "That is why it is so nice of you. When you got your own troubles and—"

She had risen and was facing him. He wasn't nearly as far away as she had thought. He must have come closer. He must have come soft, and him a heavy-built man, too. And when she looked up into his face, she didn't recognize it. It was twisting itself all out of shape. He looked suffering, like somebody who has a stroke and struggles to tell you how he feels but can't make the words.

She thought he was having a stroke.

He was not having a stroke. Something had started to claw its way out of him, like a crazy cat trying to claw out of a dark sack,

[305]

and the claws were, it looked like, cutting his insides to pieces. The thing had started to claw out as soon as she began to thank him for being nice.

So he burst out, in his throaty, choked-up voice: "There's something—something I got to tell you. I got to!"

She was staring raptly at that tortured and yearning face. She thought how that face—that man—was struggling to tell her something. She didn't think what the *something* might be, for the important thing was the twisting urgency to tell her. It was her he had to tell it to.

And on that instant she was aware of the sudden urgency in her. She had to tell somebody how awful it still was, again was, even after all the years, as though those years had meant nothing, and therefore her life nothing. She heard her own voice: "He did it to me. He did it to Jasper, and Jasper just a baby, just born. He ran away from us. For three weeks, and got drunk, and—"

"What—what?" Nick Pappy was demanding, staring down at her intense face, feeling things go askew, like the floor tilting.

"—and he ran away to Chattanooga and lay round with them, with those dirty women, and the things they did, and he left me and Jasper just born, and the things they did, he and—"

She was looking up at him, and the words came out of her mouth, with her hands moving in a strange, weaving, lost way, moving only from the wrists, and with her blue eyes staring up at him with that intent demandingness that he answer something, explain something, do something.

He could scarcely figure out what she was saying, except that her husband had run off a long time ago and done her wrong, a nice woman like her. It was the fact that there was no excuse for her to be telling it, that and the suddenness just bursting out of her without any relation to what was going on in him, that made him feel that everything was tilting and falling and he was going to slide down the tilting floor. That lack of relation, the suddenness, the shocking fact that whatever it was bursting out of her was bursting out for him, for Nicholas Papadoupalous—it was all

[306]

like snatching a curtain back and there she was, standing there shining white and not a stitch.

It was all that. It was, too, the way the light from the window hit her hair. Even the white hairs in the yellow hair helped. They made it all look paler.

So he was standing there with his arms around her, and she was holding on to him. She was holding on, as though she couldn't stand up.

He was thinking: *Jeez, Jeez.* No, his lips were whispering it over and over, while his mind was saying: *It's Mrs. Harrick, it's Mrs. Harrick.* He realized that he had never thought of her in exactly this connection.

She had her face against his chest so he couldn't see it, but all at once, seeing her face in his mind, he thought: *She is near getting to be a old lady.*

Then his mind said something it had never said before: *I am old. I am old as her. I am near getting old.*

Then she lifted up her face and looked at him, and he saw the crinkles in the skin at the sides of her eyes, and the lines of worry in her forehead and how much gray there was, and he was thinking, or knowing without thinking, that this was the first human face, it seemed, he had ever looked into. Really looked into, just for its humanness.

At that, some bone-shaking happiness broke over him, so he said out loud, with breathless discovery: "Jeez, Jeez."

With that happiness he felt his arms tightening, felt her softness being crushed against his chest, and leaned his face over her.

But her eyes weren't looking at him now. She was looking beyond him, out the window. And she was saying: "But, oh—it's not dark. It's not dark yet."

He felt her pushing back from him, but he held his grip.

"Something's wrong with me," she was saying. "What's wrong with me?"

He looked wildly out the window, and saw that there was still some light, but going fast. The notion whipped across his mind

[307]

he could just hang on to her for a minute or two, he could just start working on her, and her a woman hadn't had anything in so long and not too old yet, and then it would be dark.

But he knew something had happened. Even if he got her down, it would be nothing. It would not be worth doing. It would be just like one more thing a man got drove to, and not knowing why. The only difference being on a kitchen floor. It looked like he couldn't ever remember on a kitchen floor.

His arms had fallen from her.

And he wondered why, all at once, when he was driving along at night sometimes, sixty or seventy, just giving the Cad a work-out, he had the notion, sometimes, that he might just head over the bluff side.

She had crossed to turn the light on. The light fell sudden, like a clap of thunder, if a clap of thunder did not have any noise but still had its power. Every smallest object in the kitchen seemed to leap into its proper place, into its proper being, as though they had all been drifting out of line, forgetting themselves. The objects were like soldiers snapping to attention. The night was, suddenly, black outside the windows.

She brought the mixing bowl and the spoon. She got the flour and stuff. She went over and sat in a chair, while he bent over the bowl.

After a while, not turning, he heard her voice: "You've got to excuse me—Mr.—Mr. Pap-a-doup-a-lous."

She managed to get it out very well.

"Just something went wrong for a minute," she said. "So many things happen to you you get all mixed up, and not knowing."

Bending over the bowl, he couldn't think of anything to say. Then it came to him: "Sickness in the family, it's awful."

He was thinking, with a strange, disturbing happiness, how it had been to look into a face, just for its humanness. Not because it was her face, Mrs. Harrick's, even if she was a nice woman. No, it didn't really have anything to do with her, personal, you might say.

[308]

It was not personal, even if maybe she had been ready to fall on the floor for him. And whatever had been was all over now, he knew that much. It wasn't any more than if they had both happened to have the same dream, but lying asleep far apart in their separate houses, and neither of them knowing what it meant. Yes, he knew it was over and done, and didn't mean a thing.

It was just that he had never really looked into a human face before. Just for the humanness.

Mixing the stuff in the bowl, he felt shy and happy. Then he tried to remember what it was he had been in such a pain and sweat to bust out and tell her before she broke in on him and they started the grappling. But it didn't come. Not until she now said: "I know John T. will like his waffles."

That reminded him. When they had first come into the kitchen she had been saying how nice it was of him to come to make the waffles when he had his own troubles, and the thought that then had started to claw out of him was how mean he felt trying to make money when her boy was in the ground, making money out of the fact her boy was stuck down there. He had been trying to say that he came to make the waffles not because he was nice but because he felt so awful.

Now as he mixed the batter he tried to find a way of saying that. But he began to figure that if you had been on the raggedy edge, you might say, of falling on the kitchen floor with a woman, it would not be polite to her, and her a nice woman, to say how that had not been what was in your mind in the first place, to start the groaning and grappling. It would get her embarrassed to think she had been about, maybe, to get on the kitchen floor for a guy that did not have it in mind.

So he did not say it. He thought about her face again, but not in a personal way, and felt happy again. It was a kind of happiness like having money in the bank so you did not have to go bankrupt.

[309]

X

Standing in the back hall, at the foot of the dark back stairs, down which she had just groped her way past the stacks of old *Saturday Evening Post*'s and *Life*'s and *House Beautiful*'s, Jo-Lea waited, afraid to budge, or breathe, and heard her mother's voice up front in the living room, just as though she had not ever stopped hearing it saying the things it had been saying at supper. Or the things it had been saying for always.

She stood there in the hall, by the back door, entrapped with listening to the voice, not the voice dim now from up in the living room, but the voice in her head saying what it had first said ten days ago and what she had been hearing every minute, asleep or awake, and might keep on hearing forever:

You will tell me exactly what happened.

You have disgraced yourself. You have disgraced the mother who loves you.

Now you will tell me. You will tell me the name of the degener-
ate to whom you, with no thought for your own welfare, much
less for your mother's peace and pride, have surrendered a
woman's most precious possession.

Now you will tell me, or I—

But she had known that if she told one thing, said even one
word, she would never be herself again. She would cease to exist.
She wished she were dead, but if you aren't dead you have to
exist, and if you have to exist you have to be yourself, or it is
worse than being dead, or anything.

Now she stood in the hall, hearing the voice from up front, and
the voice in her head, not able to open the door and go to a
place where she could not hear the voice.

If such a place existed.

For, all at once, she had the terrible feeling that that voice was
the world. It, that voice, was the thing that held everything else
together, and if the voice stopped, the whole world would blow
away, like the last puff of smoke that rises up from where you
have burned a pile of dead leaves, when you had thought everything completely burned, and then is snatched away into nothing by a single, wickedly aimless twitch of air. Maybe if she
stepped out that back door and couldn't hear the voice, everything, herself included, would just puff into the air and be gone,
without a sound.

So she stood there, her hand frozen above the knob.

Then she thought: *All right*. And touched the knob, wondering
if there would be a flash of light, like an explosion, when the
great puff came.

She already knew, of course, there wouldn't be any sound. It
would be like an explosion if you were totally deaf. But there
might be the great flash. She was excited, suddenly lifted up inside herself. She had opened the door.

Nothing happened.

She was so surprised, and grateful, with some unexpected
sweetness flooding her being, that she found herself saying:

[311]

"Mamma, I love you—Mamma." She was really saying it out loud, as when, years ago, she had been naughty and had confessed and her mother had forgiven her.

Finding that nothing had happened and the world held together—that seemed to make everything different and easy. With a sense of exculpation, of absolution, of disembodied blessedness, as though she were little again and forgiven, she drifted in the evening light across the back lawn, past the building that had once been a barn and was now the garage, into the alley, down the alley toward the place where alley dwindled, and was purified, into lane, and on to the place where she, lying on her bed in her room upstairs, had known, somehow, she would go. But now, going there, she did not realize she was going.

In fact, if Jo-Lea did realize what she was doing, she would have to realize too what would happen as a consequence of doing what she was doing. And then she would not be able to do what she was doing and had to do. Therefore, in that deepest wisdom, which underprops thinking and realizing, there was no thinking or realizing, as her feet were guided, by that wisdom, along their necessary path.

That path was necessary for Jo-Lea Bingham because Matilda Bollin Bingham, trapped in her own necessity, had found it necessary, that evening, sitting at her table, on the white cloth of which floated diamonds, circles, and squares of drained and ghostly color from the stained-glass window on the west wall, to thrust forward, on its long, taut-tendoned neck, her long, sallow face, as though to make the hangman's work easier, and to say: "I told you—I have always told you—touch pitch, be defiled."

And to say: "She is your daughter—but you would not listen."

And, rubbing, with a slow, secret grinding motion, the pointed tips of her decorously expensive brown kid shoes into the carpet, to say: "To permit her to consort with people like that—but you would not listen."

And, while the saliva gathered and rose sweetly about her lower gums, to say: "Not only to permit her to go—but to take her, accompany her yourself—to a public place. In the company and society of those people. Oh, if my father knew—if he—"

And to say: "But God in His Mercy has perhaps withheld the newspaper from his hand!"

And, with knees clamping together while the shoe soles rubbed the carpet with inexorable motion, and the saliva gathered, to say: "So now your daughter's name is in every newspaper in this fair land of ours—discovery made by Miss Jo-Lea Bollin Bingham, age sixteen, of Johntown, Tennessee—oh, they omit nothing, they must be sure to drag the name of Bollin in the dust—who had accompanied Montgomery Harrick, age eighteen, the brother of the trapped man, into the woods and—oh, did you attend?—accompanied into the woods—"

And to say: "And now—now to compound felony—to pile Ossa on Pelion—to heap shame on my head—this—to have it noised far and wide and bruited about that—that this degenerate brother of Montgomery Harrick has left some degenerate girl pregnant with his degenerate child. Not that it is significant what happens to one more degenerate of Johntown. But—"

And, at that moment, Mrs. Bingham had turned her dark eyes with the yellow-streaked eyeballs on her daughter, and stared at her with a dawning discovery. Then, with a delicate exhalation, she had said: "Ah."

She had said, "Ah, so that is it! So it is he, that Jasper Harrick, the prize reprobate of Johntown. Pray, miss, will you admit it now? Is that the—"

Mr. Bingham had, that very instant, finished masticating and swallowed the last of his splendid strawberry shortcake, made on hot biscuits well soaked in butter, by Esther Lindley, colored, one of the two privately employed cooks of Johntown. So when

[313]

he rose from the table, he was quite ready to go. He did not seem to know that his wife was there. At least, he did not look at her.

"Daughter," he said to Jo-Lea, "go upstairs, will you please. Your mother is not feeling well. We must let her have quiet."

The girl slipped from the chair and noiselessly retreated into the hall before Mrs. Bingham had managed to rally and to say: "Feel—feel—who cares what I feel?"

But Mr. Bingham had followed into the hall, calling after his daughter: "I brought home some new magazines. They are on my bed upstairs. I brought a *Seventeen* for you, Honey-Baby."

He stood in the hall, thinking how his daughter was not yet seventeen, feeling sweet that she wasn't yet, but sweet also that she would be, standing there in shadow in a moment of sweetness, before he remembered how things were.

It crossed his mind that things were getting worse. There had never before been anything quite like this at the table tonight. He did not know what he could do. But he squared his shoulders and marched to the living room, and out of long habit picked up the Nashville *Press-Clarion*. There on the front page was the headline:

WOMEN OF STATE RALLY
Mother's Committee Formed to Guard Sweetheart and Unborn Child of Trapped Hero

Fund Tops $20,000

Then, as he lowered himself into his easy chair, the kind that brings your knees gently up, the kind executives rest in to fore-stall the coronary, he thought of his daughter, upstairs now with her trouble and the stony integrity of her secret, lying on a bed reading a magazine called *Seventeen,* and he thought he was going to cry.

At that moment, Mrs. Bingham entered from the dining room. He stirred in the chair.

[314]

"Oh, don't bother," she said. "Pray continue with your paper."

"I was just thinking," he said. "I was thinking that she will tell me—"

"The degenerate's name!" she exclaimed. "Well, she won't. If she won't tell her own mother."

"It was because she loved him," he said. "And if she loves him, he's probably a nice boy, and he—"

"Will what, pray?—See, you can't say it. Well, I can say it. Marry. But, as I have told you, I will not permit it. One of these louts who—"

He stirred in his chair. "All right," he said. "But you can take her away. We can work it out. You can go to New York. Or Europe. I have enough money. I—"

"You will do what I have said," she said. "You promised to make the arrangements. It is the man's place to take the responsibility. Have you made the arrangements?"

He swung himself forward in the chair and its patented mechanism responded handsomely and he was rising to his feet, crying out: "It's too awful! To do that to her—just a little girl—"

Mrs. Bingham was standing before him. "You should have thought of it earlier," she said quietly. "It is your fault. You insisted on bringing me to this town. Years ago. For opportunity, you said. Opportunity for what? Opportunity to have your daughter go and—have her do what she has done. Then, oh, no, you wouldn't even send her away to school, to a place befitting her station. You said you had to have her by you. But was she by you when—when she— Oh, don't put your hands over your eyes. You cannot hide the truth."

Mr. Bingham took his hands from his eyes.

"Yes, it is your fault. You let her go with those boys. Consort with them. Go to those parties at the high school. Those dances. Well, what do you say now?"

He said nothing. He sat down in his chair and let the mechanism drop him back. He closed his eyes and thought of himself dead, and being lowered gently down. He wanted to die.

[315]

But that passed, and his body tensed with a ferocious desire to protect Jo-Lea.

From what? he thought.

From himself, from Timothy Bingham, and the humiliation he had agreed to visit upon her body.

God help me, he thought.

His daughter was not, however, reading the magazine called *Seventeen.* She was, at that moment, lying on her back on her bed, feeling the weight of herself, staring at the ceiling, feeling the certainty grow in her that she would walk down the back stairs and away into the twilight, not thinking beyond that, but feeling forward beyond it into the shadowy compulsion that was like setting your foot down in the dark on a soft woods-path, with the leaves hanging close on each side in the dark, but you couldn't see them.

By the time Mrs. Bingham had entered the living room, and finally found again the full flow of her discourse, Jo-Lea was setting her foot down on a soft woods-path, where leaves, on each side, hung fat and flesh-soft and breathlessly close but were scarcely discernible in the gathering gloom.

She had taken the back path up the Sumpter ridge which Monty had once showed her. It was longer, but this way she wouldn't have to fight up through the crowd. Far off, through the woods, she could hear that writhe and rustle of the crowd, as though some tremendous creature were just waking up and yawning, and stretching itself in the trees, as though in grass. She could hear the hum of voices, like distant surf, and then, in a lonely moment of silence, the whistle of a train, muted and sad with distance, off in the valley. Then the hum and heave of voices flooded over again.

Now, all at once, far off, beyond the woods, the singing started. They were singing Monty's song:

[316]

"All the bullets in Korea
    Could not make my Brother fear.
    My Big Brother, he was brave,
    But he's lying in a cave—
    Oh, God, bring him out to daylight bright and clear!"

She stopped in the path to listen. It was dark in the path now. She thought how Monty loved his Big Brother. Her eyes filled with tears. She would go on, and find Monty. Her heart overflowed as she thought of Monty, who loved his Big Brother so. She would find him and hold his hand.

At that thought, she was filled with the desire to lay her head on Monty's shoulder and tell him all that was happening to her. She would tell him about her mother's voice and how she had not told her mother anything, and couldn't tell her mother anything, and what it was like to be taken to that doctor in Chattanooga, where her mother had taken her for an examination, and to not even be able to tell your right name, and how her father was sweet but couldn't help her and—

And with that she thought that Monty couldn't help her either. She couldn't tell him anything, not even about the baby. She couldn't tell him. She thought: *Oh, he's just a boy.* She was swamped by a sense of desolation and loss. It was as though she had just had Monty, a man, to protect her, and all at once he had been taken from her.

She thought: *If he were only a—*

The thought stopped, and she saw the image of Jasper Harrick, alone on a gray boulder above tumbled water, wearing a red shirt, playing his box, his head thrown back, singing to the solitude.

But Jasper was in the ground.

So she went on and found Monty, and held his hand, as they sat at the edge of the crowd in the glade. The box across his knees made it possible to hold his hand and not worry too much

[317]

about anybody seeing. The people now were singing "Rock of Ages." Then Mrs. Harrick came, and Mr. Pappy and two other men carrying the wheel chair, with Mr. Harrick in it. They found a good place to set the wheel chair. They fixed a folding chair for Mrs. Harrick. Mrs. Harrick looked awful tired, but she seemed to be holding up. "Your mother looks awful tired," she said to Monty, and squeezed his hand.

For a minute, she thought he did not know or care that she had squeezed his hand. Then, ducking his head down a little under his hat brim, he said, in a low, quick voice: "I ain't talking about it. I ain't talking about the way things are."

But he still did not squeeze her hand back. It looked like he would, after the way they had been together, and all. She was hurt, and embarrassed, as though she had been caught doing something wrong.

Then the squeeze came. It was quick, and timid, but it came. She felt better. She felt her heart filling up.

"Monty," she whispered, "I'm praying for Jasper. I am praying all over for him to be saved. It is like my whole body was just praying for him."

She squeezed his hand again, and he returned the squeeze.

"I want your Big Brother to be saved," she whispered.

Brother Sumpter was praying now. He prayed for that poor boy in the cave. He prayed for his relief, and for his salvation. He prayed for the souls of all who were here, on whom the weight of sin lay, in darkness like the cave. He prayed for their relief and confession in Jesus Christ.

Jo-Lea shut her eyes and tried to think of what it would be like to be saved. To confess yourself in Jesus Christ and just flow away in darkness like sweet tears. If she could just tell somebody all her trouble and be happy. Happy, oh, happy. People cried out, they were so happy.

Brother Sumpter prayed for that poor girl who had committed carnality with that poor boy in the cave. He prayed that the fa-

[318]

ther of her child might come out of the cave to her. He prayed that they might see their error and rejoice in Jesus Christ.

Jo-Lea shut her eyes.

She opened her eyes and looked, slow, all around. She was trying to see what girl it might be who had that thing in her which Jasper Harrick had put there. There were lots of girls here tonight. She knew that they were all looking at each other sidewise, and wondering. Then, with a shiver, she wondered if they were looking at her. She shut her eyes and, with a shiver, tried to think what it would be like to have that baby in you that Jasper Harrick had put there. Would it be different? With her eyes shut, she saw Jasper Harrick's face. He wore a red shirt and was looking right at her.

She felt a hand on her shoulder, and almost jumped out of her skin.

One of those strange men was leaning over her, and nodding and smiling, leaning close, holding one of those things on wires near and saying into it himself: "—and as a special feature of our coast-to-coast news offering from the mouth of the cave where the hero Jasper Harrick is imprisoned, I shall present Miss Jo-Lea Bingham, the girl who was walking on the mountain with the brother of Jasper when she discovered Jasper's boots and guitar at the cave mouth. Now, Miss Bingham—now, Jo-Lea—will you tell us—in your own words—"

She kept shaking her head at that man. Words wouldn't come. They wouldn't. Men were changing lights and cameras. Another man, all of a sudden, was there. "Hold it, Wes," he said, quick and low, out the side of his mouth, away from the microphone that he was holding his hand over: "I got to goose a chirp out of wren here for the nine thirty, then you can can her like salmon, for all of me."

They were pulling her up.

The second man was saying: "Don't be shy, Jo-Lea. Tell us now, you were walking on the mountain with Monty Harrick?"

[319]

She nodded. She managed to say yes.

"Now tell me, Jo-Lea, you and Monty, you are sweethearts, aren't you?"

She couldn't say anything.

"Tell me, Jo-Lea, tell all the people everywhere, for everybody loves sweethearts. Jo-Lea, tell them— Well, you do go steady, don't you?"

She managed to say yes, she reckoned.

Then he asked the other things and then the other man pulled her and the lights were on her and the cameras and the man who smiled even more and looked right into her eyes was talking to her.

When they let her sit down, she thought she was going to be sick. She thought she was going to faint. She held on, though. She held on to Monty's hand so tight, she could feel the sweat squishing slick between their palms.

Brother Sumpter prayed again. He prayed for salvation. He prayed for the salvation of that poor girl with her guilty secret.

People sang again. They sang "Throw Out the Life Line."

Brother Sumpter preached again. He said that whoever lives with a guilty secret lives in a dark cave and cannot breathe for the weight of sin. He cried out that those who were in the dark cave should come into the daylight bright and clear.

Some came. They confessed themselves and wept for pain and joy, and fell down on the ground, safe in Jesus.

The lights were on them, brighter than day, and the cameras were grinding.

Jo-Lea held Monty's hand as tight as she could. She had to hold tight, it looked like.

Brother Sumpter was preaching again. He said that what had been done in the dark should be brought into the light. He implored that poor girl to come from the darkness where she lay with the weight of her sin in her, to come forth to the love of Jesus and the love of all good people. He implored her not to lie alone in the dark with the weight of sin, but to come forth.

[320]

Jo-Lea shut her eyes, and wondered what it would be like. She hung on tight to Monty's hand.

The people were singing "Almost Persuaded."

Some rose, and cried out, and were saved.

It was the cry of Miss Abernathy that made Jo-Lea open her eyes.

It was the strangest cry she had ever heard. It was a thin, wailing cry of lostness, like somebody falling down a well, a well infinitely deep, it seemed, for the cry kept going on and on, falling, spinning out thinner and thinner, but somehow sharper and sharper, with depth and distance, like a hot needle going into your brain.

Then it stopped.

It was perfectly still now. Nobody made a sound. You could hear the steady, soft, oily sound of the cameras turning.

When Miss Abernathy got her breath back, she cried out: "I have lain down in the dark. I have lain down in the dark, and, oh! it was shameful."

She got her breath back, and standing up before all the people, old Miss Abernathy, with her crazy rat's-nest gray hair all wild and her eyes glittering in the lights, cried out that it was shameful.

Brother Sumpter stood up there and prayed for her.

She stared at him for a moment, as he stood up there, his head lifted and eyes squinched, praying for her, then she began to move. Drifting with a creaky, but weightless motion, as though smoke drifting might make some kind of soft, almost soundless creaking from its sad staleness in an air that never moved, Miss Abernathy was moving. She hung on to people as she moved. She hung on to the backs of chairs. She stood and shut her eyes and tottered, while his prayer went on. Then she opened her eyes and moved again.

She was not moving toward Brother Sumpter. She was moving toward the place where the Harricks were. She came to Old Jack Harrick and tottered there, and looked down once into his twisted and grooved old leonine face, then drifted past him. She sank to the ground before Celia Hornby Harrick, who had once, a thousand years ago, been a young girl just come to Johntown to teach the third grade and had lived in Miss Abernathy's house. She seized the hands of Celia Hornby Harrick, and begged forgiveness.

She had, she managed to say, ordered a wedding present for Celia Hornby, long ago, when she was going to marry John T. Harrick. The present had come. It was a dinner set of Wedgewood china, twelve of everything—yes, twelve of everything; oh, it was beautiful—but one night, the night before it was to be sent, she had got out of her bed, she had risen in the June night, yes, it was June, and the moon up, and found her father's ebony walking stick, and opened every package, and put all the pieces on the floor of the parlor, and weeping all the while as though her heart would break, had beat everything to pieces. By the moonlight that fell through the windows, she had beat them until she had to lie on the floor by the pieces to catch her strength.

Later, she had got up and put all the pieces into the boxes and stored the boxes in her attic. Her father's ebony walking stick was up there, too, right now. With the boxes.

Her neck all at once gave down and she laid her head on Celia Hornby Harrick's lap and wept for forgiveness. Mrs. Harrick looked like she might faint. Monty got up and went to stand behind her, she looked so bad. But she pulled herself together, and laid a hand on Miss Abernathy's rat's-nest old head.

All the people were staring at Miss Abernathy and trying to catch what she was saying. Those who could not hear asked those who could. But Jo-Lea could hear. She stared at her and heard every word, or almost, and felt wild and sad at the same time, as though she herself might have to lie down, night after night, in that crazy, falling-to-pieces old Abernathy house, all alone. all alone in the dark.

And while all the people were staring at Miss Abernathy, and while Jo-Lea was feeling the wild, sad feeling, she became aware of someone pulling gently, very gently, at her dress on the side away from where Monty had been. She turned to find the slick-faced boy crouching beside her.

"It was me," he whispered, fast. "It was me got them to put you on that-there TV. Hadn't been for me, they wouldn't seen you come in. I told 'em."

She didn't know what to say. He was pulling at her dress, staring at her, saying he had done it. He got her hand and drew it down and pressed it against something. "Feel it," he whispered, "feel it." He wadded something soft and silky into her hand. When she looked down, he pulled it out of her fingers, spreading it in the shadowy space between them. "Look," he whispered. "Yores, they's yores, huh?"

They were her drawers. She stared down at them, knowing they were hers, remembering.

"Yeah, yores," he was whispering, "and you took 'em off fer him. You take 'em off fer me, and I won't show nobody I got these here. I won't tell nobody. You do hit fer me."

As she stared into his face, he was whispering: "Yeah, you done hit fer him, I'm good as any Jasper Harrick. If you done hit fer him you might as well fer me, but if you don't—yeah, if you don't—"

She lifted her head and flung her gaze wide around.

It was then she saw Mr. and Mrs. Bingham entering the glade from the other side. "Oh!" she cried, "oh!" out loud.

She had forgotten, she had simply forgotten, everything being so strange, that every night at nine thirty her father turned on the TV for the Nashville newscast.

She jumped up. "Oh!" she cried in anguish.

Jebb Holloway, crouching in the cave mouth to remove the carbide lamp and set it on the rock shelf inside, heard Isaac Sumpter crawl out of the last crawlway behind him. Then he put his miner's head rig back on. If he was going to be on TV in a

[323]

minute to tell how Jasper was dying, it would look better to have the rig on. He wiped his dirty hand across his face. It would look better, with a little more dirt smeared on his face.

Then he crawled out and stood up, and Isaac Sumpter rose beside him.

They came out just in time to see Jo-Lea Bingham jump up like she was a filly that had backed into a bee bench and upset the hives.

They just stood there, goggle-eyed, while everybody stared at Jo-Lea as Jo-Lea said she was the one that had lain down in the dark and had in her that baby that Jasper Harrick had put there.

They saw her stand there, with her face white as flour and her eyes squinched shut, and say it, and then break and run. She ran out the upside of the glade where there were no people, into the woods.

"Hot diggity!" Jebb Holloway breathed. "That Jasper," he breathed reverently.

"Yes," Isaac Sumpter echoed, very low, "Jasper." He felt a dry, dusty feeling in his chest.

"Diggity," Jebb Holloway said, "I shore bet it was juicy."

"As a peach," Isaac Sumpter said, and was overcome by a painful, inexorable envy for Jasper Harrick. But why, he did not quite know. Because he had had that little Jo-Lea Bingham, who was juicy as a peach. Or because he lay in the cool, cool dark, and did not suffer.

XI

At first Nick Pappy could not quite latch on to what that little Bingham girl was saying when she stood up there and squinched her eyes shut. He got the sense of the words, but they were not making sense to something else which was in his head. Then he thought: *For Chrissake, it is not that Cutlick, it is her.* As he thought that thought, it was like losing money.

Then he thought: *But the bastard would pay more to have his own daughter fixed up.*

So he felt better again.

Then he thought: *But, for Chrissake, if she has already up and sung like a canary, then—*

Again it was like losing money. It was like going bankrupt.

For if she had stood up there and confessed to Jesus, there was sure no sense in her old man putting out good money when everybody in addition to Jesus knew now she had been on her back.

So he sat there thinking that thought, and it was like bleeding to death.

It was like it had always been. A man got set up and then he got knocked down.

But there was still the cave. He was taking in good money right now, if that boy with the close-screwed eyes did not rob him. Maybe if things held on big for a time, he would have enough to pay off that note and maybe raise some on the hotel deal. He better get hold of that Isaac and get something on paper how they stood. He wished he had done so already, but that fellow was always running back in the cave. You could not talk money very good with a fellow who was busy being a hero and saving a human life like he was. But maybe if things held on big.

Then he noticed that Isaac and that Jebb fellow were coming out of the cave mouth. The TV fellow was talking to them. What Isaac told the TV fellow made him jump like he had sat on a hot griddle. He started motioning to people to do this and to do that. They began swinging the cameras and things. They were bringing one closer over this way. Then the TV fellow laid his hand on Isaac's shoulder and said: "Isaac Sumpter and Jebb Holloway, the devoted friends of Jasper, have just come out of the cave from the trapped man."

He was turning to Isaac now and he made his face go long like he was not feeling so good. He said: "Isaac, tell us."

"There's not much to tell," Isaac said. "I went first till we got to the fourth chamber—where the pit is. I shouted to let Jasper know we were coming, then I waited for Jebb. Jebb came, and he insisted on being the one to crawl around the pit and go in the last gut to Jasper. Well—I let him go. I didn't see Jasper. But Jebb—here, Jebb—"

And he turned to that Jebb fellow.

The TV man was making motions to the fellows who had the cameras swinging over here close. Two other guys were coming

[326]

closer with their mike things. They were coming closer to Mrs. Harrick. The camera was coming closer and looking right at her.

Nick Pappy thought: *It is going to be bad.*

But she was not noticing the camera, it looked like. She was so busy staring over at that Jebb fellow. That Jebb fellow was getting all set. He gave a smile, then wiped it off his mouth with the back of his hand, like a man had finished eating a $2.50 special but did not find a napkin handy, and got himself set to talk.

Nick Pappy saw one of Mrs. Harrick's hands. It was clamped on the arm of the wheel chair. It looked like it would break that chrome chair arm or bust itself trying.

Nick Pappy thought: *It is going to be real bad.*

That Jebb fellow, he had started.

He said: "Like Ikey said, I wanted to be the one to git to Jasper. I had me a premmy-notion, or one of them things. I wanted to talk to my pal one more time. So I taken out across the edge of the pit. I don't mean it is something you kin do with yore eyes shut. It is not no picnic, with that hole right there, black and way down, and you hear the water bubbling and sloshing in the dark way down, and you scrabbling on the edge. What I mean to say is—"

"Tell us, Jebb," the TV fellow was saying, reaching out to pat that Jebb fellow on the arm, leaning his face close and making it go serious and sick-looking, "—tell us about Jasper."

"I'm a-gitting there," that Jebb fellow said.

That camera was swinging closer on Mrs. Harrick. It looked like it was sneaking up on her. It was not too close, but the guys with the mike things were closer.

And that Jebb fellow was saying: "—and Jasper, he said, 'Pray fer me, tell 'em to pray, fer it looks like I can't hold on. It looks like I'm a goner. The cold a-crawling up me, and—'"

And Nick Pappy thought: *He dies now and I will not pay off the note. That girl confesses to Jesus and he is dying. They is all against me. A fellow gets set up and then—*

The rage and the anguish shook him and he shut his eyes.

[327]

It was the cry of Mrs. Harrick that made him open them.

He opened his eyes from the darkness of himself to see her shrinking back under the powerful light on her, with her face lifted into the light and her hands up in outrage and protest as the camera purred. In that instant, Nick Pappy saw how the grief on her face, and the glaring light, made everything come strained and pure, as though it were a face outside of Time altogether. He thought it was the most beautiful thing he had ever seen.

With that thought, was the thought: *And me, I was trying to make money.*

He could not bear it. He felt that he was going to suffocate.

Then, as though he had made a final effort from under a great weight, he was on his feet. The air rushed burning into his lungs. He had plunged toward the guys with the mike things. He had shoved them aside. He had shoved the camera back. He was yelling: "Leave her alone!"

He had never felt strong like this.

He was yelling: "I am going in. I will get him out. I will lift off that rock!"

He plunged toward the cave mouth.

There was Isaac Sumpter backed up against the cave mouth, with his hands up, pressing him off, staring at him, saying: "You fool—you Greek fool!"

He was grabbing Isaac Sumpter by the neck. He felt the little bastard clawing at his face, but he didn't care and it looked like he just couldn't let go.

That was when he felt the crack on the back of his head, and in the split second before the explosion went black, felt another one in the same place. But the second crack seemed sweet and gentle, like somebody just patting him.

Lieutenant Scrogg, with weary expertness, had pistol-whipped him across the back of the head with a Colt .44. But Nick Pappy did not get the details until some time later.

[328]

Meanwhile, MacCarland Sumpter, out of a need deeper even than his need to go and minister to the dying man, out of the need to escape the anguish of the uncertainty which, until that moment, had been unacknowledged and denied, had entered the cave. He had done it so quietly that nobody realized what he was up to until he had already got too far for protest to do any good.

Nobody had noticed because Lieutenant Scrogg and the doc had been trying to decide what to do. Jasper needed a stimulant, Dr. Maddux said, to bolster his strength and maybe he could hold on. "Just get about two cc. of caffeine and sodium benzoate stuck in him," Dr. Maddux said, "then maybe the diggers—"

Lieutenant Scrogg called for a volunteer, preferably somebody who had given hypodermics. Before anybody had spoken up, somebody said Brother Sumpter had gone in.

"Brother Sumpter is older than I am," the doctor said, in a worried, inward tone. "Maybe I ought to take it in myself."

"Doc," Lieutenant Scrogg said, looking down at Dr. Maddux's front, "no offense, but Brother Sumpter is a lot skinnier."

Then he added: "And a hell of a lot crazier, if you ask me."

Hicks Lancaster, who kept the Plymouth garage in Johntown, and had done a little caving, volunteered. He had given hypodermics, too, he said. But he never got in. Somebody figured out at the last minute that there was a good chance of meeting Brother Sumpter in one of the guts, then how the hell would you ever get 'em out? It is hell to crawl backwards out of a tight gut. So Hicks Lancaster had to wait around for Brother Sumpter to come out. If he was ever going to.

When the first call for volunteers had come, some people had looked over at Jebb Holloway. He was sitting over at the side of the cave mouth, looking sick and beat up. He looked so bad nobody had the heart to suggest he go in. He had done his part, you had to admit.

He sat there looking really sick, and like he was worried about being sicker.

Wes Williams was speaking: "—and now all the eyes of the world are on the mouth of the cave from which, we trust, the brave padre will soon emerge. Is it too much to—"

Another man was holding a watch and making a sign to Wes, who nodded, not breaking stride.

"—pray for, that the padre's news will be good?"

As the last syllable of Wes Williams died on the air, another man began speaking into his microphone: "Folks, this is Goober Godolphin, on his regular eleven P.M. radio newscast for the Knoxville *Sentinel-Press*, station QRT on your happy dial. The happy station for happy folks. Good evening, folks, I am speaking from the mouth of the cave at Johntown, the spot where the hopes of all the world turn tonight. In the ground now with the trapped man is—"

My father, thought Isaac Sumpter, who was lying across one of the sleeping bags in the cave mouth. He was so tired he couldn't move. If he had not been so tired, he thought. If he had not been near dead from what that Greek had done to him, he might have stopped his father. He was too tired to think, though. Just give him five minutes and he would start thinking again. He would have to start.

Jebb Holloway was up at the mike now.

Famous last words, Isaac Sumpter thought, with tired irony that did not please him.

Let him have it, he thought.

Let them all have whatever they want, in the wide world, he thought, with grim benediction. He felt purged of desire, high and pure. It crossed his mind that this was, perhaps, like happiness: to move in this serenity, as under calm sunlight.

But with a grinding pain, he knew it was not for him. His father would come out, and deprive him.

[330]

Perhaps, though, the old man would not make it. He might be too old, too weak.

Oh, no, he is strong, Isaac Sumpter thought, *when it is to deprive me.*

He lay there and thought of all the deprivations of his life, the long lovelessness, the loneliness, the defects of pleasure, the joyless rooms, the cheap food, the seedy clothes, the contempt of schoolboys, the sneers of strangers, Mr. Haworth's voice on the phone from Nashville saying: "Tittlebum, Mr. Tittlebum," the white thighs of Goldie Goldstein closed tight against him in their last refusal, the sardonic laughter of her friend, that Eustacia Pinckney Johnson, on the telephone—"Yes, Ikey, and I got my curiosity satisfied as to why Goldie fooled with you, and the answer is, she is a fool"—the letter of expulsion from the Office of the Dean, and—

And what?

All else.

He did not say, but he knew that all, somehow, was the strong work of his father. It was all that mystic strength of his father. All the old fool's weakness and age and idiocy and poverty and defeat turned into a mystic strength when turned against Isaac Sumpter. The old man would take him upon a mountain and bind him and set a knife at his throat and—

He rose, suddenly, on the sleeping bag, and clutched at his throat. He must have been asleep, he thought, and lay back down. He had to think. He knew he had to think. He had to think of something, something to do when the old man came out.

If he came out. With a leap of the heart, he thought of the old man falling, falling into the dark sound of water.

But no, he, Isaac, would be ruined anyway.

Yes, just as things seemed to be on the rise. Just as he seemed ready to break away, for good and all, and never come back. He would be deprived of this, his chance, as he had been deprived of all else, and of—

Of what?

Of my mother, he thought.

Ah, he thought, *ah.*

And with the certainty of truth: *He killed my mother, so I wouldn't have one—so I wouldn't have her.* And he thought, sinking into a wave of sweet weakness, if only he had now the loving hand on his head in the dark, then all, everything, would be all right.

And he heard his name.

He pulled himself up, like a swimmer, from the dark, coiling depth of the wave.

The microphone was thrust at him.

"Now, Isaac," the voice said, "you must be proud of your father's heroic exploit. Do you wish to say a few words?"

"They should have stopped him," Isaac was saying, "they should have—"

He brought himself up short. He had heard the edge of hysteria in his voice. He had felt his voice shake. He took a deep breath and began again: "What I mean is, the crawlways are hard. He is an old man. He is my father. Oh, not that I blame anyone, but—"

He let the word die away. He handed the microphone back to Goober Godolphin, known in the trade as the Fog on Lookout Mountain, or sometimes, more affectionately and simply as the Fog.

"Excuse me, please," Isaac Sumpter said, and withdrew, and lay on the sleeping bag. His mind just wouldn't work. But he had to think of something.

At least, here, in the cave mouth, he would be the first to hear the sound of the old man's return. He would see the old man's face. He would read the old man's face. But then—then what?

They were singing again, outside, Monty's song, but in a distant, half-hearted way. Or was it sounding that way to him, simply because he seemed to be falling? No, not falling. Floating. For it was as though he had already fallen so far into the dark that he was at some center where gravity did not exist, and he

[332]

was floating like a feather in the dark at the hollow center of the world.

It was sweet to float in that darkness where nothing pulled you this way or that, where there was no gravity.

All at once, the old man was there. He had not heard him coming. But he knew he was there, and opened his eyes.

His first reaction was a lift of the old anger: *He would deprive me even of this. Even of peace.*

Then, with a look that froze the anger within him, the old face, under the carbide flare, was staring at him, strained and stained, furrows more deeply furrowed by the light falling across the old flesh, streaked with red dust, the red dust black-splotched here and there with sweat, the lips moving in a thin, dry soundlessness like dry leaves moving on stone in a passage of air so slight there is no sound except the imagined sound in your head. And the old eyes yearned out at him from among all those individual and disparate things which were parts of a face but not a face until you saw the eyes that, with their awfulness of yearning, seemed, almost, to bless him.

And he thought, in that split instant, as the anger died: *He would deprive me even of my anger.*

And with that, he was aware of a deeper anger which had stirred at the fact of the non-anger. But no, that deeper anger became a kind of non-anger, too, and beneath it the deeper and rawer anger—and in that moment he felt a disorientation, a dizziness, at the entrapment in the infinite series of unfoldings, in which each new reality denied the reality of the last reality of anger. He grabbed at the stone stanchion of the wall.

Then the old man said: "He is dead."

For a second, Isaac could not put those words into the context of anything. Sure, Jasper was dead, he was in the pit, deader than mackerel, but how could the old man know that, what was he saying? Then the implication hit him. He thought: *He is saying that he has seen—that he has actually seen—Jasper.*

[333]

Then he thought: *But he is lying.*

Then, with a certainty as chill as death, he thought: *But he cannot lie. It is impossible for the old fool to tell a lie.*

"Look here," he said to the old man. "Look here, are you saying that you—" He put out his hand to seize the old man's arm.

The old man looked down at the demanding hand. Then, effortlessly, he reached his own free hand around, lifted his son's touch from him, meeting no resistance, and without a word to answer the question, with the hissing carbide still on his brow, rose into the open air beyond.

Isaac Sumpter could not, for a moment, move. But he could tell the very instant the crowd discovered the old man standing there. He could catch, as it were, the communal intake of breath, and hear the sudden silence as the old man moved forward.

He thought: *I've got to get out of here.* But he couldn't move.

Then he heard the moan and stir—like somebody stirring in pain, in bed, at night, in the next room—that moved off down the ridge, under the dark trees, the moan and stir that meant that the old man had now said that Jasper Harrick was dead.

When Isaac Sumpter did get out into the open, his father was standing on the shoulder of limestone to the right of the cave, from which he had preached to the people. His arms were lifted, as though he were about to pray. But he was saying: "There is one thing I must tell you. Jasper Harrick, dying, knowing he was about to meet his Maker, told me that no girl or woman was in trouble because of him. He said it before he died, and in the knowledge of death, and I must tell you."

Even before the full import of the words had sunk into his consciousness, something in Isaac Sumpter was saying: *Ah! this is it.*

This was the stroke the old man, the old enemy, had withheld. And the *ah* in his mind was, in its way, too, like joy. He could leap forward now, to the dangerous fact, and in that leap escape the yearning in the eyes that had, somehow, in that moment in the cave mouth, unangered, and unmanned him. He stepped into the open, before his father.

He saw Jebb Holloway crouching in the edge of the crowd, trying to make himself small, trying to creep away, trying to be nothing. *He is nothing*, Isaac Sumpter thought. *The ambition of Julius Caesar and the I.Q. of a pissant, the crud.* Then, with a quick exhilaration: *Nothing, unless*—and he felt gay, ready to burst out laughing—*nothing, unless I goose him to glory.*

He swung to the people. "Listen!" he called out. "Listen!"

The murmur of the crowd died.

"Father," Isaac Sumpter asked, "where did you find Jasper?"

The old man looked down at him, and for a moment, with the same flicker of anger at being unangered, Isaac Sumpter thought he saw that same yearning in the old eyes. Then the old man was saying: "After the fourth chamber, son. Like you said, son. Over the shelf by the pit, and into the last crawlway past the pit. Right where you said, son."

"Good," Isaac Sumpter said, to whom, to what, wasn't quite clear.

Then he swung toward Jebb Holloway.

"Jebb, come here," he called, and Jebb, hangdog as a hound with egg-yellow on both jowls, managed to get up.

"Jebb," he said, "Jasper told you about that girl? Is that true? Yes or no!"

Jebb gave him a long look of hate, then swung his gaze despairingly at the old man on the rock above, as though he might save him. He turned again toward Isaac.

"Answer, Jebb," Isaac said, almost tenderly.

Jebb nodded. "Yes," he managed.

"You hear," Isaac called out, strong and clear. "And I affirm that Jasper Harrick told me the same. I affirm it."

He turned his back on the crowd, and took one step toward his father, looking up at him. "Father," he said quietly. But in the absolute quiet, the word was clear.

[335]

"Father," he said, and took a step closer, and lifted up his hand, as though reaching up to give a hand to help the rickety old bones to step down. "You are an old man," he said.

He waited. Then: "No one would have blamed you for not going into the cave."

He waited. Then, with voice quieter, more tender: "And no one, Father, will blame you if you did not go all the way."

Again, he waited.

Then: "Through that last gut. Over the shelf by the pit, into the last crawlway. No one will blame you."

Then: "No one will blame you, for we know—we know, Father—that somehow, somehow in the very goodness of your heart, you think you did go."

The voice had become very gentle.

Isaac Sumpter stared up at the old man.

Then: "But, Father—Father—did you—did you—"

Suddenly Isaac Sumpter flung his right forearm across his eyes, and the strength seemed to go out of his body. He cried out: "I can't—I can't!"

He stood there for a moment in that posture of despair. A woman's voice, very clear and pitiful, then said: "He's crying—he's crying—for it's his own father."

At that, Brother Sumpter, who had been staring, in a kind of darkening, incredulous hypnosis, lifted his gaze to the woman's voice, and peered out at the crowd, as though trying to find her.

"Look at him!" a woman's voice yelled. "Yeah, look at him. Him a preacher and lying!"

"Yeah, and somebody ought to fix him!" a voice yelled.

"Yeah, fix him!" yelled the woman's voice from the crowd.

"Lady, I'll fix him," yelled a man, and detached himself from the crowd, fortyish, gaunt and powerful, in overalls, red-faced, unshaven, drunk. He jerked Brother Sumpter off the stone, with a quick, snapping motion that released him to fall on one knee.

But the Greek had raised up from the cave mouth, and had stepped in front of the crouching, white-faced old man.

[336]

"Get back," the Greek said, not loud, to the man, and to another man just like him. "Get back or somebody will get killed."

"Yeah, and maybe it will be you," the first man said.

"I don't care," the Greek said, "I don't care who, but somebody will get killed."

"Yeah, yeah," the man said. But that was all.

It was all except the jeering. A voice yelled here and a voice yelled there. "Yeah," one yelled, "him a preacher and lying!"

And somebody else: "Yeah, lying—fer that girl—she said it was her!"

And another voice, from the dark of the trees: "Whoop-ee! And she ought to know!"

"Boy, would she know!" another voice yelled.

Then somebody burst out laughing, on the other side of the glade, in shadow. He, whoever he was, didn't seem to be able to stop laughing. He kept laughing and laughing, as though he couldn't ever stop, as though the night on the mountain wouldn't ever be over, and he would never, never, get caught under a rock, not him, down in the dark ground, and, boy, was he ever glad!

When Jo-Lea stood up and said what she did, Monty was standing behind his mother's chair, where he had gone because his mother looked so cut up by old Miss Abernathy's goings on. When Jo-Lea said what she did, he felt as though his guts had just turned to water. He had to hold on to the chair to stand up. And there was a pain in his head, just inside his forehead, as though the words she had said were all there, like hot stones grinding and grating together. When she bolted for the brush, he couldn't move.

Even when Mr. Bingham had jerked from Mrs. Bingham, leaving her standing there before everybody with her jaw gaped open, and headed for the brush after his daughter, Monty could not move. It seemed as though he could not believe in anything that was happening. It was like a dream you were caught in but would wake out of.

Then he woke out of the dream. But the reality he woke into was exactly like the dream he had waked out of, with the only difference the fact of being worse for being real. No, there was one more difference: you could move. He was running into the woods on the upside of the glade.

He was well into the woods, ripping into brush like a blind mule with the dogs on him, before he had the good sense to stop and listen. He didn't hear a thing, except, of course, that stir and murmur the crowd was always making. He had been grading up the mountain all the time, instinctively following the line of flight Jo-Lea had elected at the start. Feeling his own knees shake and his heart pump, he figured no girl was going to hold the upgrade very long, at that pace. He ought to catch her soon. He took off again, not running now, more westerly, for it seemed more open that way. At least, you had a sense of sky breaking here and there in that direction, above the absolute dark of the trees. But he found himself running again, and his breath coming again in a kind of sob and gasp. Durn it, he had to stop that running. He would tear himself all up.

He wondered if Jo-Lea was tearing herself all up in the dark.

He wondered if she had fallen down somewhere, maybe bleeding or with an ankle broken, and nobody to pick her up.

He stopped and listened. He thought he heard a voice. Then he did hear it, off up the mountain and more east. The voice calling must have been Mr. Bingham's voice. Very faint and far off, it was calling: "Jo-Lea—Jo-Lea!" Then, more faint and desperately thin in the dark: "Honey—Honey-Baby!"

For a second he wondered how Mr. Bingham, him as old as he was, way over forty, had got so far up, and in the dark. Then he was sure Jo-Lea wouldn't be up that way. She knew where the old timber road was—the road they had made to drag out crossties, long back when there were some crossties worth cutting on the mountain. He had showed her the road. She must be bearing toward it, no matter how she had headed out of the glade. She had enough sense to know the way it lay, and to head toward it. She would miss the crowd that way, too.

He headed straight west. Then it came to him that he was going to hit the road too far downgrade. Maybe she would come in above him, and he would be running away from her, not after her. He took bearing a little upgrade, and plunged on, holding his hands out to keep brush off his face. He began to get bigger patches of sky. The stars, he thought, the stars were so high. Then he wondered why that would come into a fellow's head.

Then he broke through the last brush, all of a sudden, and knew he was in the old road. He looked up and saw the sky. He was sweating and panting. He stood there with his head thrown back to take a couple of big gulps of air, and he saw the stars again. They were so high.

He headed down the road, half running. Even here you didn't dare really open out and run. There were rocks and ruts and deadfall, and even with the openness to the sky, not enough light to tell. He stopped twice to yell Jo-Lea's name. There was no answer, so he plunged on. He was running again.

Durn it, he thought, *durn, I got to stop it.*

But he didn't stop, for then he thought that, in the dimness, he had caught movement. Then he was sure of it. Then it was gone. The road was smoother here, and grassy, his feet could tell.

He almost ran right past the place. What stopped him, he didn't know—some slightest movement caught out of the tail of his eye, the faint glimmer of some whiteness of flesh she could not hide. He checked himself, and swung like a basketball player. He was standing over her as she crouched beside the road, in the brush.

He didn't have enough breath at first. Then he said: "You heard me. You heard me and wouldn't stop."

Then: "You hid. You were going to let me run on."

That was what seemed important to him then. He could not even remember how he ever started chasing her in the dark, in the woods. He had called her, he had chased her, and she had hidden from him in the brush, crouching down there in the new June leaves, in the dark.

He looked down and saw the glimmer of white that was her face. He reached down and fumbled for her hand to draw her up. His fingers found her wrist, and closed on it. As he drew her up, the motion of her rising to face him, the contact of his fingers on her flesh—something—brought everything back to him, how everything had started.

He stood there before her, holding her wrist, staring into her face, which, in the starlight, glimmered less dimly now, and the weakness was in his gut again, and the grinding, stony pain in his brow.

Then he realized that he had to say the words. He had been running wild in the dark over the mountain to find her and say the words. So he said: "Is it—is it true?"

She was staring at him, her eyes shadowed in the white glimmer of her face.

"Say it," he said, tightening his grip on her wrist.

Slowly, she was nodding at him.

"A baby—" he said. "You going to have a baby?"

After a second, she nodded again.

"Say it," he said.

He couldn't make out what was going on on her face. Something was happening there, but he could only make out the shadow and glimmer.

"Say it!" he said.

"Yes," she said, whispering.

"All right," he burst out, "all right!"

With that, whatever weakness had been in his gut and the pain in his forehead were gone. All he felt was a kind of light-headedness, as though he were growing tall among the dark trees. He might reach out and break a tree with his hand, just reach out in the dark. It was a feeling as though, for the first time in his life, he was himself. It was as though he had never been Monty Harrick before.

"All right!" he said, his head reeling with the suddenness of life. "Well, it's mine. I know it's mine, do you hear?"

The words were bursting out of him, as though they weren't his. Or rather, as though he were the words: "I don't know what kind of durn foolishness bit you—I don't know and I don't care—I don't believe a word of what you said—I know it's mine! Do you hear?"

He was gripping her wrist, and she was staring up at him from the glimmering white of her face, and he could hear her breath.

"Say it," he commanded. "Say it's mine!"

He pulled her to him. He released the hold on her wrist and thrust his arm around her waist to draw her to him.

Rather, he began that motion. But somehow the instant his hand had found her waist and recognized the slenderness and the softness, the words she had said were in his head: *I am praying all over for him. It is like my whole body is praying for him.*

It was, all at once, as though she were again saying the words aloud—and that was the answer to him, to Monty Harrick, and all his chance of hope and pride.

Even in the instant as her waist went pliant under his hand, and she was looking up at him, the words were in his head, and his hand dropped from her.

She stood there for a moment, abandoned, seeming about to sway. Whatever she had been about to say, she did not say. All she did was to stare at him, then give a shake of her head in desperate denial, and flee down the track in the dark.

He did not pursue.

As she fled away under the starlight, he was paralyzed. He was paralyzed by a sense of betrayal. She had been his, and now she was not. Jasper had been his Big Brother, and now he was not. He felt alone, and powerless, as though a dark wind were driving over the mountain, bending down the trees and stripping him bare and white in the darkness. It was as though the wind had snatched even his name away.

But that was not the worst. The worst came a minute later, after the outrage, after the impotence. The worst was to realize how crazy he, Monty Harrick, had been to think that anybody, Jo-Lea Bingham or anybody else in the world, would turn to him, when Jasper was there. He thought of Jasper walking down a road at night, tall and laughing under the stars.

He could not hate Jasper any more. He could not feel betrayed. He could not hate Jo-Lea. All he could feel was the cold despair of the recognition of the logic—no, even the justice—in the rejection which he suffered.

He began to go back up the old road. After a bit he swung east into the woods, bearing up toward the cave. He heard the noise the crowd made, a noise louder now, swelling and confused. He heard a yell, far off somewhere. He stopped, listening. His first thought, with a start of the heart, was that Jasper had been saved.

Then, with a kind of horror, but a horror that came with, somehow, a calm and detached recognition, he realized that he did not care whether Jasper was saved or not. He did not know what he cared about now. If anything. He went on in the dark.

There was more sound eastward and north in the woods, the murmur and swell of voices, a yell now and then, and always, but with slowly increasing volume, that distant stir and heave as though a great beast were shifting in the dark, crushing down brush and saplings, breathing. But the boy wasn't paying attention to that. He heard it, and at the same time did not hear it. His finger tips felt numb.

Even when something stirred close to him, very close, he didn't at first pay attention.

Not until he heard the voice, not much more than a whisper, but harsh and hoarse: "Git on, you bastard—git on away!"

[342]

In his numbness, he stopped stock-still, and turned. He made out the forms, rather a sense of darker darkness in the shadow of a tree, merging with the darkness of the trunk, and caught the whiteness of faces. Then from under that blackness of the tree there was the voice again, hoarser now, with a murderous throatiness: "Git on—git on, you bastard—or I—I'll—I'll—"

He moved on off, groping up the ridge, his hands up to ward off the brush or boughs. Some fifteen paces on, he stopped to try to get his bearings. Over to one side, he heard a stir, whispering, a woman's giggle, a muffled protest.

He stood as still as death, trying not to breathe, as still as you do when your hands tighten on the rifle and you wait for the dawn deer to show around the boulder. But now, here, nothing would show. His heart was making a hollow, painful thump in the dark of his chest. His chest seemed as big and deep as a cave, an enormous emptiness where nothing could ever happen except that painful thumping in the dark.

Far off, on the mountain, a man's voice yelled: "Whoop-ee!"

He stood there, not moving, suffering with the constriction of his breath, hearing his heart.

Then he was aware of another stirring, farther up, toward the left, the west. With his hunter's tread, he picked his way up the ridge, a course between the spot where he had heard the other noise, and now this one. He stopped again. Again there were sounds, the stirrings, the monstrous, massive stirring far off in the woods, the smaller stirrings nearer at hand, the sibilances, the murmurs, the hoarsenesses, the distant yell, the throbbing in the night.

There was a sound very near. He knew it. Rather, where there had been sound, there was now absolute soundlessness, breath withheld, muscles tensed, lips bitten. Not thinking why, he leaned over and touched the ground. There was grass here, not brush and dead leaves and fallen twigs, but soft grass. His fingers touched the grass here, touched it there. Then he straightened up, and stared at that spot where he knew there should be sound,

[343]

but where there was not. He felt himself sucked into that focal spot of deeper darkness and desperate soundlessness.

And all at once he had the terrible certainty that Jasper, his Big Brother Jasper, and Jo-Lea were there on the ground, on the grass, in that spot of denser darkness and bitten lips and unbearable immobility. Ah, he thought, if he stood there and never moved, then they could never move. They would have to lie there forever, and suffer in the dark.

He held himself rigid and motionless, and his heart leaped with a ferocious joy.

But the voice said: "Oh."

It was a woman's voice and it said: "Oh, I can't stand it—God damn, I don't care if—if—"

He fled up the ridge.

When he stopped, he stood gasping for breath. The thought, all of a sudden, was in his head: *That's the way it is. That's the way.*

Then he thought it couldn't have been. Not Jo-Lea and his Big Brother. Jo-Lea had run down the mountain. Jasper was in the ground. But standing there panting, he then thought: *It don't matter. It don't matter a durn. It's the way the whole durn world is.*

But the voice said: "Hey."

It was a voice so casual you couldn't believe that it was coming out of the dark. It was a woman's voice. "Hey, Buster," it said, "you got a match?"

For a moment he couldn't answer. He was not even sure there was a voice. Then he fumbled in his pocket, and found some. "Yes," he said.

"Well," the voice said, "what you waiting for, Buster? Light me up, Buster."

He managed to get a match lighted, and leaned toward where the voice had been. The face that lifted up at him sudden in the light held a cigarette drooping straight forward over the

[344]

fleshy, boldly outthrust bulge of the lower lip. The dampness of
the lip caught the glint of the match flame.

For an instant that was what he saw. Then he saw her face.
It was the face of a woman of thirty-five or so, roundish under
disheveled brown hair, the brownish skin sweat-damp and
catching the match glint on one cheek. He saw that the eyes were
staring up at him, straight into his. The eyes were big and pale
blue. He couldn't believe that pale blueness coming out of the
face, out of the dark all around.

The woman was crouching on the right knee, with the other
leg lifted forward, the foot flat on the ground, with her skirt,
some sort of light cloth, crumpled back to expose the white
fleshiness of the left thigh.

"Hey, Buster," she said, letting the words come out around
the cigarette that jerked and twitched toward and from the flame
with the small motion of the lips. "You're shaking. You're shaking
so, I can't light the damned thing."

With that she reached out with both hands and took his wrist
to steady it.

Before she could thrust the cigarette into the flame, a voice,
a man's voice, from the left, so close the boy jumped, said: "Give
the little booger a drink and maybe he'll stop shaking."

Monty looked at the man caught there in the match flare,
squatting against a tree, sharp, hard face staring out, shirt open
down the front on a hairy chest, bottle in his hands.

"Yeah," he was saying, holding out the bottle into the match
light, "be polite and give the gentleman a drink."

"Yeah," she said, thrusting the cigarette into the flame, and
drawing two or three times with a sharpness that made the tip
glow viciously with the rhythm of her suction. "Yeah," she said,
"I'll be polite, yeah, I'll give him something."

She blew a puff of smoke suddenly into Monty's face, so that
he flinched and his eyes blinked. Still grasping his wrist with
both hands, she rose abruptly from her crouch, with a quick,

[345]

fluid gymnastic ease, even as the match burned his fingers and he let it drop. And all in the same second, she had drawn one hand from the grip on his wrist, but had tightened the other, and drawn his hand forward and down in the dark.

"Yeah," she whispered harshly, "yeah."

The man sniggered over in the dark. "Don't mind me, buddy," he said. "I'm just resting up."

"You oughtn't need no rest for what you did," she said. Then her cigarette tip glowed in the dark, and Monty felt the gust of smoke in his face, and the whisky smell.

"Go on, buddy," the man's voice was saying from the dark. "Then I git rested and I'll show her the difference betwixt a man and a boy."

"Who'll show who what?" she demanded, gripping the boy's wrist, drawing his hand.

"Don't mind her, buddy," the man was saying. "Been living in Chicago and she's a great talker, and mean as a scalt cat. But, buddy, she'll shore swing it fer you."

"Yeah," she said, and the cigarette tip glowed up so sharply that he caught the sudden, incongruous pale blue of the eyes leaping at him, for that split second, out of the dark.

"Yeah," she whispered huskily, and blew the smoke into his face, and he felt his hand drawn against her and held there. "Yeah, and what do you think of that muff, Buster?"

"You better grab holt, buddy," the man's voice was saying. "Grab holt while you kin. Think of that feller laying up yonder in the ground. Suppose he hadn't ripped off that last little strip of nookie, and it tender. Yeah—"

The whole durn world, Monty Harrick thought, *it's the way it is,* and felt a surge of angry strength rise in him. *All right,* he thought.

And the woman said: "Ah." She dropped the cigarette.

But the man's voice was saying: "That's it, lay holt, son. Suppose you had turned hit down, and it was you laying up thar dead in the ground and—"

[346]

Monty Harrick jerked back. He stood there free, suddenly shivering with cold.

"Dead—did you say dead?" he demanded.

"The word done come," the man's voice said. "Done found him dead and—"

The woman's hand had found Monty Harrick's, drawing him.

"Yeah," she was saying, "it's a cold hole he's in—but you, sweetheart—come here, sweetheart—"

Then he heard her scream after him: "You little son-of-a-bitch!"

She screamed it again, but it was far off now as he plunged up the ridge.

Then he could hear that man laughing. It must have been the man.

Monty Harrick crouched beyond a beech trunk at the upper edge of the glade, waiting. Almost everybody was gone from the glade, just two patrolmen, old Dr. Maddux, and a couple of grown boys hanging on. Lieutenant Scrogg had sent in one of his men, a scrawny fellow for a patrolman, with Hicks Lancaster. Hicks Lancaster carried the needle-load of caffeine and sodium benzoate, but nobody took it seriously.

Lieutenant Scrogg was walking around now, kicking up the dirt. "They have sure wore out this grass," he said. He looked at his watch. "They ought to be out soon," he said.

That was all that was going on now in the glade, until the commissioner from Nashville broke through the brush and Lieutenant Scrogg said: "Jesus, the commissioner," and at something just short of the double started across the glade to greet him.

"They gone in to verify," Lieutenant Scrogg said, as soon as he had disposed of the amenities.

"You been having you a time," the commissioner said.

"You ought to seen it," the lieutenant said.

"I did. On TV. And I've been getting the radio on the car

[347]

coming up." He stopped, and cocked his ear to the moan and whisper and stir down the mountain, punctuated with far *whoopee's*. "What's the celebration?" he demanded. "Home-coming Game?"

"We had to shove 'em back in the woods," Scrogg said. "We had to bust a few heads doing it. Once the word got out the booger was dead, folks got a little out of hand, you might say."

"What did you let 'em for?" the commissioner asked, without heat.

"Christ, boss, give me a army and I might of kept the lid on. I done what I could. I did get worried for a minute though, when that preacher come out from the ground and said no girl was knocked up. It looked like they might of lynched the old poop. Because he claimed no girl was knocked up. Maybe would have if it hadn't been for that fool Greek."

"What Greek?"

"Just a fool Greek. Local."

"Well, get on with it."

"Like I was saying, things sort of got out of hand. Folks started hooting at that preacher, thinking he was lying about going all the way in to the fellow caught. Then some toughs was gonna fix him. But that Greek, he is built like Zybysko used to be, and is as crazy as a Brahma bull with a cocklebur up his ass hole, and he took the preacher's side. He stood up there, sweating and wall-eyed, and swore somebody was going to get killed. And they might have, if you didn't shoot him from a reasonable distance. It would take a elephant gun to bring him down off his feet the first whack, and, dying or not, if he laid hands on you he would bust somebody. As for us, we was busy trying to crowd folks off down in the woods.

"The old man, he just stood there lifting up his arms to the folks like he was begging something, but they sure-God never gave it to him. Not anything he might of craved. All they did was hoot and yell and call him names. The women the worst. The old buzzard, he shut his eyes, and let his arms fall, and his face was

[348]

streaked with that red dust and where it was all sweaty it looked black. He was streaked like a zebra in the face. He was a beaut, standing up there.

" 'Bout the time we got the folks crowded down into the timber, I looked around, and I thought he was going to faint. But the Greek grabbed him. He jerked away from the Greek, and yelled, 'Don't touch me!' Loud and shrill. I figured the Greek had done something, like starting a private lynching or something, so I run toward them. But old poop was about to fall, and the Greek grabbed him again, just to prop him, I figured. But you know what happened?"

"No," the commissioner said.

"The old man, he pulled away from that Greek again, and busted out, 'Don't touch me. I am not worthy. I am not worthy of your touch.' Saying that to a Greek."

"What wasn't he worthy about?"

"I figure he never made it. Crawling far in, I mean, and come out and lied about talking to Jasper and all. Him being a preacher, it started to prey on his mind."

"Well," the commissioner asked, "what made the old fool want to go in for?"

"I figure it had gone to his head," Lieutenant Scrogg said. "All the TV and such. He is human and it went to his head. A poor old hillbilly preacher like him and he finds himself in the Big Time. He had to keep on top."

"You don't think he made it? All the way?"

"Like cow patties are porridge. So he came out with that horse apple of a lie about how Jasper said he never knocked up nobody in his sweet life. Just after that girl had confessed, too. That was what was so dumb."

"Well," the commissioner said, "just suppose the chick does not lay the egg. Then what?"

"Listen, boss, are you playing dumb? That chick is the daughter of the local folding money. She is the legal and legitimate daughter of the guy who is the local mother of money. He

[349]

brings it forth. There is going to be a lot of whitewashing. The egg will not be laid. I bet Baby-Girl is on her way this minute to Nashville's best abortionist. Who is it, by the way, since old Doc Pickerell had his trouble?"

"You in trouble, Lieutenant?"

"Naw," Lieutenant Scrogg said, and grinned, "but if you had to be, statutory and all, you could do worse than what that Jasper had for the condemned man's last toot. She is nookie-built. She is evermore built."

"So you think the Bible-thumper was lying?"

"Yeah, but even if he wasn't nobody would believe him. Sure, folks believed him when he first come out and didn't say anything but that Jasper was dead. But as soon as he said Jo-Lea was not knocked up, they would not believe that for pignuts. It is a lot more fun to believe that that Jo-Lea is knocked up. She is nookie-built, and it is fun to think of her getting it. Folks believe what they want to believe."

"You are a pragmatist, Lieutenant."

"I'm a what?"

"Skip it," the commissioner said.

There was a burst of yelling down the mountain, in the dark.

"They have enthusiasm," the commissioner said.

"It is the same old kind," the lieutenant said. "Red-eye and nookie. They are also enthusiastic about not being dead in the ground."

The commissioner cocked his head, listening.

"If I had a-had as many men as Dwight Eisenhower had on D-day, I might of kept the lid on," Lieutenant Scrogg said defensively. "I did pretty well the first couple of nights. To be honest, though, I admit that as long as that hillbilly was stuck in the ground, it sort of dampened the spirit of fun. A fellow can't help but wonder a little how he himself would feel stuck down there, and it shrivels the pecker. Also that old bush-league, retread Billy Graham was goosing 'em with the hot handle of the Devil's pitchfork. He was holding down enthusiasm.

[350]

"But things changed fast, once that preacher come out of the ground and said Jasper was dead. Sure, they'd believe that much of what the old poop said. OK, Jasper was dead, but they were not. Most of 'em not even saved. Hadn't even got fanned by an angel's wing, in passing. Well, you can figure it out, so durn glad to be alive they had to prove it. All over the mountain corks started popping out of whisky bottles. It was booze like a gully-washer.

"I went down in the woods a-ways, dark as the inside of a widow woman's best black silk bombazine bustle, and you could hear the brush crashing where they fell. I tell you, down yonder there is fraternizing amongst strangers. There is clapp-swapping amongst the non-introduced. It is damned near like cordwood, the way they are stacked. If cordwood could talk and grab hold and took any interest in that kind of goings on. I had to pick my way out of the woods.

"But not much harm going to be done. Black eyes and hang-overs in the morning. Maybe a couple of guys will get cool-cocked and let lay. Or carved by a switch blade. Some dame will turn up and claim she was raped. But mostly the damage will just be knocking over some fences and spoiling the Sumpter sassafras crop and rubbing the bark off post oaks like a wild boar honing dried mud off his back, where folks can't get ground space."

"Maybe we'll get off lucky," the commissioner said.

"Everybody except that Jasper," Lieutenant Scrogg said. "And his last toot was juicy."

Monty Harrick, crouching behind the beech tree, waiting for people to go away from the glade, heard every word Lieutenant Scrogg said.

[351]

Hell had not yet really broke loose on the mountain before Isaac
Sumpter got his mind made up. He got on his phone, there in
the cave mouth, and got the Nashville airport. It felt funny,
funny and fulfilled, to be calling the airport. Knoxville was a lot
closer, he knew that, but he explained to himself that he didn't
know where the airport was there. Then, in an access of candor,
he admitted that that was not the reason he was electing Nashville. He had had to elect Nashville. Three weeks ago, in humiliation and despair, he had been driven from that city. Well, he
was coming back. Long enough to spit on that sacred earth, then
grab a plane and fly away forever.

So he made his call. He had never been on a plane.

He grinned sardonically inside himself, at himself, and the
callowness of pleasure. There was, in fact, one part of himself

so certain that he deserved, and would have, all success and all pleasure that any pleasure, when it came, could give only a kind of grim and arid satisfaction of fulfilled prediction. Life-to-be-lived was already life-lived, the future was already stale with sardonic recollection. And there was, he learned, an American flight to New York, 7 A.M.

Then he took the back lane down the mountain.

He went up to his bare wooden goods-box room, turned on the naked light, glanced once, avidly, with an avidity of, as it were, expiation, around at the nakedness and poverty and ugliness of the room, knowing somehow that the image of this special place would go always with him and give an edge and a salt—and a desperation—to all the enjoyments of luxury and beauty that would, so surely, come.

He stripped naked, washed himself in the china bowl, with water from the china pitcher, dried himself, and hurriedly dressed. He wondered why he was not tired. He was tingling with energy.

He packed his clothes, a bare minimum, flinging the rejected items, clean or not, into a heap in the middle of the floor. He took the wallet out of the top drawer of the bureau, and counted the money. He had just about enough, he thought, to make it. He would be in New York tomorrow before the banks closed. Before the Dutch Trust closed.

From the floor by the bed, where he had tossed it that hot, quivering afternoon a thousand years ago, he picked up the Cambridge edition of the poems of John Keats. A moment, he hefted it in his hand, trying to decide.

The words came full and plangent to his tongue:

"Thou wast not born for death, immortal Bird!"

He again said the words, out loud, for the first time realizing fully the trance of power and the triumphant liquidity of the syllabification.

God, he thought, in that instant of joy.

He repeated the line, and then:

> "No hungry generations tread thee down;
> The voice I hear this passing night was heard
> In ancient days—"

Ah, all seemed as clear—as clear as the triumph of life. All seemed to be only as it had to be. How could anything be otherwise? He felt like a man who lifts his head and, in that moment of recognition, steps forth to tread the joyful measure of necessity.

He flung the book back to the floor, slammed the lid of the suitcase down, locked it, picked up the suitcase, and was taking the first step to the door, when he heard the noise downstairs. His first thought was to run out the back way. Then he remembered that the keys to the car were in the bowl in the front hall. But that wasn't the real reason he waited, counting the slow steps on the stairs, waiting for the knob of the door to begin slowly to turn.

He set the suitcase on the floor, and waited.

The knob turned, and his father, very slowly, entered the room.

"I—I saw the light," the old man said.

"I was packing," Isaac said.

The old man looked down at the suitcase, then lifted his gaze back to the boy's face.

"You don't have to go," the old man said, very quietly.

"No," the boy said, "but it's through no defect in your good intentions."

The boy was standing almost directly under the naked light. The eyes of the old man staring at him had to blink against the light. The boy wished to Christ he would stop that blinking.

Then the old man said: "I had to go in the cave, son."

"All right, you went in," Isaac Sumpter said. "You went in and you found the poor bastard where I said and—"

"Yes," the old man said humbly, "I found him where you said."

[354]

"—and he was out of his head and told you a bloody lie, so why didn't you pray with him and get the grief over and come on out and keep your mouth shut? You would have been greatly admired. From coast to coast, I may say."

"He wasn't out of his head," the old man said.

"Who wouldn't be?" Isaac Sumpter demanded. "Stuck in the ground."

"He wasn't out of his head, son. He was dead—"

"Dead! But you said—"

"Yes, I said it. But he was dead before I got there."

"Then you—you—lied? But you—you couldn't lie. I thought you wouldn't tell a lie."

"Yes, I lied. I had to tell my lie to undo the lie you told."

"But what the hell made you? You heard what that girl said. She admitted it."

"I don't care what she admitted. That's between her and God. But Jasper Harrick never said that, or anything else to you. You never got near him—so don't you understand I had to lie—for the sake of Jasper—for the sake of the living—for the sake of truth—for the sake of . . ."

"For the sake of ruining me. That's what you tried to do." He took a step toward the old man. "Well, you tried. But I am not ruined."

The old man's eyes had stopped blinking against the light. They were fixed on him now with that yearning which, all at once, he could not bear. *I got to get out of here,* he thought.

"You are my beloved son—" the old man was saying.

I got to get out of here, Isaac Sumpter thought.

"—and you killed Jasper Harrick," the old man concluded.

For a moment Isaac Sumpter was frozen. Then he came unfrozen and took a step toward his father, speaking very fast. "Now, look here," he said. "I knew you would say something like that. I was just waiting for it. I tell you I thought he was dead."

"Your action prevented food being carried to him."

"I tell you I thought he was dead."

[355]

"He was," the old man said, "but he hadn't been dead long. He was still warm when I touched him."

"I thought he was in the pit. Anybody would have thought he was in the pit. You saw the pit, didn't you?"

"Yes."

"Well, anybody would have thought he was in there."

"But he wasn't."

"Well, it is not my fault," the boy insisted, speaking fast, the words tumbling out, clean and sharp and fresh, as though prepared and straining to be said. "It is definitely not my fault. Look, be logical. Don't you see"—he hesitated, for the clincher—"he would have died anyway."

"Yes, I guess so," the old man said. "It looks like he was caught pretty bad. Worse than you said."

"Yes, I guess so," the old man said.

"So you see! It's not my fault. He would have died anyway."

"It was not yours to decide," the old man said. "And he had to die alone. All the time you were running in and out of that cave with your lies, he was dying alone."

"But it's all the same," Isaac said. "He is dead. He couldn't have been saved!"

He stared into his son's face, studying it, as in hope. Then he said: "There is such a thing as justice."

The boy looked across at him, wondering, in the absolute silence and the naked light of the hanging bulb, if he had ever seen that face before. "Well," he said then, with a harsh indifference, "what are you going to do?"

"I don't know," the old man said.

The boy looked at him another moment, then stepped closer, leaning. "You got your knife, haven't you," he demanded, "Father Abraham?"

The old man's head was moving with an infinitesimal motion, from side to side.

"I'm waiting," the boy said.

He waited.

"You don't really need a knife," he said. "You can just use the telephone. Just call the police."

He waited again.

"I really can't wait longer," he said.

He picked up the suitcase, and moved toward the door, swinging wide of the unmoving old man as though he were a natural obstruction, a post or rock. Past him, he paused, and turned. "Listen," he said, "I am leaving. I am taking the car as far as Nashville. Now. Tonight. I will send it back with a driver. So you won't be inconvenienced."

He took another step toward the door, paused, and turned.

"So you funked it, Father Abraham," he said, and with a sudden surge of gaiety in him, like likker hitting the stomach, stepped toward the door.

But he did not open it. His hand was on the knob, when he heard his father's voice.

"Just one thing, son," the voice said. "The heat pad—you remember the heat pad?"

Isaac Sumpter stood there with his hand on the door. *This is it*, he thought. Then: *This is it, and he waited to the last to tell me.*

He saw, in his mind, the heat pad where he had left it, just inside the fourth chamber, flung down and forgotten.

God, he thought, with sick defensiveness in the cold gut-clutch of that moment, *God, a fellow can't be expected to remember everything*. If he and Jebb Holloway had come back in to seal the crawlway beyond the pit, he could have fixed it. Or it would never have mattered. But now there was no telling, there was no telling. Now when everything had worked out—oh, now it was not fair!

Then standing there, he wondered, in a kind of out-of-time clarity, how he could ever have expected things to work out. After the first lie when he came out of the cave the first time and met all the eyes and told the lie, he should have known he was trapped. Oh, it wasn't Jasper Harrick, it was he, Isaac Sumpter, who was trapped. He was trapped by something in him that, against all logic and all possibility, had made him tell that lie. No, he had not told the lie out of his mouth. Something in him, but not himself, had told the lie through his lips.

Oh, what a fool! he exclaimed inwardly, sick of himself, sick with fear.

It was not, not at that instant however, fear of the consequences now. It was fear of that thing that was in him but was not himself, that had seized on him and spoken through his lips. He was standing there sick and shaking. For that thing in you was what you could never escape.

"It is all right, son," the old man's voice was saying.

Then the old man's voice said: "Look—look here, son."

But he could not look.

"Look at me, son," the voice was saying. "I want to tell you something," the voice was saying.

He turned slowly around to confront the old man.

"Don't worry about it, son," his father said. "I carried it across the shelf. I carried it across where Jasper is. I came back and got it."

As the words came out, and their meaning grew in him, Isaac Sumpter felt growing in him, too, the weakness, the suffocating sweetness, the insidious fear of unmanment. He felt the gush of gratitude, the welling of tears in his heart, the beginning of the terrible self-betrayal which love is.

Then he heard the words in his head: *I've got to get out of here.*

His palms were sweating.

But he mastered himself.

"Well," he said, with flat, indifferent factuality, "nobody asked you to."

He got out the door and five or six steps down the stairs. He stopped, and looked back over his shoulder, up the stairs, expecting to see the old man at the door, looking down at him. But the old man was not there.

Not seeing that face yearning down at him there had a

[358]

peculiar effect. He suddenly felt betrayed. He felt lost. He felt the fear of being thrown absolutely upon his own frail resources, alone, dropped into a sea, at night.

He called back up the stairs, toward the blank rectangle of the doorway. "I'll write you," he called. "I'll write you as soon as I'm settled. Don't forget—I'll write!"

Then he felt better. He went down the stairs, found the car key in the old cut-glass bowl, where dust in the bottom was like velvet to the fingers, and went out the front door, down the steps, and out the gate, feeling much better. He opened the trunk lid of the old Studebaker, flung his suitcase in, and flipped the lid down with a brisk snap. He was feeling definitely good.

Then he was not feeling so good. At the snap of the lid, it was as though there had been a knife, after all.

The old fool had saved him. The old fool had done that and he could never escape that fact. That fact was like a knife blade plunged between your shoulder blades, and you take a step away, and another, and another, waiting to fall.

After they got to the Harrick house, Nick Pappy was the first to go.

They had got the wheel chair established in Jack Harrick's room, and Nick Pappy had stood there a moment, sweating his white shirt to his shoulder blades, standing with heavy unease at the edge of the group under the electric light. Then, all at once, he knew he didn't belong here, in the middle of the night, not with Mr. and Mrs. Dawson here, real Johntown folks, members of the Baptist Church, and that other woman, all of them trying to spend the night here and take care of Mr. and Mrs. Harrick like good Christians.

No, there was no use for him here, and for a second he couldn't figure out how, for Chrissake and in the first place, he had ever got here in this log cabin, with the bugs butting their noses off against the screen trying to get in. It was like a dream.

But it was a for-Chrissake funny dream for a Greek to be having.

Greek: he thought.

He had edged toward the door, somehow yearning to be in the Cadillac, where he would feel better. But then he saw Old Mr. Harrick over there, staring at the window where the bugs kept bumping soft trying to get in, and if one of those bugs busted in, the dark would come in, too, like a dam broke, and it would drown that light out in no time, before you could say Jackie Robinson.

He wondered why anybody would want to just be saying Jackie Robinson. Not that he had anything against Jackie Robinson, or them you called the colored people in general, as long as one of them did not ruin a lot of good meat, meat costing what it did, and fall in the pit and barbecue himself and cause trouble.

Trouble. But his mind closed on the thought, for it looked like a man just couldn't keep thinking about everything.

He went over and put out his hand to shake hands with Old Mr. Harrick. It was funny, how Old Mr. Harrick looked up at him a second like he didn't know him and didn't know why he was putting out his hand. Then, it was a for-Chrissake funny thing he did, for he sort of lifted up his hand not like to shake hands but up with the kind of grip like he was going to table wrestle, the way they used to do down at the restaurant. A man didn't know exactly what to do, if somebody was reading the meter backwards like that. But all at once the old man got the right score, and shook hands.

Nick Pappy didn't say anything. He couldn't think of anything to say. He was again about to edge out the door, not saying anything to Mrs. Harrick either, but she looked up and she was looking at him. So he went over and shook hands. He couldn't think of anything to say to her. He looked down at her face, and thought she was about to cry. Then he wished she would cry, for it must hurt to have that many tears all stacking up inside you and crowding to get out. It might bust your eyeballs, like a head of steam blowing the coffee machine if the valve got stuck. For a second he tried to remember what it had been like that afternoon in the kitchen. But he could not remember.

But he wished she could cry. She was a nice lady.

It was then she said: "Thank you, Mr. Pap-a-doup-a-lous."

And he thought maybe he was going to cry.

But he didn't. He didn't say anything either. He made the door, and he made the Cadillac, and he eased off down the lane in the Cad, but he didn't seem to feel better because he was in the Cad and things didn't seem to get much better when he got to his house; at least he still thought maybe he might cry, and he sat in the car in front of the shotgun bungalow awhile, watching a street light down the street. He was just too tired, he guessed, to get out of the Cad and go in the house where he lived, and go to bed.

He tried to think of all the places he had lived, the rooms, and the beds he had slept in. It looked like if a man could think of all those things from the very start up to right now, just as they came, from that room by the fire escape in the Bronx, listening to his aunt boozed to the eyeballs in the next room, up to right now and the shotgun bungalow with the pink silk-shaded floor lamp in the living room and the couch with the tapestry sofa cushions showing the harem scenes, then a man could know how he had got to where he was, even if it was here in Johntown, Tennessee, where he was sitting in the Cad and staring down the street to the street lamp that was not yet getting pale and sad in the dawn.

It looked like it was not right for a man to live a long time and wind up somewhere and not know even how he ever got there. A man ought to have something and if what he had was a yellow Cad and that, all of a sudden, was not enough to make him feel like a man, then he at least ought to have a way of knowing how he got where he was. A man ought to have that much to feel he was a man.

He let his head sink forward against the wheel, and closed his eyes.

[361]

When he woke up, he noticed that the street lamp down at the corner was looking pale and sickly. He leaned out of the car and looked eastward toward Skunk Tail Mountain. The sky was getting pale off the shoulder of the mountain. He had better get him some rest, he thought, if he was to get on the job and see that that guy with the close-screwed eyes did not rob him to death.

He went into the house. He closed the front door as soft as he could behind him, and the paleness that had begun to come into the sky and touch the top leaves of oak trees and make the tin roof of the coal shed back of the bungalow look white as frost, was completely blotted out. It was dark as pitch inside, and there was the faint odor the still air of a house has at night when a woman lives there, and you notice it when you come in out of fresh night air. Nick Pappy felt a little sad thrill of excitement. Then, standing there in the dark, he decided no, it was no use. It was like a guy dealing cold hands of poker against himself in the mirror and hoping to get rich that way.

But he groped his way over to the door of his wife's room. He tried to hear her breathing. He opened the door a little and looked in. Some paleness that was not quite light oozed in around the window shades of the two windows. He could make out the hump under the cover that was his wife, and the shadowy blur that must be her head. He could not decide why he was standing there.

Then he realized that her eyes were open and she was watching him. He caught the faintest glint from that blur which was her head. But he didn't give a sign. It was like it might be dangerous to move or give a sign.

He knew she was watching him.

"I never said I would," her voice said from the shadow.

He moved his tongue over his dry lips. "Would what?" he said.

"Even if I had said it, I would not do it," she said.

"Would not what?"

"Not after I seen."

"Seen what?" he said.

"I seen her on TV. I seen her stand up before the people and say it. She is not that Cutlick one you said. She is a little girl and I ain't going to do it to her. She is little, and I ain't doing it to nobody like that. I do not care, now or never, if you do go bankrupt. I don't care if I get sent to the poorhouse and die, I am not going to do it to no little girl like her. I am an old bag and about everything has been done to me as they can figure out can be done, backwards and forwards, but I ain't going to do that to her. You can put that in your pipe and smoke it, Mr. Big."

Then, very deliberately, she lifted up the sheet and pulled it smooth, and let it come down over her face and head.

Nick Pappy looked across at the blankness of the sheet, and it seemed as though he did not know where he was, or when, or what was under that sheet in the paleness of air that now was more like light. It was as though he had loved somebody and they were dead and the snow was falling on their grave. For a minute he was afraid to move. He was afraid that if he moved he might slosh out of his heart even a drop of what it was that was there past brimming full. Besides he did not know what it was. It had never been there before.

Then he thought he knew. He moved very carefully across the room, hoping the floor boards would not creak, and lowered himself into the chair by the bed. For a moment he sat with his hands on his spread knees, looking at the sheet. On each side of the slight hummock that was the head, he could make out the fingers that grasped the edge of the sheet and held it smooth. He reached out and took the hand near him, and drew it to him. He held it cupped upward in his own cupped palm, and looked down at its emptiness.

"That's all right," he said, after a minute, to the hand. "I didn't know, either. I just didn't know."

After another minute he said: "There was a lot of things I just didn't know."

[363]

After another minute he said: "Do you want me to get you a glass of fresh water?"

She did not answer. But he got up anyway, and went out to the kitchen, where, he noticed, it was lighter because there was no shade on the window, and got a glass and filled it from the jug in the electric box.

When he got back the sheet was off her face, and the light was stronger. He held out the glass to her. She didn't say anything but she took it. Somehow, he felt shy about looking at her as she did it, or even as she drank it. When she had finished, she held the glass out to him, and let her head drop back on the pillow. As he took it, he could have sworn she sort of smiled at him, but he couldn't be sure, not with the light yet as weak as it was.

He sat back in the chair, and saw that she had closed her eyes. For a little he listened to her breathing. He could tell she was not asleep.

"You know," he said, in a voice that sounded twisted and somehow hurt him to come out. He waited and tried again: "You know, I want you to get well."

He waited.

Then: "You are going to get well quick now."

He struggled to think of a future—the future—even a day past the today that was dawning, and promised to be a scorcher, and that he would have to spend trying to take care of things on the mountain to keep from getting robbed blind. He tried to think of a day different from what today would be. Somehow, deep in him, pale and thin as the groping sprout of a potato forgotten in a dark cellar, hope, or something like hope, probed upward.

He leaned in his chair and took her hand again.

"You get well," he said, staring down at the closed eyes. "Then —I tell you what. We'll go on a trip. Just you and me. You and me."

She did not say anything, and did not open her eyes. But the hand, palm upward, remained lying in his own. He was looking

[364]

down at the palm when he realized that the rhythm of her breathing had changed. She must be asleep now.

He lifted his eyes to look at her face. The light was better now. She wouldn't be a bad-looking woman, if she got shaped down some, he thought. For a brown-haired woman.

As he looked at her, and the light came on toward day, he wondered what she had looked like when she was a little girl. Fifteen or sixteen. No, eight or nine, just a little girl. He wondered where she had lived.

He would have to ask her, some time.

As fast as that old wreck of a Studebaker which was his father's car would take the turns, he rolled down out of the high country in the dark. Now and then he met a big trailer rig booming east up the grade, and rode past with the Diesel fumes in his nostrils, and more rarely a car, usually at this time of night a new car, as he could tell from the white-glaring, arrogant thrust of the headlight beams, undimmed, like a blow in the face, long before the car ripped past with a sound like tearing silk. *The bastards,* he thought, feeling his impotence as he jiggled the light button on the floor board.

He passed the settlements, sleeping exposed and shameless in their poverty, under the starlight, like an animal killed by a passing car and knocked to the roadside, and the towns, with the melancholy prosperity and sad pretension of new gas pumps and chrome and glass on store fronts. On the outskirts of Biggerston he passed a new brick house, not big but with two stories and an awkward jackleg imitation of the classic white pillars of Confederate graciousness, and a spotlight on one corner of the house illuminating, even at this hour, a patch of newly installed lawn with a concrete fountain and a couple of painted wooden jigsaw herons standing guard beside it.

At that sight, snatched quickly back into darkness, he thought of himself remembering it forever, all the years of his life, as he would always remember this night of his flight. But that sight—the new white pillars, the spotlight on the fountain set in that mortician's artificial green of scarcely sprung grass—would go with him, forever and ever, to negate, somehow, the very flight he was making. It would be like a tiny ulcer in his brain, unhealing forever and oozing. He felt physically sick, and did not know why. He thought: *Jesus.*

At Crossville, he took the south fork of Route 70, stepped up his pace, somewhat worried about time now, and beat on through the settlements and crossroads clusters and little towns—Bon Air, Sparta, Peeled Chestnut, Liberty. Somewhere along there, while it was still dark, he saw a light on in a house up a draw. He couldn't really make out the house, just the dirt track leading whitely in starlight across a field to a black clump of trees where the light showed, and where the shack, it probably wouldn't be much better than a shack, must be. He wondered what they would be up for, with a light. Getting ready to go on a journey, or just take some beef cattle down to market at Nashville, a child sick, somebody dying, somebody getting born—anyway, people living up there, caught in their mess of living up there across that hard-scrabble, limestone-pan field, over yonder where the lane now led, white in starlight, to the dark clump of trees.

He felt some dry entrapment of the heart, a clutch of terror and despair, unresolved, and thought, *Jesus,* and set the accelerator pedal to the floor. He beat on. He was worrying about time. The house with the light, all the other houses, were snatched away, one by one, mercilessly and mercifully, into darkness behind him. As that single glowing spark of reality that was himself fled westward, all things behind sank, at that withdrawal, into their undifferentiated sleep of nothingness and the darkness of unreality.

He realized he had branched off Route 70, probably at Sparta. But he could still make it by cutting across country to Murfreesboro. It was coming light now. With the first sunlight leveling behind him and touching the jumble of roofs, he hit Murfreesboro, and broke loose, northward. He would make it, he was near now. He saw a highway sign saying:

SMYRNA, TENNESSEE
See the Historic Home of
Sam Davis
Boy Hero of the Confederacy

"Ikey Sumpter," he said aloud, "Boy Hero of the Confederacy." His heart bubbled with gaiety. He was light-headed with gaiety. He passed through Smyrna, the little string of stores on the highway, houses set back in maples. He saw a red traffic light ahead. "Fuck the light," he said, and giggled with delicious gaiety, and barreled right through.

It didn't matter. There was nobody on the street. He saw the milage sign for Nashville. He thought, suddenly, that he might not stop at the airport. He might drive right on to Nashville. Right through Nashville, out West End Avenue, on out to a bed where, in a shadowy room, Goldie Goldstein would be lying white and blurred and ripe in her dawn drowse, her dark hair loose on the white pillow, the sheet twisted down about her waist, a bare arm outflung, the pink filmy stuff of her gown twisted, by the position of the arm, tight across the near breast so that the nipple pressed hard up through the wispy fabric, her lips slightly parted with their dreamy breath.

He would stand there, and he would whisper: "Hey, Goldie," and if she tried any monkey business, it would sure be different this time. But she wouldn't. Oh, no. Not now. Not now, for things were different now for Ikey Sumpter, the Boy Hero of the Confederacy, and if she wanted that million babies like bunches of grapes hung off her, he would sure oblige her right now with Jew Baby Number One, he would hang one on her, for she wouldn't be expecting this visit and wouldn't be armed, and to hell with her, for he would be up and out and long gone on his way.

[367]

To hell with her, for the traffic light for the turn off to the airport was coming up ahead on the highway and was green. To hell with her, for a fact, for who was she, and he took the turn off. He rolled on into Berry Field, parked the car, made the arrangement with the U-Drive-It people to deliver the car back to Johntown, picked up his ticket, checked his bag, and found himself standing in a telephone booth, the apparatus to his ear, a dime, between thumb and forefinger, poised in the air, and the image in his head of Goldie Goldstein lying deep in her dawn drowse. He would just give her a tickle and let her know he was passing through.

But who the hell was Goldie Goldstein? She was the Jew Girl. *She was a Jew Girl I used to rip it off of, back in Nashville, yes, when I was a kid, and, frankly, without any exaggeration*—

His mind—rather, the stance of his mind—was implying the anecdote, the event accomplished, the thing which in its *doneness* would be, somehow, a joy greater than the *doing* had ever been.

The world was full of stuff that would make her look like dirt. Why should he waste a dime on Goldie Goldstein?

So he didn't.

He stood there with the dime, between thumb and forefinger, poised over the coin slot. Before the plane lifted to bear him away, he had to make some contact with somebody, it didn't matter who, in Nashville. He had to wipe out, somehow, the pain with which he had left that city three weeks ago. He stood there, caught in that need, but with no name, no number, in his head.

Then his glance fell on an old man, poor, dirty, derelict, with a parcel tied with string, who was sitting over there on a bench. What the hell would such a guy be doing on a plane? That thought—the man's age, his dirt, his poverty, his paper parcel—was a personal affront, a diminution of his triumph, a smear on his pleasure. Then the old man leaned over and picked up from the dirty floor a discarded newspaper. The old man opened the mixed-up sheets, idly, and fixed on something. The sheet held up to the view of Isaac Sumpter was the front page of yesterday evening's *Press-Clarion*. There was the headline:

WOMEN OF STATE RALLY
Mother's Committee Formed to Guard Sweetheart and Unborn Child of Trapped Hero

Fund Tops $20,000

Looking at the paper over there, he thought of Jim Haworth. That would be splendid. He would just wake Jim Haworth up and give him the news, just a little item: *Isaac Sumpter left this morning, by plane, for—*

He thought of that bastard Haworth clawing from a bourbon-blurred sleep to pick up the telephone. It would be splendid. He would have to look in the directory for the home number, but that was little enough trouble to take for a friend.

He got the number, and you could tell that that bastard was hit. He did not like it one bit. Even the satire of his congratulations to Mr. Tittlebum was weak and sad.

"Shall I spit on Jersey City, that rock from which you were hewn?" Isaac Sumpter inquired politely. "It won't be any trouble, it really won't, I'll be winging right over."

But that bastard was paying no attention. He was breaking in, his voice suddenly happy. "Listen here, Mr. Tittlebum," the voice was saying, "I've got a little item for you. A Jewish society note, Mr. Tittlebum. Today that Goldstein girl—yeah, the one that found you weren't much good for her purposes and kicked you out—yeah, this is her wedding day. Oh, yeah—and she's marrying a guy named Blumhof. *The* Gorham Blumhof.— Say, do you ever read the big financial ads? Well, you're rich now and you better start reading the ads of that brokerage firm of Blumhof, Borstein and MacIntyre in New York City. Goldie's

[369]

going to own about half of it, and there's a branch in Paris, France, and she's going to live there, and, boy, will she have fun! And am I glad."

Isaac Sumpter held the telephone, from which no sound came now, and something most horribly blocked his breath.

Then a sound came from the telephone. "And how do you like that, Mr. Tittlebum?" the voice asked solicitously, just before there was the click of the severed connection.

He was standing there, holding the dead phone, feeling sick and deprived, knowing that all his striving had been in vain, for a man suffered for his success only to find, in the end, that it was ashes, and that others, the shining ones, moved serenely off into their glory. He was standing there when the flight to New York was announced. He went out, numbly, and like a condemned man mounting the scaffold, climbed the steps into the body of the plane.

He found a seat. He knew that you were supposed to strap yourself in, and with the thin, hoarded satisfaction of that knowingness, found the straps and bound himself, more tightly than necessary.

The engines burst into life, and he waited. Then the plane roared down the slab and mounted into the morning light, bearing Isaac Sumpter, by the deep, inner logic of things in which he had faithfully trusted, to the place where he would go:

Where *he had money in the Dutch Trust:*

Where, *in the studio, they would say,* Yes, Mr. Sumpter, yes, Mr. Sumpter, when you are ready, sir, *just before he stepped calmly into a blaze of light:*

Where *he would sit in a high, spacious office, with walls tinted the cool of woodland shadow, with a suffering and hieratic canvas of Rouault smoldering on one wall, with a wide window giving over the majesty of the river and the land spreading westward:*

Where, *feeling the surge and sweep of the elevator, his face lifted to show the chiseled profile with the Bermuda tan, his eyes watching the red numbers flicker past on the indicator as floor after floor fell away, he would hear someone whisper,* Yes, that's Sumpter, yes, that's Mr. Sumpter, yes, that's the great Ikey, *and hearing that, would curl his lip in a deep, mysterious, ironic satisfaction, for he was Ikey, Little Ikey, and it didn't do any harm to be called Ikey in the world of Big Media:*

Where *it didn't do any harm to be called Ikey among those smart or beautiful Jewish girls who moved like houris across that world of Big Media, the pale-skinned, dark-eyed ones with slow, opulent thighs, the enameled, glittery ones with sharp, prancy ankles and shrewd, challenging wit and neurotic gestures and tears of vituperation at strange moments, the Bennington graduates, or the stars of Sarah Lawrence seminars—or even of Radcliffe—with tweed skirts like something grabbed when somebody shouted "Fire!" and hair hanging over the brow in careful emulation of an English sheep dog, but not so thick that it hid the possibility of the old yearning in those learned eyes—all of whom, with some slight show of statistical justification, Isaac Sumpter regarded as devised for his personal delight and nightly passport to oblivion, and from each of whom he was compelled, in the end, to exact some humiliating vengeance for an old rejection, this even when he could not remember, offhand, the rejection:*

Where, *one day, he would read in the* Herald Tribune *a flattering notice of a show of sculpture by Rachel Goldstein, and for the moment would not remember who Rachel Goldstein was —having always thought of the Jew Girl as Goldie, as was appropriate for the Jew Girl—and then remembering, he would get the* Times, *and leaf hurriedly through, hunting for a notice which, he obscurely hoped, would not be flattering, but it was, and he felt afraid, mysteriously, as though there were not enough of success in the world, and if somebody got any, even the little morsel that Rachel Goldstein now was getting, it would be taken from his own hoard:*

Where, *another day, not too much later, he would read that*

[371]

Mrs. Gorham Blumhof, wife of one of the partners of the brokerage firm of Blumhof, Borstein and MacIntyre, had died in Paris, in child bed, and he knew that Goldie Goldstein, who had dreamed of babies hanging off her like bunches of grapes on a grapevine, and had dreamed that all were to be Isaac Sumpter's babies and beautiful like Ikey, would now never be a big fat mamma who had loved Ikey for a million years, and thinking this, he, at first, felt a pang of deprivation, as though he had always expected her to come back in the end, but then a surge of relief, for now she would not be able to throw rocks at him, as she had promised, and he only wished that her husband had been killed with her, say in a car crash, for then whatever she had told him about Ikey would be expunged, but what could she have told him, for what was there to tell:

Where he was sometimes asked to tell the story of Jasper Harrick, and would do so, briefly, modestly, and obligingly, but where at all other times he tried not to think of Jasper Harrick, and not to dream of a dark weight of stone, and usually managed, for success and Seconal were readily available to him, the most famous product of Scotland was still in long supply for the export trade, and the caravan of Eastern beauties, to the faint servile clink of small gold chains, came footing slowly toward him, with humble yearning in their eyes, over the golden sands of the desert waste:

Where he, Isaac Sumpter, Ikey, Little Ikey, who wanted to be good, and had paid the price, could at last be totally himself.

XIII

Mrs. Dawson was saying something, but Celia Harrick was not listening. She was listening to the sound of the Cadillac, out yonder in the dark, as it gave one soft cough and then stirred into life. She could not hear it move off down the lane. She thought: *It goes away so quiet.*

Mrs. Dawson and the other lady were saying they'd love to stay all night and take charge. But Celia Harrick simply would not let them stay. She had to be alone in the house. With John T., she said. And Monty, of course, when he came in. She didn't know why, she said, and thanked them, but she just had to be that way.

But she did know why. She felt as though all the skin had been taken off her and she could not endure a human touch or a human voice. She could not bear the touch of the world.

When she had heard the last sound of their car fade raggedly out down the lane, in the dark, she stared for a second at Jack Harrick, a deep speculation in her eyes, and then went back to the kitchen. She got a glass of cold water, brought it back, set it on the little table by the wheel chair, and touched the bottle of pills into easier reach. She knew John T. saw her push the pills closer, and she knew that all the shaking up must have made things hurt. She saw him gripping the sides of the chair. But he didn't reach for a pill.

She wished there were a pill she could take for what hurt her.

What hurt her she found, all at once, was hurting worse because she was hating John T. because he hurt and would not take a pill. Oh, it was spite, plain spite, for him not to take the pill and make her hurt go away.

"Take a pill, John T.," she said.

At first he did not seem to hear. Then she saw him shake his head. She went and sat in a chair to one side of the window, and looked out into the dark. She wondered when it would hurt him enough to make him take it.

"You wouldn't pray for him," she said, not looking at him.

She did not expect an answer. Nor did she want one. If she said something, and just kept looking out into the dark, it would be as though she had not said it and therefore were not responsible. If now what she happened to say went over into his head, it would be as though he had thought it up by himself.

"You wouldn't ask God to take him out of the ground," she said, in almost a whisper.

The bugs were butting the screen. The moths were butting, too. They were so soft, but they butted hard and it must hurt.

"You wouldn't ever let things be right between you and him," she said, whispering.

The bugs were butting.

Then he said: "You never forgave me."

"But I did!" she cried out, in pain, and rose from the chair.

"If you had forgiven me—" he began, not noticing her, and stopped. He was staring at the dark square of the window screen.

[374]

"Go to bed," he said then. "You might as well. I don't want to."

"I did—I swear it," she said.

But he was staring at the window darkness, drawing away from her, unconvinced, uncaring. She couldn't stand it, but she did not know what she wanted. Maybe if he would take a pill.

He said: "We've got this far, the way we are. Go to bed."

She moved to the open door, then turned, with her hand on the jamb: "Oh, I want to love you!" she cried.

"You didn't forgive me."

"Take your pill," she said softly, staring at the back of his head.

He didn't answer.

So she demanded, very quietly: "Why didn't you want Jasper to come out of the ground?"

She stood in the hall a moment, wondering whether or not she had said it. It did not seem that she could have said a thing like that to him, old and dying. She stood there marveling that you could be yourself all those years and not know you could up and say something like that to an old man you had loved. It was like not knowing who you were. She was even wondering where she was, that very minute. She was wondering if anything had ever happened. She was wondering if she had ever stood on the sidewalk of Johntown, the street full of muddy snow, beside crazy old Miss Abernathy, then not old and not crazy, and had seen a Ford pickup skidding down the street with a tall man standing in the back, holding up above his own head and blood-smeared face the forever outraged, unforgiving face of the bear, like a lifted mask.

If it had not happened.

If nothing had ever happened.

If nothing had happened, then there would be no suffering and terror under the stone.

And then she could sleep.

If something had been different, he thought. But everything seemed very far away, what had happend tonight, and what had happened a thousand years ago, when he was a boy. He could remember, all at once, as clear as day, clearer than what had happened tonight, how once when he was a boy, a little boy, seven, eight, he had climbed up the Sumpter Ridge, and had gone swimming in the pool below the falls, and then he had climbed on up to the glade where the big beeches were, and the little hole in the ground under the roots of the biggest beech. He had lain on the blue grass in the glade and wondered if the sun would dry his hair enough so his mother wouldn't give him a whaling for getting in the creek. He could say it was just sweat. Yeah, and she would give him one look and say: "Jack —don't lie to your mother."

It was funny how your mother could tell if you were lying. Maybe it was because when you lied you felt funny. You wanted the lie to be true so hard that it hurt you. Maybe if you didn't care if a lie was a lie, then you could tell a whale of a lie and nobody would know.

Old Jack Harrick was in pain. He knew the pills were there, but he would not look at them. In fact, that pain was mixed up with what was becoming the pain of remembering, but he did not know why it should hurt to remember that you once were a little boy, seven or eight, who went swimming when you hadn't ought to have, and who was going to tell a lie.

What good would it do to take a pill if the two kinds of pain were so mixed up? What good would it do to take it if the pain of the *then* you were remembering and the pain of the *now* you were living were so mixed up you couldn't tell them apart? Also, with things so mixed up it was hard to know who was thinking the thought that if you didn't care if a lie was a lie then telling a lie would not hurt you—a little boy seven or eight thinking that

[376]

thought, or an old man in a wheel chair with a cancer down there that was going to kill him.

Jack Harrick, sitting in the wheel chair while the moths damaged themselves against the screen with the soft, anguishing insistence that he could not bear, wondered if, that day when he was a little boy, he had told the lie and got whaled. He could not remember, no matter how hard he tried.

Then, so suddenly he thought he might burst into tears—yes, it was the suddenness of it that tricked you—he realized that he could not remember how that little boy with the wet hair had turned into him, into the old man who was going to die.

If a man only knew how a thing like that happened, then he could die.

Then he heard the stealthy sound in the hall. His heart knocked with guilty alarm. It knocked so hard you would have thought it was he, who lived in the house, who was being caught in the disgraceful trespass, and not whoever it was who, now, crept down the hall where he didn't belong. The anger flared up in him, and he thought how, not so long ago, not so damned long ago, he could have stepped into the hall, yeah, Jack Harrick, barehanded, and grabbed whoever that was, and broken his back over a knee like a stick of kindling and thrown him into swamp water to drown.

But now Jack Harrick choked in the suffocating rage, which was his weakness. Yes, that was the guilt that he was about to be caught in, the shameful guilt: to be weak.

Jack Harrick had to force himself to face the open door, where the shadows of the hall piled up. Then he saw the figure appear in the space. The face, white against the shadows, was the face of MacCarland Sumpter.

They stared at each other, and in that long moment Jack Harrick knew that that was the man of all men whom he could not now bear to see. He thought: *If that man comes in here something will happen.*

He did not know what it would be but he knew that he could not bear it.

MacCarland Sumpter came in, and stood there.

He stood there a timeless time, staring down the distance. Then said: "He is dead."

Jack Harrick nodded, but the motion was almost imperceptible, for what need was there to nod at the oldest certainty he had?

"I came to tell you, for the fear you had not believed me. In case you do not believe I went all the way."

"I believed you."

"Nobody else did."

The telephone on the little table inside the door rang.

"You want me to get it?" Brother Sumpter asked.

Jack Harrick shook his head, and wheeled the chair to the instrument. "Yes," he said into it. Then: "Yes. Yes." Then: "Thank you."

He hung up, and wheeled himself back to the center of the room, past the standing form of MacCarland Sumpter.

MacCarland Sumpter followed, and came around to face Jack Harrick, but held his distance.

"It was the police," Jack Harrick said. He waited a moment, staring across at the other. "At least I got you told before they called. I mean I got you told that I believed you. Now you can know it wasn't because the police called I said I believed you."

"Nobody else believed me."

"They will," Jack Harrick said, but not in a voice offering comfort. It was the voice of distance and indifference.

"I do not want to be believed."

"They will believe."

"I do not deserve to be believed."

"I don't know what you deserve," Jack Harrick said, looked at him, then looked out at the dark beyond the moth-ridden screen.

"What I said was true. What I did not say was the lie. I must

[378]

tell you, though you spit on me. My son had never gone in. All the way."

Jack Harrick did not even turn. He was still staring at the white moths spread on the screen against the dark.

"Say something."

Jack Harrick gave no sign.

"All right, don't say it," MacCarland Sumpter said. "But it is true. And I let him do what he did. I knew."

Jack Harrick turned to him, and his face worked with something that strove to be spoken, then froze again into its leonine distance.

"No, I did not know," the other man said. "What I mean is, I knew and did not know. But I let him. I supported him. If I had not supported him, other people would have gone in." He paused. "Do you know why I supported him?"

He waited, but Jack Harrick did not turn.

"Do you know what I told myself was the reason?" He paused. "Well, I'll tell you. It was for his salvation. I said to myself, he must show courage. He must crawl into the ground for another. He must do something, whatever, in expiation. If he should do these things, I said, it would be the beginning of his salvation. He stood—he stands—sorely in need of salvation."

He looked pleadingly at Jack Harrick. "That much—I swear it is true. Forgive me that much. Before you spit on me." He waited, then added in a weak voice of beseechment: "Wouldn't you have done that much to save your own son?"

Jack Harrick, not turning, said: "I did not save my son."

"No, I did not save your son. No—" he stopped. "Nobody could have saved your son. For this world."

"I knew it," Harrick said. "That's what the police said on the phone."

"But that is not the point," MacCarland Sumpter said. "God does not judge the heart by the casualness of earthly consequence. And when I began to know the worst I could not accept

[379]

that knowledge in my heart. Thus I refused to save your son."

"You went in the cave," Jack Harrick said. "You did that, for what it is worth to you."

"I will tell you what it is worth. Nothing. For I was driven into the cave. The pain of my guilt, when it burst upon me, drove me into the ground. When that Greek man—a man of no obligation—rose up and tried to enter to your son, it was my shame, and I knew all, and knew that I had connived in and advertised a lie. I could not stand my guilt. I wanted to enter and die in the ground."

He waited. It was as though he had said nothing. Jack Harrick did not turn. The moths, coming out of the darkness, tapped with their soft, squashy obscenity of sound against the screen.

"But I lived," MacCarland Sumpter said. "I lived, and I compounded my guilt."

"Say you lived," Jack Harrick said, toward the dark screen. "That's enough. You're a human man, aren't you?"

"Listen," MacCarland Sumpter said, "and spit on me. Here is how I compounded my guilt. I arranged things in the cave so it would seem that my son had been there. Did you hear what I said?"

He waited.

"Say something," he said.

Then: "Do you want to spit on me now?"

Then: "All right. Listen. And then you will do it."

He came closer, leaning a little. "I will tell you. Long ago, I saw a son of yours dead—a bloody nothing, a piece of something like a dime's worth of cat meat from the butcher shop. That son of yours had come from the body of Mary Tillyard, my wife, and my heart leaped for joy that it was dead. But I denied that joy. Even in that moment, I denied it, in God's name and my vanity of virtue. But tonight—"

He leaned closer. "Spit on me," he said.

Jack Harrick, not turning, said: "No."

"Spit on me, so I can live."

[380]

"Go on."

"Will you—" MacCarland Sumpter demanded humbly, avidly, "will you then?" He waited, then said: "Tonight when that boy came forth and said that Jasper Harrick was dying, my heart leaped again. In the old joy. But now I recognized it as joy. I wanted your son to die. Because—"

He leaned closer.

"—because it was your son."

He waited, and against the night sounds his breath came with its slow rale of expectation, as he held his face closer, the cheek turned, the eyes closed.

"Now—" he said, whispering.

Jack Harrick turned and looked at the pale-fleshed, dust-smeared, sweat-blotched face that hung there in the air near him, with the eyes closed tight. "Now—will you?" the mouth whispered.

"No," Jack Harrick said.

The eyes of that suspended face opened, the face turned slowly at him, the man straightened creakily up.

"Why?"

"Because—" Jack Harrick said, and paused, then seemed to come to grips with himself. "Because," he said, "I wanted my son —my own son—to die."

"What do you mean?" MacCarland Sumpter demanded, almost fearfully.

"I don't know," he said. Then he cried out: "Oh, God, I loved my son—but—"

The cry fell away to a whisper: "—but I know it's true."

MacCarland Sumpter was staring down at him. Slowly Jack Harrick leaned forward in his wheel chair, gripping the sides for balance, lifting his face. Then on that face the lips drew back, the folds of flesh convolved, and there was the old grin, triumphant, savagely gay, sardonic.

"Now, Ole Mac," Jack Harrick demanded, "do you want to spit on me?"

The head of MacCarland Sumpter twitched a little from side to side—a conscious denial of the demand made on him, or an unconscious denial of a fact not for him to confront. He retreated, slowly, the head still twitching, and sank into a chair. He still stared at Jack Harrick.

Jack Harrick met the stare with the old grin. Then, aware of that old grin on his face, he felt that the grin did not belong to him. Putting that grin there now—it was like stealing a dead man's clothes. He turned his head away.

The grin, he thought, *it is a lie.*

He thought: *Let him look at me like I am.*

He let the grin fade from his face, and felt weak and naked.

Then something was happening in him, slow and deep. It was like cool water flowing in darkness, under bending trees.

He thought: *Now I know why I could not bear for MacCarland Sumpter to come in this room tonight. If he told me what I knew he would come to tell me, I knew I would have to tell him what I have told him.*

Then: *But then I did not know what that was.*

And then: *But I knew I would know.*

He sat there panting with that thought. It was like being trapped. It was as though everything you touched in the dark suddenly turned into small fingers that clutched and held. Each was so weak, but there were so many in the dark.

MacCarland Sumpter got up. He seemed uncertain on his feet. "We have lived a long time," he said, in a voice that showed all the years. "We have come a long way," he said. "To this."

Jack Harrick looked up at him. He felt a soft pity in his heart. "It will be all right," he said. "For you. People will believe you."

"I do not want them to. I do not even want God to forgive me for what I am."

"I don't know what God will take into His head to do," Jack Harrick said. "But people, they are going to believe you."

"I could not bear it."

Jack Harrick studied him. "Do you think you owe me something?" he asked.

The other man nodded. "I owe you a son," he said.

"No," Jack Harrick said. "But you owe me what I am going to ask you. Pay attention, will you?"

The man nodded.

"All right. You have promised. I ask that the body of my son be left where it is and the passage be sealed up. And you will stand at the mouth of the cave and preach the funeral of my son. And I will sit there. You have promised."

There was a long silence, except for the night.

"So—" MacCarland Sumpter said, softly, "so that's your revenge."

"If it is revenge," Jack Harrick said, "it will be revenge on me —on myself."

"All right. I will preach the sermon. And when I have finished, I will confess."

Jack Harrick was shaking his head. "You can't," he said.

"I will."

"You can't. For the same reason you don't want yourself believed. You will not confess because of what it would do to your son. Just like you don't want to be believed, because if people believe you they have to not believe your son."

"No—" MacCarland Sumpter cried out. "No—because I am guilty. I am guilty of worse than Isaac.—I want to be spat upon —I—"

Jack Harrick was shaking his head. "No," he said. "But is it so awful for a man to love his son?"

MacCarland Sumpter sat down again, weakly, in the chair. "I've got to hold on to something," he said. "Even my guiltiness," he added.

"You will hold on to your promise. You will preach the sermon."

MacCarland Sumpter started a little, with a faint, hopeful

[383]

movement. "Listen," he said, "if I preach the sermon and you are there, then people will know you believe me. Then they will believe me, and—"

"Yes, they will believe you."

"But, listen, if they believe me, they will believe Isaac guilty—therefore I should not preach the sermon, because you—you yourself—said it isn't so awful for a man to love his son—and—"

"Yes, they will believe you," Jack Harrick said. "But they will believe Isaac, too. Folks believe what they want to believe. They need to believe Isaac is a hero, a success, a something. So they will believe what they need to believe."

"But the truth—" MacCarland Sumpter said, and rose from his chair, shivering as though with cold.

"Take me," Jack Harrick said. "I need to believe you are a good man."

"But the truth—"

"Folks need to believe you are a good man. They got to believe somebody is. So they will pick on you and believe you."

"But the truth—" MacCarland Sumpter cried out.

"It changes," Jack Harrick said. "Truth changes. A man changes, and I reckon truth changes."

"God doesn't change," MacCarland Sumpter affirmed, and again shivered.

"Well, maybe He ought to," Jack Harrick said.

"That is blasphemy," MacCarland Sumpter said. He wandered over to the window and looked out at the night. Jack Harrick could see his shoulders shiver now and then. Then he heard him say: "I wish I could pray. I can't pray."

The moths were softly butting the screen beyond MacCarland Sumpter. Then he turned back to face the room. "Maybe God does change," he said. "Maybe I figured I knew too much about Truth. And about God. And they changed on me."

He moved toward the door, then stopped. "Maybe a man can't puzzle out those things," he said. "Maybe a man's just got to try to live. And die."

He stopped. Then cried out in anguish. "But live and die for God's sake!"

He took another couple of steps and again turned. "To help God," he said. "To help God change the way He wants."

He got to the door, turned again, hesitated. "That is blasphemy," he said. Then he asked, very quietly: "Why must I utter blasphemy, too?"

He sank into sad, slow thought, but after a moment lifted his head. He began:

> "For thine arrows stick fast in me, and thy hand presseth me sore.
>
> There is no soundness in my flesh because of thine anger; neither is there any rest in my bones because of my sin."

He turned into the dark of the hall, but Jack Harrick called him. "Mac!" he called.

MacCarland Sumpter stood framed in the dark of the door.

"Ole Mac," Jack Harrick said, "when you can pray—along toward day, when you find you can pray again—pray for me, Ole Mac. Put in a couple of licks for me, will you, Mac?"

MacCarland Sumpter nodded, slowly. He did not seem to be able to say anything. Then he went down the hall.

Does everything have to happen? Jack Harrick thought, when the sound of feet on the boards had stopped. *Can't I die before some things have to happen?* Then he sat there and sweated, thinking of dying.

He thought: *I did not want my son to come out of the ground, because somebody always has to go in the ground. If he was there I would not have to go.*

He thought: *That is it.*

It was sad to know that that was it.

But it puzzled him, why he sweated when he thought of dying. He had never been afraid of getting hurt. Nobody had ever said he was a coward. He had marks on him to show he wasn't a coward. He had that knife mark in his left shoulder, from that time he had fought that fellow from Tainter's Mill, above Johnson City, fought him barehand and him with a knife, and heft, too.

Well, the folks watching yelled, and he, Jack Harrick, he took the cut and then there wasn't much left of that fellow from Tainter's Mill. Not when Jack Harrick broke in under that knife. The fellow was broke and bleeding and any self-respecting undertaker would have refused the job. It would hurt his reputation. It was a waste, that fellow not dying, for it would have been self-defense, clear as egg-settled coffee. He didn't die. But he might as well have. He wouldn't never again draw no knife on nobody else in a friendly argument, Jack Harrick thought now with grim joy, a faint echo of the old wildness of joy when he used to come to the grapple, to the bone-breaking, to the beating of the skull on hard ground. He felt now his muscles tensing, his breath coming tight, his fingers closing.

But they were closing on nothing.

What's the matter with me? he thought.

But he wasn't a coward. He was not a coward, and he had a medal to prove same.

He had his whole life to prove same. But not his death.

But not my death, he thought.

He had his whole life to prove—

To prove what?

What had it proved—the fighting and bottle-fighting, the helling and Hell-hopping and box-beating, the anvil ringing all a summer afternoon, the pigeon-wing and "Turkey in the Straw" till the strong fell down without breath to laugh, the girls? And suddenly, he saw them all looking sorrowfully at him:

A sad hill girl, barefooted, holding the pair of precious shoes in one hand to preserve them from the stony track, a lax blue ribbon in the tow hair, the eyes sick from loneliness.

A town girl, with a long-waisted crepe-de-Chine party dress on, for the high-school dance, crouched in the Model-T, weeping in the dark.

A raddled French whore, on straw, in a cart with a tarpaulin over the uprights, rain thumping the tarpaulin, two weary men outside—brothers, cousins, pimps?—holding the shafts to keep things steady, while near half the platoon was lined up waiting in the rain, sick with disgust, waiting because they had to, and were afraid not to, and artillery fire rumbled far off, and Jumping Jack Harrick, in the inner dimness, kept saying: "How'm I doing, how'm I doing, girlie?" to which the girlie, having neither language nor inclination, said nothing, so that Jack Harrick's heart was full of anger and despair.

Mary Tillyard, Tillie Tillyard, in dogwood time, in the dark, giving her strut-bust moan.

A farmer's wife coming down past the barn, footing the good pasture grass on a hot afternoon, panting like a dog, down to the cane brake, leaving her baby tied to a bedpost with a length of clothesline.

Jessamine Abernathy, the rich doctor's daughter, with gentle eyes in her ugly face, accepting without complaint the humiliations which Jack Harrick had to mete out to her because her father was the rich doctor.

And the others, all of them—their names, he hadn't even known the names of some—wanting something from him, always a different something, but something, and always something he didn't care whether, in their emptiness, they ever got or not.

Even Celia Hornby, when, in the dogwood-dark, he had flung himself at her feet, caught in the terror which had come over him immediately after the thought: *I am not ever going to die.*

Yes, he hadn't cared what even she had wanted or needed, what emptiness she had to fill to be herself. All that had mattered was his own terror when, not knowing for a second whose hand he held in the dark, he had been caught in the vertigo of his own non-being.

[387]

Well, that had passed. It had just been a second. He was Jack Harrick. And a girl, even Celia Hornby, knew what she was getting. She was getting Jack Harrick.

That was what his life had proved.

That he was Jack Harrick.

But who was Jack Harrick?

I am me, I am me, he thought, and saw the white moths, with their frail, wayward plunging, come out of the dark to butt so sadly and softly the screen that kept them from the light.

But who was Jack Harrick?

And he thought that he, the old man sitting under the electric bulb in the bare room, sweating in the wheel chair, could not possibly be Jack Harrick.

No—for Jack Harrick, he knew then, was nothing but a dream. He was a dream dreamed up from the weakness of people. Since people were weak, they dreamed up a dream out of their need for violence, for strength, for freedom. Sitting there, he hated them for their weakness, for all their praise and envy, for the hands clawing at him for his strength, or in supplication for it. Old Jim Duckett, patting and clawing: "Yeah, yeah, Ole Jack, and him high-stepping!"

He hated them for their weakness, which had made him what he was.

No, he knew then, as calmly and indifferently as morning mist parting on the mountain, the weakness was not theirs. It was his. Out of his own weakness, he had dreamed the dream of Jack Harrick. And from that, all had followed.

But who was he?

He thought: *I am an old, nigh-illiterate, broke-down black-smith, sitting here in the middle of the night, and my boy is dead.*

Maybe he could die now. Maybe if he had known earlier what he knew now he would have been able to pray for his boy. Maybe he would not have been afraid to go into the ground, under the stone.

Are all men like me? he wondered.

[388]

He wondered about that quite a time, it seemed. *Are all men like me?*

What had Ole Mac said? Then he remembered:

> . . . neither is there any rest in my bones because of
> my sin.

How did it go on? He could not remember. Then he said it:

> "My wounds stink and are corrupt because of my fool-
> ishness."

How did it go? Then:

> "For my loins are filled with a loathsome disease: and
> there is no soundness in my flesh.
> "I am feeble and sore broken: I have roared by reason
> of the disquietness of my heart."

How did it go? How did it go? Then:

> "My lovers and my friends stand aloof from my sore;
> and my kinsmen stand afar off."

He said the words. Then he stopped. He was wondering if there was a stink. Perhaps there was one he could not smell. Because it was his.

He was wondering this when Jo-Lea Bingham, who had been crouching for a long time out in the dark by the hydrangea bushes, managed, at last, to muster up her courage and tiptoe into the house and down the hall, where she saw the light. She had no place else to go.

[389]

Jack Harrick, hearing the noise, if the breath she was trying to suppress could be called that, swung the chair toward the door. At first he didn't think she could be real, standing there so still, and so white in the face. Then he said: "You haven't got any place else to go, have you?"

She shook her head.

"Come on in," he said.

She did not move.

"I don't know why you said it," he said. "But I know it isn't true. So come on in."

She managed a step inside the door, like a timid swimmer managing the first step into cold, deep water.

"Come on," he said. "Closer."

She managed another couple of steps, staring at him.

He looked at her, and thought she might cry.

"It's awful," he said, "you running around in the night."

He studied her again.

"You're just a little girl," he said. Then: "Come closer."

She obeyed him.

"They all got too much for you," he said, "didn't they? Folks and things?"

She took a quick-flung look, almost desperate, over her shoulder, then around the room, as though something might be lurking.

"Things got out of hand," he said, "didn't they?"

He waited.

"Don't worry," he said, then. "That's the way things do, sometimes. They get so a person can't tell one thing from another, sometimes."

Then: "Why don't you sit down?"

She shook her head.

"Anyway," he said, "everybody will know it's not true. Before he died, Jasper said it wasn't true. To Brother Sumpter."

"Oh," the girl cried out. The tears came up into her eyes. She looked like she was trying to cry, but couldn't. It seemed as though what had started out to be an effort not to cry was now an effort to cry, but the tears would not come.

"Anyway," the man said, "anybody would know that Jasper wouldn't done it to you. Little like you are."

Maybe, he thought, she was going to cry after all. Maybe she would make it.

He said: "Anyway, Jasper knew you were Monty's girl. He knew Monty loved you. Monty told him."

He did not know what was going to happen to her, at first. She was white enough in the face already, and one cheek scratched where a briar or something had got her in the dark, and her big eyes popping with the grieving darkness in them. But her face went like chalk all at once, and she seemed to be spinning into distance. It was strange, how, looking into her face, when she went even whiter, and her eyelids flickered open and shut two or three times, you felt how things must feel to her, spinning away.

But she didn't faint. She stood there a second, and then dropped to her knees, right by his chair, the way she had that first afternoon, when she came running in from the ridge to say she had found the boots and the box. That first afternoon she had flung herself down before him, gabbling out what she had to say, grabbing him by the knees as though he, Old Jack Harrick, in that chair now for life, death, duration, and discussion, could do something. So now she flung her head on his knees, and cried. He let her cry for a reasonable time.

Then he said: "You going to have a baby, though?"

He felt her head nod against his knee.

Then he said: "You crying about Monty?"

Again he felt the nod. He laid his hand on her head, feeling her hair.

"Yeah, you love Monty," he said, and patted her head. "You just got Jasper and Monty sort of mixed, didn't you? Like a dream gets sort of mixed with daylight, before you wake up good. But you know, that was just a way of loving Monty, too.

[391]

Monty loved his Big Brother. He'd talk to you about his Big Brother, wouldn't he?"

He waited, and after a little while he felt the head nod against his knee.

"Yeah," he said, "and it will all be all right now."

She lifted her face up, staring at him. "Oh, he'll never believe it now!" she cried.

He nodded. "Yes, he will," he said.

"Oh, no!" she wailed.

"Listen," he said. "Listen careful. Do you know where he is?" She shook her head.

"Well," he said, "he has crawled in the ground to his Big Brother. I know exactly how it's got to be. When folks finally got away from that cave and finished their doing and botheration, Monty would just go on quiet in. I know it. He has gone all the way, for he is Jasper's brother and he is brave. He will hold his Big Brother's hand, and tell him good-bye. And Jasper will tell him about you. What I mean is, Monty will know it just like Jasper could really tell him. He will know it in his heart."

The girl had dropped her head back down on his knees. She was crying soft and easy now.

"Don't you worry," he said. "Monty will come out of the ground, and he will love you forever."

He patted her head, letting her cry. Then he picked up a lock of her hair, looked at it glisten darkly in the light, and let it slip across his hand.

"You got beautiful hair," he said. "It is soft and silky. It feels good to the fingers."

She had stopped crying. Her head lay relaxed on his knee.

"You can sleep here tonight," he said matter-of-factly. "Anyway, Ceeley needs you. Go in, and hold her hand. It will help her sleep."

She rose to her feet, in a slow, drugged motion, and stood there.

"I'll call your father," he said. "So he won't worry. I bet he has torn up that mountain. I'll call him. He is a good man."

She went slowly toward the door. There she paused, held the jamb, and smiled back at him, a thin, cobwebby smile, for the tiredness, but with a little glisten in it, like some dew that had caught on the cobweb and not dried off yet.

When she had gone, he wheeled over to the telephone, found the number, and called it.

"Mr. Bingham," he said into the phone.

Then: "Jo-Lea is here. She came in.—Yes, she is all right.—Yes, I bet you were.—Well, she is all right now. It is all straightened out, Mr. Bingham, that fool business.—No, Mr. Bingham, just girl-craziness. Yeah, Jasper sent word out before he died. Anyway, Jasper wouldn't been into something like that. As for Monty, now Monty has made a mistake, in a manner of speaking. But it's a human mistake, Mr. Bingham. With him loving her. He's a good boy.—You make me happy, saying that, Mr. Bingham.—Yeah, we're going to keep her here tonight, with your kind permission. She'll be a comfort to my wife, too.—Good night, Mr. Bingham."

Mr. Bingham, face scratched from the brush, body bruised from falling over stones, his voice hoarse from calling the name of his daughter on the dark mountain side, had come home a few minutes before to get a flashlight and go again on his search.

"You will call the police," Matilda Bollin Bingham had said.

"I won't have police chasing my little girl. She is just hiding somewhere, scared to answer me," he had said.

"I will call them. I can bear the burden of this shame," she had announced. She had started from her chair, saying: "I will call them this instant."

[393]

"I think not," Mr. Bingham said, and laid his hand on the phone.

"You would balk me?" she demanded.

"I reckon so," he said.

At that instant the phone rang. It was Jack Harrick.

The conversation finished, Mr. Bingham stood there with his hand yet lying on the instrument, while a joy flooded his heart. It was a simple joy beyond all consideration, the joy that a little girl, who happened to be his daughter, was no longer running in the dark on a mountain, not knowing where to go. He shut his eyes, and thought how so many things did not matter now.

"Was that the Harricks?" Matilda Bingham's voice was demanding.

He opened his eyes.

"Yes," he said.

"I presume I have the gist," she said. "So you will get right in the car and go get her. Even if she is—"

"She is my dear, sweet little daughter," he said, "and she is going to spend the night at the Harrick's."

"I wash my hands of it," she said, portentously rising to her feet. "Of her. Of you. You have debauched her. When I think of my poor father, sitting in Nashville, reading the—"

"Your father," Mr. Bingham murmured, as though to himself, as a thought unfolded like a blossom in his head. "The poor old gentleman," he murmured, "he must need you. And," he added as the last petal calmly unfurled its beauty, "nobody else does."

She sat back down.

"As a matter of fact," he said musingly, "I am not exactly a poor man. I have worked hard and accumulated. I think that one-half of my estate would make a comfortable settlement for you. If you live simply. We can have it put in writing tomorrow in time for you to catch the one P.M. bus to Nashville. To spend a few days with your father before you go to Nevada. Or would you prefer Alabama? I hear it is quite easy there, too."

[394]

That didn't quite end it. It was necessary to point out that she would probably not do her case much good if she ever got on the stand. "Look at your feet," he said, noticing them with new interest. "Look how they're just chewing their way down into the carpet. You know, Matilda, I think you would probably blow up on the stand."

Then there was the clincher: "And if you insist on being nasty about things, do you think Jo-Lea would be of much help to you?"

"You have poisoned the mind of my child," Mrs. Bingham said.

"Have I?" Mr. Bingham asked calmly, knowing now it was in the bag.

He went upstairs, got some fresh clothes out of their room, went down the hall to the guest bathroom, bathed, and dressed himself. He did all this without thinking beyond the next instant.

When he had dressed, he came back down the front stairs and, without a glance into the living room where his wife sat, went on out to the front porch. He went over to the side of the porch and sat in the swing, leaning his brow against the chain by which it was suspended. There was a trellis to screen this part of the porch from the street, and on the trellis the moon vine was blooming.

He pressed his brow against the chain and tried not to think of anything. There would be so much to think about soon. Now he closed his eyes and let time, and the night, flow over him. From downtown there came, somewhat mollified by distance, the racket of cars, an occasional backfire, the gnashing of bumpers, the blatting of horns, all punctuated irregularly by the irascible screech of a patrolman's whistle as he tried to unsnarl the traffic of Johntown.

Thousands of people, he didn't know how many, had come here because a poor boy had got caught in the ground, and had lain there dying. They had wept, and prayed, and boozed, and sung and fought, and fornicated, and in all ways possible had striven to break through to the heart of the mystery which was themselves. No, he thought, remembering Brother Sumpter with his arms lifted under the floodlights, to break out of the dark mystery which was themselves. Now Jasper Harrick was dead, and they could all go home.

He did not want to think. But things came into his mind. He thought of Jasper Harrick lying deep in the ground, and not thinking. He thought of Old Harrick dying in the log house under the old cedars, and Mrs. Harrick grieving for her son. He thought of his own daughter up yonder, up the cove, resting after the terror of flight and darkness and the foot on the stone, resting now with a new life glimmering deep in her.

He thought of her lying there asleep, and then knew he was about to think of what had happened to her with that Monty Harrick. But in the same instant he knew that his mind could not bear to come to that thought. So he sat there, sweating in his distress, behind the blossoms of moon vine.

Then it occurred to him that if he could, just once, think of what had happened to the pretty little body of his Baby-Girl, then everything would be all right. But he wasn't quite ready yet.

At that thought, he felt again the strange stirring of excitement and expectation, shading over into guilt, which he had felt that first day in the bank, listening to the soft *click-clack* that came as Dorothy Cutlick operated the posting machine. He thought about how strange he had felt that day with Dorothy Cutlick working the machine to make that *click-clack*. He had been awfully cut up then, enough to account for anything, but it was strange, any-way. It would tear any man up to be waiting for that Greek to come, when you had to ask him what he had had to ask. Yes, that was it. But it was strange how it sort of excited a man too.

Well, he thought, he could manage things now, without any Greek. He had almost done a terrible thing to his daughter, but he would try to make it up. That Harrick boy was a good boy. Even if he was what people called a hillbilly. He remembered how he had called Jasper Harrick a hillbilly, and, thinking of the cave as a tourist attraction, had wanted to know what money was to a hillbilly. He had said it right before Jo-Lea, too, sitting right at his own dinner table. Now Jasper Harrick, hillbilly or not, was dead in the cave. Sadness grew in Timothy Bingham's heart. Was it sadness for the death in the cave, he wondered. Perhaps, but not only. Sadness, too, for all the sad foolishness a man did and said before his own time came to die.

Jasper's brother, he reminded himself, was a hillbilly, too, and he was a good, clean-cut boy, and had never been in any trouble. He had made high marks in his graduating class at high school. He remembered reading that in the Kobeck County *Weekly Herald*. Well, he, Timothy Bingham, would work things out. He would get them married, and send the boy off to college. Yes, a little money was a good thing to have, and he had worked hard and accumulated. He would send the boy, and Jo-Lea—yes, of course, her too—away somewhere, maybe over to Chapel Hill, in North Carolina, for he had heard it was a good school, or maybe up North. He would make them little visits. But not too often.

Then, in his mind, he saw Jo-Lea sitting with a baby in her arms, her head bowed in a gentle light to look at the baby's face, and Monty Harrick, who was sort of a nice-looking boy, seated at a table, leaning over a book. He thought it was just like an advertisement, a life-insurance advertisement maybe. He thought of it now, not as a fantasy, but as a picture, in color, in beautiful, rich, subdued color, full-page, in a big magazine, perhaps in a Christmas issue. The sweetness flooded his heart. He could not understand why the thought of the picture of them—Jo-Lea, Monty and the baby—should be even sweeter than the thought of them as real.

The picture, he guessed, was more outside some of the trouble of life.

He wanted Jo-Lea to miss some of the trouble. He wanted her to be happy. Then he remembered that once, long ago, he had wanted Matilda Bollin to be happy.

That thought was a pain, but a pain which converted itself

into a savage irony, as he thought: *Perhaps she has always been happy, perfectly happy in her own way.* Even tonight, in the bitterness of conflict, she had, perhaps, known what her happiness was and had known that she was moving toward its final fulfillment. She would get on the bus and go to her father's house, and live there, and the dark nameless grievance of life would now have a name, a name which would do as well as any, and she could sit by the ravaged, senile man out of whose loins she had sprung, and name over that name for the outrage of life, hour by hour, all day long.

Then he realized he was crying, or about to, for sitting here on the dark porch, on a summer night, behind the screen of moon vine with the blossoms open, was like sitting on such a porch, in Nashville, a million years ago, behind vines, waiting for Matilda Bollin to come down and go to the dance over at Peabody College, where her father was a professor. The pathos of life possessed him. How could it happen to a man that he should have sat behind blooming moon vine then, and now, in the same life? How could things be in the same life?

He rose from the swing. He could not stay here. A man simply could not sit around and think about life. He squared his shoulders. If a man just did one thing, and then the next thing as it came along, he wouldn't have to think about life. So he couldn't stay here, behind the vines.

He was down the front steps now. But where could he go? He went to the iron gate, opened the gate, and stepped out onto the strip of concrete walk. Some light was coming up into the sky. He found his feet going the familiar track to the bank. That was a place he could go.

As Mr. Bingham, under the first paleness of dawn, moved with his usual brisk tread toward the bank, he did not know that Dorothy Cutlick was watching him from the shadow of a maple across the street. She had been standing there for a long time, ever since she had heard about Jo-Lea on the radio. Her heart grieved for him, for she knew how he loved that little girl.

But she had one little piece of good news for him. There was a note on Mr. Bingham's desk saying that she had had a call from the bank examiner, and all he had wanted the other day was to know if his gold pencil had been found. He prized the pencil, because it had been a gift from his mother.

The pencil was on Mr. Bingham's desk, too. She had found it.

She was glad she had found it, because now Mr. Bingham wouldn't worry. He was inclined to worry. She knew that. She reckoned, though, it was all right now about Jo-Lea, since he was going down the street, like usual, except it was awful early. She hoped he did not have to be worried about Jo-Lea any more and everything was all right.

Hoping that, she felt a wave of sweetness at the thought—no, the image—of Mr. Bingham leaning above Jo-Lea with a gesture of solicitude. Her breath caught with the sweetness.

Then she remembered how, long ago, after Sim Cutlick, her own blood-father, had come to the bank, and Mr. Bingham had had to shoot off the pistol, and she had been so ashamed she thought she would die, he, Mr. Bingham, had patted her on the shoulder.

From the protection of her maple shadow, she watched him go down the street. She realized that he must be going to the bank now to open up. She started to follow him, walking down the other side of the street, not trying to overtake him. She would go too, to help.

But then she realized that it was too early for that. She would have to go back to her room and wait till eight o'clock.

Having hung up from his call to Mr. Bingham, Jack Harrick started to wheel himself back to the middle of the room, but he noticed the guitar propped against the end of the bureau, where somebody had left it. He wheeled over and picked it up, then

[399]

wheeled back to his old place, beside the little table. He stared down at the box across his knees. He rubbed his finger lightly across the wood, inspecting it. No, the dew didn't seem to have done too much harm. He ran his right forefinger down the *E* string, so lightly as to make no sound. But when he lifted his finger, he could see the string quiver, ever so little.

Or was that a trick of the light? Or of his eyes? Maybe he had winked his eyes.

It was my box, he thought.

Then: *It was Jasper's box.*

Then: *It is Monty's box.*

He did not know what to make of those facts. They hung in his head, the three facts. They were like three strings vibrating together, and he strained to catch the melding sound, but could not. He felt, suddenly, his sad ignorance of life. There were so many things in the world he could not hear, and did not know.

Are all men like me? he wondered, with the wonderment he had had just a little while ago before the girl came in.

Are all men bone-ignorant and bone-proud, like me? he wondered.

Then he wondered how he would want to have the question answered. If all men were like him, then he would not have to feel so bad. He would be no worse than the others. He could take comfort in that.

He tried to take comfort in that. It was a dry, hard comfort, like lying on the bare dusty ground, in the dark. It was like walking hard all day across a dry, bare country, and when night came just lying down on that same ground.

But, he thought, if all men were not like him, then some were better. That meant he would have to feel worse for being himself. That meant he would have to know how slow and blundering he had been. *I am feeble and sore broken*, he thought: *I have roared by reason of the disquietness of my heart.*

It would mean he would have to feel worse.

[400]

He looked down at the box. He had played on it, his songs, break-downs and revels, toe-smashers and breath-snatchers. Jasper had played his own songs, the ones he used to make up out of his solitariness and his own head and sing down by the river, and girls cried. Monty had closed his eyes and sung because his Big Brother had gone into the ground.

Every man's got to make his own kind, his own kind of song, Jack Harrick thought.

He wondered what kind could be his own kind now. Not one of the old puncheon-busters, and him sitting here in a wheel chair in the middle of the night.

He thought of Monty standing up there, his head lifted, eyes squinched shut, those TV lights on his face, the hat with the drake feather canted over one ear, his right heel lifted, his fingers on the strings of the box, and he, Jack Harrick, did not know why but he thought he might cry. He thought of Monty standing up there and singing for his Big Brother.

Then he thought: *Monty is in the ground. He has gone in to hold his Big Brother's hand.*

Then he thought: *Oh, Monty, he's not like me. My son is not like me. All men are not like me.*

But he didn't feel worse from that thought. He felt better.

He looked down at the box. Ever so lightly he touched the strings, and listened for the faint sound.

"God damn it," he cried aloud in the middle of the night, "Monty—he's just a boy, and he—he's gone in! He has gone in to Jasper!"

He struck the strings, one chord. Then he began to play. For a minute he played the tune, getting a hold on it. It had been so long a time, and his fingers had lost their sleight. Then he started again. He began to sing:

> "He is lying in the ground,
>   And he cannot hear a sound.

[401]

He is lying under the land.
There's nobody to take his hand.
He is lying where he may no more be found."

Then:

"He is lying under the land,
But I know he'll understand.
He is lying under the stone,
But he will not lie alone—
I'm coming, son, I'm coming, take your Pappy's hand."

Then:

"I will come under the land.
In the dark take your Pappy's hand.
For I'm coming—"

It was then that Celia Hornby Harrick, wearing a nightgown with a ribbon collar, and some sort of light summer wrapper, but barefoot, as though she had suddenly been called from bed, came in.

He let the box sink down across his knees, and looked at her.

She came toward him, soundless on her bare feet, and stood very close, looking down at him. Then she crouched by his knee, her right arm lying loose across the knees, looking up at him.

Old Jack Harrick laid his hand on her head, not the weight of it, just lightly. She opened her eyes and again looked up at him. After a minute, she said: "John T."

He didn't answer.

She was looking up, studying his face.

"John T.," she said. "Oh, John T.—I never saw you before!"

"Hush," he said, "hush."

"Maybe it's because—because I never was me before."

"Hush," he said, and held his hand on her head.

"Oh, John T.," she cried out, but the cry was almost joyful, "don't die—don't ever die!"

He was patting her head.

After a while, he said: "Ceeley, you used to teach school. You taught the third grade, when you came to Johntown. It was the third grade, wasn't it?"

She nodded, under his hand.

"There was always some pore little slow scholar," he asked, "wasn't there? That couldn't keep up?"

She nodded.

After a while, he said: "That's me. Yeah, Ceeley, I was always a poor scholar. But I'm trying. I'm trying to learn, Ceeley."

She reached up and drew his hand from her head, and laid her cheek against the back of it. She felt the bones in it.

"I was a pore scholar," he said, "but—"

She rubbed her cheek against his hand.

"But—" he tried again, but didn't go on.

Then he tried again, even though he didn't know what he was trying to say. "I reckon," he said, starting all over again, "I reckon living is just learning how to die. And—"

He stopped, then tried again.

"—and dying," he said, and stopped.

"—it's just learning how to live," he said.

She was rubbing her cheek against the back of his hand when he withdrew it. He reached over, picked up the bottle and fished out a pill, picked up the glass of water, and took the pill. He set the glass down, and, avoiding her gaze, picked up the guitar and adjusted it to position. All at once, he hit a big clanging chord that filled the room.

"Let that anvil ring!" he cried out, and lifted his head up.

"John T.," she whispered, looking up at him. "Oh, John T."

He dropped his gaze to her, then grinned, rather sheepishly.

"I don't want to bust the box," he said. "It's Monty's box."

[403]

ABOUT THE AUTHOR

ROBERT PENN WARREN was born in Guthrie, Kentucky, in 1905. He entered Vanderbilt University at the age of sixteen and graduated *summa cum laude;* he went to the University of California for his master's degree, then to Yale University, and in 1928 to Oxford as a Rhodes Scholar.

Mr. Warren began his teaching career at Southwestern College (1930-31) and Vanderbilt University (1931-34). He moved to Louisiana State University in 1934, and was one of the founders and editors of *The Southern Review.* From 1942 to 1950 he was Professor of English at the University of Minnesota (and Consultant in Poetry at the Library of Congress, 1944-45). From 1951 to 1956 he was a member of the faculty of Yale University.

In 1939 Mr. Warren published his first novel, *Night Rider* (reissued by Random House in 1948) and won his first Guggenheim Fellowship. In 1943 came *At Heaven's Gate* and in 1946, *All the King's Men* (Pulitzer Prize). His fourth novel was *World Enough and Time* (Random House, 1950). *Brother to Dragons: A Tale in Verse and Voices* appeared in 1953, and his fifth novel, *Band of Angels,* in 1955. Mr. Warren has also published four volumes of poetry, of which the most recent is *Promises* (National Book Award and Pulitzer Prize, 1958); a short-story collection, *The Circus in the Attic;* and such influential textbooks (with Cleanth Brooks) as *Understanding Poetry* and *Understanding Fiction.* Mr. Warren's *Selected Essays* was published in 1958.

Mr. Warren lives in Connecticut with his wife, Eleanor Clark, whose most recent book is *Rome and a Villa,* and their two children, Rosanna and Gabriel.